To the library staff Bognor Campus

Warm regards

11/9/9

The Lords of the Moon

Book One

The Ice Crown

by

Sean Beech

Published by

MELROSE BOOKS

An Imprint of Melrose Press Limited
St Thomas Place, Ely
Cambridgeshire
CB7 4GG, UK
www.melrosebooks.com

FIRST EDITION

Cover designed by Kenneth McLeod

ISBN 978-1-906561-10-9

FSC
Mixed Sources
Product group from well-managed
forests and other controlled sources
Cert no. SGS-COC-2953
www.fsc.org
© 1996 Forest Stewardship Council

Printed and bound in Great Britain by:
CPI Antony Rowe, Chippenham, Wiltshire

First and foremost I would like to thank you the reader for purchasing this book and in doing so helping the National Literacy Trust to improve literacy amongst our children.

My wife deserves special praise, her patience and understanding has been greatly appreciated. I love you.

Finally special thanks to my daughter Tamara for some of the ideas; my good friends Lucy and Roger for their support; Kenny for the cover design and in some little way to each and every person I know, they say an author bases his work on life experiences and in some way you may have shaped this or my future books and for that I thank you.

Sean

Chapter One

Morkin was enjoying himself; it appeared that at last he was going to fulfil his destiny. He had known for the last ten years that he was special. That he was descended from the kings of old, and was as such, the sole surviving successor to the throne of the Lands of the Moon.

The Realm of the Moon, as it was currently referred to, used to be known as the Kingdom of the Moon, but due to the fact it had no king or queen at present, it was as per royal decree from the time of Morkin's great-grandfather known as a realm whilst no king or queen was crowned. Morkin's coronation should have taken place many moons since, but for the treachery of one of the Lords of the Moon, who on Morkin's father's death stole the Ice Crown for the Order of the Dark Knights. The crown though had never made it to the Dark Knights' lands; mysteriously disappearing from Lord Vermount's saddle pack somewhere en-route. For twelve years the Lords of the Moon had searched for its whereabouts and up until today there had been no clue as to its fate.

Today was Shadow Day in the realm, the day when the Moon and the Sun competed on equal terms for their length in the sky. A day of partying and celebration. A day of feasting and games, and this was the first year that Morkin would be allowed to compete in his own colours, bearing for the first time his standard of the red fox. Thus he had spent the entire evening beforehand grooming his horse, Dancer, a fine stallion standing at over eighteen hands tall, with a pure jet black coat that shone with vigour and power. A coat only broken by the tan brown of its hooves and the white crescent it wore like a crown on its forehead. Morkin, having been around horses all his life, was now a fine horseman, his squire though seemed to think that he was a great horseman, but Morkin was humble enough to realise that this was just flattery reserved for a king-in-waiting. No, he was a fine horseman because it was in his blood, he had felt it the very first time he had sat on a horse; the quickening of his heart, the excitement that ran coursing through his veins, the adrenaline pumping and yet, also, a quietness, an understanding, almost an empathy of being at one with another living thing. He knew how the horse felt and it was this understanding and ability that singled him out from the other riders in the Keep and made him a fine horseman. Not a great horseman, not yet, not until he had proven that to the people, and that was surely only, a matter of time, he thought.

So he had spent all yesterday evening grooming his horse, brushing the horse's coat until it had shone, a deep black sheen full of vigour and life. "The turnout of your mount at all times depicts the qualities of its rider." He repeated the words to himself again and smiled. Lord Luxor, his guardian and mentor, had said those very same words to him eight years ago when he had been given Dancer as a gift on his fourth birthday; and every day since, Morkin had insisted on grooming and caring for his horse himself, despite his rank and the fact that his household had some of the best squires in the land at his disposal to groom and stable it for him.

So it was with great surprise that he found himself summoned from his room in the Keep of Ishfern this morning. It was Lord Luxor himself who had interrupted his dreaming and dragged him half asleep to the stables. He had found himself astride Dancer and halfway to Crescent Wood before he had started to fully wake up. Lord Luxor had been his father's champion, a great bear of a man, with golden shoulder-length hair which was as unruly as the man himself was disciplined. He stood at over a head taller than any man Morkin had seen or heard of and his strength was legendary throughout the land. Luxor himself was not of noble birth, but had earned his title from

Morkin's father with his years of loyal service, courage and skill in battle. No man, either noble or common born, begrudged Luxor his title or position as Morkin's guardian. He was, it seemed, universally liked by all, which had as much to do with his ability to get on with all manner of people, as with the power his position afforded him.

Luxor had sworn to protect Morkin on the King's deathbed and as such the loss of the Ice Crown was a particularly sore point, least not discussed too often in Luxor's company despite his good nature. After all, a man as proud as Luxor would only take what he deemed as a personal failing in good humour so far.

The ride to the woods had not only started to wake Morkin but also to raise his spirits, as only riding a thoroughbred stallion could. The gentle sway as Dancer seemed to effortlessly drift and flow across terrain that was as rugged as it was beautiful. Their breath forming clouds around both beast and rider in the cool morning air, as lush green meadows brimming with buttercups and small daisies passed by underneath. The soft gentle sound of water in the nearby brook as it rushed and hurried past rocks and over stones on its own epic journey to the sea and beyond. The gentle, twittering song of a thrush in a nearby tree, calling out, singing to its mate contently, as it enjoyed the feast of insects and grubs found in the early rays of the warming sun; the gentle warmth of which complemented the cool breeze blowing down from the grey snow-capped mountains in the distance. Strange, thought Morkin, he had never seen snow this late in the year on the peaks, at least not that he could remember. Yes, the day was beautiful, not a cloud in the sky and today was going to be very special; he could feel it in the air, in his heart, in his bones. Today he would compete in the games under the banner of the red fox. Today would be his first step to becoming a man and hopefully with the recovery of the Ice Crown, the King.

Morkin was a practical prince, he knew he was the king in all but name, yet the Lords of the Moon insisted that he could not be king until he was crowned as such. All twelve of them unanimously agreed with this, including Lord Luxor. They had argued that this was the law according to royal decree and that the Ice Crown was the only crown that would make a person of royal descent the monarch of the Moon lands. The problem was that whilst this was the case, no one person had overall command and rule in the Lands of the Moon. Each lord rightly or wrongly, without a king to guide them, had become more and more likely to instigate policies and laws in their lands which could be to the detriment of those surrounding them. This had at times had serious implications on the rest of the land. The most recent of such an occasion was when Lord Garish had ordered his people to grow rice in their fields so he could feed them with less cost to himself. This had involved the damming of the river Cool that ran through his lands at the southern border in order to provide enough water for the rice to grow. His people thrived on the cheaper food source, thus increasing his tax revenue. Unfortunately, the damming of the river resulted in a drought downriver in the lands of Lord Finbar. The river ran dry and his crops failed, resulting in famine and death amongst his people. The situation was only resolved when Lord Finbar had summoned his army and marched on Lord Garish's lands. Only the timely intervention of Lords Luxor and Marekin had prevented what could have boiled over into a civil war in the Realm of the Moon.

After this incident the Lords of the Moon had become even more wary of each other and despite knowing in their hearts that Morkin was their regent and king, until he was crowned as such, they refused to take counsel from him. Some even went as far as to make him unwelcome in their lands until he was crowned.

The people of the Realm of the Moon liked Morkin as they had his father. They could see he was a fine young prince, of even temper and possessing a good heart. They had known peace from before their eldest grandfather's grandfather's time, when the first King of Moon was crowned by Serevent, the dragon queen, and thus the Moon lands had been given to the rule of man. It had been their reward for helping defeat and banish the Dark Knights from these lands; the Dark Knights who at the time had spread their empire from the distant Cestere Sea to the snowbound peaks of Fennigan Mountain. They had burned the land and laid to waste its natural beauty in their search for raw materials to fund their empire. The Fey, the Wolves of

Fennigan and the Ice Dragons had nearly lost the battle and were facing extinction before the massed hordes of their army. They had been massacred in their thousands in a vain attempt to defeat the foe and finally, as all hope slipped away and defeat loomed over them like a dark cloud, a saviour arrived from the west; from across the Tamor Ocean, an army of men arrived as if summoned by the gods. This army, the army of men, had helped turn the tide of war and eventually they had driven the Dark Knights and their Order back to the Cestere Sea and won their prize.

As their reward the men were given the Lands of the Moon to settle in peacefully. Their leader, Sutur, was crowned king with the Ice Crown by Serevent, the dragon queen, and her powerful eulogy was engraved forever in the minds of men:

> *'As long as your line shall live and the crown be in its place, the Kingdom of the Moon shall have a king and will thus be safe.'*

Serevent disappeared as of then and has never been seen since. Some say that when she relinquished the crown that she gave up her hold on life, others though say that it was her time to pass on the crown as it had been passed to her, a keeper of the fortunes of the Moon lands. The Wolves of Fennigan, if you believe the tales told by the mountain people, are still around. Once considered an ally of the Moon lands, their appetite for sheep and other livestock had now made them into an enemy of the people and most now stayed well clear of Fennigan Mountain and their surrounding forests for fear of the wolves.

The Fey, if you believe some, are still here; people of the trees who still haunt the woods and forests, appearing and disappearing as if ghosts. Many believe that they are all just that: ghosts of a once proud people, the remnants of a past that is now gone, who will not let go of their ancestral home and thus deprive its use by those of the living world. Others though insist that they have seen living, breathing Fey, and that they choose to live in solitude, that they are angry with man for having their lands, which so many of their kind bled and died for. Whichever truth you decide to believe, the legends of the Fey still live, and they are still recognised by all in the land as the best archers, hunters and athletes ever seen. No man could hope to compete with a Fey in such sport.

And as if to heighten the myth and strengthen the legend further, the annual games held around the country have seen on many occasions a stranger appear to compete in the archery competitions and then disappear again, having beaten all other competitors. Always hooded and never waiting to collect their prize. A Fey or something else? Nobody knew for certain. But what was certain was that if the Fey were alive, they were not introducing themselves to man for whatever their reasons, and had not done so since their land had been taken from them and given to the rule of man.

The people of the land were on the whole honest hard-working country folk. They knew that Morkin was their king and accepted this fact, and despite the lack of the Ice Crown, many believed he should be crowned regardless. It was a measure of the lord of whose lands you were on as to how you heard this opinion. In the lands of the lords who were tolerant and assured of themselves and their people, these opinions were openly expressed. This, however, was not the case in all the lands within the Realm of the Moon. Lords Calebar and Thorins had made it an offence to question them over the Prince and their people did not openly discuss their opinions on matters of state. There were also people in the realm who believed that after twelve years of self-rule by their lords, that there was no longer any need or want for a king, especially if it upset their status quo.

The worst offenders and the two most anxious never to see the coronation happen can be found in Morkin's own ancestral lands: Mr Grabbit and Mr Such. Both have made a very tidy profit out of the discord and envy caused by the current Lords of the Moon's distrust of each other.

Mr Grabbit, or Sir Grabbit as he likes to be called, a title given to himself only to sound more official, works as a tax collector in Morkin's lands. He is an extremely large and grubby man, whose paunch is only equalled by the size of his palate. A man so large of girth that he uses a rope to tie his trousers up; a man so large and round, it is reckoned that if he fell over he would roll; a man with a particular appetite for horse. Not just any horse, mind you. No, the horse he likes best, you see, is the horse which is taken in lieu of monies owed to him and then eaten in front of its poor owner. Grabbit's size is not all fat though. No, Grabbit is also strong and surprisingly athletic when need be. Yet despite his size and grotesquely brash manner Grabbit is considered to be very sly and almost weaselly in character; and it is just these trait's that give him the unerring ability of being able to justify his methods and actions to all and sundry. Mr Grabbit, rather unsurprisingly, is the royal tax collector, appointed to the post by Morkin's father on the recommendation of Mr Such.

Mr Such, in stark contrast, is a fastidiously clean and well-turned-out dwarf of a man, and whilst Grabbit is considered weaselly in character, Mr Such could definitely be considered weaselly in appearance. His character though is somewhat more cunning and devious, a thoroughly ruthless and viciously nasty individual; the sort of person that will seem charming and seductive, whilst all the while working out your worth before robbing you blind. You see, Mr Such is a lawyer! He was also, at the time of Grabbit's appointment, a particularly good lawyer who worked for and was trusted by the late King. Mr Grabbit's appointment as such went unquestioned and his position has never been rescinded. Mr Such's sole motivation for having Mr Grabbit appointed to the position was that of greed. The fact that he could not stand the man was neither here nor there, he immediately recognised the financial possibilities of having Mr Grabbit as the royal taxman and the two of them have for the last fifteen years made a rather large fortune out of Morkin's lands and its people. This has been made all the more easy in the last twelve years as Morkin, despite being the lord of his own lands, is still, until he is crowned king, unable to rule over them. The twelve Lords of the Moon thus share equal governance over his lands and as such never seem to agree on any matter of importance, each thinking the other is trying to gain an advantage over them. As a consequence, Morkin's lands have been left lawless for Such and Grabbit to plunder freely.

Morkin, despite his tender years, was no fool; he knew and fully understood the perilous position his country was in and what his people faced. They were on the brink of civil war, most of the lords distrusted each other. They were a broken and disjointed country that lacked leadership and guidance. As such they were vulnerable both from inside and outside influences. The Dark Knights rode again in the east, and until the Ice Crown was retrieved, he as the rightful heir and protector was unable to do anything about it.

Yet today was different, today something would happen that could help to change all that. He did not know how he knew it, but deep inside he did, and despite the fact that he now rode beside Lord Luxor, he was reluctant and hesitant to ask the question that now nagged at him; *On this day of all days, why are you taking me for a ride to Crescent Wood?* If that was indeed the destination. He decided though, hesitantly, that patience was called for. Lord Luxor would tell him as soon as he saw fit, after all if any man knew and understood what today meant to Morkin it was his mentor, guardian and, most of all, friend. *If he has brought me all the way to Crescent Wood today of all days it is for a very good reason*, he thought to himself. His stomach interrupted his thoughts with a low grumble. *He could have thought of breakfast though, I'm famished.* This thought had no sooner entered his head when an apple bounced off it and landed in his lap.

"Owww" exclaimed Morkin.

"Breakfast," laughed a smiling Luxor, "I bet you thought I had forgotten, hadn't you, lad?"

Lad, thought Morkin as he rubbed his head. "I bet you will still call me that when you eventually find me my crown, Luxor, and I am your King."

The look of anguish on Luxor's face immediately made him regret that last remark. "I'm sorry, it was not meant as a criticism, Luxor, I am only jesting. I know how much the crown's loss has hurt you and how hard you have sought to find it."

"Do not worry yourself over a sensitive old fool, lad! But you are right, its loss does annoy me. I should have slain that traitor when I had the chance, lad, I never trusted that one." Luxor smiled as he

8

rode over and fondly ruffled Morkin's brown hair. "There, that's better, looks more like mine now, a real man needs wild hair, you know, it attracts the ladies and scares the enemy."

"Attracts the ladies, eh?" Morkin laughed as he ran his own hands roughly through his hair. "There," he smiled, "now they will be unable to resist my charms."

"Ahh, lad, one day the ladies will be falling over themselves to attract your attention and it won't be for your hair! However, for now they will have to make do with old Luxor."

Encouraged by their banter, which overcame his hesitancy, Morkin was just about to ask why they were going to the woods when over the horizon he saw three riders on white horses galloping towards them. Even at this distance Morkin could tell that the riders had ridden hard over a long period of time and distance. The horses' stride was short yet they were still being driven at a gallop, white clouds of steam snorting from their nostrils as they sucked in and blew out the air needed to keep their huge muscles going. The riders were all dressed in armour, the sun shining off the breastplates of each in a dazzling and blinding radiance that caught the eye of all those watching. The large pendant held aloft easily recognisable as Luxor's own, a green snarling dragon with red flames roaring out of its mouth, fixed across a white background, and the edges of the pendant trimmed with bright gold. Morkin was spellbound, he loved to watch a horse and rider as one in full gallop, there was something majestic about the fluidity of the shared movement and graceful actions, a truly magical sight full of power and energy. Even more enhanced when the rider and horse are dressed as if for war.

WAR! The thought seemed to come screaming into his head, it hit him like a sledgehammer and knocked him sideways. His world seemed to spin and tumble, he felt light and dizzy as if the world itself were spinning out of control, round and round, faster and faster.

"Oww." How can a thought hurt so much?

"Ha ha ha ha, so much for a would-be king's horsemanship."

Morkin's vision slowly cleared. Above him sat a hooded rider on a white battle charger. The horse was sweating heavily, yet it was obviously well cared for and well ridden. Morkin looked up at the rider, boots of fine leather that were, judging from the visible creases, very soft and comfortable. Good boots for riding, he thought, and expensive. The leggings above the boots were a deep green, like the colour of the leaves on a mighty oak tree in the full of summer. A scabbard of highly polished leather with metal leaves embossed on its surface hung loosely from the rider's belt. The sword's hilt, just visible, was plain and functional yet at the same time showing a rare craftsmanship in its make, hinting at the quality of the blade hidden within the scabbard below. No doubt a functional blade which was designed to be used, and again hinting that the owner was adept and skilled in its use. It was a sword designed for fighting and yet still managed to possess a distinct powerful beauty. Morkin's gaze continued upwards; what he had presumed in the distance to be an armoured breastplate shining in the sun was in fact a waistcoat of what appeared to be metal leaves, each individually fashioned, each overlapping the other in a manner that provided the wearer with protection, yet allowed them an ease of movement that a fixed breastplate would not. Morkin had never seen such craftsmanship, and the material used to fashion the leaves was unknown to him, but he assumed they would be strong enough for their purpose. The rider wore over his head and shoulders a rich, emerald-green cloak which seemed to shimmer and shine with a life of its own in the morning sun. The hood was pulled down over the rider's face so that Morkin could not distinguish any features hidden beneath, yet he was sure it was the rider who had laughed at his misfortune moments earlier.

As Morkin made to get up, the rider turned his horse suddenly so that its rear came quickly towards Morkin and sent him sprawling again backwards onto the grass.

"Oii," Morkin shouted, "mind your horse." But the horseman had already moved off towards where Luxor sat astride his mount, watching events unfold with a surprising nonchalance.

Morkin struggled onto his feet. Oww, my head still hurts, he thought as he felt round the back of his scalp. Good, no blood and nothing broken, it seemed. He looked around and saw that Dancer had not gone far and was now contentedly grazing on the grass at the side of the path. Dancer, sensing he was being watched, looked up, and Morkin was sure that if a horse could laugh then it would look like Dancer now did with his upper teeth bared, as if he too found Morkin's misfortune amusing. His thoughts, however, were more concerned with the stranger. It was obvious that the rider had known who Morkin was and that he had no real regard or respect for his position. Most people, Morkin reflected, were struck dumb on first meeting him due to his rank and position. Yet this person had openly laughed at him. Well no, that was a bit unfair; the person had really laughed at his misfortune more than at him; indeed the more Morkin thought about what had happened the more he could see the funny side of it himself. Here he was, a self-confessed horseman, toppling off his horse at the mere sight of three strange riders in the distance. It was just as well they were not trying to do him any harm. Yes, he must have looked ridiculous. Morkin now started to laugh out loud, amused at his own misfortune. The rider glanced around on hearing the laughter, and Morkin was certain he saw a flash of teeth in a smile beneath the hood, but it was gone as soon as he had seen it.

The stranger had now reached Luxor and the two were in what appeared from this distance to be a deeply agitated conversation which Morkin was unable to hear any of from where he stood. The conversation lasted a few minutes and finally the unknown rider gave out a piercing call and threw something onto the ground beside Luxor's horse, before galloping off. His two companions, who all the time had waited off to the side, now dug their heels into their mounts and galloped off after the rider, who it would appear was their leader. By the time Morkin had remounted Dancer and ridden over to where Luxor was now standing, his mentor had dismounted, picked up and put whatever the rider had thrown down onto the ground into his pack. Luxor himself now looked worried. Morkin had never seen Luxor worried before and found this rather unsettling. He had seen Luxor fight on many occasions, and Luxor had even saved Morkin's life on one occasion four years ago when he had got into an argument with what had turned out to be a couple of thieves. Rather than being robbed, Morkin had decided to argue with the men. It had happened whilst he was out riding one day alone, they had come out of nowhere as he sat at a crossroads, deciding on what path to explore next.

He had always thought that the line 'your money or your life' was a bit corny and that no one really used it. So when the two men with their swords drawn had come at him and uttered those very same words, he had laughed as only an eight-year-old can. This only served to irritate the two men, but the more they insisted that he hand over his money or his life was forfeit, the more Morkin had laughed, until he finally blurted out between fits of laughter that if they were serious they would have to come up with a more original line than that. At this point the men had had enough.

"Just kill him, Fref," the bigger of the two had said.

Fref had duly advanced and it was only at this point that Morkin realised that he was indeed in peril. He had dug his heels hard into Dancer who, shocked at the sudden pain in his side, had risen up onto his hind legs, kicking out his front hooves at the same time at the approaching man's head. Dancer had come down with a thud, the man had gone, and as Morkin had leaned forward to see if the man's body was below him, a rough callused hand had shot up and grabbed him by the collar and pulled him off Dancer. He had landed flat on his back, the air driven from his lungs, his vision blurred by the tears forming in his eyes.

"Got yer, ye little bugger," shouted Fref, "I got him, did ye see me? I got him." Spit flew out of his mouth at Morkin's face, followed by the foul smell of rotting teeth and stale ale.

"He tried to kill you with his horse, Fref. Kill him," the other man shouted from where he stood watching events, his hand still clutching his sword.

Fref smiled, a grotesque pitted black smile and pulled out a short knife. "Gone and dropped me sword, but never mind, soon finish you with this," he laughed, stabbing the knife in short, sharp thrusts into the air above Morkin's face as if to emphasise his point.

Morkin's first thought as he was hauled off Dancer was that he was going to die. Now having seen Fref above him, he knew he wanted to live, he was not going to die like this, he was a king and he was going to fight, after all why else had Luxor trained him all these years? Certainly not to lie here and die. As Fref leaned forward with his knife, Morkin brought his knee up hard into Fref's groin. The look of glee and malice on Fref's face quickly changed to confusion and then pain as he crumpled forward. Unfortunately for Morkin, Fref landed right on top of him in a writhing, cursing heap. By the time Morkin had managed to free himself from under Fref, the other man was towering over him. The pain was immense, a sea of red clouded his vision and slowly the surrounding scenery faded to black as Morkin slumped backwards. The man brought up his sword again to strike down on Morkin's prone body.

"I would not do that if I were you."

The man looked up at the voice and smiled. "He's ours and we need the money, so bugger off."

Morkin had recognised the voice immediately, it belonged to Luxor. He was safe, he thought as he drifted into the darkness.

"He is the King and belongs to no man. If you wish to partition the King, then please do it in the customary manner." Luxor smiled at the man, a smile that stated clearly 'I AM NOT JOKING' in capital letters.

The man gazed down at where Morkin lay and then looked back at Luxor. "Might be too late, but as you can see this fellow here called Fref," he pointed with his sword at the groaning Fref, "was trying to rob the King, it was only my timely intervention here that saved his life!!! I think!!" A sullen shrug of his shoulders accompanied the words. "Never was much use with a sword, seems I may have hit the King by mistake?" The question was left begging to be believed as he looked away briefly, trying to calculate the distance back to the woods.

"Very well, if what you say is true, then the King will pay you handsomely for saving his life," Luxor replied. "Please be so kind as to kill the man you called Fref, the accepted punishment for attacking the King, and I will personally double the reward!"

13

The man looked at Fref and then at Luxor. Fref was by now more aware of the situation and had proceeded to crawl back towards the woods.

"Well, come on, he is getting away!" commanded Luxor, trying to hide his amusement.

"How much?" asked the man. "How much of a reward for saving the King's life?"

"Ten ras sound reasonable?" enquired Luxor.

The man smiled.

"But only when the guilty man is dead!" Luxor smiled again.

The man looked sorely tempted for a moment as he watched Fref crawl away.

"Ah! I'm afraid he is my brother-in-law and my wife would kill me if I killed him, Sir, and then there is the little ones to look after, all ten of them, Sir. They are an awful handful and so many mouths to feed, and then the pigs, not been a good yearrr …," the man stammered, now becoming afraid.

Luxor had raised his hand, "Enough, go and take Fref with you, but be warned, if the King does die today as a result of your hand I will return and take my vengeance on you both, and trust me it will not be a swift death!" He paused, letting the words have the desired effect, the growing fear in both men becoming more evident as they inched backwards away from the prone figure of the young Prince. "I can see he stirs now so be gone, you are both pardoned this time!" Luxor was no longer smiling, the men had ran.

Morkin had discovered that day that he was never truly alone. Luxor, it seemed, was never far away. Morkin smiled to himself, the troubles he had caused this man in the years gone by, and here now he saw Luxor troubled. This did not auger well, suddenly the good feelings of the day seemed to evaporate like a morning mist in the heat of the sun. What will the day hold for me now? he thought as he dismounted beside his friend.

Chapter Two

The mist descended from the mountain top, shrouding Ranabin in a cloak of damp air.

"If only I could remember where it was," he said to himself, "and this mist does not help in finding it," he harrumphed.

Ranabin stumbled over a pile of rocks, slipped and landed with a thud on his bottom.

"Well, I'll be ...," he exclaimed, "here it is all along."

He picked up his stick and leant on it whilst he rubbed his bottom. The problem with growing old, he thought, is I have less padding on my bottom to cushion my fall. Ranabin was now at least 150 years old. He was not naturally clumsy, but he did spend rather a lot of his time falling over. This, it could be said, was due to the fact that he spent most of his life halfway up the mountain of Stant, which for its sins was usually covered in a thick, wet mist that made things rather slippery underfoot. This meant in turn that Ranabin spent rather a lot of his time on his bottom. Today though was different; you see, today Ranabin was coming down his mountain, which is why he had brought his stick. The stick itself was a plain old stick, fallen off a tree a few years since, nothing overly special about it apart from at the moment it was Ranabin's favourite stick. He used it to lean on, he used it to walk with (not that he really needed it) and he used it to chop off the heads of various plants and flowers as he walked, pretending to be a famous knight fighting off the enemies of his kingdom.

It was in just such an adventure that Ranabin had today lost his stick. He had been trying to strike the head off a particularly tough and vicious dandelion, when his stick had slipped out of his hand, soaring away on a spinning arc off the side of the mountain ledge he had been standing on. It had quickly disappeared from view into the mist, with the only trace of its existence being the clatter it made as it bounced off the rocks below until it had found its current resting place. Now that it was safely back in his grasp, Ranabin started to sing to himself:

> "*Semor cemest si mi*
> *A grand old mage I be*
> *Semor Cemest si mi*
> *My bladder's full, I need a pee.*"

With that he hitched up his robe and after a few minutes he let out a satisfied sigh and continued down the mountain.

Ranabin himself was, well, you could only describe him as being wiry. No real muscle or bulk as such, but having spent all his life up a mountain, he was tough and agile. He was, however, prone to slipping, which he blamed mostly on his choice of footwear as opposed to the damp weather. On his feet were a pair of sandals which were made of wood. He had been given them as a fortieth birthday present, and when new they had gripped the slopes of the mountain with a sure-footedness of their own. Now unfortunately that grip had eroded away and the sandals slipped and slid on every wet surface; despite this though Ranabin felt very attached to them and refused to get a new pair. His robe was, when clean, a light green colour, with speckles of blue and white. The choice of colour was for no other reason than him liking it and the pattern when he had seen it at a market ten years ago. This by coincidence was the last time Ranabin had come down his mountain. His face was clean-shaven and apart from a broken front tooth, another unfortunate fall last month, his only distinguishable feature was his eyes. You see, one was blue and the other was green. Ranabin knew that eventually they would both turn white, but at the moment they were his pride and joy, and as far as he knew, the only success in his studies.

Ranabin was one of only five mages in the land. He was by far the youngest by at least 150 years, with the oldest mage, Sin, apparently, if you could believe him, approaching his 750th year. So in terms of being a mage, Ranabin was just like a child, which was very much how the other four mages treated him. This annoyed Ranabin so much that as a result he very rarely visited the other four. The fact that Ranabin did not have a tower was also frowned upon by the other four. It was also very much a sore point with Ranabin. He did have a tower five years ago, and even if he had said it himself, it was a very fine tower indeed. But in a rather unfortunate use of herbs, fertilisers and fire it, well, it was technically still there, as he often told himself, but unfortunately it was also over there, there and there as well, just not all together, a sort of scattered tower.

Today was one of those days that Ranabin had to visit the other four. He had been summoned. Four equally as obnoxious and annoying birds had come and sung to him this morning. Ranabin had no real idea what they were twittering about, but the fact that they had all come at the same time and were all singing the same song at his feet on a mist-covered mountain slope could only mean one thing! The other four wanted to talk to him.

Next time I'll make the mist thicker, he thought.

All mages were supposed to be able to talk to the birds in a sing-song twittering sort of fashion, but Ranabin much preferred talking to the worms, mainly because they hated birds, which of course ate them, and because the four other mages used the birds to summon him. But mostly because the perpetual mist on his mountain meant he did not meet many birds and therefore had not really bothered to learn the language. If the truth be told, he had no real problem with any animal or creature in general, including birds, it was just those four birds in particular that he disliked. No imagination between them, he thought, each bird identical to the other, small with a red breast and a coat of greeny-grey feathers. But the thing that most annoyed him was that after their twittering they sang the same song over and over again or a version of it.

17

Now Master Ranabin
He's a twit
Talks to worms
Below his feet
Always sat upon his seat
Cause perhaps he has smelly feet.

Of course Ranabin was not really certain that he couldn't talk to the birds. The fact of the matter was quite simple; Ranabin could talk to the birds if he really wished it. He simply chose not to as he did not very much like what they had to say. This was further exacerbated by the fact that the only birds Ranabin had any contact with on his mountain were these four, which made him even less inclined to talk to them. This led him to the natural conclusion that all birds were probably as rude and irritating and therefore not capable of holding a worthwhile conversation.

Worms on the other hand, well if truth be told, the conversation, although not rude, was not much better. Their whole conversation seemed to centre around the water content of their soil, how many children they had and complaints of birds of which they at least had a shared poor opinion of.

"Ah, here is the spot," smiled Ranabin to himself.

He sat himself down on his bottom and looked down. Below him stretched out a steep slope of green damp grass that was interspersed with a random grey spattering of rocks and boulders. A copse of trees and shrubs grew halfway down the slope, blocking his view of the remaining ground, but Ranabin knew his mountain well and was fully aware of the path that lay ahead. The mist had cleared on this slope, leaving only thin tendrils of soft damp cloud that lingered around sporadically in the cold morning air, Ranabin's own breath adding briefly to their number as thin tendrils formed at the end of his nose each time he breathed out, only to rapidly diffuse again into the air, its brief existence consumed immediately into the enormity of the world. The sky beyond was a crisp mountain blue, promising a warmer day to come when the sun eventually climbed the sky. This was Ranabin's favourite spot on the whole mountain, the ledge that he was now sitting on gave way to a slope that fell sharply away in front of him at almost a vertical angle. This was the best part about living on a mountain, thought Ranabin as he sprang up and leapt off over the edge of the ledge with a whoop of glee.

"Yippeee, whooaa!"

He landed on one foot, off balance, his momentum carrying him forward. Just as it appeared as if he would topple over, he managed to utilise his stick to tip himself backwards and plant his other foot onto the damp grass. He was now sliding down the mountain, accelerating as he went. His robe billowing out behind him, flapping around his knees, the pattern now indistinguishable against the green grassy background as it danced around his frame. The cold damp air rushed past him, the moisture in the air making his nose run and blurring his vision as he tried in vain to blink and wipe away the gathering moisture and snot. Glasses, thought Ranabin, I need glasses, I can't see a thing. Oh no, not that rock again. A grey indistinguishable shape was hurtling straight at him. He leant hard to his left, as a large grey shape with streaks of green across its surface blurred past him on the right.

I'm sure that rock moves, he thought to himself. No time to daydream, Ranabin, he thought as he braced his knees and crouched down lower, arching his slender frame forward. The increase in speed was immediate. Here we go, he thought as a green bush grew bigger and bigger in front of him as he hurtled towards it, up and over, he pushed up and jumped into the air. Just in time, he thought as he felt leaves and twigs brushing and tugging against his ankles and sandals. "Must remember to tuck my knees in. Ah yes!! This is the way to fly," he laughed out loud, the excitement mounting as his flight upwards reached its apex. The ground below his feet was a blur of greens, browns and greys as the undulating terrain flew by beneath him. His descent was slow and graceful as he leant into the slope, the ground now less steep as he approached the bottom of the mountain.

"Prepare for landing, feet down," he shouted out against the rush of air blowing into his face. He straightened his legs and leant further forward.

"Here we come," and he bent his knees slightly to prepare for the impact of the ground that was rushing up to meet him beneath his feet.

"YES!! Perfect," he was again sliding down the remainder of the slope on the damp grass with a slightly smug grin on his face.

"Time to stop, I think," and he collapsed backwards and continued to slide on his bottom. The act had the desired effect and his descent slowed until he was at last sitting at the bottom of the slope, his legs splayed out either side of the first tree of Mark Wood. Ranabin looked down and chuckled in relief, "And not a moment too soon!"

Now Ranabin was never what you could call well turned out, but at the moment he was a sight. His legs were covered in thick mud and grass up to his knees. There were twigs and leaves growing out of his sandals, his stick seemed to have sprouted branches and some leaves and, to top it all off, he had a huge greenish-brown stain up the back of his robe. Ranabin stood up carefully and began to pick the twigs and leaves out of his sandals; he was interrupted by a familiar and irritating song.

> *"Now Master Ranabin*
> *He's a twit*
> *Who cannot keep*
> *Upon his feet*
> *Prefers to slide*
> *Upon his seat*
> *A really un-endearing feat."*

"I'm coming," cursed Ranabin as he shook his stick at the birds, who just hopped out of the way and then fluttered off into the woods, singing as they went, their chirping and calling slowly fading into the distance.

Must be something terribly important today, if they have sent those cursed birds after me twice, he thought. Now which way? He looked around, surveying his options. Ah yes, here it is. The path was very obvious now that he had seen it.

———◇———

In Icebar Tower, watching Ranabin, sat the four senior mages of the Moon. Sin, as the oldest mage, sat closest to the fire which sparkled and hissed as he spoke to it, its green flames seemingly responding to the very tones of his voice. Sin was getting old now and he knew that his time here was nearly over. He could not leave and continue his journey, however, until Ranabin had come of age, as only then could a new mage be born from the fires of Ester. From even before the time that the imps had ruled these lands, there had always been five mages to keep the land healthy. The Mage of the Peoples of the Moon lands, the Mage of the Animals, the Mage of the Air, the Mage of the Water and the Mage of the Land itself. It took 150 years to train a mage in each discipline and only when they were ready could they then be promoted through the five, starting from the land, to water, to air, to animals and finally on to the mage of the peoples of the Moon lands.

Ranabin, although he knew it not at this time, was the Mage of the Land. It was now his time to move on to being the Mage of the Water, it was time for a new mage to take his place. Sin, who had now been all five, was now nearly translucent with age; at times he seemed to disappear entirely from view only to flicker back into vision again after a few seconds. These periods of disappearance were becoming longer and longer as the days and years progressed, and eventually Sin knew he would disappear from view forever, and the cycle would begin again. The only problem was that despite having 150 years to train and master his skills, Ranabin was not yet ready and the 150th year ended in two full moons' time. If he was not ready by the end of the year then Sin would disappear without a new mage being born, leaving only four mages, and the balance of the land would be altered and become out of phase, with potentially disastrous consequences. The four remaining mages would each as a result wield too much power and the land itself would suffer. The powers of the people would grow and the land would be stripped bare.

History, it seemed, was repeating itself. Sin knew what needed to be done, but why was it always Ranabin? It was as if the fates were always stacked against him. The same cycle as last time, 1500 years ago when it had also almost ended in disaster and every 300 years since. But this time it is even worse. This time the dragons are no longer around and the Fey no longer have an interest or so it would seem. The Wolves of Fennigan are not what they once were and the humans, since the loss of the Ice Crown, have no king to unite them. To expect a saviour to come from the sea again would be too much to ask from the current water mage, Anabar. They had each played their part every 300 years. Fazam, the Mage of the Air, with the dragons, now that was something special, Sin thought. Five hundred dragons, each with their own markings and colours, flying over the Northern Mountains from who knows where, led by Serevent, their queen. They had swooped down from the heights onto the Dark Knights, who had never stood a chance beneath their fiery breath and razor-sharp claws. My word, was it really that long ago?

"*Saramuch.*" The flame turned to yellow.

"*Celum.*" The flame turned to light purple.

"Sin, are you playing with the fire again?" asked Acab.

Sin did not reply. Ah, Acab, he thought, how could I have forgotten your masterstroke, the Wolves of Fennigan?

"Was it really 900 years ago that you summoned the first of the Fennigan wolves, Acab?" asked Sin.

Acab looked over at his friend, "Ah yes, the wolves, I do believe it must have been, let's see, humans, dragons and, yes, wolves. Why do you ask?"

"Ranabin."

"Oops," said Sin almost immediately as the fire jumped.

Just at that moment in the woods Ranabin, who had been walking along the path, fell flat onto his bottom. "Oww," he exclaimed loudly.

"You've done it again, Sin, haven't you?" enquired Acab.

"Yes, but this time it was accidental, I forgot I was facing the fire."
Both mages laughed.

"Oh well, soon it will be my turn," Acab sighed, when he had
finally stopped laughing.

"Do it again, Sin," shouted over Anabar from his seat by the
window in the tower.

Fazam and Anabar both watched as in the distance Ranabin
again slipped over and landed on his bottom. They were both laughing so much that they never heard their own names being shouted
into the fire; they both slipped off their seats and landed with a thud
on the hard stone floor. They both looked over to see the two older
mages bent over, looking at them with huge grins on their faces. All
four then burst out in laughter, whilst intermittently Sin would shout,
"Ranabin," into the fire, until eventually all four mages were rolling
on the floor in fits of hysterical laughter and unable to talk.

⊰•◆•⊱

Meanwhile in the woods Ranabin was having a terrible time of it.
It seemed that at the moment he just could not stop falling over. He
had no sooner stood up, when bang, he was again on the ground, it
was almost as if he were drunk on ale, yet he knew this was not the
case as the last time he had drunk the stuff was over ten years ago,
the same time he had bought his robe. Was I drunk when I bought
it? he thought, Oh well, good taste then.

Finally he managed to make his way along the path until he came
to a stream. I'll sit here for a while and try to clear my head and rest
my aching body, he thought. He watched as the water gently flowed
past, listening to its soothing song as it traversed the rocky stream
bed. The water was clear and very inviting, reminding him of how
thirsty he had become. Ranabin leaned forward on his knees, gently lowering his hand into the water, his other hand took a firm hold
of a grassy divot growing on the side of the bank. The water was icy
cold to the touch; he brought his hand up in a cup shape towards his

23

lips. The water tasted as good as it looked, cold, crisp and fresh. He lowered his head towards the water and thirstily cupped more into his open mouth.

———◆———

The four mages in the tower had by now recovered from their mirth and Sin was once again looking into the fire.

"So what will we do with him?" asked Acab.

Sin continued to look deep into the flames thoughtfully.

"Sin, did you hear me?" Acab had turned to face him.

Sin raised his hand, Acab stopped and looked into the fire himself. The Dark Knights were there, rampaging over the land, the scene changed, a tower burning, a dragon swooping out of a cloud-filled sky, flames spewing forth from its mouth. A crown, shining brighter and brighter now became the focus of their attention, the rest of the fire disappearing into the background as if the flames themselves were in the shade of the crown's brightness. The light became blinding as it filled the room of the tower, then bang. The light vanished, leaving behind a dark, empty void. The howl following it started off as a low grumble as if struggling to find its power, and then suddenly, it burst into the room, shaking the walls, knocking the four mages to the floor as it reverberated off the ceiling and floor, looking to escape. The window smashed, sending shards of glass and timber showering down to the foot of the tower as the howl fled out into the woods, a trail of birds taking to the air in alarm marking its progress outwards, through the trees until it could no longer be seen or heard.

"What on earth was that?" asked Fazam, to no one in particular. Sin and Acab looked at each other as they slowly picked themselves off the floor.

"Did you see that? What does it mean?" Acab asked as he looked at Sin.

Sin looked at his oldest friend and sighed. "Come, we need to talk before Ranabin arrives," he crawled back to his fire and resat on the matting on the floor, "and you two, come along, we do not have much time, he will be here soon."

———◆———

Ranabin stood up in the stream he had just fallen head first into, he was soaked through. The water cascaded off him in angry torrents as if annoyed that he had taken it away from the stream. What on earth was that? he thought to himself. He had been leaning over the stream when he had heard a very loud howl. He had nearly jumped out of his robe, thinking some manner of hideous forest beast was about to pounce upon him. All that had happened, however, was that his hand had slipped off the bank and he had fallen head first into the cold water. He now looked around warily, listening and looking for any signs of the owner of such a noise. His nerves were on edge and he stood shivering and shaking, which was not totally as a result of the cold water. Slowly he regained some of his composure and decided that there was no obvious imminent danger to himself. He still remained hidden in the stream though for another few minutes until eventually the result of the coldness of the water and the pain in his joints made his mind up for him and he scrambled up the muddy bank on the far side. As soon as he left the water though, he noticed that his robe was completely dry.

"Well, I'll be …," he laughed, "that has never happened before."

He had completely forgotten the mysterious howl now, as he thoroughly examined his robe. Hmmmm, a bit damp under the armpits, but apart from that it is completely dry, he thought. He walked back over to the stream. Looking at it suspiciously, he again knelt down and slowly lowered his hand into the stream. His fingers broke the surface of the water, causing a small eddy to form as the water diverted its course around the new intrusion. It was cold and wet exactly as it was before. He pulled his fingers out. They were now completely dry, no trace of any water on them at all.

"Well I never," he exclaimed out loud, "a magic stream."

The slow realisation that he had just drunk from the stream made him slightly nauseous as he thought what this water would do to his insides. He looked at his hand again and fascination got the better of him. He plunged his hand back into the stream and pulled it back out. Again it was completely dry. Wet, dry, wet, dry, wet, dry, he continued to push and pull his hand in and out of the water, laughing as he did so. Well, well, well, thought Ranabin as he walked back into the woods, let's see, shall we? He turned round and ran straight for the stream and jumped right into the middle, the water splashed up over his robe and head as he landed. Then bending down, he continued to scoop the icy water up over his head, causing him to take sharp intakes of breath each time he did so, followed by a whoop of delight at his own childishness. Once he was thoroughly soaked he decided that it was time to get out. He waded towards the bank and again scrambled up until he was once more standing on the edge of the trees.

As before he was completely dry, now he was out of the water. "Oh look, and clean as well," as he examined his robe. His robe was now as clean as it was on the day he had bought it, the colours were once again vibrant and bright. He studied the intricacies of the design as if his eyes had never seen the full pattern before, it felt as if the robe was now alive and its beauty had been awakened from a long dormant sleep. He was feeling very happy with himself and, if the truth be told, a little smug. I know where I will be doing my laundry from now on, he grinned.

<hr />

Up in the tower, Sin, Acab, Fazam and Anabar were now sitting in a circle on the mats on the floor. The fire was in front of all of them as they circled it, the heat had been turned down and it was now just a pale low flame in the hearth. To look at them from the outside it was plain to see that they were all very similar in stature, the same lean, wiry frame as Ranabin. All of them wearing a different coloured robe though. Sin was in black, red for Acab, purple for Fazam and blue for Anabar. They were all clean-shaven with short mousy-brown hair. The only discernable difference between all four apart from the robes was the colour of their eyes and their translucency. Sin, as already mentioned, was so translucent that at times he would disappear from vision, and at other times he was only visible as a faint whiff of smoke which barely differentiated his outline from the surrounding environment. His eyes were completely white with no trace of any colouring.

Acab was still visible all the time although his appearance was blurred and distorted around the edges as if he had been smudged, his was an almost opaque appearance. His eyes were totally clear like glass, with only thin green veins visible around the outside and a slightly darker chiselled glass effect in the centre where the dark pupils should have been.

Fazam's skin was very thin and wispy and the colour of watered-down milk, his thin yellow veins easily visible below the shallow surface. His skin shone like a pearl in the light and gave an impression of depth, strength and fragility all at the same time. His eyes were like a multifaceted crystal, stained with the faintest tint of blue. They shone and sparkled as they caught the light and could at times appear as if they contained a multitude of colours and textures, although if you were to stare at them for any length of time you would find them both foreboding and unsettling but all the same fascinating.

Anabar, the last of the four was just pale, a white sallow skin with no other colouring, as if it had never seen the sun. His eyes were completely blue, a light blue similar to the sea on a hot, clear, sunny day. They held depth and clarity, no visible pupil and no white to surround it, just the light blue that reminded everybody that met him of water.

They were now in deep conversation, and judging from the tones and animation, there was obviously some disagreement between the four.

"I tell you he has the ability," Fazam stated angrily.

"He was always the lesser of the five, the weakest, the clumsiest and the least able," Acab retorted.

"Ability only comes from belief," Anabar stated calmly.

"Agreed, but whose belief, his or ours?" Acab asked.

"The belief of the Lands of the Moon," Fazam was now becoming very agitated in his defence of Ranabin.

"Oh come on, Fazam, we all know that the people of the Moon lands no longer have any belief in us or indeed in themselves. The people of the land are in themselves the land; and what is a land without its people and a people without their land?" Acab retorted.

"And whose fault is that, Acab? Theirs or ours? We have hidden away in our towers for over a hundred years just watching. How can they have any belief in us if we no longer have any belief in them?" Anabar watched Acab as he talked.

"Enough," Sin had listened intently to the argument, "this conversation is totally irrelevant. Ranabin is our only hope so there is no point in arguing about his virtues or vices. He is the one who has inherited the power this time, and only he will know how to use it and be able to do so."

Laughing, Acab replied, "Yes well, that's the point, is it not! It is very plain to see that he does not know how to use the power."

"When the time comes he will have to be able to use it and we have to believe in him and guide his path. After all, if we four who are of him as he is of us do not believe in him, then there is no hope," Sin replied as he stood up to indicate that the conversation was now over.

"Now let's prepare, he will be here soon." Sin looked at the other three, "Come on, we have not a lot of time left."

Chapter Three

So that was the prince-to-be-king, thought Carebin. Not much to look at now, but I do see some potential in the young man.

"Come quickly, we must arrive before them and prepare," he called out to the other two riders. He then leant forward and whispered into the ear of his horse, it flicked its ears and snorted in response and their pace quickened as the three horses stretched out their long legs and seemingly flew over the terrain; such was their majesty and ease in the gallop.

In the distance the Crescent Wood grew closer and closer, drawing him home. The green trees a welcome sight after the grey mountains and the rolling plains of the Moon lands. After three years, Carebin the Fey was returning to his people. He had much to tell them and many a tale to enthral a people who for too long had hidden in the sanctuary of their trees away from the world.

Tales of grey snow-covered mountains that reached up so high that it felt as if you were actually in the clouds. Tales of distant seas that rolled and crashed onto sand and shingle beaches, of strange lands where the sun blazes hot throughout the day in a constantly cloudless sky, contrasted by the cold moisture of the nights that seemed to replenish and refresh the land for its next assault from the sun. Of the strange creatures he had met, some forgotten, some considered to be a myth, the ice trolls, the wolves and others too bizarre to mention. Tales of happiness, of laughter, of adventure and tales of losses and of sadness. Hopefully tales that would excite and inspire his people to once more travel the lands of their forefathers as the once proud and illustrious Fey of old had done.

He knew though, deep in his heart, that this would not be an easy task. The Fey Elders, the leaders of his people, were protective, cautious and suspicious, and as they formed the council, they in turn ruled all Fey. They remembered well the price of Fey blood paid during the last war. The elders had vowed then never to lead their people to war again and had thus hidden their people in the woods and forests of the Moon lands, and using the ancient faerie magic, they had concealed their presence from the humans and other inhabitants of the land, woods and forests. Occasionally an elder would wander into the realm of man to observe their path, but no longer did the council appear interested in the fate of the land or its inhabitants, until three years ago, he closed his eyes and let the memories occupy his mind.

That had been the first time Carebin had been summoned to the council and he remembered being shocked as he approached to see a man in the middle of the circle of elders. The man appeared to be drugged as he lay on his back, staring blankly with completely white eyes at the canopy of leaves overhead. The elders sat in a circle around the man, who Carebin now knew as Luxor. The elders were chanting the song of the woods, inviting the spirits to return to their domain. The Fey used the spirits to ascertain the truth and righteousness of any important information they received. For the elders to use them on a non-Fey was unheard of for hundreds of years. Carebin sat and watched as the air in the hall of trees became thicker and denser. A cloud of thick particles forming then started to shimmer and shine and dance all around them before finally migrating towards the elders, leaving a faint trail of wispy coloured smoke in their wake. It formed a ring of bright multicoloured light around the elders as the song they sung reached its peak and the light began to shine more brightly as the words of the song became fuller and deeper.

"Cabar te on felor,
Cabar te on felor,
Harry to full aman
Set an to sarebarh
Se te on Towd."

The ring of light turned white and rushed towards the prone body in
the centre, bathing him in a brilliant white that made his whole body
glow. The light grew brighter and brighter until nothing could be seen
within, the body of the man now invisible to all around. Then noth-
ing, just complete silence and darkness. When their eyes had finally
adjusted to the darkness again, the body of Luxor had disappeared,
it was as if it had never been there.

An elder looked up, "Ah, Carebin, you have come as requested.
Good, sit over there."

Carebin again looked around and now saw a chair in the centre
of the circle of elders. The chair was like nothing he had seen before,
it seemed to have sprouted out from the very ground. Its legs were
thickly wound vines, stretching up, round and round each other. Two
of the vines stretched up further to form the back of the chair, the other
two bent over to form the seat, the leaves and the branches from the
vines interweaving and knitting with each other to provide the sup-
port for the seat and back. Carebin stepped between two elders in
the circle and crossed over to the chair. As he went he looked for any
sign of Luxor but could see no indication anywhere that the human
had ever been in this place.

Carebin slowly sat down on the chair, testing its strength. As he
lowered himself into the chair though, he was immediately surrounded
by an intense white light. The elders around him began to fade out of
focus, their shapes becoming indistinct as his whole world became a
sea of bright iridescent white light. His world had started to spin as
he lost all his bearings, he tried to focus on something, anything, he
tried to stand but seemed to be held in place by a mysterious force.
He shut his eyes, trying to shut out the light, screwing them tighter
and tighter until he could bear the brightness no more, it seemed to

be burning into the back of his head. Then, just as suddenly as it had arrived it was gone, rapidly fading away into the background.

"Open your eyes, Carebin, it is quite safe," the same voice as before, but this time it felt as if it was coming from inside his head.

"Open your eyes and see the truth, Carebin."

He slowly opened his eyes, blinking as he did so; he was up high, high above the Lands of the Moon. He grabbed for the chair in panic to stop himself falling.

"Relax, Carebin, let go, you will not fall. Your body has not left the circle of elders. You are on the dream path, Carebin, remember all that you see, it may save your life and the lives of many. But be warned, do not believe all that you see, as the truth of it is dependant on the heart, Carebin, not the eyes."

Silence followed and filled his mind. Relax, he thought, breathe. He opened his eyes and relaxed, he swooped down through the clouds, the feeling of cold, damp air rushing over his face seemed too real to him and he grabbed again for the chair. Relax, he thought, taking another breath, so this is what it is like to fly, to soar like a bird. A rider on a horse came into view on the mountains below. He was galloping hard, looking over his shoulder now and again, fearful and scared as if he was being pursued by hell itself. He had a sack tied to his saddle, an eerie yellow glow just visible through the coarse material even at this height, accompanied by what appeared to be, to his ears, a low humming noise.

I'm too close, thought Carebin, as he soared straight at the horse and rider. He threw his hands up in front of his face, as he shot through the image and it disappeared, he looked back to see a dark empty void. Where am I? he thought, sweat dripping down his forehead as he battled with himself, trying to regain his composure. The world was now entirely black, a complete emptiness about it, no light, no sound, just a dark thick blackness that seemed to stretch and stretch forever all around him. Then from the distance up ahead, singing. It came straight at him, the sweet soft notes floating gently towards him as if carried on water. The song was so gentle and peaceful it seemed to surround him with a deep soothing feeling of happiness. He tried to pick out the words, but they would not stay in his mind, they just surrounded him and then vanished, the next immediately taking the last's place. He peered into the darkness in vain, trying to find its source, hoping that it would never end; he could listen to these notes forever.

Flame burst out from the darkness, rousing Carebin from his thoughts, the song was gone, his peace with it, leaving an emptiness inside his head. Riders now appeared inside the flame, dressed all in black, riding completely black horses. Too many to count, but they seemed to be surrounded by the flames, riding through them, but no sound, yet he could see their mouths open and close as they seemingly screamed and shouted at each other. Carebin leaned forward, trying to see the insignia on their shields.

The howl seemed to come from nowhere and everywhere all at once; the howl of a wolf that echoed off the darkness surrounding him, chasing him. He forgot where he was as he tried to run, the noise now seemed to be pursuing him, his mind in turmoil as he tried in vain to flee the sound, he tried to stand, to escape. He fell.

He tried to rise, but the world was now light again, the wolf's howl was gone. His limbs were not responding, he felt very cold as he started to shiver and shake. His head was thumping and the pain of opening his eyes to the light was unbearable.

He awoke some time later on a bed of the softest heather, woodland flowers surrounded him, their sweet scents tantalising and teasing his senses. The tree branches seemed to drape over him, surrounding him in a sea of light green, yet the sunlight seemed still able to trickle and filter in with a new gentle radiance. His head felt light and empty, he felt that his body was no longer attached to him and had to look down just to reassure himself it was still there. He tried to rise, but thought better of it as his giddiness rose instead.

"Rest, Carebin, rest for now." The same voice yet again, a deep commanding voice, yet nobody was in sight from where he lay. He lay back and closed his eyes again, to be instantly rewarded with deep, peaceful sleep.

When he opened his eyes again he looked up and saw an older Fey sitting beside him.

"You have rested sufficiently?" without waiting for a reply, "Good. Are you hungry? Thirsty?" Again without waiting for a reply, the older Fey seemed to summon someone in the background who had obviously been waiting, to fetch food and water for Carebin.

"How rude you must think I am. I do believe I have failed to introduce myself. I am Fengar. We have not met, but I am well aware of you, Carebin." The last almost sounding like an accusation.

"Your visits to the human games to shoot arrows, your reluctance to accept the rulings of the elders, your continued persistence in putting the lives of your people at risk, Carebin. What have you to say to all of this?"

Carebin looked at Fengar, who was sitting beside him. He saw everything in this Fey Elder that he disliked about his people. The older Fey was arrogant and assured of his righteousness in every aspect of the Feys' lives. He had the air about him of somebody that was used to being obeyed, with no room in his life for sentiment, personal opinion or questioning of the way of the elders. He was obviously an elder of some standing, but since Carebin took no interest in the Fey council, he did not know that this Fey was in fact the Supreme Guardian of the Western Fey and as such was a very powerful individual.

"It would appear that you have already made your mind up about me, so there is little point in having any say, is there!" Carebin replied scornfully.

Fengar though was unperturbed by Carebin's scorn.

"I am merely repeating the observations of the wood and forest, Carebin. If I was to listen and take heed of everything I heard, I would never be able to trust or judge anyone fairly." Fengar smiled as he continued. "No! I have no opinion of you as of yet apart from what I have just seen and the fact that you appear to be a very resourceful and adventurous young Fey." He paused as the food and water arrived. "Eat, Carebin, I need you strong."

Carebin looked at Fengar, as he grabbed the bread and water. "Strong for what?"

Fengar looked around him as if checking they were alone, he then leant over, his face now inches from Carebin as he whispered, "First tell me what you saw and then we will see."

Carebin chewed on the bread he had just bitten into, it was as usual delicious. No human could make bread that tasted this good, he thought. The natural honey and nectar used tasted divine as it slowly melted on his tongue. The water from the pitcher was perfect; a clear, crisp, cold and refreshing drink taken from the unspoiled waters of the River Cool. He suddenly felt guilty and self-conscious as he realised that he had not offered this Elder any food. He held his plate out. "Sorry, excuse my manners, would you care to share my food?" he smiled sheepishly at Fengar.

"Thank you, Carebin, I think I will, if you do not mind."

They both ate in silence for a few minutes, caught up in their own thoughts and savouring the quality of the food.

"Now, if you please, Carebin, can you tell me what you saw?"

"I saw a man lying on the ground in the centre of the elders!" Carebin looked at Fengar as he said this, trying to judge his reaction.

Fengar seemed to just ignore this statement, "No!! Tell me what you saw whilst sitting in the chair."

Carebin concentrated and looked at the ground as he tried to piece together what had happened. Fengar waited patiently, watching the young Fey with obvious concern on his face. Carebin eventually looked up into the face of the Elder and recalled all that he had seen and heard including the voice. He must have looked down again at some point because as he finished speaking and again looked up to where Fengar was sitting, there was now nobody there. His chair had gone as well and he was completely alone again.

Was I still dreaming? he thought to himself, but then he saw the remains of the food still lying where they had left it. But I never heard him leave! It is as if he just vanished! He slowly sat up, he felt refreshed and invigorated, as if by telling his dream to the Elder he had somehow released what had been draining his strength. He felt full of energy and life, almost as if he were reborn. He looked around, he never tired of the beauty of his woodland home; the thick canopy of leaves and branches as a roof, to keep the glare of the sun *and the worst of the rain off them, thick sturdy tree trunks as walls, which were as strong as any human's keep, the soft earthy floor with its generous covering of leaves, grass and moss, the constant changing colours of the seasons, a rich tapestry of ever changing hues and textures. How dull it must be to live in a house and be surrounded by the same colours and textures, he thought with a rueful smile. Yes, despite his adventures and visits to the humans he was very much a Fey at heart.*

No matter how much he thought his peoples' decision to hide away from the outside world was wrong, he also on occasion very much appreciated the solitude and peacefulness this self-enforced exile afforded. He firmly believed, however, that his people could have both very easily if they chose it. He was determined to reopen their minds to the world outside their sanctuary.

As he sat taking in his surroundings, Fengar was back in the circle of the elders. Unbeknown to Carebin at the time, they were coming to the decision that would alter his entire life and set him on the journeys and adventures to follow; some of which he reflected he had just returned from.

"The visions were clear and confirm the human's truth."

"Indeed it would seem so, if what you say is true."

"Do we now question the truth and sincerity of our own kind? This youth has no reason to lie or deceive, he has no knowledge of events. He spoke from the heart and it was true, our ancestors have never falsely accused or falsely led us before."

"You are wise as usual, Fengar, and I am misguided; however, our caution has saved us and kept us safe, since the time of the dragon."

"Indeed you are correct, but caution can only serve for so long."

"And who is the judge of this length of time? How do we know it is now and not in the future?"

"The ancestors have spoken, have they not? Do we now choose to ignore them, when they have always guided our path? Surely that would be the path to destruction, as we have always trusted them

before."

"Again your wisdom has truth, Fengar, however, the land is not as it once was, it is no longer our land, perhaps the ancestors are misguided in themselves or perhaps there is other magic now around to confuse and trick them."

"My friend, you are right to ask questions, and it is your earned right to do so. This council though will decide the question, not you or I or any other individual, as has always been our way. All I can do is provide the truth. The ancient ways of our people are sacred and honoured. The human today arrived by their will, of that we cannot dispute! Agreed?"

"Agreed," a chorus of assent.

"He was also returned to his realm unhurt, a sure sign of the trust of the ancestors and the truth in his words. Agreed?"

"Agreed."

"These words were confirmed by one of our own kind's visions. Agreed?"

"Agreed."

"Then the decision we make here today is based on our sacred traditions and customs, and is entrusted and empowered by them. Do we now turn our backs on them because it does not suit our own desires or will we be true to our ancestors and the Fey people and accept our fate as is their will?"

The light appeared as if from nowhere and Carebin, without really understanding why, stood up and walked towards it. It was not the same blinding light as before, this was a soft glow, hovering at about head height in the trees to his left. As he approached it, the voice returned; it seemed to come from nowhere and everywhere at once.

"Are you, Carebin of the Fey people, loyal and true to all the Fey and the Elder Council?"

Carebin looked around, trying to source the voice, before reluctantly answering as he was feeling slightly silly and embarrassed to be talking to a light, "I am."

"We, the Council of the Elders, have listened to your vision and

the wisdom of the ancestors. Do you accept our judgement as being truthful and wise, Carebin of the Fey?"

"Your judgement of what?" Carebin asked hesitantly with mild concern.

"You have seen some of what you should not have seen. You saw the man; however, your vision was true. His words and yours are of the same breath. You therefore are the chosen."

"The chosen?" Carebin enquired. "What does that mean?"

"These are difficult times for the Fey people, we stand at a junction on our path. The way ahead is not as clear as it once was. We ask that you seek out the truth of the visions, Carebin of the Fey."

"The truth! What truth? I do not understand!"

"The Dark Knights ride again, it is their time, these lands have no king. You walk with the humans, Carebin of the Fey. We do not have the answers to the questions. What we do know is of little consequence, and what we do not know is anarchy. The time of the changing is approaching, yet all is not well. Find the truth in the visions, Carebin of the Fey. You have until the third Shadow Day from now to return."

"Return from where and what happens after the third Shadow Day?"

"From wherever your path may lead you, Carebin of the Fey. Time, however, is only eternal to immortals and it still may be too short even for them. The third Shadow Day from now is when the council will sit to decide the path of all Fey. We will sit with or without your advice, Carebin of the Fey. We would very much like your presence, we will not, however, grieve your absence. The fate of the Fey may be in your hands, Carebin of the Fey, or perhaps may be not!"

"When do I leave? How will I travel? Where do I start?"

"You have already started, and you left the moment you stepped into the circle, Carebin of the Fey. Your horse awaits you."

The light diminished in front of his eyes, fading in a blink into nothingness. Carebin turned at a sound behind him, there she was, true to their word. His horse was standing contently grazing the tender grass where once the wood had been empty. The white mare was his most prized possession. She was descended from his family's blood-stock and was considered to be one of the finest amongst all the Fey's horses. For a people that lived in the woods and forests, this would not at first be as great a boast as it seemed. However, the Fey had a way with all animals and their horses roamed the plains of the Moon lands and were perceived by most to be just wild herds of horses, such was their freedom. Yet they were very well trained and always answered to their owner's calling as if a telepathic bond existed between Fey and horse. For Carebin's mare to have been called here without his consent or knowledge could only mean that his mare had known before he did that he was leaving the wood.

The mare looked up at him as he approached and snorted her hello.

"Hello, my beauty, it looks as if we again get to ride the plains together." Carebin produced a mushroom from his pocket and the mare gently nuzzled his outstretched hand to accept the treat. Carebin continued to walk down her side, running his hand along the mare and onwards, down the mare's side and flank, a gentle pat and once obviously satisfied, he moved as if a blur, springing up onto the mare's back, a deft movement practised over the years and helped by his agility, having spent his life living in and around trees.

He leant forward and spoke gently to his mare, at the same time rubbing her neck. With a soft whinny, the mare tossed her head as if in confirmation and set off along the path leading out of his realm.

"Follow the dream, Carebin of the Fey, let your instincts guide you," the voice trailed off as Carebin moved further along the path into the woods beyond.

It was hard to think that that was nearly twelve full seasons, three whole years ago. Carebin had in that time travelled the length and breadth of the land, and he still felt he was no closer to understanding the visions that he had had. His two companions would not be allowed entry to his realm, he was sure of that. Yet after spending the last two years of his life with them, he was reluctant now to part with their company. Crescent Wood was now just over the next hill. How much will have changed, he thought and then remembered with a smile that probably very little, as usual in the Realm of the Fey. They were of course waiting for him for that. They would be waiting for him to give them guidance. The enormity of this had only become apparent after he had left his home three years ago, and at first it had been too big a burden for him to carry. It had sucked at his soul, emptying him of life. The enormity of his responsibility, one false step or one wrong word could condemn his people to a fate that he could not contemplate or bear.

He had spent the first six months of his journey hiding, skulking around aimlessly and avoiding every living creature. He had felt an outcast, not sure of how to go on and not willing to return a failure to his people. He hid in caves on the mountains, living off what he could catch or pick. His unhappiness during this time had nearly driven him mad, the Fey did not live like this, they enjoyed company, they enjoyed the trees. He was homesick; he missed the woods, the forests. His mare had deserted him during this time, she had returned to the plains far below, fed up with his company.

Yet slowly things had improved, he started to enjoy the new solitude and freedom the mountains gave him. He still did not know where to start his pursuit of the answers to his vision, yet now it did not seem to be such a heavy burden to carry. It was almost as if he knew that fate would guide him when it and he were ready. This, he realised now, had been an essential part of the journey for him. The new-felt inner peace that he had was essential for allowing the ancestors to guide him along the path chosen for him. This realisation had made the journey from thereon easier, and he had no longer worried about his path. It was out of his hands, just like now as his journey reached its end. The ancestors would be able to judge what he had to say and they would be able to make sense out of the things that he had discovered. He had grown in the last three years, more so than at any other stage in the thirty years previous to that. He now felt calm and serene at all times even in crisis, as if he had finally grown up to fulfil his potential. A new empathy and understanding existed with all living things, not just his mare, but a deeper wider understanding of the world that he lived in. He was stronger both in physical stature and that of character. But mostly he felt humble and at peace with himself and others for the first time in his life. Carebin did not know what would happen now, he knew that he would be able to talk from the heart and let the words flow, he knew what the ancestors wanted and he now knew why they had chosen him. He was going home. But for how long? he asked himself, I'll soon find out.

Carebin called over to his two companions, and after a brief discussion, he left alone, heading into Crescent Wood along a familiar track, the trees slowly swallowing his form, until he could no longer be seen from where his companions had now lit a small fire, beside a small stream.

Carebin's mare certainly seemed to know the way she should be going. She followed the track into the wood, deeper and deeper until he sensed a difference in the air, almost as if the air was now fresher, newer and more full of life. The trees also looked different, not in their physical shape, but they looked healthier, their leaves a richer, deeper, fuller green, their branches stronger and straighter. It was almost as if he had entered a different wood altogether, a wood that was more loved and cared for than the one he was in a second before. Carebin was home, he had passed through to the Realm of the Fey. He knew he was being watched from the trees, but he paid no heed. Whoever watched him would surely know he was of them, no one could pass into their realm unless they were blood or invited.

The mare carried him along the track at a gentle walk until she came upon a small clearing in the trees, the canopy of leaves breaking to allow the sun to shine down on the carpet of rich green grass. Carebin dismounted as the mare had already decided that this was as far as she was carrying him. She lowered her head to graze on the tender new shoots of grass at her feet. As soon as Carebin's feet hit the ground, he heard the voice as before, the same voice of three years ago.

"So, Carebin of the Fey, you have returned to your people. Did you find all that you sought and did you seek all that you found?"

"I have found many things and have the answers to many questions, some asked and yet others still not thought upon," his voice was calm and serene.

"Indeed you have grown in wisdom, young Fey. Come then and tell us the answers we seek, and then perhaps we will know the questions you may yet seek."

The light descended slowly from within the canopy of leaves to Carebin's right, it hovered just at the edge of the clearing and as he turned to face it, it backed off into the woods as if beckoning him to follow. Carebin followed it down a path as it led him back to the circle of the elders.

"Enter the circle, Carebin of the Fey," the voice commanded.

The chair was already there waiting for him; it was exactly as if he were back here three years previously, everything the same, bar him, he was very different. How much so, well, the elders would surely find that out for themselves. He sat down and allowed his mind to go blank as the light descended upon him, encompassing his entire being, drowning out all vision and sound. The last three years shot past his vision almost as a dream, yet more, he felt he was reliving the whole experience. The solitude on the mountains, the meeting of his companions, the snow faeries' dance, the ice trolls' hall, the lady in the mist, the Wolves of Fennigan, the Dark Knights and the Ice Crown. The memories and experiences of the last three years of his life came washing and flooding over him, they were all around him, at once a vision and then a blur as they continued to flick past his vision over and over again, faster and faster, until it was all just a coloured blur of light, the sounds now blending into a cacophony of noise, until he could no longer keep track of his thoughts. The ancestors were delving deeper and deeper into his mind, seeking the answers even he did not know he possessed. His last thought as he drifted off towards the light, the sight of the King falling.

Chapter Four

The warmth of their huddle of bodies in the cold, damp cave felt good. Their stomachs were full and there was no sight or smell of any humans around. They knew they could sleep peacefully today and enjoy the shelter that the cave afforded them from the storm that raged outside. The wind had increased in the early evening as the snow had begun to fall, driving it relentlessly down onto the pack as they had stalked the fallow deer in the forest. They would have preferred to have gone down the mountain for the easier pickings of the humans' sheep and goats, but Fent would not let them. He had insisted on staying up in the mountains on this night and they had not dared to disobey him.

So they had hunted, like they had in the past, before man had come to these lands. They had stalked their prey, keeping downwind to close the distance. Smelling it, delighting in its scent and the taste it would surely bring to their hungry mouths when they finally caught it. As they had closed in on it though, the deer had heard something, its senses alert to danger. It sensed their presence; it shot up and ran, bounding over the fallen trees, tearing through the undergrowth. Its agility allowed it to dart this way and that, changing direction effortlessly, and at times even in mid-air, its flight now joined by others of its kind in the forest. The flight of one had now become a stampede of quarry and predators each in its own race for survival.

The wolves were slower and less agile, relying on their strength, teamwork, stamina and intelligence to catch their prey; their target the weakened, slower, less-agile animal, sighted as its flight was not as brisk, its movement lacking in fluidity as it struggled to keep up with the herd. Its smell of fear hung in the air as the wolves closed in on their quarry. Fent had planned it well, he lay in wait, his pack driving the fleeing deer towards him and the ambush. They waited, listening to the noise as it came thundering towards them. This is what he had missed, the thrill of the chase, the joy of the hunt. He slunk lower to the ground, his powerful hind legs poised to propel him forward as the prey passed.

He leapt, feeling the air rush past him, the shock clear on the deer's face as too late it saw him and tried to alter its course. The warm salty taste in his mouth as his teeth sunk into the soft velvety flesh. The blood pumping into his mouth as the deer lay side by side with him, locked in a deadly embrace, its life slowly draining away, seeping into the forest floor. Its legs twitched and its eyes finally went dull. It had been a good hunt, they had caught two more deer at the same time. His pack were getting better, they were becoming stronger and he was content for now as he lay amongst them, drifting into sleep.

He woke in the early evening, feeling refreshed and alive. His plans for his kind were slowly taking shape; the Wolves of Fennigan were once more becoming a powerful presence in the Moon lands. Yet the very essence of their being was missing and this was Fent's shame. He had thought long and hard about it over the harsh winter months, the result being their presence now as a pack on the southern slopes of Fennigan Mountain. He had to make his kind strong again, they had to run free, they needed to have a powerful presence, to be once more a force to be respected in the Lands of the Moon. This was his dream, his ambition, his desire and he would work them hard to achieve it.

He stood up, shaking his huge torso, loosening off his powerful limbs, bringing them back to life, the rest of the pack aware of his temper, watching him from their huddle as he padded over to the mouth of the cave. Stopping at the entrance, he sniffed the early evening air, tasting its scent. The wind carried the aromas of all the forest and the mountain for miles around to his nose. Detecting nothing of interest in the air, he relaxed and surveyed the scene around him. Good, tonight I will gather the packs, tonight we will begin our journey back to our rightful place in these lands, tonight we will begin to bring back the pride of the wolf to these lands.

He turned to his pack and growled and snarled at them, "Neas, Fen, Sar, go and fetch the others, bring all the packs to An Sumn clearing by tomorrow dusk. Go now!" he snapped the last. Fent watched as three young wolves immediately sprang to their feet and ran out of the cave. They fanned out, each heading in a different direction, and eventually blended into the darkening landscape; their paths marked in the crisp snow now the only indication of their passage.

"The rest of you, up! There is much to be done in preparation for tomorrow night. The ground needs to be cleared and prepared, you will not rest until it is so," he barked his commands as he ordered the pack. "Pareen, you are in charge, you know how it should be done, ensure it is so," the last was aimed at a shy wolf skulking in the background. Pareen was his younger half-brother, and as such was very anxious to please and impress his older sibling. Unfortunately, in his eagerness to please, Pareen usually managed to disappoint Fent, who as a result had little or no patience with him. As Pareen was about to leave, Fent snapped at him, "Do not let me down." The snarl on his face underlying his meaning.

Fent, his orders issued, gazed out of the cave over the white snow-covered ground once more. The storm during the day had been strong, the snow had settled all over the forest and mountain, transforming the landscape from a mixture of greens and browns into the thin white tapestry he now surveyed. This will make things harder, he thought, the snow crisp and cold under his paw as he stepped forward. The humans will find it easier to notice our movements and numbers in this snow. He could not remember the last time it had snowed this late in the year, it had not been a consideration in his planning. "Never mind, hopefully it will not lie for long," he growled out loud. None of his pack though were now around to hear his thoughts.

Fent was a powerful wolf with a dark grey thick winter coat, that only now was starting to thin, showing traces of white underneath and over the belly. The body beneath, strong and muscled, toned from the constant hunting and fighting he was involved in. He was big, even for wolves of Fennigan Mountain, his size matched by his strength, cunning and fearlessness in battle. No wolf now challenged Fent for his right to lead them. He had assumed leadership over all the packs two years ago by easily defeating the last challenger to his supremacy. That had been the last of the outer packs' challenges to his domain and now he ruled them all, as it had been in the time of his father and as it should be, the blood in his veins having descended from the great wolves of old, a proud and noble race, who in their time had rescued the Fey and saved the Moon lands. They themselves had been slain years later, suffering the shame of having man rescue them as they once had been the rescuer. This shame of being beholden to man was only surpassed in recent years by the theft of their Ancients' Howl. Stolen from them twelve years ago, it was this theft and loss that now drove Fent relentlessly in his goal, the fate of his kind tied between the two, the howl and pride as one intrinsically linked and bound as one.

He knew what he had to do to get it back and tonight he would put that plan into action. Tonight the Wolves of Fennigan would once more hunt the Lands of the Moon, seeking the one whose death would recapture their call and once more his kind would be able to call to their gods, once more be able to travel freely, once more be in command of their own destiny. There was no other way, they had been promised, and although Fent had no love of their kind or trust in them, he could see no other way to recapture the howl, the Ancients' Howl, the spirit of their kind, their connection to their gods, stolen from them by a man, robbing them at the same time of their pride and destiny.

It had been a long and hard journey to this place, and at last he had managed to unite all the packs. At last they would all work together. Yes, tonight was the night. His excitement rose. He raised his head towards the full moon as it broke through the dark evening cloud, he opened his mouth, sucking in the cold night air, filling his lungs and then howled, his voice carrying out into the night sky, travelling miles over land, reaching into the hearts of all animals, exciting and scaring depending on race. Or that is how it should have been, despite his best efforts, no sound came, just a rasping emptiness where once there had been pride, joy, love, fear, hope and passion in the notes. He felt empty, incomplete, a vital piece of him missing. Soon, he thought, soon my gods, my shame and my father's shame will be avenged and we will again become a race to be respected and feared.

He left the cave, leaving his pack to his bidding. Turning left, he made his way up the slope that led to the mountain summit, the ground under paw becoming more and more rocky the higher he climbed, the valley and trees below sinking into the distance, the cave now no longer distinguishable amongst the myriad of rocks and outcrops below him. No longer able to walk up the slope, he was now bounding from rock to rock, his muscular frame making lazy work of the treacherous climb and footing. He leapt into the air, judging the distance perfectly, landing with a gentle, agile grace, his soft paws hardly making a sound; he leapt again, the landing awkward, his rear paw slipped as the rock beneath it crumbled slightly, he scrambled with a new urgency, trying to right his balance and gain purchase on the rock. His other rear paw slipped as more of the rock crumbled away, sending a small cascade of stone tumbling down the mountain. Both rear legs were now frantically fighting for grip, his body slowly sliding backwards, more rock giving way. His front paws were now flat on the rock surface in front of him as he lowered his entire body down onto the rock, trying to gain as much purchase on its treacherous surface as possible. His left rear paw was now scratching at thin air, he stole a glance over his left shoulder, the drop below him plunging down what appeared to be the whole height of the mountain, down to the forest below. The fear coursed through him, he strained his huge muscles, renewing his effort, willing himself up the rock. More rock gave way under his weight and he felt himself slip further down over the precipice, his grip on the rock giving way, his attempts to get back up now frantic as he realised he was falling back and he would fall to his death, to abject failure, his plans thwarted by his own clumsiness.

The horn's note cut a clear path through the evening air. It seemed to be all around him, echoing off the rock faces and reverberating around the mountain. The stick hit him full on the nose before he even saw it. He snapped at it out of instinct, missed, and in the process slipped further down the rock, both rear legs now scratching in mid-air. The stick swung again at his nose. This time he saw it coming and timing his bite better, he snapped his jaw shut onto it, feeling it splinter and crack in his powerful jaw. The warm salty taste of blood trickled over his tongue, as a splinter of wood drove itself into his gum. He held on despite the pain, his vision now focussing on the other end of the stick, held by a powerful-looking outstretched arm.

"Ah, Fent! Should I push or should I pull?"

Fent recognised the voice and was very sorely tempted to let go at this point, surely death would be better than rescue by this man.

"What was that, wolf? I cannot hear you!"

This last question was followed by the sound of laughter from over the edge of the rock. "Oh silly me, you cannot answer me, can you, wolf? Without letting go, that is. What a predicament. Well, let's see; I now have the opportunity to kill an enemy of my people. Just a little push and then I let go."

The stick was suddenly thrust forward, forcing Fent back further off the rock until only his head, shoulders and front paws were resting on its rough surface.

"Ha ha ha ha ha. Look at him, the supposedly powerful leader of his race. It's pathetic," the voice mocked him.

Fent hung on, his survival instincts keeping him holding on to that stick, that faint glimmer of hope and life. His jaw ached as his heavy body pulled down on him, inviting him to death below. Suddenly the stick pulled back, almost slipping out of his jaw. He was slowly dragged up the rock, scraping and scratching his body on the rough, sharp surface even through his thick coat. Fent's feeling of relief at once more being on solid ground was soon overcome by the profound indignity of his rescue. To make matters worse it was Vangor, the Dark Knights' second in command that had rescued him. His hatred of this man was immeasurable, he hated this man more than any other he had ever met. One day, he thought, as he slowly and painfully stood up on the rock. His senses took in his immediate surroundings and the men who accompanied Vangor. There were thirteen of them, all heavily armed and dressed in their customary black clothing, each wearing their red crescent emblem on their breasts and their shields which at the moment were hung from their horses' packs. Fent quickly allowed his senses to ascertain the worth of each individual in turn; they were all weak, he surmised, mere followers, relying on their master for their power and authority. Vangor though was different, here was a man to be feared; he was ruthless, cunning, powerful, ambitious and brutal as Fent and his kind had found to their cost on many occasions in the last few years.

Vangor smiled at Fent. "How's your howl coming along?" he smirked, which encouraged the men behind to laugh. "Oh yes, I seem to recall that you have lost it, how clumsy." The men, encouraged by their leader, started to shout their own insults at the wolf.

Vangor allowed his men to continue shouting their insults at the wolf, he enjoyed watching the reaction of those mocked, measuring their worth by their reaction to the insults. Fent though just stood and stared straight back at Vangor with dark piercing eyes.

"You know it pains me to have to rely on the likes of you and your kind, but my Lord commands it, so it shall be." Vangor had walked over to Fent and bent down, pushing the stick in his hand into Fent's hairy face. Still the eyes seemed to burn into him. "But mark me well, wolf," the last word spat out, "you fail me and I will find a much more gruesome death for you and your kind. In this weather a man can always use a nice new fur coat," Vangor sneered. He drove the stick at Fent with these last words and it hit him with such fury and power that he lost his balance and fell to his side. Vangor spat at him and then, turning on his heel, walked away towards his men, who, encouraged by their leader's humiliation of the wolf, increased their own derisory shouts and insults.

Fent, his anger rising, sprang to his feet, growling as he did so, his teeth visible in his powerful jaw with smears of his own clotted blood clinging to their white surface.

The sword swung past his head, the blade singing in the air, a blur of silver-white metal. Vangor now stood facing him again, the men behind now silenced by the sudden change of events. Vangor's sword was now delicately poised in his right hand, his left now loosely held his shield, which moments before had been across his back, its emblem of the red crescent emblazoned proudly on the jet-black background. Vangor had his left foot slightly further forward, resting his perfectly balanced weight on his false right foot as he watched the snarling wolf in front of him. Fent circled to his right, watching Vangor as the man moved in turn, always seemingly perfectly balanced, able to attack and defend in equal measure, the sword tip always pointing directly at Fent's head, the shield held close to the body. This adversary will have to wait, Fent thought as he swallowed his anger and let go of his temper. He loosened his stance and stood up straight, never taking his eyes off Vangor, his pride though not allowing him to totally submit.

Vangor watched the wolf as it stopped snarling at him, a smug look crossed his face. "Nice doggy," he taunted. He wanted the wolf to attack, he knew it would be an easy kill, it always was when an enemy let anger dictate their actions, he wanted to play with this wolf first, though.

"Lost a bit of your ear along with your howl, wolf." Vangor pointed with his sword at a matted blood-soaked lump of fur to Fent's left.

Fent allowed his gaze to follow the path of the sword and saw for himself a small piece of his ear, lying on the rocky surface. It was only now that the pain in his ear began to register as his anger and the adrenaline settled down. His hatred of this man increased, he had been beaten easily and he knew it. He had allowed his anger to nearly get himself killed. He swore that it would not happen again. He knew that despite his hatred of this man, he had to work for him at this time if he wanted to restore his and his kind's pride.

Vangor stood watching and waiting for Fent's next move. Despite the ease with which he had fought off the wolf, deep down he was scared of the animal. It was a supreme being, designed for killing, its instincts bred and honed over the centuries for the hunt and the kill. He knew this wolf well and he knew he was a dangerous adversary, he thus made sure at all times when dealing with it to keep it at a distance and to show off his undoubted skills with his blade in the hope of deterring its obvious desire to kill him.

Vangor at thirty-eight had been a soldier all his adult life, running away from home at fourteen to join the Dark Knights. Starting as a foot soldier, his size, aggression, ambition and ability with a sword had seen him rise up the ranks very quickly. He was a dangerous man to have as an enemy and to many he was also considered to be as equally dangerous to have as a friend. His ambition and ruthlessness had got him to where he was now. Only the Lord Tarebeth, the commander of the Dark Knights, gave Vangor orders and even then the details were left for Vangor to decide upon himself.

The stealing of the Wolves of Fennigan's howl had been Vangor's doing. For too many times now the armies of the east had tried to take the Moon lands and each time they had been thwarted in their hour of victory by the Armies of the Moon. This failure was a source of irritation and embarrassment to the Dark Knights, their glorious history tainted by this one country that on each attempt had managed to defeat their army. Yet now they had Vangor and thus felt they were sure to succeed, with him leading them.

Vangor had studied the history of his people and in particular the battles for the Moon lands. He had noticed the common link between each defeat and the links to the Moon lands. He was amazed that nobody had questioned the reasons behind the defeats before. Armed with this information, he had set off on his journey fourteen years ago to discover the real reason behind why his people had failed to overcome and conquer the Moon lands. Disguised as a tramp, he had travelled alone in the Moon lands; mingling with the people and listening to their stories. Travelling between towns, working in the fields during harvest, buying drunks ale in taverns, he had travelled the length of the land for two years with no end to the puzzle and no obvious clue to the reason behind the seemingly powerful Moon army. He had become frustrated and angry with himself and decided to return to his people, yet the idea of failure made him make one more journey into the forests of the northern Moon lands. He was later to discover these were Fennigan Forest, but at the time he knew not where he was or the name.

It was in Fennigan Forest, beneath the snowy peaks of Fennigan Mountain, that he found the wolf cub. It was wandering around in the clearing he had just stumbled into, he was hungry and tired and sorely tempted to eat the cub at first, yet it had been skinny and bony and would not have satisfied his hunger, so it had lived. This, it turned out, was the luckiest and best decision he had made in his life. He decided as he was not going to eat the cub that he could do with the company. For the next three days he had fed it, travelling down into the meadows to the south, stealing milk and livestock from the local farms and small holdings. The cub had trusted him immediately; it had a voracious appetite, and despite his best efforts he never seemed to be able to sate its hunger, yet it thrived. It slept beside him at night, sharing his warmth. It hunted with him during the day, seemingly as keen and eager to learn from him as he was from it. He watched as it moved, marvelling at its strength and agility even at this age, as it leapt and ran around the clearing in a seemingly perpetual state of motion. It encouraged him to practice and improve his own techniques as he tried to mimic the fluidity of the wolf cub. He strove to perfect his own movements and hone his skills with his weapons, so that now he was considered to be the fastest, most agile and lethal swordsman ever known to his people. It was on the third day, as he had sat and watched as the wolf cub seemed to effortlessly glide around the clearing, that he became aware of a presence in the trees surrounding them.

At first it had just been a sense of something else being out there. This feeling had rapidly changed and the hairs on the back of his neck had stood up as he became aware that he was being watched, and not by one set of eyes but by a whole multitude of eyes; whatever was out there had him surrounded. His senses were good; even the wolf cub had not noticed the change in the forest, until as he watched it, it finally sensed something in the air, stopping, sniffing, its curiosity aroused, as part of whatever was out there watching them had obviously moved upwind, to circle them completely.

The startling thing was the cub's reaction; instead of being fearful of the smell and running back to him as he had expected, it seemed to be excited as it yelped out a small bark and ran straight off into the forest, leaving Vangor on his own. His disappointment was momentary, as he realised what was watching from beyond the trees could only be a pack of wolves. His theory was confirmed when he took a pace towards the trees where moments earlier the cub had disappeared, he was met by a low feral throaty growl which stopped him in his tracks, sending goose bumps racing down his spine. This wolf meant business, the low growl an obvious statement of intent; if he proceeded any further he would no doubt end up as its dinner. A thought which did not endear itself to him. Taking a step backwards, the growling disappeared. He had then sat down on a fallen tree stump covered in moss, its surface damp to his touch. The darkness of the forest surrounded him, it was almost as if whilst in the cub's company he had never noticed it. He listened, using his ears to sense the danger out there. He was sure that the vast majority of the pack had now left, yet he could still sense the presence of a few wolves around him, a sort of rear party to stop him following. He did not know why but he was sure that if he remained where he was for the time being that he would be quite safe. As he settled down to wait for night to come, he started to plan his journey home; he would make his way south out of the forest and then follow the road to the east.

As the day drew to a close, his mind started to piece together the information and tales that he had heard on his travels. The stories of the dragons, wolves and men were not new to him, as he had heard them all before from his own people, only this time the perspective was different as they had been the saviours of the Moon lands and thus as such revered in the history of these lands. The reason why these races had appeared as it by magic at the end of each battle had so far evaded his knowledge. The only feasible explanation, as far-fetched as it sounded, was the use of magic, but as to where the magic had come from and its source, he was none the wiser. The tales of the Fey had promised much, yet he had found no evidence of their continued existence. The wolves that he had encountered on his travels were the same as in his own country; they hunted and they ate, a wild pack of dogs, in essence, just a little larger and a bit more fierce. This pack of wolves, he realised, had been different; there seemed to be an intelligence behind their actions that he had not seen in wolves before. Yet the only hint of any real power he had seen in these lands had lain with the King and the Ice Crown, which if rumour was to be believed had been passed down by the dragons. The Ice Crown had become the main focus of his attention and thoughts for two years now, he had believed its capture to be the key to victory, yet so far it had evaded him.

The howl came from nowhere and yet everywhere all at once, it was definitely a wolf's howl, but not just any howl. It was beautiful. The forest seemed to spring to life as the clouds parted in the night sky to reveal a moon shining so brightly that the forest was lit up with a soft white glow as brightly as a hot summer's day. The music of the howl danced around him, flowing over him, drowning him in a sense of well-being, a sense of belonging. His senses seemed to come alive, almost as if they had been dead before; he could feel the forest, not just see the trees but the living, beating heart of the forest. The deer grazing amongst the trees, a dormouse scurrying around in the grass, its small legs scraping and scratching at the thin soil, the squirrels in the trees, the owl as it took flight from a branch, its huge powerful wings beating softly in the night air, and then finally his senses homed in on the wolf.

A big beast of an animal, bigger than any wolf he had ever seen. It stood atop a rocky outcrop in a clearing, its coat a deep dark grey, with flecks of white protruding from within as it moved its neck, huge paws planted firmly on the rocky surface, with big muscular hind legs. The body, despite the thick coat, gave the impression of pure muscle which gave way to a thick muscular neck, topped off with an almost regal-looking face. Deep dark eyes surrounded by white patches that glistened and shone as it raised its head to the moon. It was almost as if it were singing to the moon, the beauty of its voice as it spoke to its pack was mesmerising. There must have been over 200 wolves in the clearing, all sitting on their haunches as if in a trance, listening to the song. The moonlight was bathing them all in a soft iridescent glow that seemed to shine off their coats as a sea of white and grey.

"The cub has returned."

The words seemed to spill into his mind as his cub, the one he had looked after, came into sight, playing in the grass with others of a similar age.

"The man goes free, we thank him. We honour him as he honoured us. Now we honour the Ancients' spirit."

The singing howl continued, but a new voice came thundering into Vangor's mind, demanding his attention.

"Be gone, man. I sing now to my gods and your honour. Be gone before I finish my song; we hunt tonight and all is prey that walks within the range of my song. I, Raon, leader of the Wolves of Fennigan, thank you for the life of my son, Fent. Be gone, as once the hunt starts it will not stop until blood is spilt and the hunger sated. Be gone."

Vangor staggered backwards as if slapped in the face. His confused and distorted senses were finding it hard to readjust to reality and back to their normal state. He shook his head as if to clear it and grabbed his water bottle, forcing water down his throat in deep satisfying gulps. The forest exploded with sound, the howl of earlier was nothing compared to this, it was as if the soloist had now been joined by the remainder of the choir. The night sky, which had been dark and empty except for the odd star, was now lit up; blue, green and red lights danced across its vastness, their movement in the night sky seemingly matching the notes of the howls from below. He was sure he saw an image of a wolf's head fleetingly shoot across the sky in-between the dancing lights. The sight was mesmerising, he stood staring in awe at the beauty and majesty of the moment.

The giant wolf's head shot back into vision in the sky as the song seemed to reach a crescendo of noise. It was as if all the wolves in the clearing were now singing in chorus. The giant head hovered in the sky, its giant eyes seemingly searching the forest below as if seeking out its prey. As Vangor stood and stared their eyes seemed to meet, holding each other's gaze for a second, Vangor was frozen to the spot and in that instant, the head swooped down towards him, its giant mouth snarling, revealing huge teeth as it made directly for him, the lights seemingly dancing in the sky in the wake of its flight. The sudden movement had broken the spell; Vangor realised that the howling had stopped, the hunt was on and he was now the prey.

He leapt down from the fallen tree stump that he was now standing on, rolling forward, he sprang to his feet as behind him the mouth of the giant wolf's head snapped shut onto the air where he moments earlier had stood. In the distance the howling of the pack changed to a different note, a more feral howl as they sensed his presence, the giant wolf's head was now gone, having led the pack to its prey. Turning to his right, he ran downhill towards the trees. He crashed through the bushes surrounding the clearing, his momentum ripping a path through their thin branches which whipped at his arms, legs and face. He threw his arms up instinctively as the branches lashed at him, seemingly determined to take his eyes out, a ripping sound as his cloak snagged in a branch and was then torn free. He burst into the forest, the trees randomly spaced on a downward slope, enabling him to increase his speed of flight, yet he knew he could never outrun a pack of wolves. Think, where am I? He searched his memory from the days spent hunting with the cub. The Pool of Fennigan, it was his only real hope, how far though? Can I make it? The thoughts rushed through his head, as he darted quickly to his left, changing direction in an instant, leaping over a fallen tree trunk, its dead branches cracking as he ploughed through them. He landed heavily, his left ankle twisting under him, his weight thrown forward; letting his training take over, he allowed his weight to carry him forward and tucking his head in, he rolled forward and sprang back onto his feet. His ankle was painful but seemed to be holding at the moment.

The pack were close now, he could sense their presence which was confirmed by a noise of a branch snapping close by and of something close tearing through the undergrowth around him. Dark shadows flickered amongst the trees in the distance, their shape indiscernible in the light. How much further? Yes, right down here, he recognised the rocky outcrop in front. His breathing was hard now, his legs ached, his lungs were screaming out for more oxygen as his heart pounded in his chest. A flicker of movement on his left, the wolf leapt through the air. Vangor saw it in time, throwing himself forward underneath it as its teeth snapped into thin air. He was up and running again, fear driving him on, the fear of being ripped to shreds by the baying pack giving him more energy and strength than he knew he possessed. The wolf crashed straight into a tree, all the air driven momentarily from its body. He grabbed hold of an approaching tree with his hand, using the force as a pendulum to swing his body around it in a sudden change of direction to his left, as another wolf careered past, its momentum carrying it further down the slope as it tried frantically to change direction as well.

Not far, he thought as he ran for the clearing ahead. He knew the clearing gave way to the cliff above the Pool of Fennigan. It was not a big drop to the water below, and although he had never swum in the pool, he was certain that it would be deep enough to dive into from here, well, certain enough to try it when chased by a pack of wolves. He burst into the clearing, his face and arms bleeding from the cuts and grazes, his legs tiring, aching and screaming for rest; he staggered across the clearing, fifteen paces, fourteen paces, the cliff top grew closer, his sanctuary so close, the relief rising in his soul. Behind, the pack burst into the clearance; they were about thirty paces away, led by Raon. Vangor found new strength; he was not going to die and he rushed for the cliff top. Raon was closing the gap with easy, effortless leaps and he was at last within striking distance. He felt no sorrow for the man; he had been warned, he had tried his best but like all humans they were curious and now it would cost this man his life. He could taste the blood already; he liked the taste of human blood, it was not always available and was therefore a bit of a delicacy for him. He leapt at the back of the man, his teeth bared, ready for the kill.

Vangor slipped, his foot catching on a hidden root, he fell head first before he could compensate, landing inches away from the cliff edge, his hand could just reach over into the thin air. A dark shape roared past him overhead, disappearing over the edge, it let out a howl of rage as it tumbled down, splashing into the water below. Vangor wasted no time, he scrambled to his feet and launched himself off the edge, after the wolf, and away from the pursuing pack.

Vangor's relief was short-lived as he hit the water with a thud, his world rapidly changing into a watery whirlpool as his momentum from the fall drove him deeper into the depths. He kicked hard, driving for the surface. His head hit something that moved quickly above. Breaking the surface, he was met by a flurry of teeth and claws as Raon tried to bite into him; missing his arm by inches, he snapped again, this time his teeth sinking into the soft flesh until they hit bone.

Vangor let out a cry of pain and rage as Raon sank his teeth into his left arm. The water around transformed into a bubbly torrent of crimson as the blood leaked out. He clenched his right hand into a fist and drove it into the wolf's face, hitting it hard on the left eye. Raon felt a pain soar through his head, his vision on the left darkened as blood filled the orbit, clouding it in a red mist. He let go of the man's arm, realising that he was at a disadvantage in the water. He made off for the distant bank; overhead his pack were watching from the cliff, howling at their leader, a few of the younger wolves trying in vain to scramble down the cliff to their prey.

Vangor, realising that the wolf was hurt and that he had the advantage in the water, had a tough decision to make. He could pursue the wolf or make for safety downstream. His left arm was painful but he still had full function and strength, the bleeding had also slowed to a trickle. He kicked out hard; filling his lungs with a big gulp of air, he ducked under the water, pulling his knife out of his boot as he did so. The wolf was a good swimmer, yet he was soon directly beneath the dark shape as it made its way towards the bank. Vangor drove up for the surface, his hands in front of him, the knife blade dulled in the dark water. It penetrated the flesh above, sinking easily into the soft underbelly of the wolf. Vangor's head broke the surface as his hand tried to pull the knife free.

Raon felt the knife enter, the sharp pain ripped through him, his strength seemingly draining from him instantly. A calmness overcame him, he knew what he had to do. The wolf stopped moving, its legs were no longer kicking. The only movement now in the water was caused by Vangor's attempts to free his knife from the wolf. Yanking down hard, the knife eventually sucked free, a flood of bright red blood pursuing its exit from the body. Vangor nudged the wolf, was it dead already? Surely not, but still it did not move, its great grey coat now red with blood, the wolf slowly began to sink, air trickling from its cavities. Vangor, still wary, trod water, his arm aching now as he watched the huge creature sink down into the darkness. Up on the cliff, an angry crescendo of howls reminded him he was not yet safe. The pack were now even more determined to catch their prey and make him pay.

Vangor kicked forward, heading towards the river that ran out of the pool's southerly bank. Sharp teeth closed round his foot, the bite hard, puncturing his leather boot, entering the soft flesh, snapping through the tendons and scraping onto the bone beneath. He swallowed a big mouthful of water as the weight dragged him down. Raon intended to take the human with him; if he failed all was lost, the ancient song entrusted to him would not be able to transfer to his son, his slayer had to die for this to happen. His powerful jaws clamped shut even harder, the bone between them splintering and cracking beneath the force, even as the dark water poured into his now open gullet. His death was now upon him as he sank down, his great weight dragging the helpless Vangor down to join him in a watery grave.

Vangor drove his knife into the jaw of the wolf, levering and prising at the teeth in a vain attempt to free his foot. The powerful jaw of the wolf, however, was locked tight and as he sank further and further down, Vangor realised that he only had one chance left to save his own life. It took all his remaining strength, the pain unbearable but better that than death. His foot sank down with the wolf as Vangor kicked up for the surface, blood trailing in his wake from the stump of his leg. Raon's last sight as his vision faded was that of his prey disappearing; he knew that he had failed, his kind doomed, he was shamed.

Vangor broke the surface of the pool, gasping for air. A lightning bolt struck a tree to his right, lighting up the whole sky in an eerie glow. The air was thick with rain as it pelted onto the surface of the water and drummed into the ground. The wolves on the ridge had gone. Green light shot across the cloud-filled sky in a myriad of patterns, illuminating the dark clouds with a strange green glow around the edges. A bolt of it broke free and shot down to earth; it hit the side of the cliff, an eruption of rocks and stones cascaded down into the turbulent water.

Vangor, his pain and exhaustion forgotten, swam for the far bank, away from the cliff. A great roar swept through the air as the image of a wolf dived from the sky, straight into the middle of the pool, its body seemingly made from the green light, a streak of green still glowing in the sky, marking its flight. The water now bubbled and hissed, small whirlpools forming around the pool. Vangor felt himself being dragged backwards; he swam harder, panic now taking over, the current though too strong as he was sucked into the middle of the pool. He travelled round and round in ever decreasing circles, the last of his energy used just to keep his head above the tumultuous water.

The downward pull became overwhelming. A final lungful of air as his head vanished beneath the surface, the last attempt to cling to life. The darkness deepened as he was pulled quickly down into the deep water, his last breath almost gone as his lungs now screamed for more air. Open your mouth and breathe it in, he thought, end the pain, his whole body now racked in agony. The water entered where only air should be, his vision blurred, he was a child again playing with his hoop and stick. His first fight, the bloody nose and sore fist. The Battle of Stone, his first command. The darkness descended like a veil.

The green light had at first seemed a blur, then it was closer, a huge wolf coming for its revenge. Too late, I am already dead, do what you may. It had swum straight into him, entering his body, his vision had cleared, the pain gone, his limbs once more strong, a rush of air as he found himself propelled up through the surface of the water. The sky now clear, the moon once more lighting the sky, he took a huge breath of air; it tasted good. He felt sick, he vomited, the water ejected from his mouth; he did not care, he was alive, but how?

That had been twelve years ago now. It had taken him another ten years to discover the full truth of what had happened that day. He had stolen the Wolves of Fennigan's ancient song from their leader by slaying him, it had cost him his foot but it was a price now he would have gladly paid over again. Its spirit had rescued him from the water, as was its duty and his right. Yet a human could not control such a spirit. It had nearly ripped his soul apart, but eventually Vangor had tamed it, he now knew how to use it, he could not call the ancient spirits and sing to them, but he could now speak with their kind. Fent was the same cub he had spent those three days with. Now Fent wanted what he considered to be stolen back. Vangor wanted the King of the Moon lands. He had failed once already by trying to steal the Ice Crown. The Lord Vermount had been easily duped, but had been incapable of completing the task. The fool had lost the Crown on route and never realised it. Vangor could still remember the look on the fool's face as he proudly presented a turnip to the Lord Tarebeth. The Ice Crown was never found and as far as could be ascertained it was still missing.

Vangor therefore intended to rid the Moon lands of its only heir to the crown and thus make its recovery irrelevant. This was going to be Fent's job. Vangor had easily convinced the wolf that he would help return their Ancients' Howl to them if they brought him Prince Morkin. Dead or alive he did not mind, but he wanted to see the body. Vangor knew that the only way that Fent could retrieve the spirit of his ancients, was the same way that he had received it. Fent had to slay him and live. This was not going to happen as far as Vangor was concerned. He was not sure if Fent knew this or not but, none the less, he would deal with it at the time. For now Fent did his bidding and that was all that mattered.

Fent sat watching Vangor, the man seemed to have slipped off into his own thoughts for the time being. He was staring straight through Fent as if he were no longer there. Fent marvelled at the man's clothes. He had seen clothes on many humans but not as marvellous as Vangor's. Every item of his attire was black, the boots a dark dull black leather, the right one easily disguising his wooden foot, black leggings above hugged the shape of his legs. A black tunic just visible below a black waistcoat, the only adornment, the red half-crescent moon-shaped buttons, barely visible yet each lovingly and intricately fashioned. His sword scabbard hung at his left side, it was a strange design that curled and coiled up when the sword was withdrawn like it was now, the only visible detail that of a snake's head at the top with an open jaw to accept the blade. The sword was in Vangor's right hand, held loosely, pointing at the ground now, in a relaxed grip. Its blade was also black with a deep sheen to the metal, a small piece of matted fur stuck to the tip, where it had cut his own ear. The hilt of the sword designed as two interlocking fangs of a snake, presumably to match the design at the top of the scabbard. Vangor's left hand held a small metal shield, totally black, with the only decoration that of the red crescent moon, depicting his loyalty to Tarebeth, above that of his own red raven emblem emblazoned on to its surface.

The face of the man was unremarkable; clean shaven and black haired, no scars or wounds from battle, a sign of a raw recruit or a master swordsman, a young face still, seemingly untroubled by the rigours of life. The eyes though held it for Fent. There was something wild and untamed in this man's eyes. They burned with passion and anger, pride and duty, they were almost feral in appearance. Fent knew those eyes from somewhere in his past, they invoked memories; this was a man to be feared and obeyed. This man though must die, but first he had more pressing matters to attend to.

Something stirred in Vangor at that moment. He returned to the present as if on cue and again focussed on Fent.

"You know what is required of you, wolf. I trust that you are now ready. We require him by the next full moon." Vangor swept his sword to the sky in a long lazy swing, as if by doing so he would summon the moon to appear from behind its cloud. "You do know the price of failure!" the piercing glare seemed to burn through Fent.

Fent growled in reply, "You have mastered our tongue well, human, answer me this. Where did such a talent emerge from? Not since the time of the mage have we spoken with your kind."

Vangor's senses became alert. What had the wolf just said? Had he heard properly? Mage? He had never heard mention of any mage in his travels across these lands before now.

Fent noticed the surprised look on Vangor's face, it had been a momentary show of emotion and he now knew that his hunch had been correct. Now to see how much information he could get from this man.

"Tell me then, wolf, do you still converse with the mage?"

"Personally no, but I cannot answer for all of my kind."

The anger in Vangor's voice was evident in his reply, "I suggest you remember quickly, wolf." His sword now held more tightly in his grip.

How far can I push him? thought Fent "I can only answer with the truth as I know it. I have not spoken to a mage in my lifetime, however, my kind travel all the Moon lands. I will enquire within my kind if it interests you so much, human."

Vangor stared at the wolf; this animal was not as stupid as he first thought. Let's play the game then and see what he wants. "Watch your tongue, wolf, my blade likes the taste of your blood," his sword swung up to emphasise the point. "Where would a mage be found in this land then, if you have not spoken to one?"

Fent sensed the change in Vangor's tone of voice; although very subtle, it was to his ears very discernible. "I will seek your answers within my kind, if you answer me one question."

"Be assured, wolf, you will tell me what I want to know, however, I will tolerate your insolence for now. Ask your question." Vangor was enjoying this game, he knew what was now coming and he wanted to see Fent's reaction when he revealed that it was he who had slain his father.

Chapter Five

The hamlet of Falesh was small, even by the Moon lands' standards. It was also very grubby, it comprised a pier, a tavern and two houses, one for the tavern owner and the other for the ferryman. Despite this the tavern thrived, it was always full, the reason being the village's close proximity to the Cestere Sea which was less than a mile from the tavern. It was the only tavern in the Moon lands that was close to the Cestere Sea and therefore was always full of a mixture of travellers, seamen and thugs.

"Mr Grabbit," the small bespectacled man pushed through the crowded tavern towards the large man sat in the corner.

"Mr Grabbit."

The fist crashed down on the table, sending cutlery and crockery flying. The effect was immediate; silence settled uncomfortably in the packed room, a few patrons were already diving for cover, knowing full well the rage that would follow. The table flew through the air as if in questioning response to them, scattering a path before it, and it was closely followed by the small man, his nose now bloody and flattened across his face.

"That's SIR Grabbit to you," the voice boomed.

The tavern keeper nervously fingered the bludgeon hidden underneath the grubby bar. He let out a sigh of relief though as Grabbit, seemingly satisfied that his doubtable honour was now restored and that the man had been suitably chastised, was now settling back down into his chair. He returned to cleaning his glasses, spitting into the next one and wiping it with a small brownish cloth that hinted of once being white many years ago.

"Wench," Grabbit bellowed at the passing tavern keeper's daughter, a young girl of fourteen with blonde hair, freckles and an eternally cheerful disposition. She glanced over at her father, who nodded his consent, and then looked at Grabbit.

"Fetch me more ale and pie, I seem to have spilt mine," he laughed, "and he is paying," pointing at the prostrate man on the floor. "Get him out of my sight," he commanded at anyone and everyone in the tavern.

This tavern was a particular favourite of Grabbit's, more for the choice of clientele than any testament to the food, which was more often than not stale, or the ale, which likewise was more often than not watered down. This particular tavern was the favourite of all the undesirables in the Moon lands. A veritable cesspit of what, by many standards, were considered the dregs of society. Grabbit was in his element; these were his kind of people and he was the worst of the lot. He revelled here in his power; he was lord of all in this environment, a prize thug lording it over the rest.

The barmaid hurried over with his ale; she tried unsuccessfully to avoid Grabbit's groping hands and she nearly threw the pitcher onto the table in her eagerness to escape the foul man's advances. She was one of the lucky ones, as so far Grabbit had not insisted on her company in the back rooms during his many visits. This was solely due to the fact that her father was easily able to deal with Grabbit and his kind and partly down to the fact that Grabbit did not want to be barred from the establishment, a virtual certainty if you molested this tavern keeper's daughter.

Somebody at the far end of the tavern was now attempting to entertain the drinkers with a song, his attempt though was easily drowned out by a table of seamen who preferring their own words to his tune were becoming more voracious and raucous as the verses progressed. The tavern was packed with a variety of characters in various stages of intoxication, most at this hour littered the floor, a few covered in vomit, not always their own, others barely breathing if indeed they were still alive. Olaf, the hired help, would come round now and again and throw some of the bodies out into the gutter, for no other reason really other than to create space for the next drunk to fall into. Olaf was the real reason that there was usually very little trouble in the tavern. He stood at over seven feet tall, with arms and legs as thick as tree trunks, one of only two men in the Moon lands that made Grabbit look small, the other being Lord Luxor. Unfortunately, his intelligence did not match that of his size. He was in all ways a simple man; he followed simple instructions and was fiercely loyal to the tavern owner, by virtue of the fact that he had rescued Olaf from a cruel circus master as a child. Even Grabbit was mindful when Olaf was around and he never offended the tavern keeper or his family if he could possibly help it.

It was Olaf who now stood in front of him, grunting in a nasal fashion, "Le-le-le-let-tt-er, letter, M-M-M-Mr Grabbbit," as his enormous hand thrust its way up in front of Grabbit's face.

Grabbit looked up at him; the man is an imbecile, he thought (not much of an insult coming from Grabbit), as he took the letter from the giant's hand, "T-t-thank yyou, Olaf," Grabbit replied, enjoying the confused look on Olaf's face as he mimicked his stutter. A few men who were sitting close by laughed, but not loud enough for the tavern keeper to hear.

"Wh-where did it c-c-come ffffrom, Olaf?" Grabbit continued, enjoying making the man look a fool.

Olaf just looked over, seemingly totally oblivious to the fact that Grabbit was making fun of him, and then pointed at the small man on the floor that Grabbit had just punched, "Hee haad it." Olaf smiled at Grabbit, his face lit up in a black toothy grin, as if very pleased with himself.

Grabbit looked at the man on the floor, took a silver coin out of his pocket and tossed it at Olaf, who was still grinning at him.

Grabbit waved his hand to dismiss Olaf, "Thank you." His attention was now on the letter as he turned it in his greasy fingers. Seeing no outward sign of its origin on the yellow envelope, he ripped it open; a small piece of crumpled yellowing paper fell out onto the table. Grabbit peered into the remains of the envelope to make sure there was no other content, he then crumpled it up and threw it over his shoulder, picking up the paper before it absorbed any more grease from his table, satisfied he carefully and slowly read it.

MEET ME AT VON BRIDGE
TONIGHT AT MIDNIGHT
S

Grabbit stared at the note and then looked over at the prostrate man, who was now being picked up by Olaf to be ejected from the premises.

"Wait!! Leave him be, put him in the corner and look after him," Grabbit bellowed over the noise in the room.

Olaf looked over, confused; he looked at his boss, who on hearing this had looked up from the bar and now nodded at Olaf, grunting his permission before walking over to where Grabbit was sitting.

Grabbit handed the tavern keeper a purse of coins. "For the food, ale and his safety," he stated, pointing over at the man who Olaf had just lain down on a bench in the corner. The tavern keeper weighed the purse in his chubby hand, considered the amount and grunting his agreement, left Grabbit to his thoughts.

It was unusual for Mr Such to contact him at all out here. To send a note was unheard of, especially by such an incapable messenger. Grabbit almost felt sorry for the man he had just punched; Mr Such had not briefed him very well but his pity was only short-lived. He looked at his watch; it was an hour's ride from here to the bridge so he still had plenty of time. He trusted Mr Such, in so far as you could trust a lawyer; they were a good partnership but something made him very uneasy about this unexpected meeting.

───◆───

The plan was simple, he thought; the three men he had hired in the tavern had ridden out for the bridge over an hour ago. They would be there by now, their job was to make sure Mr Such did not have any nasty surprises in store for him. They would remain hidden unless required, half a bart, fifty ras each upfront had secured their services for the night, the other half to be paid when he was safely back in the tavern after the meeting. It was more money than he liked to spend, but he wanted loyalty and reliability and for this amount of money it was almost guaranteed; he was sure they would kill to protect him if need be, to get their other half a bart.

Satisfied with his plan, he rode out of the hamlet ten minutes later, leaving by the southern road and crossing the bridge fording the river Cool before then turning north to follow the dusty track to his destination. His path was lit by a near full moon as it shone out of the night sky. The air still held some of the warmth from the heat of the day. A full belly, a head full of ale and the gentle sway of his horse, all combined to induce Grabbit into a gentle slumber as his horse picked its unhurried way along the track.

The world was quiet as horse and rider entered a wood half an hour later. Too quiet, but Grabbit was not as alert as he should have been. The arrow pierced his horse in the chest, its squeal of pain and anger jolting Grabbit to his senses. He freed his feet from the stirrups just in time, allowing him to jump free as his horse reared up in pain and then toppled to its right, its great weight crashing to the ground. Grabbit was unarmed as his sword now lay strapped to his pack and that was below the thrashing, dying animal, giving him no immediate hope of retrieving it. Curse my stupidity, he screamed to himself, but they will pay for this. A frantic search around ensued and he eventually found a stick which seemed large and strong enough to offer some sort of defence in his hands. He swung it round his head a few times, testing its length as it swished past in a sweeping arc.

Satisfied, he skulked down behind a bush to wait, listening and watching, his eyes trying to penetrate the darkness of the surrounding trees. The silence was complete, no sound from the trees, none of the night sounds that he would expect to hear were present, there was somebody out there, but he could not tell where. Always an impatient man, the wait became too much; he leapt up with anger and frustration and rampaged towards where he presumed the arrow had been fired, his stick blindly hacking a path clear in front of him, his huge frame crashing through the close undergrowth which tore at his clothes and skin in revenge.

Fifty paces on, puffing and panting from the effort, he slumped against a fallen tree in a small clearing. He was momentarily lost now, his anger and frustration spent; he tried to work out exactly where he was. The sky above held no clues as cloud now covered the stars in a white fluffy shroud, the moon's light only just highlighting their shape. The trees around all looked the same, dark and featureless in the poor light, the ground everywhere he looked seemed to be covered in low brambles. Faint images of loose branches, tree stumps, dark rotting leaves and an odd clump of grass were barely visible interspersed over the ground. Still no sound. Somebody was out there, he could sense them now, like prey can sense a predator. Grabbit was normally very self-assured and confident but he was now out of his natural environment; he now felt very unsure, he felt threatened for the first time in his life and it frightened him.

The arrow hissed past his ear and thudded into the trunk of the tree behind him. It buried itself deep, to the hilt, into the tree, the shaft now protruding from the trunk like a feathered branch, visibly shaking gently from the vibration of flight and force of impact. Now he was very scared!!!

"Who are you? Come out, I have money, here." He threw a few ras into the surrounding trees, they shone briefly in flight as they spun and then clinked to the ground, lost in the darkness.

Still nothing, complete silence. Grabbit raised his stick up in the air in front of him, an act of desperation more than any real hope of defence. The arrow hit the stick coming from his left, tearing it from his surprised grip, both then spun to his right before toppling to the ground an arm's length away. Grabbit ducked down lower, he reached out desperately with his right hand, hoping to retrieve his weapon, his fingers scratching and feeling blindly in the dirt, he was now too afraid to raise his head high enough to look to where the stick had landed. His fingers thankfully found it, just touching its surface at the tips, his relief was short-lived though as another arrow whished past, plucking the stick from the ground and sending it further away, out of reach from where he now hid.

Grabbit, now terrified, all sense of bravado gone, flung himself to the ground, trying in vain to blend into the woodland floor. The next sound shocked and angered him, Mr Such's small squeaky voice idled out to him from the trees in front.

"An impressive archer, hey, Mr Grabbit? No, don't raise your head, you can stay kissing the dirt for now."

Grabbit had risen to his knees on hearing the voice, only to fling himself back down again, just in time as another arrow sang in the air, whistling past where his head had been seconds earlier.

"So why the hired thugs, Mr Grabbit?" Mr Such enquired. "Most rude of you!"

"S-s-sorry, Mr S-S-Suc," stammered a nervous Grabbit, now very much regretting his hiring of such incompetents.

"Not as sorry as they now are! My friend is very good with the bow, as you can see, and has exceptional eyesight even in this darkness. Do you not agree, Mr Grabbit?"

"Y-y-yes S-Sir." Grabbit was now shaking, he had underestimated Mr Such and was not sure what would happen to him now.

"Do not worry, Mr Grabbit, I have need of you, your life is quite safe for now." Mr Such seemed to have anticipated Grabbit's concerns and he needed him focussed. "But please stay down, my friend still has an arrow notched and apparently once notched it has to be fired, something strange about custom and tradition or something like that. Seems like a waste to me but I will respect my friend's customs as I am sure you will."

Grabbit grunted his confirmation; he had no intention of moving.

"Good," Mr Such continued, "you have put me at a bit of an inconvenience, Mr Grabbit. I hate the outdoors as you well know; so much mud and dirt, and it plays havoc with fine silk. I will of course deduct a suitable fee from your pay for the cleaning. Say twenty barts!! Yes, that should cover it."

Grabbit just grunted again. Twenty barts was a fortune, more than he had paid his thugs, yet his life was more dear to him than any amount of money.

Taking the grunt as confirmation of Grabbit's agreement, Mr Such continued.

"Excellent, here's the deal, Mr Grabbit. The boy Prince, Morkin, has left the Keep. Rumour has it word of the Ice Crown's location has arrived in the land. If he becomes King, Mr Grabbit, then all this is over. He will arrest and hang you. As for me, well, my fate, I am sure, would be a lot worse. Your job, my portly friend, along with my friend here, is to make sure that Morkin does not find the Crown. You will join his party, Mr Grabbit, you will befriend him and then, if need be, at the right time you will kill him. It must of course look like an accidental death, Mr Grabbit. Do you understand? Any questions?"

"L-Lord L-Luxor," stammered Grabbit, still trembling on the ground, "he will not let me near the boy."

"Leave Lord Luxor to me. I have plans for him. You just concentrate on the boy. Now if you have no further questions, I will take my leave. Oh, by the way, my friend, Lorigan here will sit with you until morning. Do not move before sunrise, Mr Grabbit, or Lorigan will be forced to kill you on my instructions. Enjoy the company; I will leave you two to become better acquainted." The faint sound of twigs snapping to his front followed by a small chuckle marked Mr Such's departure.

Grabbit cowered in the undergrowth; his joints ached, the cold seemed to seep into his skin from the ground, he longed to rise, to stretch, but his fear of the arrows kept the longing in check. The hours seemed to crawl by, dragging their heels. The sounds of the night slowly returned to the woods, an owl hunting in the trees, small creatures scurrying in the undergrowth, all the sounds amplified in the night air. Sleep must have come at some stage as Grabbit woke with a start, forgetting momentarily where he was; confused and disorientated, he nearly stood up, awareness gripping him suddenly at the last moment. The sky was lighter now, dawn was approaching, the blackness that had encompassed him was now a dark grey as the sun rose in the east, hidden at present by the trees and the mountains. The dark grey of morning slowly lightened and the area around Grabbit became more visible. The dark featureless shapes of the night softened to reveal low bushes and pine trees surrounding his location, the leaves on the bushes now visible and distinct as at last the light grey gave way to the colour of the day as the sun bridged the distant horizon.

Grabbit's surveillance of his surroundings was interrupted by a shadow falling over him. He glanced up to see a tall figure standing there, a figure clothed in a cloak of green, which seemed to shimmer in the early morning light. As he stared, the cloak appeared to blend into the background of greens in the trees, making it hard for Grabbit to distinguish the shape above him. The hood of the cloak was up, hiding the features of the wearer. A large bow hung loosely behind its right shoulder, the upper curve of which was just visible and indicated its true size and power.

The voice, when it came, was not what Grabbit expected; he had expected a rough, gruff, powerful voice. This was sweet, soft and gentle, almost childlike yet it still conveyed conviction and authority, as it told him to rise. He did so gingerly, his limbs and joints aching, his body was tired and sore, he was cold and now he was again angry. Angry at himself and angry at Mr Such for humiliating him, but most of all he was angry at this Lorigan who had kept him in this spot all night and shot at him with arrows. He glanced around as he stood, shaking his weary limbs into looseness and life. Lorigan, he thought, did not offer too much that would concern him at close quarters; yes, he was obviously lethal with a bow, but now on closer examination, he was a thin creature, lacking any real power. The cloak hid his stature well, but his arms looked thin and the torso thinner. Grabbit grinned to himself. I'll crush this Lorigan and have pleasure doing it, he thought.

He stepped forward. Lorigan stood and watched the giant of a man as he did so. Grabbit offered out his hand as he approached Lorigan. Lorigan stood as still as the trees around and did not acknowledge the gesture. Grabbit shrugged his shoulders and grunted to himself, "Suit yourself," as he stepped past the tall figure of Lorigan.

For a big man Grabbit could be deceivingly quick, especially in a fight. He had transferred his weight onto his right foot as he walked past with Lorigan on his left. He spun round quickly, driving his bunched fist into the area where Lorigan was standing. His fist continued through thin air, as a blurred shape shot into the air and over Grabbit's head. He was now off balance, having thrown his huge weight behind the punch, expecting it to poleaxe Lorigan. He struggled to regain his balance and threw his right foot quickly forward in front of him. Too late, something hard hit him in the centre of his back, his legs lost all their power and strength and he tumbled face first onto the grass. He tried to push up, using his arms to raise his torso. Another blow hit him on the nape of the neck and his arms now lost their strength, and he again fell face first back onto the grass. His whole body now seemed to be powerless, as if all his strength had been drained out of him, even the weight of his own body now crushed his chest, making it hard to breathe, and it seemed as if it was only his eyes and neck that had any power left in them as he struggled to look around. A boot came into view beside his face, dark green in colour and from this close it almost seemed to have a velvety texture to it. The legs and then an arm came into view as Lorigan knelt beside the prostrate Grabbit. Lorigan grabbed Grabbit's hair, pulling back on it roughly, lifting his head back until they were looking at each other. This was the first time that Grabbit had seen the face under the hood; it was childlike, a pale white complexion with unblemished skin, the eyes slanted downwards at the outer corners and were separated by a long thin nose that protruded like a thin beak. Thick, long blonde hair flowed over the shoulders and half covered the small ears that were rounded to a point at the top.

"Elf," Grabbit spat the word, his hatred visible and undisguised in his tone of voice.

Lorigan smiled, revealing small, sharp, pointed white teeth, "Lorigan of the Fey, at your service." The smile disappeared, an angry look swept over the face, hardening the features. "Never again call me elf," Lorigan snarled at Grabbit. The eyes seemed to bore into his soul and Grabbit flinched. "And never try that again, human," the last word spat out as if distasteful to the mouth, "or I leave you here for the forest creatures to dine on. You will watch helpless as they gnaw and pick at your flesh, unable to move, unable to stop them. Madness will take you before death, but death will arrive, human, a long drawn-out death. The long death of the Fey reserved for the condemned, human."

Lorigan let go of Grabbit's head, which dropped to the ground again; Grabbit, unable to prevent his head falling, cursed out loud. Lorigan stood up and with a blur of speed was gone, at least as far as Grabbit could see from his prone position.

"Wait," Grabbit roared out, "wait, don't leave me!" His cry was met by silence.

Grabbit panicked, he was truly scared now; he looked around as best he could, his vision limited to about three feet to either side of him. The exertion and effort required just to turn his neck left him gasping and fighting for air. His body was totally useless, it just lay there, his huge muscles unable to move; he was completely paralysed.

The silence seemed to stretch for hours as he lay there, nothing happened, his fears slowly subsided, he still could not move but he was alive and Mr Such had need of him, he was certain of that, and almost certain that Lorigan would come back soon. With this thought he settled down, relaxing his breathing some more, allowing his fears to further dissipate. The first sound came from his right, a small scurrying of feet that made his heart race with fear, then came the scratching noise. He felt something on his leg, he screamed out, scaring it off with the sudden noise. He could hear whatever it was as it now scampered through the undergrowth around him, the sound seemingly amplified as it became the sole focus of his attention. The hairs on the back of his neck were standing upright, he was sweating, the salty liquid running down his forehead into his eyes, making them sting. He tried to wipe his forehead on the grass, but it seemed to make no difference.

A fox cub came into his field of vision, it sniffed the air, smelling Grabbit, curious yet timid. He shouted at it and it darted back out of view.

"Help, Lorigan. Please help, don't leave me. I will behave, I will do what you ask, don't leave me." Grabbit was now sobbing, the tears mixing with the sweat and streaming down his cheeks, fear and frustration making his voice tremble.

The fox cub appeared again, it stood watching him, assessing him, smelling the air again. Grabbit shouted at it, it darted away but was back within seconds. He shouted again, this time it just stood looking at him. It came closer, sniffing him, its cold nose pressing against his warm skin, its paws scratching at him as it climbed over his body. He felt it scramble up his back and then he felt it lose its grip and topple over the other side. For a moment he thought it had gone. He almost jumped when the cold nose touched his right hand; he tried to pull it back, realising he could not move it, he again shouted out. The nose disappeared, leaving a cold wet patch on his hand, the air making it feel colder as it blew over it.

"Ouch," a sharp pain in his finger made him cry out. He roared out again in a vain attempt to scare the fox, his voice now croaking and brittle. He felt the rasping tongue as the cub licked at the blood from the finger it had just bitten, the noises he made no longer able to scare or deter it. It nibbled tentatively at the soft warm flesh, not sure of itself but enjoying the taste. Grabbit lay there, sobbing, he could feel the cub chewing on his finger. He knew it would not be long before the smell of fresh blood brought other more voracious predators. They would not be happy with just a finger, the thought of it making the bile from his stomach come up into his mouth. He swallowed hard, trying not to be sick. Too late the vomit came, it was hard to clear his mouth, it was up his nose and it slowly seeped under his head into his hair. This was worse than his worst nightmare, he had always dreaded drowning, but this was even worse. How could his friend Mr Such allow this to happen?

There were other noises now, he could hear them; something else had smelled the blood. They sounded larger. How long would he live for, how long would the pain last? He hoped he would black out before it was too bad. Hopefully night would bring the wolves, death at least then would be swift, he thought, now resigned to his fate. He closed his eyes, trying to black out the sounds around him. The fox cub had been startled moments earlier by something in the trees, it had fled back into the woods. A flurry of movement, low feral growls and sounds of an animal in distress behind him had momentarily raised his spirits as he hoped that whatever was out there was now dining on the cub.

The voice startled him, it came as a whisper floating on the breeze; at first he thought he was dreaming, but reality soon focussed his mind. He strained to hear the voice as it seemed to sing and float around him as if on a cloud.

"I am Lorigan of the Fey, come to me and you will be free. I am Lorigan of the Fey, come to me and you will be free." The same words over and over in a soft dreamy voice.

"Yes," Grabbit croaked, his voice now painful from all the shouting, "set me free, please, I beg you, set me free."

"Come then, come to me."

Grabbit struggled to hear the last. I cannot move, he thought, how can I come to you. His anger rose within, another game, he thought, but wait, his finger moved. It was weak and felt like it no longer belonged to him, but yes, it moved. Relief washed over him and tears stung his eyes. I will live, he thought, as slowly power and strength seemed to seep into his limbs again as if by magic.

The tears rolled down his cheeks. "I can move, thank you," he croaked into the trees.

"Come to me," the soft singing voice floated over to him, "come to me."

He crawled on his hands and knees, he crawled because he was unsure if he was able to walk yet and he was anxious to get to Lorigan as quickly as possible. His right index finger was covered in blood, the tip of it was chewed and mangled with bits of flesh hanging off but he no longer cared or felt the pain. He had been humbled by a Fey, but again he no longer cared as he was alive and that was all that mattered.

Lorigan watched the huge man scramble to her on his hands and knees. She smiled to herself as she knew that Grabbit would cause her no more problems. He would do her bidding now, she was sure of it.

"You are free, Mr Grabbit, if I have your oath and your loyalty?"

Grabbit meekly gave her his word; he knelt at her feet and swore his loyalty. It was the first time in his life that Grabbit had given his word to somebody and actually meant it; he was scared of Lorigan and awed by her power. He had underestimated her, taking her frail stature as a sign of weakness, yet she had bested him with an ease and power that Grabbit could not fully comprehend. It was this that scared and also fascinated him. His thirst for power over others was such that he longed to know Lorigan's secrets, no matter the cost, so he had given her his oath, he had sworn it and he had meant it.

They ate then, Lorigan producing a rabbit that she had caught earlier. They talked as they ate, or Grabbit asked Lorigan a lot of questions, which with good humour Lorigan answered. He discovered that Lorigan was indeed a female Fey, a fact which, much to Lorigan's amusement, annoyed Grabbit, who was obviously not pleased he had been beaten by a female. A male Fey he could just about deal with, but a female, before today he would have said it was impossible. He eventually managed to swallow his remaining pride when Lorigan threatened to leave him back in the woods for the animals to dine on, the thought of which drained all colour from Grabbit's face as he stuttered his apologies. Lorigan left him to sweat a little before she smiled again at him.

Lorigan revealed in that time that she was an outcast, a condemned Fey, sentenced to death in the same manner that Grabbit had faced just a few hours earlier. He shuddered on hearing this, the terror still very much in his own mind. He did not ask her why she was condemned as he knew she would not have told him. They stayed in the woods, talking all through the afternoon, Grabbit was fascinated by the Fey race, her stories and her life, and finally she had told of how she had come into the service of a certain Mr Such.

It was obvious when she spoke that she had an unfathomable hatred for her people. She wanted revenge on them, and as it appeared that they were now going to help the boy Prince, Morkin, it was logical that Mr Such would now after many previous attempts to recruit her services finally get her to agree to help on this special assignment. Grabbit wondered what her role was to be and how she planned to exact her revenge but did not press for details at this time; he was left in little doubt though that this would involve killing people.

Finally exhausted, Grabbit fell asleep, leaning against a tree trunk. Lorigan covered him with a blanket from her pack and settled down in the clearing. The stars sparkled gently in the night sky, the sounds of the night gradually surrounding them. Lorigan felt at peace, she liked Grabbit, he was her kind of human, simple and effective, easy to control yet also useful. He had nearly hit her, he had got close, closer then any human before, it had scared her and she had therefore scared him even more. Yes, today had been entertaining, she thought as she pulled her own blanket over herself, her bow loosely strung beside her and her blade close by. She looked over to where Grabbit was gently snoring, and satisfied all was well, closed her eyes to embrace sleep.

Morning brought the early rays of the sun which danced and shone through the droplets of dew, coating the surrounding foliage in a glittery watery sheen. The air was cool, the cloudless night sky having allowed the heat of the previous day to escape and the sun's strength not yet sufficient to warm the chill out of the air. Grabbit sat up and stretched, his breath causing small clouds to form each time he exhaled, he looked around. Lorigan was already up, she stood motionless in the clearing, staring out into the trees. Without turning, she sensed that Grabbit had roused from his slumber and motioned for him to follow her. She set off in a long loping stride, easily negotiating the undulating terrain and obstacles in their path. Their journey was short, a mere twenty minutes, but even so the pace had left Grabbit short of breath. They approached the two horses that were hobbled beside a tree; they both looked up on hearing their approach.

Lorigan approached her dappled mare, running her hand lightly down the flank and onwards to the legs. She untied her horse's front legs and then gracefully with a fluidity of effortless movement swung up and onto its back. She sat there looking at Grabbit, the look on her face evident that he should hurry up and join her in mounting his horse. His horse was larger and thankfully saddled, as he drew nearer he noticed it was his own saddle on the horse, a flash of anger crossed his mind at the memory of its slaughter and his lack of alertness. The thought was brief though, his fear of Lorigan still fresh, so he quickly untied the horse and by comparison clumsily struggled up into the saddle.

Their journey took them out of the woods and along the track, leading to Von Bridge. The sun had heated the early morning air sufficiently now to make it comfortably warm. The birds were singing in the trees, to their left a kingfisher swooped down into the nearby stream, disappearing momentarily from view beneath the bank only to emerge moments later further down, with light droplets of water cascading off its bright plumage and a shiny fish trapped securely in its orange beak. As they approached Von Bridge, Lorigan led them off the track, three bodies lay there in the grass face up. Each had an arrow buried firmly up to the quills penetrating out of their chests. They looked strangely at peace as they looked up at the rising sun, their eyes fixed in a vacant stare, their mouths though filled with buzzing flies as even now the flesh had started to slowly rot. Grabbit almost felt sorry for them; he had faced what they had faced, they, however, had never stood a chance, they had been expendable and thankfully for now at least, it seemed, he was not. Lorigan watched him impassively, judging him, measuring his reaction, knowing full well who these men were. He had shown courage in the woods, she thought, more than most, he had broken as they all do eventually, as even she had, but he was strong and seemingly not too emotional. The Fey Elders would yet have good cause to regret her escape from death, she thought.

She leant forward and spoke into her mare's ear. It immediately rose up onto its hind legs, kicking out its front legs and letting out a loud snort. Lorigan sat perfectly balanced on its back as it leant further and further backwards, seemingly stuck there, effortlessly defying gravity, waiting patiently for the mare to thunder back to the ground before immediately setting off at a gallop along the track and over the bridge, a cloud of dust gently blowing in the breeze marking their passage.

"Come, Grabbit, do not dally with the dead," the voice again as if a whisper, yet it travelled the distance between them with crystal clarity. Grabbit dug his heels into his horse and pursued Lorigan down the dusty track, over the bridge and onwards towards Crescent Wood.

Chapter Six

Morkin was half out of his saddle when the howl erupted from nowhere and seemed to pass over them like a wave. His horse Dancer, not easily spooked, rose up on its hind legs suddenly, the whites of its eyes enlarged and its nostrils flared, startled by the sudden feral noise. Morkin was thrown off him, for the second time that day, but thankfully landed on softer ground this time. By the time he raised his head though, the noise was gone and once again Dancer was calm and unperturbed as he stood beside him, looking down at his master. Luxor was calming his own mount, he had managed to stay in the saddle, whilst all around him men of the Royal Guard were either doing the same or were gingerly and rather embarrassingly picking themselves up off the ground. Ever alert for danger, Luxor's hand rested easily on the hilt of his sword as he calmly surveyed the ground around them, his eyes quickly covering the terrain in sweeping arcs. Once satisfied that they were in no immediate danger, he swung himself to the ground and crossed over to where Morkin was still lying and pulled the young Prince up onto his feet.

"What was that?" Morkin enquired.

"Wolf," Luxor replied bluntly, his mind obviously on other matters as he walked away towards his horse.

Morkin chased after him and grabbed his cloak, "Wolf? Where? How?"

Luxor turned to face him, the look of mild irritation on his face just barely disguised, "Listen, boy, I have no time to explain, we have

81

to ride, we will be late." Luxor took the final few steps to his horse and swung himself up into the saddle. Morkin stood and stared, his mouth slightly open, lost in his own thoughts.

"Come on, boy, hurry." The urgency in Luxor's voice encouraged Morkin into action and he ran over to Dancer and swept himself up into the saddle. All around them the Royal Guard were also now remounting their horses as Luxor barked out his orders.

They set off at a brisk pace, a new urgency in their passage. The gentle canter of the morning had become a trot as Lord Luxor led them towards Crescent Wood. The tops of the first trees of their destination were now just visible as they poked above the distant horizon, breaking up the skyline with their dark ragged green edges. The dust from the path rose up in billowing clouds under the thundering mass of hooves, choking the riders at the rear of the group and covering the horses and riders in a fine, white, dusty sheen.

They saw the fire beside the stream as they breached the summit of the last hill, the smoke rising straight into the air in pale white puffs. The two men sitting beside the fire looked up briefly at the approaching riders and, seemingly unperturbed by their presence, returned their focus to the pot that hung above the flame. Luxor pulled his horse up beside the men and Morkin, now closer, recognised them as the two companions of the rider they had encountered earlier. His curiosity heightened by their presence, he wondered where their companion was. Luxor meanwhile was issuing orders to the Captain of the Royal Guard, and once satisfied, he turned his attention to Morkin and beckoned him to join him.

Luxor led Morkin away from the camp, leaving the Royal Guard and the two strangers in the distance until Luxor was sure they could no longer be overheard. Morkin noticed as they rode away that the Royal Guard seemed to be setting up camp; they had all dismounted and were busying themselves with the drilled routine as if their stay here was going to be prolonged. Some of the senior men had joined the two strangers at their fire, everybody seemed to be relaxed and at ease apart from Luxor and himself.

"Your patience does you credit." Luxor's voice interrupted

his thoughts and he brought his gaze back onto his guardian and mentor.

"You must be wondering why I have brought you out here today of all days, young Prince," Luxor continued, "believe me, it was not my intention. I also had plans for today. I was looking forward to competing against you in the games; it is not every day a lord gets to beat a prince, especially one he is sworn to protect." Luxor flashed a smile at Morkin.

Morkin smiled back and shrugged his shoulders. "Perhaps, but I hear you are getting old? Is that the reason you brought me here, scared that I might have beaten you? Yes, that sounds more like the truth, old man, age is creeping up on you and I believe you have brought me here because you cannot face the humility of being beaten by a twelve-year-old."

Luxor laughed, his laughter carrying over to his men, whose gaze fell on them both briefly. "It is true I am old, boy, but I would need to be a lot older yet before I could be bested by a pup such as yourself. Especially," Luxor continued with a smirk on his face, "one that still cannot stay on his horse."

Morkin glared at Luxor, the words stung his pride, he bit his tongue though. "Fair point, Lord Luxor. So pray tell me if not for the fear of being bested by myself today, then why else have we stolen away from the games and who was that rider earlier?"

"Ah, curiosity finally surfaces," Luxor smiled, baiting the young Prince, judging his reaction.

But Morkin was used to Luxor's games after all the years spent in each other's company and would not give him the satisfaction. He looked away as if the conversation were now a mere distraction for him.

Luxor again laughed, his laugh could become infectious at times and Morkin now smiled over at the man.

"Alright, lad." Luxor dismounted and signalled that Morkin should join him on the ground, as he sat on a high grassy tussock beside the stream. He glanced around and, once satisfied that nobody was within hearing distance, he started to tell Morkin what he knew so far.

Morkin sat and listened as his mentor told him about his search for the Ice Crown, how he had in his search come to these woods three years ago. How he had discovered the long-lost people of the Fey as if by magic, emerging through a silvery mist to find their hidden lands. They had questioned him and then, as if from a dream, he had awoken in his own bed in the Keep of Ishfern, his only memory of the whole experience that of a white light and trees, the rest seemed to have faded from memory, slipping through like water in a sieve, refusing now to return. He had returned to the woods that very same day, searching for three days, walking every path yet never finding the Fey people again. He had started to believe that perhaps he had dreamt it all in a drunken sleep, the experience nothing more than his own imagination fuelled by his desperation to find the Ice Crown. He slowly forgot the experience, confining it to a bizarre episode best not discussed for fear of ridicule, until one day almost a year later, Carebin had come to seek him out.

Carebin of the Fey had, it transpired, seen him that day in the woods, in the elder circle and had spent his last year before their meeting again in isolation, sent by his people to find their path. He had during this time seen Luxor again by chance one day whilst he was out riding and, recognising him immediately from the circle, had sought him out. They had spent an evening together talking and once more the reality that had become a dream became once more a reality.

Luxor continued explaining what had transpired to Morkin and finally added, "It was as if the memories and details were always in my mind, but were hidden from me, they all then came flooding back as if released by Carebin's words and presence. He had been sent into the dream world after me to ascertain the truth of my words and to discover the path which his people should follow. He told me of the Crown and a few other truths from my own dreaming that he sought the answers for. I trusted him and gave him two of my men to ride with him and it was arranged that we would meet here today, by which time his search would be over, the passage of time afforded by his kind would be spent and he would have to return to their midst."

Luxor stood up and crossed over to Morkin; he knelt in front of him, clutching both of his hands in his own.

"My oath to you is true, Prince. I have sworn to protect you with my life. I would gladly slay the demons of hell for you, yet I fear that our paths will not lie together from hereon and I fear I will not be able to fulfil my oath to you. I thus make a new oath which I hope you will accept in its stead; if you are slain away from my side I vow that I will pursue your slayer across the mountains, seas and deserts of this world. They will know no peace in their lifetime, their life will be forfeit and that of their men. Their death will not be easy and they will regret your death before their own is upon them. This is my vow to you, my Prince."

Luxor now knelt humbly on the grass at Morkin's feet, with his head bowed. Morkin knew the pain and anguish this man felt, and knew that Luxor out of all of the Lords of the Moon would avenge his death if so required. He reached forward with his own hand and lifted Luxor's chin so that their eyes now met.

"Lord Luxor, you have served me well, you have been a loyal and true friend and you have kept me from harm and shown me guidance. All that I am today is because of you. Through no choice of your own you have been as a father to me and I could have wished for no one better, for this alone I am eternally grateful. If as you say our paths may now part, then I trust it is for good reason and you can trust you have taught me well! Now, tell me of your fears."

Relief washed over Luxor's face. "Sire, you are indeed your father's son, you are wise beyond your years and strong of heart. I would be truly honoured to call you King and even more so to have you as a son."

Luxor bowed his head again, pausing for thought. "We must enter Crescent Wood and find the Fey. I am not sure how this can be done but I am sure that it will come about. We must ride alone though, just the two of us, the men will stay here. What we will find and how we will be received I do not know, but Carebin of the Fey gave me this." Luxor crossed over to his pack and brought over the item that Carebin had thrown to the ground earlier. He held it out in the flat of his palm, a hand so used to force now gentle and caring. Morkin looked down, captivated by the small silver fox which, despite its size, was intricately and lovingly carved, perfect in every minute detail. As Luxor brought his hand forward towards Morkin, the fox started to glow, a soft silvery shimmer of light which increased in intensity as it came towards him.

"It is your family's royal seal," Luxor offered, seeing the confused look on Morkin's face. "It was and should still be attached to the Ice Crown."

Morkin reached out towards it, his fingers tentatively testing the surface of the metal, expecting heat, yet finding the surface icy cold. The fox now seemed to be alive beneath his touch, as if his presence and touch had awakened it from a long dormant sleep; the light glowing from it was now a deep yellow full of depth and vitality which bathed his hand. "Why does it glow?"

"The dragon magic contained within its surface will always glow in the presence of royal blood. It is a sure way of stopping an impostor claiming the throne. It glows because it is in your presence now, my Lord, it recognises you as the rightful king."

"Where did it come from? Is this what Carebin gave you? Where did he get it? Does this ...?" Morkin's mind was suddenly brimming with a myriad of unanswered questions but Luxor interrupted the flow.

"I know not the answer to these and the many more questions you may have; however, I am sure Carebin of the Fey does and we need to see him, the time has come, the sun is at its peak."

Morkin looked up as if to confirm the statement, his life seemingly no longer carefully mapped out before him, he was excited and at the same time scared. His head was spinning with questions and thoughts, which in turn brought more questions. Had his crown been found? Do the Fey have it? If so, what do they want for it? Why not just give it to me? No, surely they do not have it, but they must have news of its location. He looked down at the fox glowing on his palm; he turned it over, inspecting it, and found a small pin and clasp located on its rear surface as if at one time it had served as a brooch.

My father's seal, Luxor had said; he imagined he could feel the magic contained within its surface and his father's touch. Smiling to himself, he carefully put the fox into his pocket, the faint glow now just visible through the material.

Luxor had already mounted his horse and waited as Morkin did the same. They both turned and rode off along the path leading into Crescent Wood. Morkin had been in these woods before, yet today it felt different. Today it felt as if he was seeing the trees and undergrowth with new eyes. The colours were deeper and more vibrant, dew still hung on sheltered leaves, grass and cobwebs, glistening in the light that filtered in through the rich canopy of leaves. The air was full of birdsong as they called to one another and sung of the joy of life. A squirrel scampered across their path and ran straight up the tree to their left, its flight never slowed despite the steep ascent. Morkin marvelled at its agility as it made the vertical climb seem effortless, watching as it leapt from branch to branch and the from tree to tree in a show of daring acrobatics.

The path they followed was well worn and in places rutted; it was wide enough to take a cart along and allowed them the luxury of riding beside each other. It was a path that was obviously well used by the people who lived close to the woods and those who made their living in the trees, yet neither of them saw any sign of another person as they rode gently on, each seemingly lost in their own thoughts and at peace in each other's company.

"So how do we enter the Fey's land, Luxor? Which path do we take?"

They had arrived at an intersection on the path. The path they were on ended there, as another crossed directly in front of it, leading off both to the north and the south. Luxor looked around, puzzled, "I do not know, boy, the last time I just arrived with the Fey. I imagine it matters not which path we choose! Which would you prefer?"

Morkin looked up and down both paths, both seemed to offer very little in the way of the promised Fey lands. They both led off into the trees and disappeared from vision about 400 paces further on.

"North," Morkin commanded as if he was leading an army.

Luxor looked over, shaking his head and smiled. "North it is, Sire, would you like me to send out scouts?" he tried hard to keep the laughter from his voice.

Morkin glanced over, seemingly puzzled and then realisation struck that he was once again being made fun of. He stuck his tongue out and blew a raspberry; childish, he thought, but it was the only response he felt fitting for Luxor's comment. The path that led north meandered through the trees, they followed it around corners and up and down slopes and across a low running stream. It seemed at times as if the path would take them clear of the woods themselves without ever finding the Fey.

"One more corner and then we will turn back and try the other path."

Luxor grunted his consent and they continued along the path, which as they rounded the corner brought them into a small clearing, the trees thinned backwards and a ramshackle hut stood at the far end, presumably by the design of it occupied by a local charcoal burner. The hut though was in disrepair, the low walls and thatched roof were still intact, but the door hung loosely off its hinge, balanced precariously half in and half out of the doorway. The glass in the sole window visible from their side was all broken, the ragged jutting of clear glass making the window frame resemble an open mouth full of jagged broken teeth. The single chimney stood smokeless and redundant and there was no sign of life around. Morkin dismounted, he was hungry again, it seemed as if they had travelled miles in the woods and still there was no sign of the Fey. If they had summoned him as Luxor had said, then why did they not show themselves? His hunger made him irritable and he took his frustration out on a stone close by, kicking it hard and sending it skimming across the damp grass.

"Well?" he looked at Luxor questioningly.

"Well what?"

Morkin sighed as he looked around, "Do you have anything else to eat?"

His answer came with a thud as another apple hit him on the side of his head and rolled off into the grass at his feet. He bent over to pick it up, a movement in the trees to his left caught his eye though. He froze in place, peering into the trees, trying to see what was there. He was sure he had seen feet, a mere fleeting glimpse as they moved but now they were gone. Or were they? He remembered the boots that Carebin had been wearing earlier. Their colouring would blend in well with this undergrowth, he thought. He picked up his apple, rubbing it clean and dry on his cloak and walked nonchalantly over towards Luxor.

"We are being watched," he whispered as he passed close to Luxor's horse, "in the trees to the left. I saw movement and I am certain they are still there."

Luxor glanced around, letting his eyes sweep over the trees and undergrowth in front and then slowly to his left, yet even to his trained eye there was nothing discernable to be seen in the trees, but he trusted Morkin. He knew well the legends of the Fey folk and their ability to blend into their surroundings; if they watched now they meant no harm, if they meant harm he was sure they would both be dead, their deadly arrows piercing their bodies.

"Perhaps we are, lad, but I feel they mean us no harm. Come, let us ride on a bit further and see what comes of it."

They crossed the clearing and rejoined the path at the far end. The path was narrower here and less used. Morkin bit into the apple with a satisfying crunch, his mind slipping away into thoughts of the feast he should have been eating today: freshly roasted suckling pig; shanks of tender lamb; roast guinea fowl, his particular favourite; a feast of sweetmeats and vegetables; the local traders with their glazed fruits and sweets; the ale and the cyder; his mouth now watering at the thought, the apple now tasteless in comparison. He threw the core away absently, his peripheral vision catching its path as it disappeared in mid flight. He looked around in dismay at where it should have been, there was no sign of it, he looked up and around, he was completely alone apart from Dancer; the path was empty, Luxor had disappeared as well. He shouted out and, hearing no reply, turned Dancer around and rode back along the path he had just ridden. No tracks, he thought as he looked at the path in confusion. I have just ridden this way, there should be tracks. But the path was virgin soil, fresh and undisturbed with no trace of ever being ridden or trampled upon.

"Luxor," he cried out again.

Lord Luxor was fraught with concern. Morkin had been in front of him seconds before and then a shimmering light had enveloped him. The boy and his horse had disappeared in front of him, swallowed up by the light and then vanishing as the light had faded back to leave the path empty. He had called out but no answer had come. Realisation slowly dawned on him as a memory came back to life. The Fey have him, he thought, but why not me as well? He looked around angrily.

"I am his guardian," he shouted into the woods, "let me pass. I am sworn to protect him." He knew they watched, he could not see them but he sensed their presence. He fought back the sudden urge to draw his sword. Best not to let the heart rule the head, he thought. His anger and frustration, however, were not so easily sated and finally got the better of him; he pulled his sword free from its scabbard with a ringing sound that sang through the air, the blade shone and dazzled as he swung it in a powerful arc over his head in a majestic show of arrogance and strength. He let go of the reins of his horse and, using his knees to control and guide her, galloped up and down the path between the trees, flicking and spinning his sword from hand to hand in slow deliberate arcs, the blade singing through the air, the metal deflecting the sunrays into a dazzling and mesmerising display that was blinding to watch. His horse moved in anticipation of its rider, it never missed a stride, turning, stopping and galloping in response to the subtlety of pressure from its rider, both man and beast equally trained and functioning as one. The dust rising from the track created small clouds that obliterated the horse's hooves from view as they rode backwards and forwards. His blade now spun faster and faster in dizzying arcs and circles that barely missed him and his horse. His horse was enjoying the game, playing its part; it was trained for this

90

spectacle, it was in truth his victory dance for the games, a dance they had performed on many occasions, well developed and practised over the years. The grand finale approached as the horse rose up onto its hind legs, kicking out with its front hooves as it did so. It seemed to hang there, suspended in time as it gathered itself before launching straight up. All its hooves were now clear of the ground, it landed back down on its rear legs, standing perfectly balanced and then it took two steps backwards, as if readying itself for the bow, all the while Luxor sat in complete control astride it, using his legs as an anchor. The horse let out its battle cry, a powerful throaty snort from deep within its huge frame, a cry of victory, a cry of triumph and it then hammered its front legs back onto the path, provoking an eruption of dust and soil.

Luxor bellowed out his challenge now, having allowed his horse its glory.

"I am Lord Luxor, protector of man, guardian of the King. If any harm befalls him, I will wreak a vengeance on the Fey that no magic will be able to prevent. Hear my words, and take them to your elders, Fey. Mark them well."

The clapping which came from the woods was the last thing he expected to hear. He had expected silence, he had expected anger, he had expected the unexpected but never applause. It came from the trees to his front, near to the place where Morkin had disappeared.

"A fine show, Lord Luxor, surely today's games will be dulled by your absence?"

Carebin stepped out of the woods, seemingly coming from within the tree itself, his cloak, boots and leggings having blended him into near invisibility within his surroundings.

Luxor, his anger still burning, spurred his mount straight at the Fey, who stood and watched as horse and rider galloped at him. Carebin never moved, he stood watching and waited, the horse pulled up inches in front of him, its nostrils billowing warm air into his face, its teeth bared as if daring him now to move.

"Easy, Lord Luxor, put your sword away. I come as guarantee of your Prince's safety. He will not be harmed. The elders will return him safely once he knows his path".

Luxor looked down at the Fey, trying to ascertain any falsehood and deceit in his words. He had trusted this Fey; had he been tricked, had he betrayed his ward, had he failed in his task? He stared into Carebin, anger burning in his eyes, looking for deceit. Carebin stood still under the gaze, his eyes peering back at Luxor's; he carried no weapon and his hands were held out to his side with the palms facing the man. The silence stretched, each measuring the other.

"If you lie to me, Fey, I will make your death a slow one even by your kind's standards. I will do it to cleanse my soul and because I like and trust you. If you lie to me, Carebin of the Fey, I will kill you."

There was no emotion in the eyes that Carebin could read, the gaze was now cold and calculated and the words cut into him as deep as a knife.

"I do not deceive you, Lord. My people though, well, I cannot truthfully answer for them after all these years spent away, but I sense no deceit in them. My people may not have concerned themselves with the lives of men for some time now, Luxor, but we are an honourable race and your Prince is our guest. I am here merely as a courtesy to your people."

"Why you? You have been away from your people for three years already! Surely their hospitality stretches further than to send you to me after so short a time?"

"I volunteered. Your reputation precedes you, Lord Luxor. I hoped you would receive me and trust me as a friend, which may not have been the case if another had come in my stead. Come, let us sit and talk. I have much to say that may be of interest to you."

"He is safe, I have your word?"

"He is and you have, now come." Carebin gestured over to a fallen log.

<hr />

Morkin dismounted from Dancer and led him on foot by his reins. He wanted to inspect the path more closely for any signs of his travel, suspecting some trick. As he did though, it soon became apparent that nothing had covered his tracks and it was as it seemed a virgin path. Perhaps my mind is playing tricks on me, he thought to himself, he had heard of people becoming mad in the head and getting lost in the woods. He looked behind him, where they had just this minute been. Relief washed over him, his footprints and those of Dancer were clearly visible in the soil. Stopping, he stood up straight and scanned his surroundings, taking in the detail of the trees. It was hard to place but they seemed to be different, it was as if they were almost new. They appeared healthier, greener and better looked after, almost as if these were loved, nurtured and cared for. The air smelt different as well, clean and crisp like the air after a storm. It hung around the trees full of moisture, almost like a mist but not as thick and left a silvery sheen on his and Dancer's coats. He could now hear a stream in the distance, its water gently washing over its bed, singing a quiet serenade which lightly echoed off the wooded walls that surrounded him and the path.

Morkin felt a peacefulness around him, his fears and anxiety regarding Luxor's disappearance slowly fading the longer he stood and listened and breathed in the air, it was intoxicating, invigorating and calming. Realisation crept up on him, he was in the Realm of the Fey, it was he who had disappeared not Luxor. Luxor must still be outside, wherever outside was, in the other wood. Yet that had just been there or was it here, he looked around, struggling to comprehend what he had just come to realise.

"Very astute! Most humans need an explanation after their arrival here."

A tall figure stepped out from a tree less than an arm's reach to Morkin's right. Morkin jumped back in astonishment, he had not seen a thing; how long had the figure been there watching him?

"Sorry to startle you, Morkin. I forget how easily we blend into the trees. I am Fengar of the Fey. We have been expecting you. Carebin of the Fey has told us about you. A fine horse you have there, it will be safe here if you follow me."

His voice sounded almost as a song to Morkin, the words

blending into one continuous sound, a sound which was simple and harmonious, a sound Morkin found hard to follow but somehow he had understood everything the Fey had just said. Morkin studied Fengar, his attention drawn automatically to his face. Dark piercing eyes that shone in the light, a thick head of light silvery-grey hair that washed down over his shoulders, small ears that came to a point at the upper margins, skin that was as white as alabaster and lips that were a bright, full pink. So this is what a Fey looks like, Morkin thought, the image he had conjured in his mind earlier of them bore little resemblance to the reality that stood in front of him now. He had thought they might be grotesque in appearance, hence the need for the hood, but this man was almost beautiful, almost childlike in appearance and he looked younger than Morkin knew himself to look.

Fengar returned the scrutiny, then nodded and gave Morkin a small knowing smile. It seemed almost as if he could read my mind, Morkin thought as Fengar now appeared to be amused by Morkin's thoughts.

As if to clarify this, Fengar spoke, "An imagination can be a powerful tool, however it does not always bear the weight of truth well. We are not what you envisaged us to be are we, young Prince? Perhaps there is a lesson there you would do well to remember if one day you are to become the King!"

Morkin felt his face redden slightly with embarrassment; he had no idea why he had thought the Fey would be grotesque in appearance, his imagination had obviously added features to what had, only a few hours ago to him, been a myth. A tale of a people told around an evening fire, a tale which, depending on the spinner, could portray the Fey as heroic or evil. Was it any surprise therefore that he had created a look for the Fey that would best fit his opinion of them?

His thoughts were interrupted by Fengar, "Do not fret, young Prince, we are as much to blame for your people's perception of us as they are. It suits our purpose for humans to be fearful of us, as it preserves our peace and solitude. If the price of this peace is a perception of us being evil and grotesque then it is a small price and one that we are willing to pay. You have no need to apologise, your embarrassment alone serves to prove your sincerity."

Morkin had opened his mouth to apologise, but now just shut it, aping the words instead.

Fengar ushered him along a path which took them past numerous Fey going about their daily routines. Some stopped to briefly glance over in their direction but most just continued as if a human in their midst was a daily occurrence or one that did not concern them. Fey children ran around in the long grass, darting now and again between the trees in some sort of game, their rich laughter echoing through the wood, their speed and agility whilst playing so fast that Morkin found it almost impossible to keep track of their movements.

"We are agile and fleet of foot, are we not?"

Morkin stared at the children. "Yes, it is remarkable! How do they move so fast?"

"Now that is a question!" Fengar stopped and faced Morkin before continuing, "Surely the question should not be how but why? How does a bird fly, how does a fish swim? We are all different, we all have our strengths and our weaknesses, young Prince."

Morkin looked puzzled.

"A fish is surrounded by water, is it not? and that is why it swims. A bird flies to escape its predators which cannot fly. We are fast and agile because we need to be, it is our strength. The secret is to know your own and utilise it to best effect, to maximise your strengths and to hide your weaknesses, especially from your enemies. Now, as to why are we so fast and agile? Well, the answer is all around you."

Morkin looked at the trees, a sort of understanding forming in his head, accompanied though by doubt and a sudden fear.

"Are we your enemy?"

"Are you our friends, our allies? At one time the answer would have been a resounding yes, but now we will have to wait and see."

The children continued their game as Morkin and Fengar continued down the path, the trees becoming taller as they proceeded, their trunks becoming thicker and stronger. Morkin gazed upwards, dizzied by their height, but feeling compelled to constantly stare into the green canopy of leaves that formed a roof above his head.

Movement caught his eye, what he had originally thought of as just leaves and branches now on closer scrutiny revealed the Fey within them and the walls, roofs and doors of houses suspended above him and finally the walkways that snaked between the trees partly hidden within the thick foliage.

"You live in the trees?" Morkin spoke out loud.

"Of course we live in the trees. We are of the trees. We have no need for walls of stone, when our trees are stronger than your stone walls. These trees have been our home for thousands of years, long before your walls of stone and, with the grace and fortune of our ancestors, they will be our home for thousands more."

Morkin's eyes struggled to take in all the new sights. He now saw steps going up some of the trees that were so well blended into the trees that he almost missed their presence entirely.

"For our elderly," Fengar offered, pre-empting Morkin's question.

Now that his eyes knew what to look for, he started to see more wonders on every tree. A pulley system that hung from a tall tree to Morkin's left that had at first looked like a simple vine hanging from the leaves, But now he saw what he had initially mistaken for as leaves interspersed along it were in actual fact leaf-like cups. The vine itself along with the cups hung down from the heights and at its base disappeared from view within the very roots of the giant tree it hung from.

"The Fountain of the Fey."

They turned another corner and an elderly Fey female walked slowly across the path in front of them; she wore a light grey cloak that matched the colour of her waist-length hair. Her pale white skin was drawn taut over her facial features, giving her a waxy appearance that shone without expression. Despite her obvious age she still walked with a tall, straight, easy elegance that defined her stature. She stopped suddenly and looked over, smiling directly at Morkin, who was standing staring, transfixed by her presence.

"You seem to have impressed Lolas, young Prince. She is the oldest of all our Fey. She has already fought the Dark Knights, our last survivor from that battle."

Morkin, still unable to draw his eyes away from Lolas, stammered, "But that was nearly 300 years ago!"

"Indeed and she was a great warrior in her time and is still much revered by our people. You do well to receive such a precious gift as a smile from her, treasure it well. There may come a time when you will be truly grateful and in need of it."

Morkin did not know if he truly believed Fengar, surely nobody could be that old and still live. He did, however, feel elated that he had received a compliment from the elderly Fey lady. He lowered his head in courtesy as he passed, Lolas impassively watched him go and then simply vanished from sight into the trees around.

Fengar stopped at the top of a gentle slope, he gestured to Morkin to move to his right. Morkin looked to where Fengar now pointed; there was a low ornately carved table decorated with leaves and vines standing in the tall grass. On top of the table there was what appeared to be a plate of bread and a leaf-shaped cup full of water.

"Please eat and drink, after all you are hungry, are you not?"

Morkin looked over at Fengar, who was smiling at him.

"I shall return when you are ready." Fengar turned and walked down the slope, vanishing into the trees.

When I am ready, Morkin thought, what a bizarre comment. How would he know when I am ready, I might be ready now. He looked at the food, his hunger returning, his stomach gave a low grumble of confirmation and he crossed over to the table. Well, perhaps not quite ready!

The food tasted divine, the bread was indescribably good, it seemed to just melt in his mouth unlike the doughy breads at his keep. A blend of flavours seeped out over his tongue, exciting his palate, although his hunger at first overcame his desire to savour the taste in full. The water was equally as good, it was cool, crisp and refreshing and he drank it down in big thirsty gulps, letting the coolness settle in his stomach and flow outwards through his body, he shivered in satisfaction. He was so engrossed in his meal, he never noticed the audience he now had until he had finished his plate. Looking up, he saw faces of children peering out of the trees, watching him, a stranger in their midst.

A childish giggle and a few of the faces, having been seen, disappeared. Morkin smiled and raised a hand to wave at the children, the rest disappeared as if on cue, leaving the trees now strangely empty in front of him. He felt a light tap on his shoulder, he looked around to find nobody there. A giggle from above, he looked up to see a young Fey boy hanging upside down from a branch twenty feet up. Morkin struggled to contain the urge to jump up in anticipation of the child falling at any moment. A noise to his left, a blur of movement, he looked up again, the child was now gone, vanished from view. He looked left and right in quick succession; he stood up, trying in vain to keep track of the children around him. Sometimes one would be in front of him, only to be gone again just as quickly. He would see the very same child moments later up a tree only then to be down beside him again.

A small hand closed around his left hand, it was cold to the touch and made him jump, he looked down into the face of a young Fey girl; she smiled up at him, her white teeth and blue eyes etching themselves forever into Morkin's mind, she giggled at him and then was gone. Morkin laughed, they were playing with him, he had no hope of keeping up with them but he could play along in his own way. He stopped looking around, he pretended to ignore the giggles from around him, he became impervious to the taps on the shoulders and pretended he could no longer hear their voices as he stared directly in front of him. He waited and waited for what seemed like an age, judging the moment for maximum effect; he would catch them unawares. He could feel them behind him now, they were still and quiet, yet he could hear their breathing, he did not know how many there were but they were there. They could not keep their amusement quiet for long and little snickers and laughs grew closer and closer.

He jumped around, yelling out as he did so. It had the desired effect and a few of the children vanished effortlessly into the trees as before, but the rest of them, as he had predicted, fell over each other in their eagerness to flee, startled by his sudden movement and the noise. Five of them now lay sprawled out on the grass, a massed tangle of limbs and heads as they struggled to free themselves and get away. Morkin raised his arms out directly in front of him and walked in slow deliberate paces towards the children, roaring out now and again as he closed the distance on them.

The children saw him coming, they kicked and squealed in a vain bid to free themselves from each other, their frantic efforts though only tying them tighter together. Four of them eventually scrambled clear just as Morkin towered over them, they all vanished in a split second now they were free. The young Fey girl lay below Morkin's outstretched arms, unable, it seemed, to move, she covered her eyes with her hands, now not sure what to expect, a low whimper escaping from her lips. Morkin's hands closed around her waist, her scream cut short by her giggles as Morkin tickled her. She was writhing around on the grass, seemingly unable to escape Morkin's hands as her legs kicked out frantically and her hands tried to stop Morkin tickling her, her laughter and giggling now intermittent with loud piercing squeals of delight as she thrashed around helplessly on the grass.

A crowd of Fey children closed around them to watch the fun. The young girl though eventually managed to wriggle free and back to the sanctuary of one of her siblings. Morkin again raised his arms in front of him and slowly turned around as if searching for his next victim. He stepped forward as he turned, straight into Fengar.

"I see you are ready, young Prince."

"Oh, ah yes," he stammered, the surrounding area now empty but for the two of them.

Fengar led Morkin down a gentle slope and into another clearing beyond the trees. This clearing was different from the others, the trees surrounding it stood tall and straight like ancient sentinels guarding the area; they were evenly spaced and very much older than those in the surrounding wood. All their branches stretched inwards, forming a canopy of green and yellow leaves that sheltered the ground below, covering the entire clearing in a light that flickered and danced between the shadows on the ground. A group of Fey sat in the clearing, patiently awaiting his arrival, their eyes now followed his movement beneath their hoods as he made his way up the path between them to a space set aside for him. Fengar bid him to sit facing the group.

Morkin looked out at each of the Fey now facing him, their impassive stares shadowed by the hoods each wore, making them seem as one, each dressed in a sombre grey gown that stretched over their entire bodies, making them appear in the poor light as large boulders in a circle, resembling in appearance the praying stones that had been found in the south, presumed to be from a long-forgotten race that had lost its path. It was only the occasional gleam as a ray of light hit a shadowed eye that gave Morkin the comfort of knowing that life lay within. They were all silent. They were waiting for him to speak, he felt a lump in his throat and a knot in his stomach. He disliked talking in front of groups of people; he had been doing it for years, yet his discomfort had never waned during the time.

The silence was audible now as it grew, it was as if he had been asked a question and his fate depended on the answer. His discomfort grew with each passing second, his tongue felt dry and brittle like uncared for leather. What do I say? he thought to himself as he once again looked out at the circle of Fey in front of him, hoping for something from them, trying to meet their gazes only to face the same cold, blank expressions of earlier. His gaze settled on the trees in the background; as he watched they started to fade into the distance as if they were moving, he felt dizzy watching them, a nausea rising from his stomach, stinging the back of his throat, he swallowed hard. The surrounding area was now bathed in an eerie yellow glow which blurred the shapes of the encircling trees, robbing him of some of their warm, solid, familiar comfort. The light grew in intensity as it seemed to slowly creep towards them like a luminous mist, blown by an undetectable breeze. It now encompassed them, the whole of the group at its centre and Morkin could see nothing now of the outside world through the intensity of light. The air grew thicker, it smelt metallic as it pressed down on him, he felt trapped and claustrophobic yet none of the Fey seemed concerned.

"Breathe, Morkin, breathe and relax." The voice seemed to be coming from inside his head as a thought which was not his own. He took a deep breath in, almost choking as the thick metallic air rushed into his body, he coughed and tried again, this time it was better and slowly he forced himself to calm. The heaviness seemed to lift as he relaxed, to be replaced with a new sense of lightness in his being as if he had just taken off a heavy suit of armour; it almost felt as if he would float away and he found himself digging his hands into the ground beside him for reassurance.

"Welcome, Prince Morkin, heir to the dragon's crown, descendant of the kings of men. Welcome to the hall of the Western Fey, welcome to the dream state. Beware though, any falsehoods told here will have dire consequences, only the truth may prosper, choose your words wisely, Prince who would be king."

Nobody seemed to have spoken, Morkin was sure of it. He had looked around as the voice spoke, seeking its source, yet all the Fey had looked straight back, their mouths still, their expressions blank. Yet the voice was clear and powerful as it filled the space around them, spoken with confidence and authority.

Morkin's voice came as a low squeak in comparison, it struggled to penetrate the air around them; he swallowed hard and tried again, this time his voice stuttered as he struggled for the words he wanted.

"You have nothing to fear, young Prince, your heart has already shown itself to be true. You would not be permitted into the dream state if it were not so. Speak from your heart, you will be heard, your heart holds the truth." Again the voice seemed to come from nowhere and everywhere at once, as it floated around the circle and into his head.

Morkin shut his eyes; his father would have known what to say, he thought, and then he remembered the silver fox in his pocket. He closed his hand gently around it, its icy chill focussing his mind and cooling his nerves as the cold seeped into his skin.

"I am honoured to be here amongst the Fey people. For too long now our people have forgotten your past friendship. We now fear the myth of the Fey instead of embracing its reality." His voice was strong and clear, yet he spoke as a whisper.

Silence met his words, it was as if the group were considering their meaning, weighing their value.

"You speak the truth, young Prince, for too long we, the Fey, have closed ourselves to man, yet our isolation had its purpose as does every path we tread as a people."

"My father's court told me tales of the Fey. Tales that could excite, enthral and terrify a young child. The reality so far does not fit some of the myth."

"Myth and legend are tales for children, the bones on which they build the flesh that their heart dictates."

"Indeed, and my heart had your kind as a grotesque shadow of yourselves. Surely the reality would be better, especially as you are no myth or legend but a people, a race more ancient and proud than we can ever hope to be."

"Your words flatter, young Prince, yet your words cannot deceive your heart."

"My heart is true, and no man can deny it. Do you now do so in this place?" Morkin struggled to contain his anger with the challenge.

Again the silence, followed by a low grumble that shook the earth where he sat, the light surrounding them flickered, orange sparks glinted within its midst. A flash of pure white light streaked across in front of Morkin, blinding his vision with its passing; he sat perfectly still, barely breathing, he was angry, yet still in control. They had questioned his truth after admitting they found his heart to be true. He would not show fear, he thought. I will not flinch, as another flash of light shot past him, this time it was close enough for him to feel its heat against his face. The circle of Fey were no longer visible to him through the maelstrom of light and sparks that sizzled around him; the air was burning and full of electrical charge, the smell invaded his nostrils whilst his hair stood on end. Colours flashed in front of his eyes, red, blue, green and white constantly changing in a blinding cacophony that was now hurting his head. He summoned his courage, fighting his fear until he had tamed it for now.

"Enough!" he bellowed, not sure if he could be heard through the light and sound. "I will not stay here and have my honesty and integrity questioned. Either tell me why I am here or return me to my people."

The light surrounding him dimmed with his words, the low grumbling noise slowly dying away with it, the circle of Fey coming slowly back into focus as Morkin blinked into the seeming darkness. His head was thumping with a mixture of anger and pain from the lights, he brushed his hands over his head, his hair tingled to touch and the static jumped across his fingers. The Fey watched in silence, seemingly impassive and unmoved by his words.

"You are indeed your father's son, Prince Morkin. We apologise for any insult you feel we have caused you. The information we have to share though demands our caution and it would appear, regrettably, our rudeness."

Morkin paused, letting his mind calm, his hand absent-mindedly sought the comfort of the small fox; he took a deep breath in, "Very well. If this information is as grave and as important as you describe then I will gracefully accept your humble apology and assure you that no further offence will be taken."

No sooner had Morkin spoken the words, when the light again closed in rapidly, blinding him momentarily and then it was gone, he blinked and rubbed his eyes. The trees came back into focus around him, with the Fey council sitting in front. Fengar rose beside him, "Come, we have much to discuss."

Chapter Seven

Ranabin stumbled against the invisible wall and cursed. It was the same every time. He never had any problems locating the invisible tower of Icebar; he always had trouble though finding the door. The problem was that while most people's perception of a tower is of a round construction, well, it is the accepted conformity of shape after all, unfortunately for him this was not the case with Icebar Tower. It belonged to Sin and, having lived in it for over 700 years now, he had during his time added bits to it here and there and mostly, it seemed, for no other purpose than to relieve his boredom. The result was not so much a tower now as such, or at least not at the bottom, but of a conglomerate of extensions and huts thrown up out of and around the original base of the tower in a haphazard manner. Some of the added rooms, it was believed, had no entrance, an oversight that, knowing Sin, was very easy to believe.

It would not be surprising, Ranabin thought, to find that Sin had built a new extension over the actual door into the tower. The last thought, however, had more to do with hiding his frustration than on any basis of fact as he had always managed to finally find the door, even if it had taken some time. The other three mages never seemed to have any problems in finding the door and of course Sin knew where his own door was located; no, it was just typical of him. Why am I so incompetent? he thought in frustration as he banged into another wall that stuck out at an obscure angle to his left. He was sure it had not been there the last time he was here, but being sure, as far as Ranabin was concerned, was not definitive, so with a sigh he continued to feel his way to the left.

Up above, the four mages watched as Ranabin felt around and around below them. He had, much to their amusement, passed the door three times already as he fumbled around. The only reason that he had not located the door yet was because Sin had not yet pulled the lever to reveal its presence. There were many levers in the tower, each for a specific purpose, many of which unfortunately Sin could no longer remember, yet the one to reveal the door was now firmly held in his grasp. There was of course no point in having an invisible tower if people could still walk into it; the tower also needed to be able to move, to bend itself out of the way of passing animals and people which accounted for the two other levers to his right. Although on occasion Sin had forgotten to disengage those levers and a few locals over the years had been known to bounce off thin air whilst out walking in the woods; thankfully this had always been explained away by ale, even if the unfortunate person had been sober at the time. It was easier for the locals to blame the drink than to try to comprehend a more sinister or magical meaning. These levers were now fully engaged, so that Ranabin could actually find the tower, yet another failing on the young mage's account. By now, Ranabin should have been able to find Icebar and enter it regardless of its physical state and without the need of the levers.

Ranabin swore, he was sure he had been around this bit already. He turned around, leaning back on the wall as he sat down. An old rotting tree trunk faced him, its shape and the holes in its trunk made a grotesque mask that seemed to be laughing and mocking him.

"If they want me that badly then they can come and get me."

He was fed up and he muttered the words under his breath and folded his arms across his chest in defiance. He was tired and his body ached, the earlier mystery and excitement at the stream had now totally worn off. He felt like going home, back to the comfort and solitude of his mountain. His feet were sore and as if to make his day worse he was getting a blister on his toe, it felt hot and tender. Slipping his sandal off, he bent his leg up and examined it only to discover a small cut on the underside of his little toe. Must have happened in the stream, he thought as he rubbed it.

As he did so, four birds materialised out of thin air to his left at ground level. They hopped about, looked at him with their small black eyes and then started to sing.

Ranabin picked up the nearest stone and threw it at them in annoyance. The stone missed, sailing over their heads as they sang on unperturbed, the stone though rather than hitting the ground behind them disappeared in mid flight, followed by a faint clatter as it hit something hard and then rattled onto a stone floor.

> *"Old Ranabin ain't he sweet*
> *Blisters though on his feet.*
> *As he ponders on the floor*
> *Because he cannot find the door."*

Ranabin jumped up in anger, his robe hitched up around his waist and held in his right hand as he ran at the birds, flapping his left arm wildly at them. They watched him approach, judging it to perfection, hopping out of his way at the last momement and flying off into the sky, taunting him with their singing as they went. From within the tower, Ranabin could hear the faint laughter of the other mages.

He stepped into the door, into a black pool, disappearing from sight from the outside world. Ranabin hated going into the tower, it felt like he was stepping into an electrical storm, the air crackled and hissed around him, invisible energy tugged at him, sucking and pulling at him, resisiting his entry and trying hard to evict his unwelcome presence from its domain. His movements were slow and laborious, each limb requiring a massive effort of will and energy to move. The air smelt of noxious burning metal which choked his nostrils, making his breathing shallow and his eyes water. He held his breath and pushed through the choking air, feeling along the wall in the claustrophobic darkness, unable even to see his hands. After a few more strides that drained him, at last the resistance eased and he knew he was in the tower. He fell forward into light, sprawling onto a cold tiled floor as he sucked in the clean air. The inside walls of the tower flickered into focus, blindingly white after the darkness from which he had just emerged. The floor resembled a draughtboard of black and white tiles stretching out in front of him. The room he lay in was large and com-pletely empty, the walls bare and there was no furniture on the floor, nothing, not even the stone he had thrown, the only break in the walls in the far corner, a door of black wood that stood out in complete con-trast to the walls.

He stood up and walked towards the door, his footsteps echoing in the emptiness of his surroundings, bouncing off the walls and reverberating back to him, making him conscious of the noise he was making; he started to tiptoe to lessen the effect. He resisted the urge to shout out, to hear his voice echo off the walls but he did increase his pace, anxious to get out of the barren room which with every passing second he found more and more eerie, creepy and suffocating despite its size.

The door creaked as he opened it, the sound magnified in the room as the squeal reverberated around him and sent shivers down his spine. He stepped through the door into the library; this was his favour-ite room in Icebar Tower and he immediately felt more at ease.

The room was filled with ancient creaking bookcases, crammed full of volume upon volume of different books. Ranabin loved books, it was the only downside of living on the mountain. He could very easily spend the rest of his life immersed in the pages held in this room. It was the mage library and contained all the books collected over the generations by successive mages, every book treasured and considered magical in its own right and lovingly cared for by Sin, although there were a few books in the library that were definitely more magical than others. These had pride of place in the central bookcase which even from this distance was visible over all the others, towering above them, surrounded by an aura of light of its own making. The room smelled of dust and leather, a few cobwebs clung to the ceiling and over some of the older bookcases, none of which had ever seen a spider. Sin kept the webs purely for effect as befitted the age of the books, the older the books the larger the web, so that in one corner of the library the whole wall, bookcase and books were covered in a thick mesh of webs, it seemed an almost eerie and foreboding way to celebrate their status.

Ranabin looked around, drinking in the smells and sights, a childlike grin lighting up his face. He sighed deeply. Perhaps once I have finished upstairs I will spend some time down here, he thought. He made his way through the library, trailing his hand lovingly over various volumes as he went, heading slowly, reluctantly to the door at the far end that led to the spiral staircase of the main tower. One thousand, six hundred and eighty-three steps, he thought miserably, if only I had learnt to fly. He trudged up, his footsteps echoing and mockingly pursuing him up the weary climb. No doors, no landings, no windows and nowhere to sit and stop. Just step after mind-numbing step, round and round in a continuous circle to the top of the tower and then the meeting. His heart sank, becoming more and more despondent with every upwards step.

By the time he reached the top his legs ached and he was out of breath. He spent a couple of minutes leaning against the wall at the top of the stairs, his heart racing in his chest.

"Come along, Ranabin." Sin's unmistakably rasping voice echoed down the corridor in front of him.

Sighing inwardly, Ranabin pushed himself upright and walked slowly towards the room at the very centre of the tower. The four older mages were sitting around the fire, they turned to watch as he entered the room.

"Ah, Ranabin! Nice of you to join us. I trust you had a pleasant journey here, not too many slip-ups along the way, we hope?" Acab struggled to keep from laughing as he spoke. The other three just smiled at him. Fazam gestured that the young mage should sit beside him and Ranabin lowered himself onto a pale blue mat on the floor.

The fire sparkled in front of him, a mixture of blues, greens and reds, yet despite sitting within an arm's reach of its flame he felt no heat emitting from it. He was sure the fire should mean something to him, he had a nagging sensation about it, one that he felt he should be able to recollect, yet at the moment nothing came to mind. He watched the flames lick around the logs which sat in the hearth completely untouched as if they had just been cut from a tree. The flames danced to a beat of their own, gently swaying and cavorting with each other around the logs; he was mesmerised by their dance, drawn to it. He became aware that the other four were watching him and it became disconcerting as they just stared, seemingly judging him by his actions now.

Finally Sin spoke, breaking the spell of the flame, "Ranabin, the time is upon us. Your time has arrived. For nearly 150 years you have been the Mage of the Land, it is now time for you to progress."

Ranabin looked at Sin, a clear look of puzzlement on his face.

"You do not remember, and that is the way of our life cycle, yet you have been here before five times already, Ranabin. My time draws near and for me to be reborn anew, you need to progress to the next level. If you do not achieve this then my life force will disappear from here forever."

The silence was complete; all the mages were looking directly at Ranabin who was still as confused as he was earlier. His confusion and puzzlement irritated Acab.

"See, he has no idea. We are doomed, he will never be ready and never be able to save us."

Ranabin looked at Acab, meeting his glare with his own and finally finding his voice. "Perhaps if you explained things clearly instead of speaking in riddles I will better understand what it is you are trying so hard not to tell me!" he replied curtly.

Acab flinched with the retort, he never liked to be spoken back to, especially by Ranabin. Fazam interrupted the two of them, sensing the hostility growing between them, "Acab, we have already discussed your views on this matter. What is important now is that Ranabin fully understands the situation as it stands."

Acab glared over at Fazam and then looked over to Sin for support, but finding none forthcoming, conceded the point to Fazam, who looked over to Ranabin.

"Ranabin, what do you know of the Dark Knights and the war?"

"The Dark Knights?"

"See," Acab interrupted, looking again to Sin for support.

"Silence, Acab, let him think." The finality in Sin's voice was evident and Acab sighing crossed his arms whilst gnashing his teeth in frustrated irritation.

Ranabin stared back into the fire, choosing its peaceful and mesmerising dance over looking at any of the four mages around him. The flames flickered as he watched, growing brighter the longer he stared at them. The brightness seemed to be taking form, developing detail, becoming a picture. Now another and another, a flood of images flickered in front of his eyes with each blink, invoking memories from deep within. It was as if a dam of information within his mind had been breached, allowing him access to these memories for the first time. Where the memories came from he did not know or understand, but a lot of things now made sense; he knew who he was at last. It was as if he had been an orphan all these years and at last had found his family and where he belonged. His mind spun with the reality of the information, and a lot of what he saw still made no sense to him but he knew what Sin had been talking about now, even if he lacked some of the detail.

The images slowed down and finally faded away, until the flame once more danced gently in the hearth. He smiled and looked across at Acab, mischief in his eyes, "The Dark Knights have plagued these lands for millennia, their greed and lust for power insatiable and their quest for these lands so far a constant failure that erodes their pride and soul. They will come again, driven by their failure and by lust and, if memory serves me correctly, it will be soon."

Acab swallowed hard; he never liked to be wrong and he still had his doubts, but Ranabin perhaps did have some potential after all.

"Excellent, young Ranabin!" Sin croaked. "Perhaps I will be reborn yet."

The others laughed nervously as if to contemplate the consequences of failure was too much to think about.

"Still there is much to do and much to tell. It is true the time of the Dark Knights draws ever nearer again. We fear though that this time they will succeed. This land is not as strong as it once was. The humans have weakened its resolve, their coming a blessing and a curse that may yet cost us dear."

The other three nodded their agreement as Ranabin sat, intently listening to the tale unfurl.

"The humans have lost their power," Sin continued, "the Ice Crown, the symbol of their unity and power given by Serevent, the dragon queen, has gone, stolen and yet not. It did not reach the thieves' intended destination which is just as well, its power and magic protected it and us from that fate, yet now it is gone. The King is dead and the Prince can no longer unite his people. They will fight if needed but not as one, they will protect their own interests and be killed one by one, some may even sell their services to the Dark Knights in a vain attempt to hold onto their power."

Sin paused, allowing time for Ranabin to absorb this information; once happy that he at least seemed to be keeping up, he pressed on.

"The allies of men are gone. The Wolves of Fennigan prowl again, yet I fear their intentions may not best serve us. The Fey are undecided, they are lost in a wilderness and lack guidance. The dragons are gone and you, Ranabin, are the key to victory."

"Me?" Ranabin was taken aback.

"Yes, you," all four replied in unison.

Sin continued, "We have all in our time used our powers to intervene in the defence of these lands. It is our purpose, these lands are of us as we are of them; we summoned the four we have spoken of and there were others before them. Now it is your turn again, you alone have the ability and the power, yet fate is against us."

"How and what do I need to do? What can I summon and from where?"

"That is not for us to say, we no sooner have the answer than you do. Yet the time will come if you are ready and then it will all become clear."

Ranabin pondered the words, his mind struggling with the enormity and the responsibility which had now been thrust upon him.

"How will I know when I am ready?" he asked.

"Difficult to say, it is not a definitive state of being. It was different for each of us, but we can assist you on the journey, in so far

111

as we can."

"What else do I need to know?"

"Difficult to know, yet we feel you need to travel and find your answers."

"Travel, but I have only just arrived, and I do not know the questions so how will I know when I have the answers?" Ranabin could not hide the despair in his voice.

"Indeed, but the path to your destination is long and arduous and needs to be travelled."

"Where do I start then?"

"Crescent Wood! The boy Prince meets the Fey there tomorrow. You will be expected."

Ranabin considered the answer. "But that is over three days' ride from here, and I have no horse!"

"Your problem, young Ranabin, is that you have not studied hard enough. The journey is indeed three days long for a human, we, however, are mages, not human. It is time you learnt to utilise your abilities to the full. I trust you can read and know the location of my library. The book you require is on the third bookshelf."

Ranabin rose and the others rose with him. He lowered his head to each of them in turn, ending with Sin. They returned the gesture and watched as he turned to walk out of the door. Ranabin stopped halfway across the floor and raised his hand to his mouth as if to cough. He whispered four words into his closed fist and then threw them into the fire. The words hit the fire with a hiss as Ranabin reached the door, he looked over his shoulder with smug satisfaction as the four older mages landed as one with a thud on the floor, their names crackling in the flames. They did not look best pleased, he thought as he raced down the stairs, expecting his legs to fly out from under him at any moment.

He reached the library safely, much to his surprise. The four mages upstairs, however, were still on the floor, each too caught up in their own thoughts about the coming year to be bothered with exacting revenge and besides, now that Ranabin knew, it would not be nearly so much fun.

The book was not hard to find. It seemed to know that it was being looked for and literally jumped out at Ranabin as he approached its place on the shelf.

How To Be Where You Want To Be
When You Want To Be There

And in small print underneath the title:

ALSO AVAILABLE IN POCKET SIZE TITLE
There Is Here Now

Ranabin sneezed as he wiped the dust and cobwebs off the cover; it was a thin book, fewer than fifty pages in total. He carried it over to the desk in the corner of the room and, settling into the chair, proceeded to flick through the pages. Realisation dawned on him slowly as he thumbed the worn pages. He had read this book before, he had even written in the footnotes of some of the pages, his spidery writing clearly recognisable.

The portals, of course! They were spaced evenly around the Moon lands, eight in total. He checked the map on the front page. Yes, one was situated within Crescent Wood. Now where was the closest one to here? Ah yes. Now the small matter of how to use them; according to what he had just read, it was a matter of focussing his inner energy and using it to tap into the portals which were linked together. Unfortunately, it also warned that the drain on the user's inner energy meant that they could only be utilised sporadically as the user was left very weak and vulnerable for days afterwards. Their overuse also had the potential to kill the user, which was a very sobering thought.

Yet it was the only way he would be able to get to Crescent Wood in time. Sin had not insisted, but he knew that if Sin had mentioned it then it must be important that he made it. Ranabin liked the new feeling, he was important at last. On reflection the day had turned out not too badly after all. The magic stream, shutting Acab up, finding out who he really was and that now they needed him, he was important, no, was now Essential to the survival of the Moon lands. He jumped into the air, kicking his heels together and whooped with joy. Realisation hit him as he landed, the Essential part came out of nowhere, flooding back into his brain, down into his stomach and back out of his mouth, as he leant forward being sick over the floor.

His embarrassment washed over his face in a red heat as he looked up to see Sin and the others standing in the doorway, watching him with a mixture of amusement, concern, disbelief and anger on their faces.

"One more thing. The Dark Knights have a new general, Vangor! Do not underestimate him, he is very dangerous and he now knows of our existence. They are close, closer than we thought. War is upon us, Ranabin. Go now. We will aid your journey as we can."

The ground shook, the walls moved, green replaced the brown of the bookshelves. The shock threw him, he was out in the woods again, the tower gone, yet from his left he could hear Acab's voice faintly, "But why do I have to clean it up? You should have got him to do it," and then the sound was gone as well. His head hurt, it felt as if it had been hit by a brick or a magic wall. He looked around, slightly dazed, with the book still in his hands.

"Oops, can't have that falling into the wrong hands." The voice came out of thin air in front of his nose and was immediately followed by a hand which reached out and grabbed the book out of Ranabin's hand, both then disappeared immediately, leaving Ranabin sitting on the grass with a surprised look on his face.

"Buutt, oh welllll," he spluttered.

The thunder brought his mind back to his immediate surroundings as it rolled in from the grey sky overhead, followed seconds later by a crack of lightning that forked across the sky and down to the ground to his right, hitting the fallen tree trunk that had mocked him earlier with its grotesque grin and splitting it in two. Ranabin smiled. Serves it right for laughing at me earlier, he thought, as he leant forward to pick up his stick which lay at his feet. He did not remember dropping it or leaving it there, but that was how it was sometimes with his stick. The rain came hard and cold, driven by the wind, turning the world around grey and bleak. The world darkened and the shadows under the trees grew into deep dark holes void of light. He ran for the cover of a nearby oak tree, its huge canopy of thick leaves offering some protection from the driving rain.

As he crouched under a low hanging branch, he reached down, resting his hands on his robe. It was dry. He felt again and then around it, it was all dry, he was bone dry and yet he had been out in the pouring rain only moments earlier. It was like the stream all over again.

Wait a second, he thought to himself, I am the Mage of the Land and am now due to change, what comes next? He searched his memory. Realisation dawned on him, accompanied by a small smile; the Mage of the Water, that must be it. He was changing, he was becoming the Mage of the Water. He stepped back out into the rain as it pelted down around him and raised a hand palmwards up to the sky. The rain fell all around him, he watched it as it seemed to steer around him, diverting its course as if repelled by an invisible field around his body. He stood and watched as a drop of rain approached his upstretched hand, heading straight for his palm, but then at the last moment it separated and fragmented into tiny droplets and, as if it had been smashed to pieces, these then migrated around his hand and re-formed into a drop at the other side, which then continued its path to the ground with seemingly no less of a lack of force.

The novelty though soon wore off as he began to grow cold and, remembering he still had to find the portal. He decided to continue with his journey. Visibility in the rain was poor and the trees around him were now distorted into twisted shapes that seemed to constantly move when seen through the endless onslaught of rain.

Now, where to find the portal? he thought. The map he had seen was vague and drawn out of proportion. The portals drawn on the map were huge in comparison to the surrounding demographics, the one he sought would, if the drawings on the map were to scale, be the same size as half of Mark Wood, which of course was totally ridiculous, and made pinpointing its exact location on the ground frustratingly time-consuming and nigh impossible. The only clue the map had given to its approximate location was that it had been drawn over the northern edge of Mark Wood, so it was in that direction he now walked.

There was no sun to guide him, it was hidden behind the dark grey clouds, obliterated from view, so he followed the moss growing on the trees, knowing that it could only grow on the shaded northern side of the trunks. As he squelched through the driving rain, thinking of what the portal would look like, his new-found magic repelled the mud and water around his feet, leaving a rather bizarre trail of dry footprints in the soaking wet ground in his wake. Have I used a portal before, he thought? Will I be able to recognise one? It would surely have to appear as if it were an everyday item, something you would expect to find in the woods, otherwise its location would now be common knowledge to the local people; perhaps not as a portal, but of something different, something out of place, at least. But what form would it take? A tree, a mound of earth, a stick or even a leaf? He smiled at the unwelcome thought of him having to look at thousands of individual leaves in search of the portal. No, surely he would be guided to it, after all he was a mage.

The fallow deer shot up from its den just seconds before Ranabin would have stood on it, both of them seemingly as startled as each other by the other's sudden presence. Ranabin now watched admiringly as it sprang through the trees in flight, darting a jagged course through the undergrowth, his own heart beating heavily, seemingly in time with its jumps. It soon disappeared from sight, the occasional snap of a small branch the only reminder of its presence in his grey world, until that too was no more.

He looked around where he now stood, the long grass where the deer had lain was flattened and dry. The area over it was covered by a low green bush and the low branches of an ancient oak tree that stretched lazily to the ground. The tree itself leaned over towards the right at such an acute angle that it surely defied gravity, yet still it stood, clinging to the earth with huge roots that jutted out of dark brown soil. He crossed over to the tree's gnarled trunk, running his hand over its rough bark, as if drawn to it by its power. He was fascinated by it. It seemed to be desperately clinging to life by its roots, knowing that to relinquish its hold on the life-giving soil meant certain death and yet still its majesty and strength was easily able to dwarf the trees around it: a king of the woods that was not yet ready to give up its crown.

The roots where he stood bulged out from the trunk and into the soil, forming a tunnel between the two, which with a little effort was big enough for Ranabin to squeeze into. In his effort to enter their inner sanctuary he pushed himself between the roots, snapping a few of the thinner ones as he went, the act of which compelled him to mutter a small apology. The tree groaned in protest, as if those very roots he had snapped were its defining anchor in the ground. Ranabin held his breath, waiting, expecting at any moment to hear the deafening roar of falling timber, he crouched down, legs bent, nervously ready to hopefully jump clear. The ground shook for a second and then settled, as if the great tree knew it was safe for the time being, and was once more quiet in the ground.

Ranabin relaxed, he let out a long sigh of relief. The world inside the roots was dark, the only light visible trickled down through the gaps in the roots from the grey world above him and served to barely illuminate the edges of the tunnel. He waited, allowing his eyes to become accustomed to the surrounding gloom. The air smelt damp and earthy, accompanied by the faint smell of rotting timber and musty leaves. Ranabin prodded forward with his stick, feeling the ground ahead as he tentatively made his way down between the roots, deeper into the tunnel. The tunnel continued downwards into darkness, his stick as he went occasionally finding large roots growing out of the floor which when stepping over them more often than not resulted in him banging his head on its unseen cousin above. Gradually, as he got deeper and deeper, the walls and the roof of the tunnel began to close in on him, eventually forcing him to crawl. The tunnel was now harder to negotiate, with tight corners and narrow gaps that he had to squeeze and pull himself through, contorting his body around and between the roots of the tree and the surrounding damp earth. The earthen walls were claustrophobically close, the air stale and damp. He felt forward with his hands, feeling for the unseen obstacles, pushing his body along; he was tired and sweaty despite the cool damp air, the roof becoming lower now with each forward movement, forcing him lower and lower until he was lying flat on his belly, forced to wriggle and inch his way forward; his world now completely black and damp, his hands, knees and feet covered in small scratches from sharp protruding stones. He still did not know why he was there, forcing his way forward deeper into the ground like some sort of giant worm, but for some reason it seemed to be what he needed to do, so he pushed, pulled, squeezed and cursed his way along slowly; his lungs, starved of fresh air, were now labouring under the effort. The sweat ran down his face in muddy rivulets that stung at his eyes.

He pushed and thrust forward, digging his toes into the earth for purchase, clawing with his fingers to gain sufficient traction. His head hurt, he was tired and felt dirty, his hands were now bleeding from the effort, he could feel the sticky, tacky blood on his fingers and its unmistakable smell now filled the confined space. His thoughts, as he lay catching his breath, started to turn to doubts; what if the tunnel just ends with no way out? Will I be able to get out again without being able to turn around? The thought of the effort that would be required to back out of the tunnel made his head swim with nausea and panic. He fought it down again though, forcing himself to relax, knowing that to succumb to panic here and now could prove fatal. Eventually, his reluctance to back out of the tunnel convinced him that he should go forward again. His progress was now a lot slower, his initial enthusiasm spent, the adventure no longer any fun, he now wished he was not so Essential.

A faint whiff of fresh air wafted over him. It hit his face with a gentle slap, invigorating his senses and then it was gone. He sniffed the air, pursuing the smell, testing its taste with his tongue. The same damp earthy smell as before! His mind, it seemed, was now playing tricks on him; he suppressed a scream and sniffed again.

YEES, he almost cried in relief. It was there again, the faint smell of salty water, just like sea air, its freshness heightened tenfold by the suddenness and briefness of its aroma. He savoured the smell and taste, where had it come from? Surely from in front! He pushed forward again, driven in pursuit of a promised escape, each successive move bringing its scent back, stronger and for longer, until finally its aroma overcame the damp stale air of the tunnel altogether, bathing him in its promise.

His hand fell forward into a nothingness inches in front of his face, yet the world around was still dark. He felt around, feeling the edge of his tunnel and then the drop, he found a stone, he dropped it into the void in front, listening as it fell, hearing a solid clang seconds later. Not too far down, I think. He pushed himself slowly forward again until his head was once more able to be lifted up, free at last from the tunnel. He waited, looking around, peering into the darkness; wait, a faint glow, yes, to his left in the distance. It was the only discernible feature of what lay in front, yet he could now hear the promised water, the faint trickling sound of a possible stream, its sound the only noise around him apart from his heart which seemed to be pounding in his ears as if it had relocated itself for a better view.

The fall, thankfully, was short. He landed with a thud onto a rock about three feet down, the noise of his fall though echoed around him, bouncing off unseen walls and shouting back at him as if angered by its confinement, over and over again, eventually growing weaker and weaker until, finally, its death brought back a welcomed silence. The gentle trickle of the water now grew back into its place as if it had silenced itself, scared by the sudden noise in its tranquil world; its sound louder and closer now

He stood up, and nearly slipped over, the rocks' surface was slippery and wet, despite this though his immediate thought was to blame the other four mages and he very nearly cursed them. Once sure of his footing, he stood up straight and stretched himself, he was sore all over, and very thirsty. He tried to get a direction on the source of the water by listening to its song, but it seemed to be coming from all around him, the only visible point in his world, the faint glow in the distance which was now directly in front of him. His immediate surroundings were rocks, their black shapes, dark silhouettes all around him, there seemed to be thousands of them. He headed towards the light as it seemed to offer the only clue as to where he was, picking his way as he went, across and around the rock-strewn surface in as direct a path as he could manage.

He was obviously in some sort of underground cavern and as he drew closer to the light, he was able to make out more of the detail. A huge rock wall, to his left, seemed to stretch up forever, it was taller than anything he had ever seen before, disappearing out of view to meet, judging by the lack of sky, an underground roof. A roof which, if he looked directly above his head and stared upwards, could just be distinguished, he believed, amidst the darkness. As he looked up, a drop of water landed with a plop into a stagnant pool of water at his feet, accompanied immediately by a shower of similar drops all around him. It then happened, it was as if the whole cavern had suddenly come to life, all around him on the floor and high up on the ceiling, millions of small lights all seemingly turned themselves on together as if by some invisible and unheard command. Not bright lights though, no,soft and gentle lights, a gentle glow like fireflies at dusk, not bright enough to light up the cavern, but enough to soften its edges, making it less harsh, less foreboding, less dark, and revealing more of its beauty. A beauty Ranabin now marvelled at as he stared upwards at the roof, his eyes drawn to the light, luminous green areas that now glowed dimly over its surface, forming random patterns of green and black that disappeared far into the distance. But they were nothing in comparison to the crystal stalactites that hung down, those now visible reflected the green glow around them in a gentle sparkle that even from this distance seemed to dazzle. He let his eyes fall to his surroundings, peering into the darkness of the far side of the cavern and then closer to the area around him. He found what he was looking for and crossed over to a stalagmite on the floor; it was about three feet tall, a mere dwarf by comparision to the others that he now could see behind it, the faint glow of light now reflecting and refracting off their damp surfaces, creating an ever changing rainbow of colour around him.

Even these though paled into insignificance as his eyes finally fully adjusted to the world and he saw the pillars of crystal that stretched from floor to roof, two becoming one, finally ending their long courtship and marrying one another. These huge pillars now gave him the impression that it was they that held the great roof up above his head with their beautiful yet fragile strength. He ran over to one, gently running his fingers over its surface, feeling and thrilling at the texture beneath. Its surface felt rough and pitted yet smooth and ever so fragile, a small piece crumbling into his palm, reduced there to a fine powder under his gentle caress.

As he stood there feeling the crystals between his fingers, enchanted by their simple beauty, the ground shook, a few of the stalactites above his head and around him crashed to the floor, their crystal structure shattering and melting quickly into the moisture on the floor. Ranabin was thrown sideways more from the shock and fear than the ground's actual movement. Low voices followed, their deep and thunderous tones echoed throughout the cavern and serving to mask their exact origin. Ranabin cowered behind a large rock, his heart thumping as he peered around its cold surface, the hairs on his neck were raised, his fingernails were digging into his sweaty palms. He peered into the gloom around, desperately trying to discern any movement in the distance. His head now bobbing up and down like a frantic lemur behind the rock, he was too scared to keep it above the rock for too long in case he was seen, but equally aware that he had no idea where the voices had come from and was thus as equally anxious to locate them

The ground shook again, this time accompanied by a loud thud and a tearing, scraping noise that sounded like something heavy was being dragged over the ground towards him. Ranabin, expecting another crystal shower from above, instinctively covered his head with his hands, thankfully it never materialised. He turned towards the light; it had grown brighter, the cavern was now revealing all of its secrets and its size, as inch by inch the light, growing more powerful, forced the darkness to slowly retreat. Pockets of dark shadows were cut off in the retreat, fleeing to refuge behind large rocks as the true majesty of Ranabin's environment became clear. Pillars of crystal stretching up to the roof, now bathed in light, shone and sent the light dancing onwards around, the green on the roof revealed as mere algae whose faint light magic could not now compete with the new brightness. The floor around him was littered with pools of dark water, that even now in the furious glare of the light still refused to reveal their depth and secrets.

Something was coming, Ranabin was now very sure of it. He looked around again and knew he could not stay where he was. He was on one of the highest points of the cavern floor and easily visible in this light, even to his own eyes, and he knew nothing of the vision of what approached. He crawled forward quickly, slithering over rocks, chasing after the receding darkness, seeking sanctuary within its midst, yet it always seemed to be just in front of him and never fully around.

A loud snort and a grunt came from behind him. He froze behind the rock he had reached, his legs were knee deep in icy cold water, which although he still felt dry in, was still able to drive its chill into his aching joints. His teeth started to chatter, he clamped his mouth firmly shut as the noise seemed to magnify and echo out.

A movement in the light caught his eye, a shape, a silhouette in the dark and then another. The thud was louder this time, shaking the ground again, more of the crystal stalagmites and stalactites shattered to the ground, their gentle sound lost in the sound of the thuds as it echoed back off the distant walls. Ranabin felt more than saw the closest crystal pillar fall. He dived to the ground, throwing his hands up instinctively as he did so to protect himself. Expecting at any moment to be crushed under its weight. Expecting half of the roof to follow it. The expected crash never came. It was more of a tinkle and he was crushed under a shower of fine dust that briefly coated him in a sparkling sheen before melting away. There were six of them now, dragging something behind them, which every now and then would rise up over a boulder or rock and then crash back down to the ground with what was now a ground-shaking, ear-dulling thud. They were coming slowly, growing in size with each lumbering step. They were still at the far end of the cavern over 300 paces away and yet they already appeared to be over three times Ranabin's own height.

They walked with an awkward, elongated, lumbering gait, their huge arms and legs too thick to be fully bent. Great snorts of warmed air came out of their noses, forming small clouds of mist around them which made it difficult for him to discern any facial features, apart from the two dark red, fire-like glows, in place of eyes.

Ranabin watched, his curiosity getting the better of his fear for the moment as slowly and methodically they made their way towards him. He was trapped, he could not move now as they would surely see him, and he had no idea whether or not they were friendly and, judging by the look of them, was in no particular hurry to find out. As they drew closer he could see that they were a stone-grey colour, but whether this was their skin or clothing he was unable at the moment to tell.

They stopped, much to his relief, about forty paces away from him, and he crouched down further behind the rock; the cold from the water was becoming unbearable but he was of no mind to move. The first in the line grunted out some sort of command in a voice so loud that Ranabin was sure his ears would bleed, he tried in vain to drown it out with his fingers. The group gathered around the sack they had been dragging through the cavern, part of it was now pulled open and the group began to sing. It was a low whisper of a song, a lament, the sadness of it apparent to Ranabin even though he could not understand any of the words.

> *"Oor yee fo snsio dekifuy aklooppo*
> *Sferjk ksiopa erthd jooosdr qerjiio."*

The words gently filled the cavern, bouncing back on themselves, meeting each new word as they did so, always managing to complement each other as if made to match, this adding a new dimension to the song, a new depth, which with every verse grew deeper and deeper. Ranabin found himself lost in the song, humming along as he marvelled at its beauty and simplicity.

He gazed over at the group, peering around the side of the rock, and saw one of them reach down and lift a boulder effortlessly from the floor; the creature lifted the rock towards its head and then bit into it, a crunching, grating sound accompanied the action, and then it threw the rock, which was now much smaller, as if it were a mere pebble onto the floor. It bounced, tumbling and crashing straight towards where he hid. He ducked as it skimmed over his head before crashing to a sudden stop behind him. The words of the song still filled the cavern as the group turned away, they had stopped singing yet its echo still lingered, the words gently marking their exit as they lumbered away, leaving their burden behind.

Their gradual departure slowly brought back the darkness as the light once more faded along with their song, until finally as they disappeared from sight, the dark silence returned and freed the shadows from their temporary refuge.

Ranabin scrambled over to the sack as soon as he felt it was safe. The object was massive, the sack made of some sort of coarse hemp material. Ranabin scrambled around it, it was at least twenty paces long and about eight paces wide, he searched for the opening that he was sure he had seen earlier. He wanted to find out what sort of item the group would discard in the empty cavern.

A pale grey face stared unblinking at the cavern roof as he pulled back the top of the sack. He jumped back in fright, expecting the deep black eyes to suddenly flare to the red of the living. It was a troll, he was looking down at the face of a dead stone troll. Once sure that it was dead, he reached down cautiously and touched the face, he was still half expecting it to spring to life; it felt cold to the touch, cold and hard just like a normal stone or boulder. Realisation brought fresh fear into his mind; he looked around at the boulder-strewn ground with a new mixture of awe, disgust and fear, he was standing in the fabled Rock Halls, the ancient burial ground of the stone trolls. He had read of it somewhere, but as with most of the Moon lands' history, this place was considered myth. He had, it seemed, just witnessed what for them was a burial ceremony, which explained the sadness of the song. Were all these rocks bodies of dead trolls? He shuddered, one of them had bitten into one. He looked around, picking up a small rock at random and examined it with new interest.

Thankfully, it did not resemble any obvious part of a body, yet it was difficult to tell, it was hard and rock-like and he did not really know what a body part of a dead troll would look like, especially if it had lain here for any length of time. He shuddered at the thought and dropped the rock, regretting it immediately though as it hit his foot and bounced off into a pool of water. His curse echoed around the cavern, chased closely by that of the splash. Had he just been climbing over the decomposing bodies of dead trolls? Yuck, he wanted to wash his hands. He wanted very much to leave this place as soon as possible, it no longer fascinated him, it now felt a lot more empty and sinister, the air felt colder, he shivered, wrapping his robe tighter in an effort to keep warm and to comfort himself.

The light in the far corner had now dimmed back to its previous faint glow, the shadows now appeared darker and more sinister. Everywhere he looked he could now see the bodies of dead trolls instead of rocks, he was surrounded by their dead decomposing bodies; his fear rose, controlling his thoughts, increasing his panic, his throat became dry in stark contrast to his wet sweaty palms. He ran, slipping and sliding over the damp surfaces, not sure really where he should go, so he headed for the presumed comfort and security of the light. His long legs carried him forward in a gangly, loping run and somehow he managed to keep his balance as he jumped and splashed towards the supposed sanctuary.

The source of the light did not, as he had expected, offer a way out, it was a single rock, resting alone on the floor of the cavern; it sat there gently humming, the intensity of its light growing as he approached, as if it could sense his presence, and once more lighting up the surrounding cavern. The stone was not entirely alone though, it rested against the cavern wall, which when he drew even closer to it suddenly sparkled into life. Red and green lights shot out from within the stone, red going left, green going right, hitting the wall and travelling up it in seconds, each colour tracing its own path up the wall from opposite ends. Travelling upwards and inwards, creating an arch of light, they lit up the surface of the rock wall, revealing the hidden runes etched into its surface. The colours finally collided at the top of the arch and exploded into a golden yellow, which then filtered down through the letters, changing the wall from red and green into a golden sunrise of letters.

Ranabin stood about a pace away from the wall which with the stone at its foot now resembled an altar; he studied the writing, trying to discern the ancient symbols and letters. He felt an urge to reach out and touch the surface of the stone, it was as if a force was pulling him towards the light, a force which he could not explain; perhaps the same force that had drawn him through the tunnel? There were too many things though that he had no explanation for in this place and he was thus reluctant to succumb to his growing desire to touch the stone. He turned his back on it reluctantly and, with a great effort of will, started looking for the door from which the trolls had entered. He took a step away from the altar towards where he assumed the door would be although he could see nothing that gave him any hope. As he did so, he became aware of the light again, the deep glow had risen from the stone and moved with him and now hovered exactly one pace behind him at head height. He took another step away and again the light moved, following him as if it were attached, illuminating his path from behind. Another step and another and still it followed him.

He turned to face it, slowly he studied it, peering into the brightness until spots danced in front of his eyes which now hurt from the effort. He took a step forward, expecting the light to move backwards, but it stayed where it was. He was now bathed in its glow, the rest of the cavern plunging back into complete darkness, his pupils now too constricted to see beyond the light. He raised his hand tentatively, expecting heat, yet feeling none and slowly his hand reached out closer and closer towards the light. His fingers touched the light, the tingling sensation was uncomfortable and unexpected. He pulled his hand back quickly as if stung but immediately missed the sensation once it was gone.

He reached forward again, this time anticipating the sensation, aching for it, longing for its warmth and embrace. It consumed his hand, obliterating it from his vision. The tingling sensation grew and grew, spreading along his arm, crawling over his flesh. It was up to his elbow now, pulling him towards the light, which was now his sole focus in the cavern. The air crackled and hissed around him, small multicoloured sparks shot out from within the light, some fizzing through the air as they slowly drifted around, others hissing in the pools of water at his feet as they extinguished their faint hold on light.

The rage in the roar shook even the walls in the cavern; it was a primal roar, vicious and ugly. It was full of anger, pain, outrage and hate. The shock of it stung Ranabin as if its force had physically slapped him, the burning red eyes so bright that he could see them despite being blinded by the proximity of the light were the only other thing visible to accompany the roar and they blazed with a fiery glow of molten wrath. Six pairs of eyes making towards him, coming quickly with a lumbering urgency, seemingly floating in mid-air, yet rocks crashed and tumbled as they forced a path over the cavern floor. A large dark shape shot through the air, over his head and crashed behind him, sending slithers of fragmented rock in all directions. One piece hit him on his upper leg, knocking him sideways as another rock shot past him. The light was retreating as if scared by the approaching trolls' anger, fading into the background and enabling him now to see the frightening shapes of the approaching trolls.

He looked around in panic, seeking the escape route that he knew was not there, his heart thumped in his chest, another rock smashed close by. He had to move, had to run somewhere, anywhere, and he had to do it quickly. He sprang up, leaping over the rocks on the floor. The ground shook as twelve burning eyes followed his path. He had no idea where to run to; his first thought had been the tunnel he had crawled through to get into the cavern, but he had no idea where it was now in the surrounding darkness. He ran towards the shrinking light, desperately hoping that in its diminishing radiance it might just highlight an escape route from the trolls. The light though had dimmed down to a faint glow as it shrank back against the wall of the altar and the air around it no longer crackled, it was as if it too were trying to hide from the wrath of the approaching trolls.

The wall held no sanctuary or any evidence of an exit, the light no longer able to illuminate the wall below and behind it as it hovered in the air just out of Ranabin's reach. Ranabin turned around on his heels, looking quickly from left to right, seeking something, anything, an escape route, a hole, anything would do. He looked up into a darkness that seemed to have suddenly closed in on him, straight into the burning red eyes of a troll, its face glaring down at him from above, his last thought as his vision dimmed was fear. His body slumped limply to the floor.

Chapter Eight

The moon in its radiance highlighted the beauty of the star-covered tapestry that was the night sky. A cool breeze gently meandered through the trees, dancing with the tall grass as it went. Morkin lay back against an old rotting tree stump that was covered in soft green moss, gazing up at the night sky above him. His thoughts drifted off to the games and the dream he had of winning the coveted champion's lance, how he would best Lord Luxor and the rest of the lords and ride triumphantly into the arena; Dancer would strut to the beat of the applause as they rode up and down; the feast later would be in his honour and every maiden in the land would fight for his favour, for the chance to dance with him. He would turn them all down, hoping, praying that she would arrive. He had no idea of who she was or even if she existed, but his idea of what she looked like had a shape and form and she was as beautiful as the night sky above.

He sighed deeply and closed his eyes; it had been a long day. The council of Fey Elders had told him to wait here, which had now been some time ago. Food had been brought to him, along with polite conversation from a few of the Fey people. But now he was tired and longed to just close his eyes and sleep but whenever he tried, his mind seemed to come alive; it had been invigorated by the day's events whilst the rest of him had been tired out. The thought of the possibility of finding the Ice Crown had filled his head with wonder, wonder which was only tempered by the deep feeling of anxiety he now felt. He could not place its origins, yet something was wrong; he knew it, he sensed it, yet he could not place it.

A shooting star shot across the sky above his head, its path disappearing and re-emerging through the canopy of leaves that obscured his view. Its small trail of light chased its wake, forming a small tail, as it continued tracing a straight path to its unknown destination. Morkin's eyes followed its progress, predicting when and where it would reappear, waiting for it, yearning for its presence until finally it could no longer be seen from where he lay.

"Beautiful, are they not?"

The voice startled Morkin; he had heard no one approaching and had felt no one's presence.

"My people call them the pathfinders of the gods. Their presence tonight is a good sign, young Prince. Come now, the elders are waiting."

Fengar stood in the shadows behind him, and even when Morkin had risen and stared straight at the place where the voice had come from, he still could not see the Fey Elder until he decided to move. Fengar had changed into a grey robe, its colour easily blending into the shadows under the trees. He was now barefoot, and Morkin noticed that he had six toes on each foot and that each toe also had a small claw-like nail, like a cat's.

Fengar smiled, his face lighting up the night, "Do not be embarrassed, it is only natural to admire and stare at what is different and unique in each of us."

Morkin was grateful it was dark and he felt his face redden as he diverted his eyes.

"I personally find it fascinating that humans can walk and run with only five toes," Fengar continued as he walked towards a small path that led back into the woods; he never looked back to see if Morkin was following, but continued his conversation none the less.

"The claw-like nails are great for climbing, which of course you humans are pretty inept at. However, and please do not take offence with any of this, I have great regard and admiration for your ability to get things done, despite your lack of the actual talents of, ohh, let's say the more evolved and mature races. Ah, here we are, Morkin. Please sit." Fengar gestured to a lump of wood in the centre of a clearing.

The elders were already sitting, waiting for him, and as before he crossed into the middle of the circle. Each was now also dressed in a grey robe of similar colouring to Fengar's. There were no obvious badges of rank or office on display. Yet it was not hard to pick out which Fey held the power. There were five of them, they sat taller than the rest and held themselves in a manner that stated power and authority. They too sat on the grass as did all the others, but it was to this five that Morkin now turned and bowed his head before he too sat on the grass facing them, choosing to ignore the lump of wood beside him. He kept his eyes lowered, waiting for them to speak. The silence as before extended, broken only by an owl calling out in the woods and followed by the faint scream of its prey dying in its powerful beak.

The voice was gentle and sweet, it sounded like it belonged to a young girl. This surprised Morkin and he raised his head to find the speaker. The young Fey girl he had played with earlier was now speaking to one of the Fey Elders. She wore a white gown which shimmered and sparkled in the moonlight and, surrounded by the contrasting darkness of the trees and the grey of the Fey, she seemed to glow in the light. Her words were low and whispered, yet clearly spoken in the Fey's own tongue and thus indiscernible to Morkin. The Elder listened, never looking at the girl, never replying; eventually she finished. She turned and looked straight at Morkin, their eyes met and shared in that instant a thousand words. His heart thumped in his chest, his stomach ached, he longed to now speak with her but she had turned and was gone.

"How did you know?"

Morkin looked around, confused. His mouth felt dry as he tried to form a reply. He licked his lips, his composure of earlier had gone, stolen from him by a glance from a girl. He shut his eyes and clenched his fists, working his tongue around his mouth, trying to generate the saliva needed to talk and also to compose his thoughts again. The minutes passed, he eventually looked up, staring straight at the five elders sitting in front of him. Their question was easy to answer yet also a trap. He laughed out loud, immediately easing his tension.

"How did I know that you five, who look like the leaders of a race, are not?"

Morkin looked around the circle again. He stood up and slowly turned around, looking as he did so for any reaction from the Elder Council. All their faces though remained blank and expressionless as they stared back at him. Each identical to their neighbour, apart from the five. He had been blind and had allowed his head to overrule his instinct. This was not a council of men and they did not play by the rules of men, yet he still had. He had looked for what he would expect of a human leader and they had provided it. As he slowly turned full circle to once again face the five they relaxed their pose, sinking back and once more becoming a part of the greater one.

"I shall not deceive you; for a moment you had me fooled. My mind was blind and if I have offended you then you have my apology. My land and my people are ruled by pomp and ceremony and it was with this that I judged this council. I can now see I was wrong and that there is no one leader here. I have met one of your elders, Fengar, and he has spoken wisely. He has told me that the other woods and forests have their own Fey Elders and if they are present here tonight, please allow me to humbly introduce myself and pay you homage."

Morkin sat down now on the lump of wood, resting back on it and closing his eyes. When he next spoke, his voice was strong and clear, full of honesty and pride. He spoke now with a new-found confidence and assertiveness in himself, addressing the circle of elders as if he was born to it.

"I am Morkin Starhult, the Crown Prince of the Moon lands, son of Magor, descended through the generations, tracing my heritage through blood to the time of the dragon and the crowning by Serevent, the queen of all dragons, of my ancestor, Lord Sutur. I sit before you and pledge my support and that of my people to you and yours. This is my oath, my pledge and *my honour*."

The words reverberated around the trees, their tone and pace pitched to perfection. Their effect seemed less so. The circle of elders seemed

131

to be waiting in the silence that now filled the space between them for Morkin to continue. The seconds dragged on and became minutes, the crickets chirped in the grass, unaware of the drama around them.

Fengar's voice finally drifted over, soft and true, "You are welcome, Prince Morkin. I will speak for the council as is our custom in such matters; our thoughts here are as one and you can be assured that you have our full attention." He paused and smiled, having seen Morkin's doubt. "It appears we have once again underestimated your powers of observation. You are right, of course, we are all equal here and, yes, there are others here from afar, but alas not as many as we would have liked."

Fengar sat to Morkin's right and although he had not been asked, Morkin out of politeness turned to face the Fey Elder as he spoke.

"Let me introduce you to Carebin of the Fey. We are aware that you have already met, although I believe I am right in assuming that you have yet to be formally introduced."

A tall Fey stepped out from the trees behind Fengar and nodded over towards Morkin. He remained behind Fengar though, making no attempt to enter the circle or approach any further.

"Please do not take him as rude." Again Fengar seemed to be able to read Morkin's thoughts. "He is not allowed in the circle now as he is not an Elder. You will meet him later and I am sure you will enjoy his company. He has a lot to tell you which may be of interest." Fengar raised his arm and, with this dismissal, Carebin blended back into the shadows.

"Now, young Prince, how much has Lord Luxor told you about the Ice Crown that your kind seek?"

The question was unexpected but Morkin hid his surprise. "Only that he has not located it yet."

"And what would you give to learn of its whereabouts?"

"I would give my oath to any that knew of its location."

"So if the Dark Knights knew its location, would you give them your oath, young Prince?" The question was cold and cut at Morkin.

"An oath is a double-edged sword, is it not? An oath can be of vengeance as well as allegiance." He spoke calmly, keeping any emotion he was feeling out of his voice.

"So which have you just given to our people then, young Prince?"

"An oath that will befit your race's actions and intentions towards mine, of course. I hope it is an oath of mutual benefit, yet my first duty is always to my people and the Moon lands."

"What would you do if you had the Ice Crown, young Prince?"

Morkin excitedly looked around as if suddenly expecting to see it; disappointed, he returned his gaze back to Fengar. He managed somehow to keep the disappointment from his voice.

"Unite the peoples of the Moon lands, all peoples and all races and make us strong, strong enough to fight and defeat the Dark Knights; who, I am led to believe, will ride against us once more and that that time is drawing ever nearer." Morkin paused, allowing his words time to take effect, before continuing, "I would hope when the time comes that the Fey, with their mastery of horses and bows, will emerge from the trees and fight by our side as once your forefathers and mine did on these very lands. Lands that have the spilt blood of our kin mixed together as one, these are our lands, not mine not yours but all of ours, Fey, human and more. A land worth fighting for still and that is my intention, with or without the Ice Crown."

The Fey council looked slightly bemused, almost shocked; for the first time showing any hint of emotion behind their blank expressions, yet it was only a momentary lapse, a brief insight that was now once again hidden from sight, making it difficult to truly tell what they were all thinking. Although no words came from their lips and nobody moved, Morkin knew that they were debating his words; he had by now grown accustomed to their obligatory silence each time he spoke. He took the opportunity to gather his own thoughts and began to study one by one all of the faces of the Fey Elders sitting facing him. Each was very similar to Fengar in appearance; the same pale skin, and yet despite their age their features bore no lines or blemishes as one would expect. He still had difficulty working out their ages but when he thought back to when Carebin was standing behind Fengar, it was obvious that he was younger than those sitting in the circle and by some considerable years. The only striking difference had been the difference in the colour of their hair; all of the elders' hair, like Fengar's, was a rich rustic grey colour which bordered on being silver and lent them an image of wisdom, maturity and grace. Carebin's hair, in contrast, was a vivid wild yellow, a yellow of sunflowers and ripe corn; it spoke of youth and summer and the freedom that the life of that season promised.

As if called by Morkin's thoughts, Carebin stepped back out of the shadows, their eyes met and each held the other's gaze. In that moment Morkin knew why Luxor had trusted this Fey. Even at this distance his eyes appeared clear and sharp, holding honesty and truth, and there was no trace of deceit or deception within that crystal clarity. They were hunter's eyes, used to taking in the world around, yet also offering kindness and compassion. Morkin resisted his urge to smile, instead he lowered his head in silent acknowledgement at the unspoken assessment of each other.

His thoughts were suddenly interrupted by movement in the trees; a wood pigeon startled to flight burst out of the canopy of leaves, its hasty flight shaking the small branches in its path; the snap of a stick underfoot then echoed in the otherwise silent woods. Surely this was no Fey approaching? Morkin thought. His answer came moments later as Lord Luxor pushed his way into the clearing and, on seeing Morkin sitting in the centre, was evidently going to advance into the circle of elders. His way forward though was suddenly barred by the strong arm of Carebin which was flung in front of his chest but even that was not enough to deter him, the hissed words from Carebin that followed though did. Luxor stood staring at the boy, slowly letting his vision take in the scene, methodically scrutinising it for any danger to the Prince. He turned to Carebin and again words were spoken which seemingly then made his mind up and, with a fleeting glance at Morkin over his shoulder, he left the clearing accompanied by Carebin, both disappearing quickly from sight, consumed back into the thick undergrowth behind them.

Lord Luxor's entrance and departure seemed to have gone unnoticed by the circle of elders and still the silence stretched out. He was pleased that his friend and guardian was here. However, he had been enjoying his new-found freedom and responsibility, a freedom which he knew would now once again be checked by Luxor's presence. His mind wandered back to the Fey girl, as he sat waiting; smiling at her memory, his pulse quickening at the thought. He had met girls before, but this one seemed to affect him differently; he could still see her face in his mind, the copper colouring of her hair that flowed over her shoulders like a sheen of satin, the deep aquamarine of her eyes, the way her nose gently sloped and curved at the tip and the lips, lips that when smiling could banish all of his sorrow. He had no idea who she was, no idea of her name or anything about her, but that mattered not; all of that would surely come in time. All he knew at the moment was that his heart was thumping in his chest and his head was giddy from just thinking about her.

"Her name is Tamora; she is of the blessed isle, a child of the Fey, whose destiny is written by the ancestors." The voice as before seemed to float on a breeze, entering his head as a thought as opposed to him hearing it.

Morkin in vain tried to empty his mind; it felt like his innermost thoughts were laid open for all to see. It felt as if he had been robbed, his stomach churned, gripped in an iron grasp. He felt sick, betrayed and violated, yet still his anger was quickening, rising, taking over his senses. He knew not from which Elder the words or thoughts had come, but it mattered not; it now felt as if all of them were inside his head, as if slowly one by one they had all crept in somehow, silently evading his defences and were even now stripping him of his dignity and soul.

"HOW DARE YOU?" he screamed the words as a thought inside his head, "HOW DARE YOU STEAL FROM ME!"

His hands now held his head and his eyes were screwed up in concentration.

"GET OUT!! GET OUT!! GET OUT!! ALL OF YOU, GET OUT!! GO!!!"

The dull pain started from behind his eyes and grew as he

screamed the words in his head. It spread quickly, seeping through his pounding brain, his head was now thumping, growing heavier; despite his eyes being screwed up tight he could still see flashes of black, white and red dancing in front of them. His head felt as if it were on fire, his brain burning, his thoughts turning to ash in the embers, he was now suffocating in its heat; each breath became harder and harder to draw and yet still he persevered, he hung on, screaming the thoughts, fighting through the pain, determined to rid his mind of the invading Fey.

They were gone; he opened his eyes, he lay on the grass, the coolness of the earth pressing against his left cheek. His mind was empty, but they were gone; where once sat a circle of elders, now there was just grass and trees. Had it all been a dream? He raised his head off the ground; it took a huge effort and he immediately felt dizzy and nauseated. His mouth was dry, very dry, his tongue was actually stuck to the top of his mouth and his lips felt as if they would crack if he dared to move them.

He gently teased his tongue to life, slowly the saliva returned, enough now to moisten his lips at least. His mind gradually came back to him, the memories of the past and the anger he had felt. He stretched his limbs; they ached, but no worse than he had felt before and he pushed himself up into a sitting position, looking around as he did so. The nausea died a little. He was not, as he had first thought, alone. Carebin and Luxor stood watching him from about twenty paces away, both leaning against a tall oak tree that marked the start of the surrounding woods. He looked over to them, focussing his mind; he made to stand up, it was then that the weakness hit him, knocking him back down to his knees. He saw Lord Luxor still standing beside the tree, unbelievably, it seemed, his mentor was not coming over to assist him.

Carebin looked at Luxor, "He has to leave the circle by his own effort, you cannot assist him."

"You have said the same thing to me three times now, yet still you offer no explanation as to why." Luxor was angry and confused. His first thoughts when they had been summoned by the council here an hour earlier had been to go to Morkin's aid, yet Carebin had forbade it with a tone of voice that so far had made him heed the words. However, now it was obvious the boy was struggling, he was honour bound to go to his aid, despite those words.

Lord Luxor stepped forward, determinedly brushing aside Carebin's arm and words. Morkin watched his guardian argue briefly with the Fey and then come towards him; he felt instant relief at his imminent aid and slumped forward onto the ground.

The flash of lightning came from above, seemingly out of nowhere and struck the ground two paces in front of Luxor, scorching the earth black and making the air sizzle and hiss as it passed. Luxor stopped in his tracks, looking up with a mixture of confusion and anger at the cloudless sky above.

"The ancestors will not permit you to enter uninvited; he has to leave by his own effort, it is their way." Carebin's words though only served to increase Luxor's anger and determination and he glared back at the Fey, muttering a curse under his breath.

From where Morkin lay on the ground, it looked as if the lightning had actually struck his friend and mentor. The flash of light had momentarily blinded his vision, the air was heavy with static and the world outside the circle had faded to darkness. He shouted out in anger and jumped to his feet, falling back down as if struck by some invisible force himself as his legs gave way. Determined, he crawled forward, fighting through the burning air. Each forward movement brought a deeper smell of burning, the air growing darker and darker and still no reply came to his continued shouts.

Luxor had turned in anger; he could see Morkin as he stood and again fell. He took a sideways step to his left and again tried to go forward. The lightning this time was fiercer and more powerful; it hit the ground directly in front of Luxor, arcing out above him and hitting the nearest tree, the trunk split with a painful cry and the tree went crashing down into the woods. Luxor travelled backwards through the air, half by jumping and half by the force of the blast, his reflexes had saved him from the full force. Clods of earth and grass hung suspended in flight beside him, only to rain down on him as he hit the ground with a heavy thud.

"Lord Luxor, please mark my words; you cannot enter the circle uninvited. If you keep trying like this, you or the Prince may die."

The breath had been knocked out of his lungs by the combined effects of blast and landing, yet as he lay gasping for air, the finality of the words he now heard gave him more reason for concern. Where was the boy? He had been crawling forward, he must have been close to … the thought was unimaginable, Luxor felt a knot of panic rising in his stomach and despite having to gasp painfully for breath he pushed himself up onto his knees and peered hopefully into the circle.

The second blast knocked Morkin sideways, the hair on the left side of his head fizzled and sparked and was now reduced to a shrivelled fine dust which disintegrated on touch. The air was so full of charge now that it hummed so loudly it sounded as if a swarm of bees were actually travelling through his ears. He shook his head, trying to rid himself of the sound as he again tried to see out of the circle. He must be close to the outside, he thought, his hand then touched the hot blackened earth; it shot back from the heat which scorched his fingertips, blisters immediately forming, and he sucked on them, trying desperately to cool the heat.

The heat forced him to edge sideways, it barred the way ahead. Eventually after what seemed like minutes the air gradually became cooler in front, the worst of the heat was now off to his left. He edged forward again and met still cooler air, the heat was definitely now to his left, the humming less audible, the darkness slowly giving way to grey shadows which then lightened to browns and then greens and then blues. He pushed forward again.

A hand reached out of the light and pulled him forward so suddenly that his arms gave way underneath him and he landed face first onto the soft grass. He was there for mere seconds before being lifted up and carried into the cool, fresh air. He looked straight into Luxor's grinning face, smiled his thanks, fatigue then conquered him and he sank into darkness.

He did not know how long he had slept, minutes, hours or days; the water when he woke though was welcome, his parched tongue swam in its freshness before finally reluctantly allowing its passage to be enjoyed by his body as a whole. It took a whole waterskin full of water to satisfy his thirst and a further skin which he then slowly savoured before Morkin felt ready to speak.

"Where are the elders?" His first question was directed at Carebin, who sat by a nearby tree.

Carebin looked over at him, pausing for thought, seemingly deciding on the best way to answer Morkin's question.

"Gone for now." The reply was short and curt.

"Gone where? I need to speak to them or at the very least to Fengar. They have questions to answer," Morkin's anger was very evident in his voice.

"They are shamed and have gone to seek the ancestor's guidance."

"Shamed! Shamed by what?" Morkin spat the words out. "Their theft of my thoughts or their banishment from my mind?"

Carebin turned away from Morkin, choosing instead to look into the trees, he was troubled by the young Prince's words. He took his time, it seemed to Morkin as if Carebin were wrestling with his own conscience for an answer. Eventually he again turned to face the young prince.

"I cannot speak for the council of elders, but for my own conscience I can only say that I am shamed by their invasion of your thoughts. We have always had the ability to enter another's mind, yet in my opinion the council went too far this time. It has never been our custom to enter another's mind without invitation, and even then never as deeply as they probed into your thoughts. The council, I hope, are shamed by this, they have requested that I look after you until they return, tomorrow."

"Tomorrow!!" Morkin's agitation was evident. He was sure the council had been going to tell him something important about the Ice Crown, possibly even its location and now he would have to wait. He stood up and walked over to where Luxor was now sitting, he seemed unmoved by the delay.

"Well?" he looked down at him.

Luxor looked up, obvious sadness in his eyes, "Well what, my Prince?"

Morkin regretted his tone of voice and shrugged his shoulders, "Nothing, it matters not," He turned instead and walked back to where he had sat before.

His frustration made him anxious and twitchy, he needed something to distract him. He could not sit here for a day waiting for the Fey council to decide on why they had shamed themselves. He had no idea of the time but knew from the sun's rays coming from the east that it was still morning and as of yet not midday. He must have slept all night as it had been late when he had entered the circle of the elders. Or had he slept for longer? How many days had he wasted? How many days did he have? And now another whole day, it seemed, was to be wasted waiting here. He paced up and down, Luxor and Carebin watched him impassively, each lost in their own thoughts. Morkin had never before seen Luxor so quiet; something obviously was troubling him but Morkin did not feel ready to enquire as to what it was. Carebin! Of course! The thought excited him, they had told him that after the council had met he should to talk to Carebin. Well, he was here now so why wait?

He spun around and walked purposefully towards the Fey.

"So, Carebin of the Fey, I understand from the council that you have much to tell that may be of interest to us both."

Carebin looked up, his blazing eyes liquid blue in the sun's rays, "Perhaps, young Prince, but not until I have been instructed to do so by the council."

Morkin, unperturbed, sat down on the grass facing Carebin, meeting the Fey's icy stare with his own. "The council said we were to talk, you and I. Is that not all the permission you require?"

"Of course we may talk, young Prince, but some of the things that you wish to hear may only be said when the time is judged to be right."

"So let us talk anyway, I am intrigued to know of your travels. My Lord Luxor speaks highly of you and that is praise indeed for somebody he knows so little about."

Luxor, on hearing his name mentioned, looked up, his curiosity aroused and overcoming his feelings of remorse and anger at having failed in his duty to protect Morkin. He stood up and walked over to where the others were sitting.

"Yes, Carebin of the Fey, I am also intrigued to learn of your travels. You have, I am sure, much to tell me."

Morkin looked at his mentor as he sat down and was relieved to see that the earlier sadness had now gone from his eyes, replaced once more by the usual fire of life.

Carebin looked at the two and sighed. "I imagine it matters not when I tell you, so I will tell you now, but before I begin, I must ask that you do not interrupt me during the telling. My thoughts will not tolerate very well any interruptions and if you wish to hear the whole tale, then I need your silence."

Carebin looked at the two humans, who in turn looked at each other and then back at the Fey. "Agreed," their voices sounded in unison.

"However," continued Luxor, "I suggest you make it a short tale as the boy here cannot keep quiet for long. Or," he scratched his head and looked at Morkin with a mischievous grin, "you could go and find us some food, boy, whilst the men talk. I will of course summarise the tale for you later."

Morkin kicked Luxor hard on the ankle, the grimace on Luxor's face testament to its effectiveness.

"Perhaps not then," he spoke through gritted teeth as he rubbed his ankle.

Carebin meanwhile looked at the two of them in wonder and amusement, not sure whether he should proceed or abandon his tale.

"We are ready," Morkin fixed his eyes on him.

Carebin looked at Luxor, who just nodded his head.

"My story starts here, in the circle of elders or, as it is known by our people, the circle of light. It was here that I first saw the human who was later to be revealed as one Lord Luxor of the Moon lands, mentor and guardian to the Crown Prince, Morkin."

Luxor and Morkin exchanged amused glances on hearing their names so formally spoken. Carebin's eyes, now the first words had been spoken, glazed over and rolled backwards into his head. His now completely white stare seemed to fix directly on Morkin, making him feel decidedly uneasy. Carebin seemingly in a trance now slowly and methodically crossed his legs and then rested his hands loosely across his lap before continuing.

Morkin had opened his mouth to speak but a tap on his foot from Luxor reminded him of his promise and he shut his mouth in silence.

Carebin's voice was soothing and rhythmical, easy on the ear, making it easy to lose oneself within its enchanting mystery of tones and words; words which were now endlessly flowing over them.

"He was bathed in light, as white as pure new snow, yet as blinding as the early rays of the sun on the horizon. There for a moment and then gone, no sound, no trace of his being. I followed into the light, my path was unclear and yet laid out before me, a maze of choices and unknown forces pushing and pulling at me, yet always guiding. My journey had begun. Yet I was not yet born, my body was a shell, an empty vessel. I knew not who I was, I had no identity, my first year away was a daze. I travelled seeking what I could never hope to find, unaware of what it was I sought or where it was located. Yet the answers were always with me. They were in me, the ancestors had entrusted me with the path, all I needed to do was trust them and let them guide me."

Carebin paused momentarily, drawing breath.

"They led me to Lord Luxor; the illusion of the light became a real man, riding fast on a hunt. We spoke at last and my path was clear. My journey was not to be alone, though; two companions, trustees of Lord Luxor, joined me in my travels. Trador, a young knight of the royal household, and another by the name of Stend, a human from beyond the fiery dunes of Mylst, a land fabled for its riders and slayers of dragons, a man of skin as dark as the scorched earth itself. At first he scared me but now his courage and loyalty will be revered and sung in Fey fables."

The silence that followed was unexpected; they both looked at Carebin and then at each other, both were sure neither of them had made a sound to disturb the tale, yet Carebin had stopped talking. The emptiness left after his voice was slowly filled with birdsong from the trees and the gentle rustle of leaves shaking in the breeze. Morkin looked back at the Fey; his eyes were now shut, his breathing gentle and relaxed as if in sleep. He watched the gentle rhythm, it was entrancing; he now felt tired, he stifled a yawn and made to get up. A long sigh emitted from Carebin's mouth and then again his voice continued. Morkin and Luxor again exchanged glances, shrugged their shoulders and returned their attention to Carebin.

"Lord Vermount stole the Ice Crown, that much is common knowledge amongst all in this land. His treachery and deceit is not uncommon amongst humans. Yet a crown of ice can no more be stolen and kept for long than can a breath from one's mouth or a handful of water from a stream; eventually they all will slip through your fingers, trickling through your grasp and returning to their natural state, especially if one's grasp is as treacherous as Lord Vermount's. It became clear very early in our journey that we were no longer seeking a crown of ice, as it is now gone."

An audible gasp escaped Morkin's lips, he could not help it, the mention of the Ice Crown had had him on edge but to hear that it was gone had been too much. He now bit down hard on his lips, drawing a thin trickle of blood, annoyed with his own lack of discipline, hoping his sound had not thrown Carebin's tale.

"Melting slowly, trickling drip by drip, some absorbed into the ground, the rest evaporating into the air. No, we cannot find a crown of ice because it no longer exists. Yet magic does not so easily evaporate and the crown's magic is both powerful and eternal. The crown itself is an irrelevance, a mere vessel for the magic contained within, which now having been freed would return to its source. No, it is not a crown you should seek, as that is long gone, but the magic that was within and that will be found with its keeper. My travels took me across these lands seeking out this keeper of the magic. My journey however did not reveal the location of the magic, yet I now know the path that must be taken by each to open the way."

Another pause, this time only momentary. "Time though is not on our side. The Lord Luxor must raise the army to defend these lands, even when his efforts in uniting the lords fall on deaf ears, he must still find a way. The boy Prince, Morkin, will be joined by three others. Only these four can hope to find the path and although one has treachery at heart, all will be required at some stage if their journey is to be successful. The young Prince must first seek out the Faeries of the Snow; beware though of your blindness. The Fey are divided in what we must do; although our division will not lead to betrayal as with some of the human lords, our path is still undecided on. I have shown them the path, and yet it is still for them even now littered with the debris of doubt and disbelief."

Chapter Nine

Vangor watched, waiting patiently for Fent's question. A light sprinkling of snow now blew onto the ridge, the wind's persistence finally negating the protection it had afforded them from the harshness of the surrounding environment. It was not yet thick enough though to lie on the now damp, bare rock where he stood, its small flakes melting rapidly on his skin and on the rocks around. The night air was cooling though and it would not be long before the icy breeze was cold enough to bring down the thicker snow that was promised by the dark clouds above. He felt good inside, despite the cold; today was turning out to be better than he had expected. The aphrodisiac of power had for a long time succeeded in shaping his future and he was still happy for it to take him onwards on their shared journey through life.

Fent's brown eyes glared at the human, a deep glare full of self-pride and hatred of this man in equal measure. He knew the question must be asked, he knew it was expected of him as the leader of his kind, yet some part of him was somehow scared. Not scared of knowing the answer but of how he would react to the answer. Would the fire that now drove him on be extinguished in the knowing, would he be consumed instead by grief, or would the answer fan the flames into a raging furnace that would burn out of control, destroying him and all that he had worked so hard to achieve? No! He could not let the fear conquer him, he had to know and he would deal with the answer as best he could.

"Do you know the name of the one who killed my father?"

Vangor pretended to be shocked by the question, whilst inside his delight was barely contained. He steeled his resolve, determined to enjoy the moment, expecting the anger and grief to consume the pathetic creature before him. He hoped it would lash out at him, he could already feel his blade biting into its bone, muscle and sinew. He would wear the pelt, it was a pity he had never taken the father's though, they would have made a fine pair of trophies.

"What makes you presume I know the answer to such a question, pup?" he sneered.

"I do not presume, human, your words deceive when your eyes hold the truth. You know the answer, so save the games for your pet soldiers. Either tell me or I leave," Fent growled, showing his teeth, the hair on the back of his neck now raised.

Vangor's men watched the exchange with a surreal fascination. They were unable to understand what was being said as their leader was growling and snapping at the wolf. They would have found the exchange highly amusing if it had involved anyone other than Vangor, who was not renowned for his sense of humour or charity, so they watched grim faced, as always ever ready to protect and please their master.

Vangor's hand again tightened its grip on the hilt of his blade.

"I am the one who killed your father. It was I that rescued you from the woods and it was I that fought him in the pool and there sent him to greet the ancients."

The words came out cold and calculated, each individually striking home deep into Fent's soul. All the time Vangor had kept his eyes firmly on the wolf, his hand holding the hilt of his sword, his body set, ready to defend or attack it mattered not, either way the wolf would die.

Fent had suspected it, he knew there was something about Vangor that he had recognised and now it had been confirmed. A red darkness descended over his eyes, turning the world around him crimson. He raised his head, instinct taking over, lifting it to the sky; he heard the laugh from Vangor, it sounded far off, it was mocking him. He tried to fight the impulse to howl, knowing it would not come, hating himself for his weakness, but the impulse, rising from deep within overcame him; something chilling and raw, a power that needed an avenue of escape, a need to be free and it had chosen its route to freedom, he neither had the strength or the inclination now to stop it. He stopped fighting and relaxed; allowing it to control him, it extended his neck, leaning him forward and upwards on his front legs to gain maximum extension. Cold air was sucked into his lungs seemingly fighting in its rush to get in, as if it were a desperate refugee trying to escape from the cold outside. His diaphragm was pulled down, filling his lungs further until finally his ribs could expand no further.

The outward rush of warm air, billowed out into small clouds around his mouth, they were now illuminated by the full moon, as if on cue it finally escaped the confines of the clouds to shine down on him. The note was true and solid, a deep throaty howl that roared out across the trees and hills with a clarity and deepness that had been unheard for generations. Snow that had that day loosened its icy grip on the rocks below in the gentle heat of the day's sun now, startled by the sudden noise, slipped down in cascades from the higher slopes, tumbling and crashing on its way to the valley floor. The force of the howl and its suddenness had thrown the outcrop into panic; Vangor had collapsed in a heap, knocked senseless by an unseen blow. His men were either trembling on the ground in sudden fear or were hiding behind the closest rock. Their horses had fled across the outcrop and down the treacherous slope at the far end. Only one remained, a tall black stallion, Vangor's battle mount, it alone stood its ground, ears pricked back, nostrils flared and teeth bared. Seeing its master lying alone on the ground, it snorted and kicked out with its front legs, its only thought was now to protect him. It took a step towards Vangor, closing the distance warily, its eyes firmly fixed on the wolf not ten paces further on.

Fent was aware of the howl, yet he knew not where it had come from or why. He also had no power over it as it rang out from his mouth. He saw Vangor being thrown to the ground by its power and at that moment he had strained every muscle in his body in an attempt to pounce onto his now helpless prey. Yet here he stood, helpless and powerless, frozen, it seemed, to the spot, unable to move, watching in frustration as the human's horse now slowly dragged him away to safety, back to his men who now cowered in fear from the howl behind their rocks.

The howl slowly changed tone, becoming a lighter note, a long steady piercing sound, a sound that could travel miles, a sound capable of striking fear and awe in equal measure into all that heard it. An ancient sound, a sound that sang the story of the wolf, a sound that many had thought they would never hear again.

The men now seized their chance of redemption and bundled Vangor onto his horse and led him away to safety. Their new-found bravery did not stretch to attacking the wolf, although a few did draw their swords as they backed away down the slope, their only thought though was to protect their leader.

The howl continued on long after the men had been driven away by the call of the wild; Fent anchored firmly to the spot, unable to move. His lungs were past empty when finally the howl died, yet still it lived as it echoed off the walls of rock around and below. He fell to the ground, drained and completely exhausted. It felt, as he lay panting on the rock with his red tongue lolling out over his white fangs, as if his very soul had torn itself free from his body and rushed out into the wilderness.

The enormity of the occasion slowly sank in. The Ancients' Howl! He had just sung it to his people. Even as he lay there he could hear a reply, a low howl came echoing along the valley, not as strong or as powerful as his had been but equally as enchanting and magical to his ears. Then another, and another. Soon the whole mountain seemed to be engulfed in the wolf cries of his people. His heart quickened and the strength slowly pulsed back into his body. He looked around at a sound to his right and saw Pareen bounding over to him. His soft wet nose rubbed against his fur.

"I am alive, so stop treating me like a bit of meat," he growled after Pareen had licked his face with his rough wet tongue.

"We heard, was it, was it, was it you? Have they returned to us, have they, have they?" the young wolf could barely control his excitement as he jumped around Fent.

Fent looked up at Pareen; he was still a little confused and shocked with what had just happened. He did not fully understand and did not know the answers to the young wolf's questions. He needed time to think; he knew that this was nothing compared to the barrage of questions he would face later at the pack council.

"Fent! Does it, does it?" The exuberance of youth oozed out of Pareen as his excitement threatened to overwhelm him.

"Silence," Fent growled angrily, curling his lips up to reveal his teeth. It had the desired effect. Pareen stopped jumping around like a cub and looked sadly at Fent.

Fent sighed, "I need time to think, Pareen. I do not truly know what happened yet, and have you not got a lot of work to do before midnight?" He liked Pareen and did not want his exuberance curbed entirely; he might have need of it later.

"It is done, we are ready, you will not be disappointed."

"They are all coming?"

"Some were not, but if they were not before, they will have no choice now but to come. The howl of our ancients is unmistakable, even after so long, even the young who have not heard it before will surely know it for what it is. It was beautiful, It was ..." Another growl from Fent curbed his growing enthusiasm once more.

"I will leave you in peace then," he turned and was gone before Fent could draw another breath.

<hr />

Vangor stirred, his view when he opened his eyes was that of rock and grass travelling past close to his face. The air smelt of damp, sweating horse and it took his mind a few moments to register where he was. His head hurt, his last memory was of facing the wolf and laughing; but why and why was he now lying face down over his horse? He turned his head sideways and caught sight of Graint, his sergeant. He opened his mouth to talk, but no words came, his mouth was as dry as the deserts of his homeland. He pulled at his wrists, trying to free them from the stirrups to which they were tied. The effort was exhausting and, despite feeling that he was making enough noise to alert his men, their journey continued uninterrupted down the slope.

"What do you think will happen when he wakes up?"

The voice came as a whisper from behind him; he tried to recognise the voice, but it must have come from one of the six new men who had only recently graduated to his personal guard, he did not recognise it and doubted there would be any strangers riding with them.

It was answered though by the unmistakable voice of Graint, a deep bellowing voice that even when spoken seemed to fill all the space around as if trying to dominate the very air into submission, much like the speaker did with his men.

"We will find out when he wakes, now get back to your post."

A scurry of footsteps marked the rapid retreat of the man and, for the moment, the only sounds were those of the steady fall of horse and human steps as they continued downwards.

Ever alert to the moods of his men, Vangor had sensed something in his sergeant's voice. Something unspoken, something which he felt would always remain so if he now questioned him about it. Their loyalty was without question, yet something had happened today on the ridge, something his men were reluctant to talk about and were obviously hiding from him. Despite the pain in his head, his thirst and his discomfort, he decided that it would be prudent, for the moment at least, to continue with a pretence of being unconscious.

They continued for what seemed like hours, the world around slowly turned to grey with the fast-approaching night. The men were anxious to get away from the scene of their shame, as if distancing themselves from it lessened its magnitude and at the same time strengthened their resolve. These were the same men, apart for the six newcomers, that had fought by their master's side in many battles, claiming victory and honour with their bravery and skill. They were the best of the Dark Knights' army, hand-picked by Sergeant Graint for their strength, courage, ability and personality, and now they had shamed themselves. They had cowered in fear at a solitary wolf and watched as their master's horse had made a mockery of their self-proclaimed bravery by rescuing Vangor while they could only watch.

They did not know if Vangor knew of their cowardice and to a man they were all anxious to discover, on his waking, their fate. To be dismissed as a coward from the army would be the ultimate disgrace; death would be a more welcome fate. They would never be welcome in their homelands again, their families would be taken, sold into slavery along with their captured enemies, with less hope of surviving though.

Sergeant Graint was worried; his was the position that every soldier in the army aspired to fill. The world had been his for the last six years, money, women and fame. He looked around his men; five he knew that he could trust explicitly, the others, the new men, they were good, he had picked them each personally having followed their careers for many years; but could he trust them now with this? He was not sure. It would only take one slip of the tongue in a drink-filled tale to condemn them all. They all had plenty of enemies and him more so than most. The answer was simple to him and a mere matter of logistics; he was lucky that Vangor allowed him total authority in the recruitment of the men.

The manner of execution though would be harder to conceal, and the longer he delayed, the more tenuous his position would become. None of them would be an easy kill and each, he was sure, would eventually come to the same conclusion as himself. First though, the new men, and then, well, he would see about the rest.

Vangor was lowered from his horse. The night had fully closed in now. The air was dark and damp; snow was again coming, perhaps within the hour. The stars peered out intermittently from behind their dark grey blanket of clouds. His gaze with the skill and ease of years of practice quickly took stock of his environment, recognising immediately the now familiar landscape from earlier in the day. He was careful though not to alert his men to his roused state, and hung limply between two of them as they carried him into his tent; the same tent they had left erected this morning in the lee of the slope, anticipating their possible need for it on the return journey.

He was gently lowered down to the soft blankets, as if in the arms of a lover, such was their care for him. A water skin was placed at his side within easy reach. The soft swish of the tent door marked his solitude. He was sorely tempted to immediately reach for the water skin now that he was alone; his instincts though told him that his patience would be better rewarded yet, if he waited a while longer.

The darkness inside the tent slowly became complete, the shadows lengthened and eventually blended into one. The voices of his men came slowly floating into his world as they settled into the routine of a night camp. He heard the guard being posted and the remainder of his men then busied themselves with their bedding or in preparing meals. He only heard one horse though as it was led to the far end of camp, it puzzled him, but he presumed the others were somewhere around; unaware at the moment that his was indeed the only mount that was left.

Sergeant Graint's voice carried crisply through the air, amplified by the stillness of the night.

"Sett, Frick, Travet." The names of three of the new men.

"Sergeant." The voices as one sounded urgent in reply and were closely followed by the sound of the men running.

"You three will be going out to fetch the horses. Now go and eat, then off with you. We move again at dawn and I want my horse."

Vangor lay back listening; why are the horses missing, how long was I out for? He was now certain that something extraordinary had happened, and for him to find out the whole story would require patience and a little guile.

He let out a low groan. Nothing. The quiet voices in the distance continued; he groaned louder.

"Silence." The order was hushed and curt.

Vangor groaned again louder still, this time feet could be heard approaching the tent.

"My Lord, are you awake?" The voice was followed immediately into the tent by Sergeant Graint, his shadow stretching out, trying desperately to avoid the light from the lamp he carried.

Vangor groaned again and pretended to try to sit up; he slumped back from the effort and the sergeant crossed over to where he lay.

"Lie still, my Lord."

Vangor stared past his sergeant, looking instead longingly over towards the water skin. Graint's eyes followed their gaze.

"Ah yes, Sire, water," he reached past Vangor's outstretched hand and pulled the water skin up. His left hand scooped behind Vangor's head, gently helping to raise it as his right then guided the bottle to Vangor's lips.

Vangor drank thirstily, his thirst for the moment now the sole focus of his thoughts. The water was tepid, yet to his dry palate it tasted as if it had just been drawn from a fresh spring. His thirst temporarily sated, he now worked a mouthful of water around his mouth, easing out the dust and grit from between his teeth and teasing the moisture into his dry lips. Once satisfied, he turned his head and spat the water onto the ground. Graint watched with faint amusement in his eyes; he knew all too well how one's mouth felt after hanging over a walking horse, your head in close proximity to the dust and grit it threw up from its hooves.

Vangor saw the amusement and registered its meaning; he laughed as he lay back down.

"My, that tasted good."

Graint smiled.

<hr />

Fent had now pushed himself up from the rock. The night was drawing in and he still had things to prepare. His confusion persisted, his mind full of irritating questions that were trying to distract his thoughts He needed to fully focus on the coming evening. He had a plan to put into place. The revelation concerning his father and then being able to howl had made him lose concentration. Nothing had really changed though in terms of what needed to be done. Yet things had changed and his plans might have to change in accordance with today's events.

Fent took the longer way down from the ridge, following the path the humans had used. He was anxious to see the route that the humans had taken and equally as anxious to make sure that they were not still close by. Vangor would not take kindly to being bested by him and would certainly seek retribution. The path they had taken led down to the east. For the most it was just rock and grass, roughly strewn together, indiscernible really as a path. The route the humans had taken though was easily identifiable, chunks of moss and lichen had been knocked off the rocks in their passage, marking their route down the slope, their passage lower down confirmed by their footprints in the snow. Fent sniffed the air, tasting it; it was blowing from the east and he detected no fresh human scent in its delicate aroma, if they had still been close their fresh scent would have been easily distinguishable in comparison to their stale one which clung to the ground around him.

He looked out over the valley below that stretched far into the distance. The whole valley a canopy of ever changing hues of green, brown, grey and white, the grass close by protruding through thin snow, stretching out down to the trees and their darker, richer greens. The scent of a fallow deer came to him on the breeze. It was down in the valley, hidden by the trees, but none the less he was aware of its presence. The smell of the deer made him realise he was hungry; it had been a full day since his last meal but he had no time to hunt now. He let his eyes scan the distance, looking for smoke or any other signs of Vangor and his men.

He would need to send his wolves further out tonight, to guard and warn if the humans approached. An eagle circled to his left, having just emerged from a rocky outcrop; its great wings taking in the remainder of the day's warm thermals as it floated around in the sky, searching for a last meal. As he watched, it tucked its wings in and darted towards the ground, accelerating with each passing blink of an eye. It disappeared from view behind some rocks, to be seen moments later flapping its great wings in a slow ascent, its prey now wriggling uselessly within its powerful talons. Fent watched until it disappeared from view round to his left. If only my hunts were as easy, he thought as he turned and headed back round and down, returning to Fennigan Forest.

Chapter Ten

Grabbit was concerned, the fact of which was in itself a great concern to him. His sheer bulk and reputation usually meant that he never had much to be too concerned about; it was normally other people who did concern and usually when they met him. But now he was concerned and he was finding out how unpleasant an experience it could be. The worst part of it was that he had lost his appetite, which was giving him even more cause for concern. Lorigan the Fey was the cause of the concern; it was not that Grabbit had developed any morals, but the Fey, he had decided, was, well, mad.

The more time he had spent with her, the more certain he had become of it. It was becoming apparent that her sole motivation for volunteering her services for this journey was that of revenge. That in itself did not concern Grabbit; revenge was a fact of life if you gave a person cause, but it was becoming clear that the Fey would use any means possible to achieve her revenge and it was this that concerned Grabbit. The Fey's thirst for revenge was such that he felt that for as long as he was with her, his own life would be in danger and that was what really concerned him.

Morally Grabbit was very happy with the Fey slaughtering her own people and indeed the boy Prince if it suited her needs and benefited him, but he felt it would not stop there. Mr Such may have employed the Fey to make sure Morkin never became King, but Lorigan was definitely working to her own agenda. Grabbit was not sure what it was, but he was sure it existed. Of course Lorigan had never really spoken of it on their journey north; indeed after the first day there had been little in the way of conversation between the two of them.

Grabbit had thought about disappearing on more than one occasion, yet he had soon found out that the Fey seemed to be able to read his thoughts; when after one such thought, Lorigan had hit him on the head with the side of her bow, accompanied by the words, "I warned you, I will not do so again."

It had taken Grabbit a while to work out just what she had meant, thinking he had done something physically wrong, but slowly he had put the two together which in itself had brought on a terrible feeling of foreboding. Since then he had tried to keep his mind blank, which thankfully was relatively easy for him, being naturally more of a doing person than a thinker.

So far the journey north had been an uneventful series of inns, meadows, trees and the occasional farm. People seemed to avoid them which was not an unusual experience for Grabbit, so he thought little of it. He just carried on plodding behind Lorigan on his horse; the only thing that was changing was his growing concern. Thankfully for him it seemed that Lorigan could not read emotions as well as thoughts, otherwise she might have taken a keener interest in the large man's changing mood.

They were now riding along a dusty path, the fine white dust floating up in little clouds around the horses' hooves. Their path as always led north and they were now riding between two fields seemingly left for pasture, the long grass was thick with wild flowers: blues, yellows and whites interspaced randomly amidst the thick greens. Far to their left, in the distance, a small group of low buildings, possibly the farm, their thatched roofs brown and weathered, a thin tendril of smoke snaking its way upwards from the chimney eventually snatched away to nothing by the light breeze, the same breeze that blew across his face. The field on their right contained a few cows, fattening themselves on the thick grass, paying no heed to the passing riders as they continued to graze contently. In the distance in front of them the uppermost canopy of leaves from the distant trees breached the horizon, their dark green prominent against the light blue sky. The land was peaceful; bird's song floated over them, accompanied by the gentle intermittent lowing of the cattle. Suddenly though, Lorigan stopped, her senses alert to something that Grabbit could not perceive. She jumped off her horse and flattened her ear to the ground.

Grabbit watched in mild amusement and puzzlement, thinking it was another sign of the madness that was obviously inside his Fey companion. The minutes passed though, and still Lorigan listened intently to the ground, then in a blur of movement she was back sitting astride her horse, a shrill high-pitched whistle which stung at Grabbit's ears escaped her lips. Lorigan seemed to be waiting for something to happen, yet as far as Grabbit could tell, everything around them still seemed as it was before. Lorigan was now peering upwards into the sky, looking for something that was seemingly hidden from view by the few light grey, fluffy clouds that remained. The sun had not yet made an impact on the day; it was still sheltering behind a smattering of grey clouds in the east, still hanging low in the sky, choosing at random intervals though to announce its presence by piercing through the clouds with its bright white rays of translucent light that cut a path through the heavens to the ground.

Then the answering call came, a high-pitched screeching noise; it sounded out from the clouds above them. Moments later a large black shape emerged into view from the clouds in the distance, travelling towards them at pace; it flew through a beam of light, changing from black to a golden brown halo as it did so, revealing the brown of its wings and the bright yellow beak. The hawk swooped down, travelling low now over the fields, barely brushing against the tips of the long grass as it headed straight for them, its powerful wings beating out, sending the grass rippling away in waves as it powered towards them, closer and ever closer. Just as Grabbit thought it would fly straight into him, it pulled up gracefully with one huge beat of its wings and landed gently on Lorigan's outstretched arm. Its eyes seemed to immediately fix on Grabbit, boring into him with their intensity, seemingly daring him to move, as Lorigan slowly raised her arm towards her head.

The two seemed to converse with each other; although Grabbit heard no sound he could see that Lorigan's mouth was definitely moving. A minute passed and then the hawk launched itself upwards, screeching out as it went, flying off towards the hidden trees that lay in front of them.

"Come, we have company." The words seemingly both an order and a statement.

Lorigan saw them first and even when she pointed them out, Grabbit still had difficulty in seeing them. Five specks on the horizon, indiscernible to his eyes from the bushes and small trees around, but now they had been pointed out to him he stared intently at them and eventually he could see their movement. It was sporadic at best and limited, which could only mean one of two things, they had either stopped to make camp or were now intently looking for something.

"Five riders and they bear the emblem of Lord Luxor. It is safe for the moment. Keep close to me and allow me to speak to them. You do not speak!!"

Grabbit was still peering into the distance; it was at least two thousand paces across the small valley to where the men were, from where they were now sitting on their horses. He could see no pendant flying, but he was not about to question Lorigan, besides she was now trotting off down the field that led towards the bottom of the valley, heading towards the men.

The valley floor was rich with wild flowers, a sea of purples, pinks, yellows and blues. A small stream ran along the bottom, filtering through the soft ground, cutting into it in places as it made its progress towards the river Cool. They could no longer see the place where the men had been, it was now hidden from view by the upwards slope and the thick vegetation that grew on their side of the valley. They crossed the small stream, cutting a path towards a shallow exit point on the far bank. It lay directly between two large banks that rose steeply out of the stream, their near vertical sides full of small holes which seemed to be the homes for all manner of birds or animals. As they rode up the bank, another screech split the air; the hawk swooped low over the trees to their left. Shouts of alarm could be heard from above them, an arrow whistled past their heads. Its aim was poor though, and the hawk easily evaded it, turning to its left as it swooped down lower and landed on a branch of an oak tree some thirty paces directly in front of them.

Lorigan made a clicking sound twice with her tongue in quick succession and then held her hand out invitingly to the hawk. The hawk seemed to eye her suspiciously at first, as if suspecting her of some sort of deceit, and then as if reassured by another click it jumped down, and glided gently over to her hand. Again the two seemed to have a conversation of sorts. Lorigan though now seemed to be agitated as the hawk flew away behind them, it kept low to the ground, turning along the stream before disappearing from sight. Grabbit watched its departure, unsure of what was going on; he was suddenly brought back to reality though when he felt a hand grab his leg and lift it, the movement was so sudden, swift and powerful that he was unable to prevent himself toppling from his horse. As he fell though, he felt, heard and saw the blur and whistle of an arrow as it sped past his head, it disappeared into the long grass on the far bank. He landed with an ungainly thud, his instincts now very much alert to the danger. He looked around; Lorigan had disappeared, her horse though still stood where it had been and was now contentedly grazing on the grass.

Grabbit's first reaction was to find cover; he was big and he knew he was at a disadvantage from a bowman lying as he was in the open ground, even when, as thankfully was the case, the bowman was seemingly not that good a shot. None the less, he knew he made a big target and he had no intention of being used for practice.

The only cover he could see lay down the slope; the stream bank was directly behind him now and about ten paces away. It was the only thing around that was now suitable for his needs. It was not ideal, however, as it would give the bowman the opportunity to approach his position unseen, but it was all there was and if he stayed where he was for much longer, then he was surely dead.

He crawled forward on his hands and knees; not sure whether his assailant could see him this low, he was reluctant to raise his head any higher though, just to find out. His luck was holding, it seemed, as no further arrows came his way. The bank was closer now; five paces, four, three, two, his hand reached over and then he tumbled down, landing head first in the icy water below. He spat some water out of his mouth as he scrambled over closer towards the bank, almost hugging its muddy surface. Once there he squatted down in the icy water, listening intently over the sound of running water for any approaching noise. He heard a snap of a twig underfoot, the crackle of dried leaves being brushed aside followed by the twang of a bowstring released under force, the whistle of an arrow loosed in the air. Then silence again apart from the rising beat of his heart, which now echoed into his ears.

Minutes passed. Never a patient man, Grabbit was restless; he hated hiding but his new-found fear of arrows had grown exponentially after meeting Lorigan. Besides, he thought, Lorigan was more than capable of dealing with the problem. He tried to relax, but it was no good, he had to look, he had to see what was going on. He turned around, slowly lifting his hands to the rim of the muddy bank. His fingers closed around the cold earth more for support than anything else, and then he slowly raised his head, inching upwards as the tops of trees came into view first, then the trunks and branches and then a man. He was standing staring straight at him, a long yew bow in his left hand, an arrow notched with the great bow pulled back into the aim, the tip of the arrow was pointing directly at Grabbit's head. Grabbit's first thought was to duck, but he seemed to be frozen now, unable to move, unable to tear his eyes away from the shiny metal point of the arrow aimed at him. He expected it to be released at any moment, yet still he was unable to move, his giant frame rooted to the spot, his muscles again seemingly powerless.

He heard the screech, he took little notice of it though; it sounded distant, it sounded familiar but his brain for now could not place it. It came again closer, a loud, high-pitched note, coming from his right, piercing the air and shattering Grabbit's transfixed stare. The arrow tip wavered, it moved to Grabbit's right as the bowman, also hearing the screech, turned his attention towards the approaching noise, sensing danger.

Grabbit shook himself, he had to move now and this was his chance. He ducked down, moving to his left in a hunched squatting motion, keeping low below the rim of the bank, but heading now towards where the bank was lower and where the stream bent round closer to where the bowman stood. He heard the twang of the bowstring, but he was moving now and did not stop to see where the arrow went. He came up directly behind the bowman, who had now turned his entire body round, facing the direction from which the screeching had come from; he already had another arrow firmly notched in his bow and seemed to be waiting for something as he peered upwards towards the top of the trees and the sky. Grabbit though saw the hawk first; it was coming at the bowman low, hugging the ground, flying directly at him from his right. Its movement though eventually caught the bowman's eye and he quickly swung around, bringing up the great bow as he did so, drawing back the bowstring with an ease that belied many years of practice, he was ready now to shoot at the approaching hawk. It seemed as if he could not miss, the hawk was now less than forty paces away and closing fast, growing into a bigger and bigger target as it did so, its wings a blur of movement as it drove itself straight for the man. The bowman remained calm, he pulled back yet further on the bowstring, extending it to its maximum, whilst all the time the tip of the arrow easily traced the bird's flight; he waited, picking his moment.

Grabbit jumped up, roaring out a guttural feral yell as he did so, scrambling up the low bank, slipping and sliding at first but then he hit the firmer ground and rushed at the man. It all happened in seconds, yet time seemed to slow. Grabbit could see each individual wingbeat, the graceful way the feathers bent and contorted under the power and then relaxed, springing effortlessly back into shape ready for the next downbeat, the dark black eyes of the hawk, unblinking, staring directly at the bowman as it grew closer and closer, larger and larger, closing in on its prey.

The bowman paid Grabbit's sudden appearance no heed, it was as if he had anticipated and expected Grabbit to emerge from that exact spot at that exact time and had already dismissed his threat as irrelevant for the moment, concentrating instead all his efforts on the hawk.

The arrow sped forward, the black feathered flights rippling and singing in the air. As it did so, Grabbit roared out again, he did not know why he was so concerned for the bird, but he did not want it to die, not like this and not to this man at any rate. The hawk and the arrow collided, a sickening sound of metal grating through tissue, muscle, sinew and bone. The hawk arched upwards in mid-air as if frozen, a pitiful, painful scream rang out and then it fell, dropping from the air in a cloud of feathers. The sound angered Grabbit even more; he was now only two paces away and he leapt at the man with a surprising agility, throwing all his weight at him, meaning to knock him to the ground, where he could kill him with his bare hands.

He hit the ground, landing in a heap, the man was gone; displaying a surprising slight of foot, he had easily stepped out of the way. Grabbit looked up, an arrow met his gaze, the man was two paces away with another arrow already notched and drawn, he could not miss. The arrowhead blinked dully at him, its metal surface dulled black so not to shine in the sun. It was sharp with barbed tips, his eyes moved up along the black shaft over the black feathers and up into the face of the bowman. A dark brown face, its skin telling of long days spent in the glare of the sun, the eyes deep brown and soulless, ringed by the fiery red mesh of engorged veins that could come only from a lack of sleep. The man returned his gaze and then smiled, revealing the blackened stumps of teeth that had been long lost to decay; not a welcoming warm smile, but a smile of malice and contempt, a smile full of mocking, a smile that Grabbit was only too familiar with.

He heard rather than saw the arrow leave the bowstring, the now all too familiar twang and whistle sounding loud and clear, he shut his eyes, gritting his teeth, steeling himself against the expected pain, hoping it would not last for long. He had seen many men die, some with dignity, some in tears, some suffered long and painful deaths whilst others had died quickly. Up until now he had given the matter little thought, now it seemed to be the sole focus of his mind, how will I die? He hoped it would be quick. The expected pain never came despite him having heard the arrow bite into flesh; the low thud and the associated sound of something hard and sharp piercing bone, he could even smell the blood, the slightly tinny aroma that now invaded his nostrils was unmistakable.

He forced himself to open his eyes, expecting to see an arrow piercing his flesh somewhere, expecting to see his death approaching. The bowman still stood in front of him, staring at him, his eyes were now somehow vacant though and no longer met his gaze. As Grabbit watched him, the man's arrow fell off the bowstring, burying itself head first in the soft ground at his feet. The man lowered his head, looking down in mild confusion, then he slumped backwards as if only finally realising he was dead, he fell silently, apart from the low gurgling noise as the air escaped from his chest.

Grabbit, confused, quickly checked himself over, still half expecting to find an arrow buried into him somewhere. Finally, once he was satisfied he was in one piece, he slowly got to his feet, he was still nervous, he expected others to be with the bowman. The bowman now lay on the ground with his chest arched upwards towards the sky, the result of which extended his neck backwards in a grotesque manner, his blood now slowly oozed out from underneath him, forming into a crimson puddle. He was now able to study the man more closely; he was clothed from head to toe predominantly in black, the only other colouring on his clothes, a band of green that ran up the entire length of his trousers on the outside leg, so dark in colour that from a distance it too would appear as if black. The band of green was matched on his tunic running down from his collar to the cuffs of his sleeves. The cloth was unremarkable, but what did catch Grabbit's greedy eyes was the glint of silver on his left ring finger. He leant forward to get closer, trying by sight alone to ascertain its worth.

As he twisted it around the dead man's finger, trying to free it, the small emblem of a fox which was engraved into the metal came into view. He pulled harder, the man's knuckle though held the ring fast and would not let it pass. His frustration was rising as he twisted and pulled and even spat on the finger, trying in vain to free the ring. He was just about to bite the finger off, such was his desperation to get it, when his eyes saw the hilt of a knife protruding from the man's left boot, it was small, black and well concealed. He reached for it, closing his hand around it greedily.

"Leave him."

Grabbit nearly jumped in fright; he had totally forgotten about Lorigan in his excitement. He was not about to be deprived of his loot though. He ignored Lorigan and pulled the knife free of its scabbard, the small thin blade was blackened and about the length and width of one of his fingers, it was sharpened to a vicious point and had a groove running lengthwise down the centre of the blade, it was perfect for sliding between a person's ribs. Grabbit had seen blades like it before; he smiled to himself, this man was a paid killer, an assassin, the small blade a symbol of his profession.

He was still admiring the small blade, when something hard hit him on the side of his head, stunning him; he nearly tumbled over, but just managed to hang on to reality. He shook his head, reaching up with his hand, which came away sticky and red with blood. He swung round, the small knife held threateningly in his hand.

"I said, leave him."

Lorigan was crouched five short strides away, her voice calm and clear, yet her gaze bore into Grabbit, daring him to defy her, her hands though were busy on the ground where the hawk had fallen. Grabbit looked at her and then briefly back at the ring, it was worth a fair price to the right buyer, but not, he decided, worth more than his life. Besides, he thought as an idea came to him, I might still be able to retrieve it.

The hawk was still alive, but for how much longer Grabbit was unable to judge, having no experience in the art of healing and knowing even less about birds. He had been orderd to cut off a small branch from a nearby tree and then strip it of all the leaves and small shoots. He now carried the shorn branch back to the stream to where Lorigan had now moved the hawk. Lorigan meanwhile had lit a fire and was now boiling water in a small metal tin hung over the flames. The hawk lay on its side, one wing tucked up underneath it; the other, matted with blood and clumps of ruined feathers, lay limply extended out to its side, a great tear in its flesh, exposing white shattered bone that jutted out in pieces like broken teeth.

Lorigan looked up as Grabbit approached, nodding her satisfaction with the branch he carried. Grabbit watched with mild curiosity for the next hour as Lorigan tenderly and expertly tended to her hawk. She cleansed and bathed the wound before grinding a mixture of leaves and herbs which she had retrieved from her pack on her horse, she then sprinkled the resulting powder over and into the open wound. The hawk all the while lay perfectly still, trusting her implicitly, following her every movement with its deep black eyes. The wound was bound with strips of material torn from Lorigan's own tunic and then finally she splinted the wing, using the branch Grabbit had cut for her. Leaving the hawk lying there, Lorigan then walked down to the stream and pulled in the string she had earlier cast into a deeper pool of water; it had two small silvery fish caught on the hooks that were tied to it and they now thrashed around madly, trying to escape their fate. Lorigan chopped the fish into four small pieces and then fed them lovingly to the hawk, which seemed grateful for the small meal. Finally she returned to her horse and came back with a large leather bag. She ran her hands over the hawk, gently smoothing its feathers, clicking away to it as she had done before as she pulled a small cloth hood over its head, calming it, and then she wrapped it in a blanket of lambswool before finally placing it gently in the leather bag, its head protruding from the top.

"Five riders," Lorigan offered, "they were following the Green Dragons. They were good, my carelessness nearly cost me my hawk and may yet do so. Revenge though tastes good." The last words were followed by a smile that sent a shiver down Grabbit's spine, such was its ruthlessness.

"They were paid assassins!" Grabbit blurted out. "This dagger is their mark," he held it up for Lorigan to see. "I have seen it many times before, thankfully not too close though," he laughed nervously, trying to hide his anxiety.

He decided, seeing no change in the expression on Lorigan's face, to press on.

"That one has a silver ring on his finger with a fox engraved on it," his hand pointing at the body on the slope, "perhaps it would be useful to enquire of its meaning. I mean show it to people, people I know, that is, who could maybe tell us who they are. No, I mean, erm, erm people who will definitely know its worth, erm no, its meaning, I meant meaning." He ran out of words and instead chose to look over in hope at the prostrate body whilst all the time counting the ring's worth over and over again in his head, each addition coming up with more and more elaborate amounts.

Lorigan stared back at the large man in front of her with total indifference; she already knew the significance of the ring with the silver fox engraved on it. She also knew that Grabbit's sole motivation for acquiring the ring would be to satisfy his greed. However, it might suit her own purposes at the moment to allow the human to believe he had duped her, she thought as she watched Grabbit squirm and almost beg for permission to retrieve it; besides there was always the faint possibility that in his clumsy manner he might actually find out something useful when he sold the ring.

"Go, get the ring if you must, but I will keep it in my possession until you can find out some useful information about it."

Grabbit glared briefly at Lorigan, he wanted to argue with her, but instead chose to bite his tongue. He walked over to the dead bowman, muttering obscenities under his breath as he impassively cut off the man's finger and freed the ring, he wiped the knife and ring clean on the man's tunic and then quickly reached down to the man's boot and freed the scabbard, he sheathed the knife and then thrust it into his pocket.

Chapter Eleven

The first thing that struck him was the smell; even before he felt capable of opening his eyes, he was aware of it, the smell of sulphur, a smell like a thousand rotting eggs. It invaded his nostrils, seeping into his body through his pores where its tendril wisps now tugged at his unconsciousness, pulling him to wake and in turn twisting and turning his stomach to nausea.

He retched, bile rising in his throat; he swallowed, it made the nausea worse, he felt as if he was spinning, his body falling, his head felt light and giddy, he was sweating and yet he felt cold. He opened his eyes, blinking into a bright yellowy-orange light that surrounded him. The nausea finally conquered his resolve and he vomited violently, sending the contents of his stomach outwards to the side, a thick viscous orangey-brown mixture that arced out and dropped towards a hidden floor, he heard the distant plop as it hit something liquid, a sudden hiss of steam jumped back upwards at him, its heat forced him to scurry backwards.

Tears coursed down his cheeks, blurring his vision further as he blinked; he wiped a mixture of vomit, snot and tears onto his damp sleeve. Slowly his eyes grew accustomed to his surroundings and he was able to focus. His brain though was decidedly slower in catching up, the last memory he had was of burning red eyes and then darkness, complete and utter darkness. Where am I? His sudden panic threatened to overwhelm him. He sat bolt upright in fright, trying to work out where he was. He found he was sitting on a hard, rocky ledge which jutted out of a reddish-orange wall behind him. The ledge itself seemed to be about four feet off the floor, it was of similar colour yet slightly lighter than the surrounding walls; small, gaseous bubbles gurgled and hissed intermittently over the surface of the floor, leaving little eddies in their wake as small clouds of yellow gas spluttered into life, there they mixed and added their contents to the already intoxicating air around. The walls around the cavern had a collection of random yellow smears travelling up their surface as if at some time they had been hit by the large gaseous clouds that erupted from the floor and had stained their surface with their rich vaporous gases. The walls stretched up on either side like giant monoliths, reaching higher and higher above his head, eventually sloping inwards to form a high, almost domed, pitted roof of dark red, orange and yellow rock, it seemed higher even than the trolls' graveyard.

Ranabin, not given to panic normally, had his second of the day now. It clawed at him, sending goosebumps crawling over his skin. The nausea returned like an old unwelcome relative, the type who never knows when they have overstayed their welcome, but thankfully his stomach was now empty and it was robbed of some of its force as he battled to compose himself. Panic was not going to help his situation, whatever it was. He felt around, looking for the familiar comfort of his stick, becoming angry with himself when he could not find it. He felt a strange loss at its absence, as if a part of him had somehow actually been severed.

Calm! Calm, he thought to himself over and over again, the very word eventually helping him to regain focus and he finally managed to relax. His giddiness seemed to ease as he did so and he once again felt able to survey his surroundings, this time though he did so with more scrutiny and intensity. The liquid floor stretched out over the entire cavern, covering the area in front of him between the two huge walls, spreading out into the distance like a small searing sea. He peered through the thick air, he was sure in the distance, perhaps fifty to sixty paces away, yet difficult to truly judge through the thick yellow fog, that he could just make out its margins as if it lapped up against solid rock, the colour change was very subtle and difficult to detect but, none the less, now he had seen it, he was aware that there was solid rock beyond. The floor looked superhot, not hot like a hot drink, but vaporisingly hot, the sort of hot which would melt metal in seconds, yet inexplicably, from where he sat he could feel nothing of its heat.

The view beyond his closed tunnel-like cavern, past the edge of the liquid floor, quickly faded into black, hiding behind its dark veil either another darkened cavern or even a wall, for now though it was impossible to tell. Encouraged by the lack of heat around him, Ranabin swung his legs over the ledge, dangling his feet down towards the floor, contemplating for one absurd second to reach down with his toe to test its surface. The heat as he did so now hit him, it increased enormously. He snatched his foot backwards, bringing it in a blur back up to the sanctuary of the cooler air around him.

"Damn, that is hot," he swore out loud and then as if to confirm it he spat a drivel of saliva over the edge, watching and seeing it fizzle, hiss, and spit; evaporating a good foot above the surface of the floor.

"Looks like I wait," his resignation was spoken aloud as if to convince himself.

He did not have to wait long though. It seemed as if only minutes had passed when a shadow entered the cavern, casting a darkness over the floor, it grew momentarily, stretching out towards him; seemingly reaching out for him as it grew and grew and then just as he thought it was going to consume him into its darkness, it receded, shrinking quickly back, as if afraid of the approaching footsteps, footsteps that now sounded as though an avalanche of rock was heading his way. Their noise filled the cavern, bouncing off the walls, sending ripples shooting out across the floor towards him, huge gushes of steam and vapour burst up out of the floor, their supercharged heat whipping the air into great torrents, which travelled straight up, hitting the roof and then rushing out and down, filling the entire cavern within a second in a thick yellow choking cloud that stung at Ranabin's eyes and stole at his breath.

A dark shape approached, its form distorted in the thick, yellow, misty air; its deep red eyes though revealing its identity as they seemed to burn a hole straight through the mist, they were staring directly at Ranabin, their intent obvious. The noise now assaulted Ranabin's senses; the heavy grinding of rock on rock gave way to an enormous hissing and spitting noise that invoked a further fury from the floor, the thick vapours and steam spreading out quickly, thickening further the already viscous cloud that filled the cavern, which was now obliterated entirely from Ranabin's view. The heat that also came with it was unbearable, it tore at Ranabin, stealing his breath from his lungs as he sucked in the hot liquid air and then tried to choke it back out again; his robe was saturated in a mixture of sweat and cooled vapour, it was clinging to his skin now like a damp rag. His hair was matted flat across his scalp, streaks of yellow liquid ran freely down his face, into his mouth, curdling at his tongue as he spat, spluttered, coughed and gasped all at the same time. He scrambled back against the wall to get away from the steam and, possibly worse, the approaching troll.

The shock of the giant hand appearing out from the yellow mist and reaching for him nearly made him faint. It was huge and looked even more brutal through his blurred vision. The thick air serving to distort its shape further. It became a constant, ever changing flow of images, giant fingers that continually blended into one another as they closed in on him; the giant hand was certainly capable of crushing the life out of him in its grip, yet as it closed around him, it held him gently and firmly in its palm, its fingers wrapped securely around him. It plucked him from the ledge as if he were a feather, the speed of his ascent making him dizzy and light-headed as the world zoomed past his vision. Each finger was the size of a giant boulder and dark grey in colour. He had expected them for some reason to be cold to the touch like those in the graveyard earlier, yet as he now ran his fingers gently over their surface they felt strangely warm and slightly moist to his touch. The heat and the moisture he now felt beneath his fingers could have been a result of all the steam and vapour that surrounded them, he thought, but somehow he doubted it, it somehow felt different, as if it was coming instead from deep within the surface.

The troll carried him in its closed fist, he was held out directly in front of it at about waist height as it waded back through the molten floor, small splashes of hot liquid splashed up over its legs as it went, the troll though seemed not to notice. They emerged from the liquid floor seconds later, the troll immediately turned sharply to its right, and now it was back on solid ground it lengthened its stride, its speed increased, its lumbering gait becoming more pronounced and Ranabin bobbed up and down in the air as it struggled to keep its fist steady. The last remnants of liquid rock dribbled off its legs as they went, forming small pools on the floor behind them which now away from the heat rapidly cooled, solidifying and leaving a small trail of new rocks in their wake. They were heading towards a tunnel, its darkness emerging in front of them and seemingly sucking them towards it.

Their journey took them down through long corridors of carved rock that were empty and dark, all save for the faint glow of the red light from the troll's own eyes. It pierced the darkness around them, bathing it in a blood-red bubble that stretched about five paces in front and to the side of them, it floated with them marking their passage. They passed through a cavern, the close walls around them retreated into the distant gloom; the troll's footsteps, the only noise around, no longer echoed back at them as they had in the tunnel. They crunched onwards over the rocky floor, the grip holding Ranabin never easing, it squeezed gently against his chest, just firm enough to make it difficult for him to take a deep breath, and forcing him to have to pant gently for the air he needed. The air here was thankfully cleaner, and he could no longer smell the rotting egg of the sulphur; instead it was a damp, musky air that reminded him of the mist-covered rocky peaks of his mountain home.

The fact that the troll's footsteps could no longer be heard echoing back at them was the only indication of the size and magnitude of the cavern they now passed through, and Ranabin, prevented by the sheet of black that surrounded them, could see none of its true size for himself. With his own blindness he considered how well the troll could see down here. Its eyes on entering the cavern had immediately grown in brilliance and were now a deep bright red, as if needing the extra intensity to penetrate the very depth of the cavern that surrounded them. It was the same colour of red he had seen in the graveyard, a red that he had then mistaken as being a sign of anger, a red that he now understood was needed to see better in a larger space. He suddenly felt comforted by this thought; perhaps he was not in real danger after all. They had certainly not killed him yet, which was always a good sign, or so he had been led to believe.

The first indication he had that they approached the far end of the cavern they were passing through was the dimming back down to a low dull red of the troll's eyes. Within five paces of which they had entered another tunnel, the walls suddenly closed in on them again, springing back from the nothingness, bringing with them for him a sudden feeling of claustrophobia as once again the footsteps, now louder, bounced back at and around them.

It was difficult to judge how far they had travelled, the distance of each troll stride was at least equal to ten of Ranabin's, and although they had been travelling for what seemed like hours since he had been plucked off the ledge, it could just as easily have been less. Ranabin had lost all track of time, and with nothing to judge it against, he had no idea if it was day or night such was his complete disorientation in this alien environment. The troll though lumbered on with a positive purpose in its stride that never faltered. He was now almost certain he was being carried somewhere important and for a specific purpose, he also knew he had no way of avoiding it; thus resigned to his fate he relaxed and his breathing became a little easier.

They turned another corner and suddenly stopped; they were facing a wall of rock that towered up in front of them. The end of the tunnel, Ranabin thought, perhaps the troll has taken a wrong turning. He had no sooner had the thought though than he was suddenly and unexpectedly lifted up, the sudden rush of air blowing his hair across his face and whistling in his ears. As he shot past the troll's face the sulphurous smell of its breath almost made him retch again and within all but a second he found himself unceremoniously dropped onto another ledge. He looked down and saw he was just above the troll's head, some forty feet above the ground, its red eyes were glaring up at him, turning as he watched to a bright fiery red as it blinked, the light from them growing brighter and brighter, lighting up the ledge he now lay on until they became too bright for him to look at any more and he was forced, shielding his eyes with his hand, to look away, to stare at the wall instead, and then he saw it. A small hole, it was dark and narrow, stretching up the wall more like a crack in the rock than an actual hole. He would not have seen it in the dark, the light from the troll's eyes throwing its shadows away to reveal the secret. He crawled towards it; as he did so the troll's eyes dimmed, the light receded and he was able to better focus on the opening. It was obvious he was supposed to squeeze through the gap, which he did with minimal effort as it offered him more room to do so than the end of the tunnel beneath the tree had.

The gap led into a narrow tunnel of smooth rock which seemed to glow, giving out an eerie, pale orange light all of its own, which, when mixed with the colour of the walls, bathed the tunnel in a fiery ochre-red. He crawled forward, sliding easily over the almost glass-like surface, the rock beneath him reassuringly cold to the touch. The tunnel bent sharply to the left and then ten paces on again to the right, it was as he rounded this corner that he saw that there was a different sort of light ahead, a bright yellow light accompanied by noise. Voices, he could hear voices singing, singing a song similar in type to that of the gentle song that he had heard in the graveyard. He crawled forward towards the light, towards the end of the tunnel, once there he poked his head out tentatively and, seeing that it had led him out onto a rock platform, he was tempted to duck back into the tunnel. He would have done but he had been seen; the singing had stopped, and he had frozen as if hoping by the very act of keeping still that he would vanish from their sight. The platform he had emerged onto was bathed in bright light. Thousands of red lights seemed to sparkle around him like stars, stars which occasionally twinkled as their owners presumably blinked. He knew what had been singing and he knew these were their eyes, yet still as if not quite believing his own instincts he frantically rubbed and blinked his eyes, desperately willing them to quickly adjust to the brightness so he could see the truth.

The light seemed to be coming predominantly from the left, its source a huge pit of molten ore, which glowed a rich golden-yellow colour, bubbling and hissing away at the far end of the cavern. This molten rock from the pit was fed into small troughs that extended out across the entire cavern floor. The hot yellow liquid within creating a liquid yellow mosaic, that lit up a pattern of intricate shapes and designs on the floor that almost mirrored those he had seen on the wall in the graveyard behind the light. The effect from where he now knelt was breathtaking. A living work of art to rival that of any he had seen in the castles and keeps of the land, not that he was by any means an expert. The entire floor was lit up in its radiance, sending a warm yellow glow high up to gently caress the roof which towerered above them.

Standing between the troughs of molten rock were hundreds of trolls, all of different size and colour; some were small as if children and others big enough to resemble small hills. Their red eyes appeared strangely dull now in comparison to the bright yellow light that surrounded them. All their eyes though seemed to be firmly fixed on him, as if he had intruded on a private party, invited yet still an unwelcome guest; the sort you invited out of politeness and hoped would not accept. His discomfort increased under the relentless gaze of their unblinking, unemotional stares; he wanted to hide, to vanish from view, to be anywhere but here. But there was nowhere to go. He had no option at the moment but to stay, so defiantly trying to match their burning gaze with his own, he glared back at them,

To his right there was another platform, slightly higher than his own and standing free from the ground. It caught his eye as it shimmered and shone with a life of its own. It was adorned with what appeared to be gold, although adorned was probably too liberal a description. It was instead piled with gold, great big piles of the stuff. In all shapes and forms, some of it bigger and higher than the very trolls that gathered in the cavern. It was strewn across the platform in such a haphazard manner that it appeared as if it had all just been dumped there by someone who had little or no regard for its worth. Despite the huge mountains of gold on display, the feature that really took Ranabin's breath away was the throne. At least he presumed it was a throne and it was the only word that seemed to fit, even then though it did not truly do justice to the magnitude and splendour of the object he was looking at. It resembled nothing of the thrones of men he had seen, making his own platform and even the mountains of gold around it pale into insignificance. He feasted his eyes on it as if all else around were mere worthless trinkets.

Its huge base dominated the centre of the platform opposite. It was adorned with a sea of sparkling reds, blues, yellows, whites and greens that seemed to dance and shimmer as one. Every gemstone that Ranabin had ever seen or heard of seemed to be there. Each carefully placed to form an intricate pattern, the result an intertwined feast of colour that flowed and snaked around and up the base, covering its entire surface. No stone appearing out of place, each placed, it seemed, to allow their individual colours to complement and highlight the splendour of their neighbours and vice versa. Each stone, in complete contrast to the piles of discarded gold strewn around it, appeared to have been lovingly and intrinsically placed as part of a grand design.

On top of this bejewelled masterpiece was a piece of quartz that had been polished to such a finish that it shone of its own accord. It had a deep milky-white sheen that sat proudly above the gemstones and dared them to take away its majesty. There were no arms on the throne. Its back was shaped as an arch that stretched towards the roof high above, its own width at the base matching perfectly that of the quartz seat. The arch was made completely out of precious metals. A rich tapestry of twisted metal; the unmistakable glow of the red, yellow and white golds; the lush sheen of the raw silver; the almost white shine of the platinum; and finally and even more surprisingly and unexpectedly the unmistakable dark rustic ochre of iron, the most precious of all metals. Each metal was expertly laced into itself, forming strands which when plaited together created a rope. It was these precious ropes that now twisted and turned through each other, round each other, ever and ever upwards forming a mesh of metallic colour that stretched high up to an apex near the roof. The outside edge of the arch was adorned with letters, each fashioned from a different metal, all then laced together forming words, words which to Ranabin had no discernible meaning.

Adorning the very pinnacle of the arch, just below the roof far above their heads, a golden dragon, its clarity and size befitting a master craftsman as its great claws snaked around the upper letters, picking and honouring them seemingly at random. Bright red flames spewed from its open mouth, spreading down and out across the wall in a rolling crescendo that extended for about forty of Ranabin's paces. His eyes were still fixed on the dragon when a loud bang shook the ground where he stood, nearly throwing him off his feet as small clouds of dust and debris rained down on him from the walls and roof above.

All eyes turned towards the other platform. Ranabin found himself holding his breath in anticipation as the gathered ensemble as one started to sing. The tune was light and full of life and, as before, the words seemed to echo back at them, joining seamlessly and in harmony with those of each new verse they sung. It was as if each song had been uniquely written for a cavern, each song using the cavern's unique acoustics and echo to full effect, no song able to be sung elsewhere.

> *"Sle ami par da, Sle ami par da.*
> *Gret age hery, Sle ami par da."*

The tune seemed to carry Ranabin off and before he knew it he was humming along. The song built to a crescendo, and then emerging from the back of the far platform came a silver troll. Not bright and shiny silver, but the silvery sheen of granite that has been polished to a smooth finish or that of the silvery shadow you get from a full moon shining at night. The troll that emerged was by no means the biggest in the cavern, yet the cavern immediately felt smaller, its mere presence now filling it more than size alone ever could. It stood facing the other trolls in the cavern, gazing out long and hard as if counting those present. Finally it turned its focus towards Ranabin who felt compelled immediately to bow his head

If the gesture was acknowledged by the troll it was not evident. It turned and slowly eased itself down onto the throne.

"Soo, huumaan, whoo iis mooree aand aalsoo leess." The voice shocked Ranabin. He had expected a deep thunderous voice, yet this was soft, flowing and gentle and in total contrast to the size of its owner. "Yoouu daaree too eenteer thee saanctuuaary oof oouur dee-aad? Foor whaat puurpoose, I aask myseelf, iif yoouu hoopeed too roob theem yoouu wiill haavee beeeen sooreely diisaappooiinteed."

Ranabin did not have a ready answer; the gentleness of the voice had caught him off guard, he had expected an angry challenge to his presence and had readied himself for it. He was used to others being angry or disappointed with him and therefore found it easier to deal with anger and contempt.

"I … I … I …," he stuttered and fell silent.

"Soo! Weeree yoouu gooiing too roob oouur deeaad oor noot?" the troll's voice was becoming firmer and more direct now, as if taking Ranabin's hesitation for a sign of his guilt.

"NO," he bristled with anger now as he shouted the word; he had never stolen anything in his life and did not like being accused of it. "I found myself there, I came through a tunnel, it was as if I was drawn there by something. I really don't know why or by what! I am sorry, I did not know it was a sacred place, I would not have entered if I had known but once I was in, I was unable to leave."

"Yoouu foouund yoouur waay iin wiith noo proobleem!"

"Yes, but," Ranabin was about to continue when he realised the troll had not finished.

"Iis iit aalwaays yoouur maanneer too eenteer soomeewheere wiithoouut knoowiing wheeree yoouu eenteereed froom? Suureely yoouu coouuld haavee leeft by thee saamee roouutee? Uunleess, oof coouursee, yoouu eenteereed throouugh thee poortaal. Aaree yoouu trying too teell uus, huumaan whoo iis noot, thaat yoouu caamee iin throouugh oouur poortaal?"

Had he heard right, the portal? Had the troll mentioned the portal? His heart missed a beat. "The portal, you know of the portal, but that is why I am here, to use the portal, I need to get to Crescent Wood," he could barely keep the excitement out of his voice.

"Soo yoouu weeree loooookiing foor soomeethiing theen" The

statement sounded like an accusation. "Aam I theen too preesuumee yoouu aaree whaat wee caall aa vaaniisheer, oor yoouu caall aa maa-gee, liittlee oonee?"

Ranabin paused, judging the value of the question, and sensing no need to disguise his identity, he nodded and confirmed it.

"Thaat iis gooood, wee haavee beeeen waaiitiing foor aa maa-gee. Iit haas beeeen aa loong waaiit. Wee truust yoouu wiill noot bee aa diisaappooiintmeent too uus."

Ranabin's immediate joy by the trolls' excitement at him being a mage was quickly dampened by the words that followed.

"Disappoint you?" he enquired.

"Yees! Wee reequuiiree soomeethiing oof yoouu. Iif yoouu suuc-ceeeed, wee leet yoouu uusee thee poortaal; iif yoouu faaiil, wee wiill siing aa smaall soong foor yoouu iin oouur saacreed plaacee."

"Sacred place? Oh yes, I see; and what if I refuse?"

"Yoouu haavee noo chooiicee, liittlee oonee. I aam Ooxgaang, kiing oof theesee caaveerns, theesee aaree my peeooplee, yoouu aaree oonly still aaliive noow thaanks too my meercy. My peeooplee woou-uld haave cruusheed yoouu too puulp by noow iif theey haad theeiir waay. Huumaans aaree noot weelcoomee iin oouur caaveerns noow, neeveer miind thee saacreed plaacee."

"But I am not a human. I am a mage." Ranabin was bristling with indignation.

"I seenseed thiis aand thaat iis why yoouu staand beefooree mee noow aas aa guueest, buut doo noot plaay wiith mee, liittlee oonee, I booree eeaasiily. Soo whaat iis yoouuur aansweer?"

"Answer! You have yet to tell me what it is I am required to do, how can I give you an answer?"

Oxgang's eyes flared bright red momentarily and Ranabin regret-ted his tone of voice.

"Reetriieevee aa smaall iiteem foor mee. Soomeethiing stooleen by aa huumaan."

Ranabin, despite being in a hall full of trolls, had heard enough; he needed to get to Crescent Wood and did not have the time to chase around, looking for a thief.

"I have no time to chase stolen items across the Moon lands or wherever else they might be," he interrupted. "I have to use the portal now! Not in a few days time, by then it will be too late. The fate of these lands depends on it. All of our fates, yours included! It all depends on me getting to Crescent Wood now." He stamped his foot down hard with the last word, he was now bristling with anger and frustration and despite the fact he must have looked comical, standing there shaking his small fist at the giant figure opposite him, any such amusement was clearly lost on the impassive troll.

"KILL HIM!" This time the voice thundered through the cavern.

The colour drained from Ranabin's face, had he gone too far?

"Silence! I, Oxgang, rule here. Do any now challenge me?" Oxgang's words no longer flowed, they were short and sharp, their meaning very clear.

Ranabin was shaking, as much with the indignation and anger as with the new fear he was experiencing. A nervous silence followed. Ranabin looked out over the trolls, none spoke, all just glared back, their stone faces set, showing no hint of emotion. Whoever had spoken did not dare to do so now. Finally after many uncomfortable minutes, Oxgang, having decided that his authority was once again absolute and unquestionable, returned his attention back to Ranabin.

"Yoouu haavee spiiriit, liittlee oonee, buut feeaar noot, thee iiteem iin quueestiioon iis heeree wiithiin theesee veery caaveerns. Thee huumaan peeriisheed duuriing hiis eescaapee aand thee iiteem stiill liiees wiith hiim. Iif yoouu aaree quuiick aand suucceessfuul yoouu wiill soooon bee oon yoouur waay."

Ranabin looked at Oxgang with puzzlement. "If the item is here, why do you not retrieve it yourself?"

"Yoouu wiill seeee, liittlee oonee. Doo yoouu aacceept?"

"If I do, do I have your word?"

"Iif yoouu reecoooveer thee iiteem, yoouu wiill bee aallooweed aacceess too thee poortaal aagaaiin, thaat iis my proomiisee."

"Again?" Ranabin asked, puzzled, his mind racing.

Yet even as he spoke, Oxgang was rising to his feet, his eyes flared from bright red to orange and finally to a yellow as bright as the burning sun. This time there was no mistaking the anger in them. The trolls gathered around, moved away, scattering backwards away from the platform, looking around them nervously for the cause of their king's sudden wrath. The scraping of rock on rock screeched out around the cavern as they did so. Ranabin rammed his fingers into his ears in an effort to drown it out. Oxgang now moved with frightening speed, he jumped down from his platform, the entire cavern shaking as he landed on the floor. One of the troughs close by cracked with the force, spilling its hot molten gold out over the floor and around the gathered trolls' feet. None of them seemed bothered by its obvious heat as it pooled into giant, thick golden puddles around their legs. Their entire focus was now on their king, as he rushed at a shadow at the far end of the cavern. The shadow was unmistakably human-like in appearance, it had momentarily slipped out across the cavern floor as if carelessly dropped, and now knowing that it had been seen, it shrank back quickly, vanishing once more amidst the shadows of the surrounding walls.

Shouted commands, an urgency now shook the place, it felt as if the whole world was shaking and moving; as suddenly startled into action, the gathered trolls who had seemed only moments before to be transfixed by Oxgang's anger now sprang into action and disappeared amidst clouds of dust. Their speed startled Ranabin; where before they had been a lumbering, almost cumbersome, moving pile of rock, they now moved with a speed and sense of urgency that defied their size and was frightening to watch. They were now hunting a prey and Ranabin almost felt sorry for the shadow's owner, he hoped he would never have cause to face their wrath.

He looked around and suddenly he realised he was alone; he smiled to himself, he knew where the portal was, the only problem now would be finding his way to it. He ran and jumped down from the platform, the fall was further than he anticipated and he landed heavily on his side, grunting, panting and cursing his own stupidity and spontaneity. Thankfully nothing seemed to be broken and he slowly stood up. He shook his limbs just to check. The cavern floor was now awash with pools of molten gold, he seemed to have luckily landed on one of the few dry areas still big enough for him to lie on. The uneven floor had left small raised islands of solid rock interspersed randomly across the cavern floor amidst a golden sea of hot liquid metal. Tunnels led from the cavern floor around him, all were full of the noise of trolls running around and crashing along. Shouted commands echoed back at him through the emptiness and it was impossible for him to tell where any particular noise originated from. The liquid floor, he knew, would take hours to cool and solidify. He did not know how long he had, but doubted it would be long enough to allow the metal to cool. He had two options, stay and be caught or jump and run. He decided to jump, hopping and leaping like a rabbit from island to island. He slipped and nearly fell into the gold on a few occasions, but his luck held and eventually in a haphazard sort of route he made his way to the far end of the cavern. It was the place where most of the trolls that now chased the shadow had left from. He presumed this was probably the safest place for him to start, as there was less likelihood of any of them still being there.

He had no idea where he was heading, he knew where he wanted to get to, but where he was in relation to the graveyard was a complete mystery to him. He presumed though that if this was the main chamber for the trolls, then somewhere that they held as sacred to them as the graveyard would hopefully not be too far away from the heart of their community. He darted into a tunnel. It was as black and dark as the cavern had been light. He stumbled against the wall, falling down, scratching his hand against its sharp rough surface. He cursed then bit his tongue in anger at himself as the noise echoed through the darkness. He stumbled on though, still not having the sense to wait until his eyes fully adjusted, his eagerness driving him forward, overruling his common sense. He thus stumbled, tripped and swayed downwards for another fifteen to twenty troublesome paces.

The improvement in his vision, when it finally came, was only minimal such was the depth of the darkness. The space in front was now only a marginally paler black than the surrounding walls and it was still hard to differentiate between the two. He wished at that moment he had his stick, the sudden thought again panging its loss as he half stumbled, half ran along the dark tunnel; the fear of being caught and his desire to reach the portal driving him blindly forward.

The tunnel seemed to stretch on and on, twisting first to the right and then to the left; if it had any branches running off it, Ranabin was unaware of them in the surrounding black that was his immediate world. The thunderous noise though had now died down, fading into the distance, a low rumble as opposed to the cacophony of noise that had assaulted his senses earlier and he was also now able to judge roughly where most of it was coming from. It seemed to be coming from directly above him, its power muffled as it filtered down through the rock. The constant slope to the tunnel he had travelled down since he had entered it had now levelled off. Ranabin though was lost, he had no idea where he was, he had hoped to have found something, anything by now that might have hinted that he was on the right path. But in the constant darkness he had lost all bearings and sense of direction. He continued on, reluctant to turn back, knowing that as long as the sound of the trolls was above him he was relatively safe and gave him the time he needed. The tunnel now seemed to stretch on forever. Time seemed to stand still in the darkness. He had nothing to judge the time or distance of his passage against and if it were not for the fact that the tunnel he was in had always been predominantly straight he would have sworn that he was going round in circles. Every piece of wall he passed in the dull gloom seemed to look familiar, every shadow and every rock the same as the last. His tiny footsteps his sole companion as they echoed lamely back at him from the walls.

Ranabin trudged on, growing more and more disconsolate with every step, the fading noise and his lack of knowledge of the tunnels and caverns had slowly eroded at his exuberance. Doubt and anxiety now crept in, in its stead. He was *lost*, he was tired, he had no way out of the tunnel and he knew eventually the trolls would find him and he was not so sure they would be as welcoming this time when they did. His feet now dragged over the rocky floor, scuffing and scraping the loose stones scattered around. A low scuffling sound seemed to mirror that of his feet to the right, making him pause, thinking at first it was just another echo playing tricks on his mind. Something shot out across his path, a small creature, its eyes blazed at him briefly as it cast him a weary glance before disappearing into the darkness on his left. His heart thumped loudly in his chest. Too loudly for his liking; he was sure its very sound would travel like a drumbeat down the tunnels, drawing the trolls towards him.

It took him a couple of seconds to realise that it was not his heart but the sound of footsteps. Light footsteps running over rock. Running towards him, coming from behind. He envied the small creature its eyesight, as he found new energy and drive to run forward away from what was now coming towards him. His momentum carried him forward, as he slipped and skipped over loose rocks and boulders on the floor. Larger rocks now seemed to be strewn all over the floor, forcing him to jump blindly over them and to hope for a secure landing on the other side. The footsteps though were getting closer despite him running as fast as he could; he could also now hear something else, something even more frightening, something larger, a low rumble that was accelerating towards him, getting louder by the second: the thunderous footsteps of trolls and lots of them, chasing them down the tunnel.

He knew he would be caught if he carried on; he had to hide, but where? The tunnel was bare, just walls and a floor of solid rock with the occasional larger, loose rock scattered around, nothing that could really offer him any sort of cover to hide behind.

"Follow me."

The words seemed to spring out of the shadows all around him, making him spin and twist his head quickly, trying to locate their source.

"Quickly now, follow me." A mere whisper, yet conveying a huge sense of urgency that had to be obeyed. A blur of movement followed in the shadows to his left, he just caught it in his peripheral vision as it sped past and down the tunnel. Ranabin ran after the shadow, still unsure what it was but choosing its company over the pack of pursuing trolls. If it had a form he was unable to see it; it flickered in and out of the shadows just long enough to be glimpsed and each time he drew nearer, it would again dart forward, blending back easily into the surrounding darkness which obscured it from view. Yet there was something about it that seemed vaguely familiar to Ranabin as he chased it, always conscious of the increasing volume of noise behind him.

He burst into the graveyard as if it seemingly sprang out from the end of the tunnel, recognising immediately the faint yellow glow over on the far side. He ran towards it, no longer concerned about the shadow that seemed to have disappeared in the faint light. The light bathed him, as he drew close to it, its glow washing over him, a feeling of safety and security replacing his fear as it drowned out his senses. The noise became a distant roar and from all around pairs of bright yellow stars burned through at him. His body tingled and sparkled, all his hair felt alive with static as it danced and swayed above his head. Green, orange, blue, red, yellow; the light surrounding him frantically flickered between each colour, faster and faster the colours blurred past his eyes until finally seemingly unable to hold on to their colour for any longer they seeped into one, blending into a blinding, pulsating, bright white. The stars appeared brighter now. They seemed so close it felt as if he could touch them; he reached out, drawn to them, they were so beautiful as they sparkled above him, his hand drew closer and closer, his fingers touched warm rock and then it was gone. The world went blank, it felt like he was floating in nothingness, all colour vanished, the stars were gone, his eyes were open yet he could see nothing.

Oxgang let out a roar of pure rage, his fist smashed into the troll standing beside him, sending its head flying across the room and smashing against the wall, its body stood in shock for a moment, until it realised, it then crashed to the floor.

The other trolls present backed away.

"FIND IT!"

The words pursued Ranabin as he now spun dizzyingly through the portal.

Chapter Twelve

The moon was full, a bright shining disc in the night sky as it bathed the forest floor in a silvery light that was almost as bright as the day's sun. The shadows beneath the tall trees were small, as if cowering beneath its gaze. The bright greens of the day now gone, replaced by a greyer, darker version that had a silvery sheen to it. A spider spun its thin silvery web in front of Fent's nose as he sat resting back on his hind legs watching it. It was almost time; they had all come, the ten packs, 300 wolves. Not just any wolves though, these were 300 Wolves of Fennigan, bigger, more powerful and more intelligent than their cousins from the lowlands. These were wolves that had been feared and respected in days gone by, a race of wolves that the other races had sought help from in time of need. A proud race whose time was coming again; tonight was the beginning; tonight was the first of many steps on their journey to reclaim their destiny, their pride and their respect.

The thought of Vangor lying helplessly on the rocks was still fresh on his mind. How he would have loved to have sunk his teeth into the neck of that human, how he would have loved to have watched the man's eyes slowly drain of life as his teeth and jaws squeezed tight around his throat, choking it from him, in his mind hoping that the human would plead for mercy but knowing in reality that he would not. The time would come, the thought *would* become reality; it was now surely only a matter of waiting. Time and patience, time and patience, but first there was work to be done.

Pareen had been sent with thirty wolves selected from all the packs to watch the paths into the forest. Fent had decided to reward him for his efforts in preparing for tonight; An Sumn, the circle of the ancients, was perfect, the young wolf had excelled himself, now the rest was up to him. The moon was full. The clouds that had earlier littered the sky had been blown away to leave a completely dark tapestry that was only broken by the full moon and the interspaced stars that twinkled and shone as its accompaniment.

The only doubt in his mind was the howl. He had felt its full power course through him on the ridge but since then he had felt empty, almost drained. He had thought long and hard afterwards about what had happened on the ridge. Did he now have the power? Had it returned to him, as was his right, or was the ridge a mere anomaly? Did Vangor still have true possession of it? He had been scared to try again, scared of being disappointed, scared of the emptiness that he would feel now he had felt its true power. He knew that to not have the ability now, having tasted it, would be worse than having never had it.

He knew they would question him tonight, he knew they had all come because they had heard it today. Not since that night many moons since had all the wolves gathered as one, not since the last time the ancients had sung to them, not since the night of his father's death. He had hated his father then, hated him for abandoning them, hating him for dying but most of all hating him for robbing their race of the ancients' song, their power, their soul, the heartbeat of the packs. The song was what bound them together, it was what kept them strong as a race, it was what set them apart from the other wolves in the Moon lands. It was their magic and without it they were just another collection of packs of wolves; yes, still bigger and stronger but as an individual that counted for very little.

Well, now they believed it was back, they believed the Ancients' Howl had called to them, they believed that once more their ancients would sing for them. Their belief was all he needed at the moment and today, no tonight, was already going better to plan than he could possibly have hoped for.

The spider had finished now, a perfect, flawless web, a deadly trap ready to catch its prey. The web shifted in the breeze, gently ebbing backwards and forwards, anchored firmly onto two branches that supported it in mid-air; the spider retreated back to its favoured branch, settling down to wait, its work complete, its trap sprung, time and patience now would deliver its prey. He must now do the same; he must lay out his plan, put it into action and wait patiently for his prey to arrive.

The moon was shining down onto the bare rock, the beam of light shimmering onto the hard, greyish-white surface, highlighting it as a spotlight would, it was the focal point in the circle. The rock itself was pitted and aged, it jutted out of the hard earth around it like a finger pointing upwards. Its surface stretched outwards and upwards at an angle pointing towards the centre of the circle and the moon above. The rock at the distal end, the end that faced into the circle stood clear of the ground, its height equalling that of two humans. The rock was a natural platform which faced into a circular clearing in the trees that stretched for almost sixty paces at its widest point. The outer edge of the circle was ringed with small white rocks, their presence in the trees unnatural, each appeared to be specifically placed to serve an exact purpose; these stones were bordered by a line of thin low plants, mostly gorse and heather which thickened steeply into brambles and bushes, and then came the tall thick spruce trees of Fennigan Forest, these stretched upwards and outwards, casting their shadows in a myriad of shapes within the circle.

The location of An Sumn lay deep within Fennigan Forest, deep within the lands of the wolf. No man had ever set foot here, very few animals dared. This was only the second time Fent had done so in his lifetime, the last time as a cub, his memory of it sparse and lacking in detail. He was full of emotion even before he approached the circle. His senses were alive, he could smell the gathered packs, he could sense their presence. All of which added to the magical aura that already seemed to surround the circle.

He should have eaten, he thought. But he had been too busy, the hours had rushed by and now he was here, they were waiting, it was time. He pushed through the last of the thin undergrowth that had grown over the path, the very path that was last trod on by his father, the only path to the rock, him the only wolf now allowed to tread these hallowed steps. The earth felt cold under his paws, cold and new, unused and at the same time familiar as if only his paws belonged on it. Could he do this? The doubt which sprang to his mind was unwelcome and unsettling. He had no choice though, he had to, he had accepted his destiny; from the moment his father had died, he had started on the journey to this point. He had no choice now; perhaps in the beginning he could have walked away, but to do so now would spell the end for his race. They needed him and no amount of doubt was now going to stop him.

The faint yelping of cubs playing accompanied by the low growls of disapproving parents that had permeated the air ceased the moment he stepped onto the rock. The Wolves of Fennigan, seeming to sense his presence, turned as one, falling into a respectful silence as they did so. Their expectant gazes now looked up at him, it was like looking down onto a sea of shining eyes, eyes that in reflecting the moon's bright light seemed almost to mirror the stars that shone above.

Fent had thought about what he wanted to say, he had planned this for years now and he had lived this moment in his dreams on many nights. But now the reality of it all was so different. In his dreams he had always had the right words by which to address his kind. Words that would inspire and motivate them, words that would become legend amongst them. Now though as he looked out across their expectant faces the words failed him. It had been easier facing Vangor this afternoon, he thought. Then it had not mattered what the human had thought, and therefore he had been able to let his instincts command his words and reactions. Here he could not afford to let instinct or sentiment cloud his judgement and thus impede his goal.

He gazed upwards towards the moon, drawn by its majesty, hoping within its radiance to find some inspiration.

The tension increased; the waiting packs were anticipating drama and leadership, so far they had been given silence. The cubs, their attention span short and their curiosity long, seeing that nothing interesting was happening to hold their attention, slowly returned to their games; their quietened yelps gradually breaking into and filling the eerie silence that hung over the circle.

The shooting star was a welcome distraction for not only the gathered packs but also for Fent. He watched as it blazed across the visible night sky, a small trail of glowing dust seemingly hanging in its wake. As the assembled packs, grateful for something happening, followed its path, their heads and eyes gazed upwards which in turn stretched their necks. It was this that reminded Fent of the howl and his stance. He waited patiently and contentedly as the shooting star continued along its path. Eventually it disappeared behind the trees, hidden now from their view, and the packs once more turned their gaze on him.

"The ancients have spoken today. You have all heard their song. Their power was returned to me for a purpose. You are that purpose, the gathering of the packs here tonight their purpose." He watched for their reaction as the words floated out over them. He had chosen his words wisely, he thought, managing, he hoped, to cover his own doubts with his choice of non-committal words.

Their gazes all held his as he looked out at them. Tarest was over to his left and he deliberately met and held his gaze for longer. If there were any that would challenge him here, it would be that wolf. His had been the sternest opposition to Fent's right to lead the packs. A cousin on his father's side, he was even by Fennigan wolf standards a giant of a wolf who preferred brawn over brains in the leadership of his pack. It had been that basic lack of subtle intelligence that had been his downfall when they had fought for the leadership of the packs. Fent had easily beaten the bigger wolf by using his cunning and intelligence in the hunt. It was a common misconception that Fennigan wolves fought for the leadership as their lesser lowland cousins did. No, that was fine for the untamed feral creatures, but the leader of the Fennigan wolves needed to be able to lead his kind in battle against enemies that fought as an army, not to just hunt food. So their challenge, although still in the form of a hunt, had been a test of leadership and intelligence as opposed to brawn. They had hunted with their packs, pitting instinct, ability, strength and leadership against each other as they tried to outmanoeuvre each other and then close for the kill. Fent had beaten Tarest easily and thus his pack had maintained its alpha status over the nine other packs, and it was they that thus had the privilege and honour of protecting the leader of the Fennigan wolves.

Tarest had initially taken the beating badly, but the weight of opinion had been against him and he had finally grudgingly accepted Fent's role. For now though he showed no signs of questioning Fent, he was just staring back, meeting Fent's eyes with cold unblinking eyes that still seemed to hint at a challenge lurking within. There was an unspoken enmity between them now that would always exist and Fent was no longer concerned by it. It had initially bothered him but over the years he had grown used to it and accepted Tarest's bitterness towards him as part of the challenge of being a leader. He also knew though that Tarest was fiercely loyal towards the Wolves of Fennigan and wanted more than anything what he now was offering them and it was this that would keep him following Fent for now.

He let his gaze linger, drawing out the moment in a silent challenge of his own. Finally, judging the time to be right, he slowly looked away, satisfaction and honour left intact for both of them, he felt. He needed Tarest's full support not his enmity for tonight at least.

"Today I met my father's killer, the same man who by that very act stole the howl of the ancients from us, depriving us of our power and reducing us to packs of feral animals." The silence was absolute, not a sound from the forest, even the cubs were again looking up at him, having pushed and snuck up to the front of the gathered wolves, into the space between the revered elders of the packs and the rock itself, their bright eyes shining up at him full of the magic and energy of youth.

"Today I watched as this man lay helpless at my feet, struck down by the ancients with the very same howl he stole from us. Yet today although I longed to tear his heart out, I was unable to do so. The ancients stopped me, they froze my muscles to the spot; I had to watch in anger and frustration as that man was carried away. I now realise that the ancients did not want me to kill him yet, I can only imagine they know he will be of some use to us in the future."

A series of low growls met these words; it was difficult to tell though by the subtle tones whether they were growls of derision, anger or support.

"The man I speak of is Vangor, he is of and from the Dark Knights, the erstwhile enemy of these lands and thus the enemy of all the races of this land."

"All men are our enemies now, the men of these lands hunt us like dogs, why should it matter where this man comes from?"

Fent had expected the rebuke to come from Tarest, yet he had remained silent. It was an elder from his own pack that now spoke, a wolf with a coat as white as the moon above them and in whose light now resembled a phantom, a luminous apparition of a wolf that was once as strong in body as it was still strong in spirit and pride.

"It is true, men of these lands do now hunt us where once they feared to tread, but that is because we are not one. We are weak and disjointed; they no longer fear or respect us. This is why we must act now. The Dark Knights are coming, these lands will once again be a battlefield, a place of sorrow, blood and pain.When it comes we must be prepared to fight."

"Fight? Fight who? The humans, the Dark Knights? I would rather kill the farmer in the meadow than fight men I have not seen. I have more reason to hate him than any other human I know."

A murmur of supporting growls spread through the packs, the hatred of the farmer for his slaughter of many of their kind was universal.

Fent was unconcerned by the rising passions; he needed their passion, and would guide it in the direction of his choosing.

"We fight to regain our heritage. We fight again to claim what is ours. The Ancients' Howl you all heard today was a mere taste of its true power. Many of you have seen its full power. You know what I talk of, you have seen when the heavens dance to our call. Today was a mere calling to arms, a catalyst for the plan the ancients have given me to lead us to where we should be. The farmer in the meadow is of little consequence."

A few growls of protest rang out, but these were soon silenced by the majority gathered around them.

"We now have two targets. The first is Prince Morkin. Vangor wanted the human child brought to him. We will capture him and bring him here instead. The second part of the plan is to avenge my father's death and return the full power of the ancients to us. To once again see the heavens dance to our song, to be guided by their wisdom and once more become the masters of this forest and mountain."

The words carried power, driven by passion and spoken from the heart; it was as he had dreamed. They carried forth over the gathered wolves spreading like a wave, and like a wave gathers speed and force as it rushes towards the shore, his words too gathered force in the form of howls.

The loudest support came from Tarest, as if somehow they had shared the same vision for their race. He roared out his approval seconds before the others, letting the words release an age of pent-up anger and frustration. It was the moment he had waited for, the moment that Fent had prayed for. With Tarest's support and force the plan had more chance of succeeding. The reply of growls and low howls picked up pace, growing into a cacophony of wild noise that reverberated through the circle and out into the night. The cubs pranced and tumbled around, caught up in the adults' excitement, not quite fully understanding what was going on.

Fent stood on his perch, watching the joy and passion as it rippled over his wolves. For too long now they had been caged by their shame, unable to fully express their passion and pride and now it was bursting out, spreading amongst them like an uncontrollable forest fire. He hoped his plan would work; the boy was the key, the bait, Vangor the prize; and then his dreams, his thoughts, well, they took him on unimaginable journeys with his wolves, and it was all coming. But only if his plan worked.

The stag crashed through the undergrowth into the circle. Its antlers stood proud and tall above it, draped in a nest of small twigs and leaves, its eyes dark and foreboding, accompanied by great clouds of breath hanging loosely around its nostrils as it drew in great gulps of air. It stamped its feet in defiance of the pack around it, as if daring them to challenge it. The wolves initially stunned by its sudden appearance had just stared back at it as if not believing their eyes. Now though they closed in on it, snarling and growling their displeasure and their hunger. The stag tossed its head left then right, the sharp tips of its antlers a blur in the air as they faced first one wolf and then the next in quick succession, never remaining still for a second.

No normal stag would enter this circle with all the packs gathered here, Fent thought as he watched the drama unfold below. The younger wolves were now closing on the stag, circling around and behind it, closing in on it and waiting for the chance to kill. They took it in turns to snap forward tentatively, testing the stag's power, their teeth bared as they played with it. The stag was a blur of movement, antlers and hooves crashing around, keeping the wolves away for the moment. Fent knew though that it was only a matter of time before the stag tired and the wolves became bolder.

"Stop, let it go," his voice bellowing from his perch was barely audible above the growling and snarling of the packs. Most of them were hungry and eager for the meal which had seemingly just been sent to them from the gods, most thus *chose* not to hear Fent's command.

Seeing his words having no effect, he sprang down from the rock, sailing gracefully through the air in one powerful leap, landing softly on the thick grass and moss around. He pushed and growled his way through the cubs and the elders with an ease that befitted his stature and size, closing quickly on the wolves that now surrounded the stag.

As he approached he could see that one of the younger wolves already had blood staining the white of its face, a small cut visible just above its right eye where moments earlier in its inexperienced exuberance it had been caught by the stag's antlers; the smell of blood filled the air, heightening the frenzy of the pack, as they now rushed forward individually. They were still, he noticed, not working as one. I have more work yet to do, Fent thought. The antlers seemed to sing in the air, a low whistle and a blur of fallow yellow and brown, blending into one. The younger wolves, having seen their friend injured, now had a lot more respect for the sharpened points. They lunged forward and back quickly, trying in turn to quickly tire the stag. The stag bellowed in defiance and pride as it swished round. Its antlers just missed two approaching wolves as they ducked back, forcing them to retreat away. Another wolf darted forward from behind and the stag spun around, kicking out as it did so. Clumps of grass and earth came flying through the air as its rear hooves kicked out, anticipating another attack and again driving the young wolves back and away. The senior wolves seemed to have formed a second circle and watched as the young males tried desperately to prove their prowess to them.

"Stop!" Fent bellowed the order, which now clearly heard resulted in angry eyes turning to fix on him.

A young wolf, barely an adult, darted forward ignoring the order. The stag turned, prancing lightly on its feet, sensing the danger, bringing its antlers down to face the wolf. It was flattened to the ground as Fent launched himself at it, his great weight easily knocking the younger, lighter wolf to the side as his momentum carried him forward. He tore away from the pain in his left shoulder, as it seared up into his brain. His left leg felt weak. A bright spray of crimson drops spread out over him, arching out and spattering onto the grass. The stag snorted at him, its antlers dripping with blood, his blood, were inches away from his face. Now closer, the black seemingly soulless eyes looked full of life and energy as they watched him, its hooves pawed the ground in readiness and expectancy of an attack.

Fent limped round, ignoring the stag as the young wolf scampered back to the safety of the pack. Fent turned his back on the stag, not as a sign of contempt, but to face the pack and dare any other to disobey him.

"Leave it. It leaves here free and unharmed. It is a sign from the ancients. A beast of pride and nobility sent to show we are on the right path. Only a stag protected by the ancients would dare enter here tonight while 300 hungry wolves wait. It goes free, now; that is the will of the ancients and my command," the last was aimed at a wolf he did not yet recognise in front of him, who seemed to be about to protest but would now no longer meet his gaze.

The stag seemed to sense the change in the wolves. It raised its head up high and bellowed deeply into the night sky, a deep croaking bark that was answered moments later by another in the distance. Three bounds later and the stag was gone from their midst, disappearing effortlessly into the surrounding forest, leaving only its scent as a reminder to them all.

Chapter Thirteen

They crested the hill in the early afternoon, leading their horses by their reins. An open plain stretched out before them, rich green grassland, sprinkled randomly with yellows, blues, purples and oranges as the wild flowers tried to add their own colour to the unending sea of green; the thick foliage of trees to their right breaking up the horizon with a mixture of browns, reds, oranges and the varying shades of green of the early leaves of the season, these were now gradually filtering into a bluey-grey, cloudy sky. The treeline they were now standing in stretched out and around, spreading out thickly to their right before disappearing over the horizon. In the far distance the black peaks of the Stant Mountains stood out proud and tall as if guarding the low valley. Small homesteads could be seen littered across the plain, marking out the small villages and farms which were a common feature of these lands.

Grabbit knew the area well; the Keep of Ishfern stood a half-day's ride away to the southwest of them, hidden now in the distance by the gentle rolling hills that surrounded it. These were his lands, well, not his as in ownership terms, they belonged to Prince Morkin, but in terms of power; he knew he wielded more power over the people here than the Prince did, a thought which always cheered him up when he thought about it. He imagined Prince Morkin bowing low to him in subjugation as he rode through the lands; he chuckled to himself, the great rolls of fat that comprised his stomach rippled with the movement. The term belly laugh had surely been coined for him.

Lorigan seemed to be ignoring him or at least was paying his joviality no heed. She was instead looking at Luxor's green dragon banner that hung limply in the air over a small stream that flowed into and disappeared within the first trees of Crescent Wood.

"Twenty of the Royal Guard and two others."

Grabbit looked over to where the Fey was looking, seeing clearly for the first time the men Lorigan had promised were there. He did not like the Royal Guard with good reason; they were the few soldiers in the Keep of Ishfern that were truly loyal to Morkin and Luxor and as such were incorruptible; equating to no profit and lots of interference, the two things that were sure to rile him. He did not know who was down there, but it did not really matter, they all knew him and he was sure he would not receive a warm welcome.

He was right. A sentry had spotted them walking towards them and they were met just within a good bowman's range by two riders. Four others now circled behind them in a wide arc, the remainder of the guard, bar their leader, watched with their arrows notched onto bowstrings, waiting for the order to fire. The other two men seemed unconcerned by their approach and mildly amused by the Royal Guards' reaction. They remained sitting by their fire, stirring the pot that hung over it, occasionally glancing over to see what was now happening.

The two guardsmen that approached were young and obviously new to their posts, their eagerness to please and lack of experience evident as they closed in on Lorigan and Grabbit. They rode up fast, their mares stretching their necks as they rose to the gallop, both horse and rider evidently enjoying the thrill of speed. Lorigan and Grabbit stood still, holding their horses loosely by their reins, watching them.

"Mr Grabbit," they almost spat the words in unison as if the very words offended their mouths when they pulled their horses up in front of them.

Grabbit did not recognise the young men. This meant that they had only recently been commissioned and within the last two weeks, and yet even so they obviously now knew all about him.

"Who is this with you?" They turned their attention to Lorigan, their contempt and arrogance obvious and they made no attempt to hide it. "A personal assistant or another thug?"

Both were full of bravado and self-importance and they laughed to each other, sharing the joke. The man closest to Lorigan leant forward, his hand reaching upwards, meaning to flip back Lorigan's hood, which she had pulled back over her head when they had breached the top of the slope and sighted the men close by.

The guard's hand never quite reached the hood, its fingertips brushed the surface lightly and then Lorigan was gone. Before the man could blink, she was sitting behind him on his horse and the cold press of metal on his throat cut short any further insults. The look of dismay on his companion's face made Grabbit chuckle; the man was at a complete loss what to do next, his hand was frozen in indecision halfway towards his sword. Finally lost, confused and admitting defeat in his inaction, he turned his hopeful gaze back towards his leader, looking for advice.

Lorigan leant forward and whispered into the ear of the guard in front of her. The man very slowly reached down and unbuckled his sword belt. It fell away with a dull clatter onto the ground. The riders that had circled behind, on seeing what was now happening, closed in slowly, judging the situation as they approached with a caution that betrayed their evident years of experience and wisdom. A man in the camp was now mounting his horse, a huge silver stallion that was adorned with a battle helmet of bright silver and topped with a red crest that flowed over and down onto its mane. This was the man Lorigan wanted to talk to; she sat impassively, watching him on the horse, her knife still pressed firmly against the young guard's throat, daring him to move. Sweat was now running down his forehead in glistening rivers, stinging his eyes, which too terrified to move, he tried in vain to blink away.

Senteth, the Captain of the Royal Guard, was well known to Grabbit, an accomplished knight possessing an easy manner and blessed with a calm demeanour. He was a natural leader who commanded his men with an ease that came from a confidence in his own abilities. He had been Captain of the Royal Guard for six years now, appointed to the post by Lord Luxor. He stood six feet tall with a shock of red hair that reached down to mid back and was always braided into a single ponytail. He was fair of face and looked younger than his thirty-five years, which again, considering his profession, owed a certain testament to his ability with a blade and his skills in combat.

He had watched the drama unfold in front of him. All of his knights were good, the best certainly in these lands; the two he had sent were inexperienced but were certainly up to the task of dealing with the fat tax collector. Even he though had been amazed at the speed and ease with which Grabbit's companion had disarmed his guardsman. Thankfully his guardsman was still alive, which meant if nothing else that they were at least willing to talk. As he mounted his horse he pondered the roles of Grabbit and his companion, wondering which of the two was in charge. If the stranger was under the command of Mr Grabbit, which seemed unlikely but not impossible, then he would be able to deal with the situation quite easily. If it was the stranger who was in fact in charge, which seemed the more likely, then who knew. He hoped it was Grabbit because at least he was a known commodity and as such easy to predict.

He calmly rode his horse over towards Grabbit and Lorigan, the red crest on its head swaying gently with the movement, his gaze taking in his men as he went, gesturing to them as he did so to keep their distance and lower their bows. He made for Grabbit, stopping five paces away, his eyes though were trying to penetrate the darkness beneath the stranger's hood, but the hood was still drawn low, hiding the entire face in shadow. He was sure though that the stranger's hidden eyes would be studying and assessing him.

He readjusted his initial assessment; he was now sure that Grabbit was the one being led by the stranger as Grabbit, usually loud and brash, was now uncharacteristically quiet, as if he had been ordered to be so.

"You have my word, stranger, that you are safe, my men will not harm you. Please release the young man and then we can talk."

"He insulted me! He would die for that in many lands." Lorigan's sing-song voice floated out gently from beneath the hood, yet at the same time its coldness and sincerity were evident and the young man visibly shook with fear.

"If there was any insult served then I am at fault, not that man. I lead these men and therefore the blame is mine. I am Senteth, Captain of the Royal Guard. Let the young man go," the emphasis on young man was very evident, "and I am sure we can satisfy your honour, if that is what you require." The reply equally as calm was filled with veiled threats and promises.

Lorigan seemed to take an age to think; the suspense hung in the air like a damp blanket, making the less-experienced guards nervous with energy and trepidation. Senteth felt sweat trickle down his back; he hated single combat or honour fights, it was a waste of good men and he had thus banned them in the guards. But he would not let this young guard die for some unknown insult he had unwittingly served from lack of experience. He had sent him to do a job and it was therefore his responsibility; he would fight this stranger if need be to the death. His guards would honour him by not interfering but for the first time in his life, having seen the stranger's speed first hand, he was unsure of what the outcome of such a fight would be. The seconds dragged on, the fight becoming more and more inevitable with each that passed.

"We will talk." The words nearly made him jump, such had been the tension and silence. "I have no desire to kill you or this boy! Not for the time being anyway. I came today in peace."

Senteth let out the breath he was unaware until that moment he had been holding and the tension slowly left his body.

"Then let us talk, come over to the fire, we have coffee and rabbit stew."

Lorigan seemed to consider it for a second and Senteth must have thought she had changed her mind when he saw the knife being pressed more firmly against the young guard's neck. His men noticed as well and, anticipating a command, all raised their bows. Senteth waited, he met the pleading gaze of his young guard but then signalled to his men to again lower their bows.

"Why not?" Lorigan said as she drew her knife slowly across the skin of the young man's neck. The blade bit lightly into its surface, a trickle of blood smearing it as she pushed the young man forward, "Just a reminder about your manners in future." The guard fell off the horse sideways, landing in a heap on the ground, his hand immediately going up to his throat, feeling the wet, sticky blood. The earlier fear in his eyes now turned to anger as he looked first at the blood on his fingers, then up at Lorigan and finally at his sword which was lying in the grass less than an arm's reach away.

Senteth had seen the blood and the look in the young man's eyes, a look he knew only too well; the young guard still had a lot to learn. Perhaps I have made an error in this one, he thought.

"Still yourself, Crean!"

The young guard jumped at the words and the anger immediately disappeared from his eyes, to be replaced by a guarded cold expression that hid all emotion. Senteth stared at Crean as he stood stock still, arms firmly pressed to his sides, head now held high and his back straight; perhaps not too much of an error then, but I will be keeping a closer eye on you from now on, he thought as he smiled to himself ruefully. Nothing further was said as Senteth led them into camp and over to the fire. Lorigan had chosen to walk her horse into camp and had given Crean his horse back as if she had been returning a mount she had borrowed with its owner's permission. Crean had silently stared at her when he took the reins, defiance and loathing very evident in his eyes. He now rode his horse back into camp, keeping well clear of Lorigan and Senteth.

Lorigan loved the politeness and traditions that humans observed, she loved it because she enjoyed pushing at their boundaries, this always made the humans feel uncomfortable around her, yet she felt always safe, knowing full well she could deal with any situation that arose from her discourtesy. The problem humans had was they were all different in terms of manners, customs and traditions. This in turn left all humans at a disadvantage and uncertain when it came to dealing with other humans and other races. They could not really understand each other and, more often than not, only managed to offend each other in their eagerness to please; it was hilarious to watch and even more fun to manipulate. Her people though, the Fey, were different, in that they all followed the one set of traditions and customs and, no matter where they came from, they were as one; one race of Fey, same rules, same manners, same laws, easy.

Yes, it was easy to rile a human, well, most of them anyway. Senteth so far had shown promise, he at least thought about his actions with an intelligence and experience that weighed up the consequences rather than only reacting to a situation as many of his kind did, especially Mr Grabbit. It was easy to see why he was in command here.

Lorigan knew of the other two humans in the camp even though Senteth chose not to introduce them. They were the humans that had accompanied Carebin; she watched them stirring their stew, her shaded eyes hidden beneath her hood as she crossed and sat by the fire. Their curiosity was short-lived as they briefly turned from their pot and watched them sit, and then as if suddenly they had remembered something important to do, they both stood and left, leaving Senteth, Grabbit, Lorigan and a burly guard who as of yet had not been introduced to sit alone by the fire. The rest of the Royal Guard seemed to be busying themselves around the camp just out of earshot, but Lorigan's trained eyes easily noted their subtle watchfulness and ever readiness to come to their commander's aid at the slightest sign of trouble. They were well trained, she thought, yet another thing to admire and remember about this man; he leads them well and they in turn obviously trust him.

"Your men are slow, lazy and unobservant."

Senteth, if stung or angered by the words, showed nothing in his expression. The burly guard to his left though clearly bristled at the insult as Lorigan calculatedly watched them both. Grabbit, who sat beside her, felt strangely uncomfortable; he had been expecting a more courteous opening exchange. He glanced over at Lorigan but kept his mouth shut, his hands though were unable to disguise his obvious discomfort and anxiety as he opened and closed them and then rubbed them together nervously.

Senteth chose to ignore the opening remark, choosing diplomacy over aggression. "This is my Sergeant-at-Arms, Sergeant Creaner, the father of the young man whose horse you chose to borrow. I must congratulate you on your choice as it is an excellent mount, one of our best."

Lorigan's eyes assessed the sergeant as she discarded the words; one to watch, she thought. Grabbit had similar thoughts for different reasons; he had enjoyed seeing the guard humiliated and now saw a potential opportunity for profit in father and son.

"My men and I were well aware of the five men who were watching us, if it is that to which you refer."

It was Lorigan's turn to hide her emotions; despite still wearing the hood, her brain jumped a move further forward. It mattered not if they knew they were being watched, let's play the game out and see what comes of it.

"They watch no more." Senteth and Creaner showed no emotion. "They attacked my hawk," she offered as a form of explanation as her hand pointed towards her horse and the leather sack that hung from its side. The hooded head of the hawk resting to one side was just visible from where they sat.

"Is the bird badly hurt?" The question from Senteth was full of concern. "I have some experience in hawking and healing if you have any need of assistance."

The offer and its manner seemed genuine to Lorigan and she studied again the man sitting opposite her, his cold blue eyes seemingly ill at place with the fiery colour of his hair.

"That will not be required for the healing, though we may require your assistance in fetching an item essential for the hawk to fully recover."

Both of them seemed to relax slightly; they were now in a conversation they both felt comfortable with.

"What item? We may already have it or similar at our disposal. We carry an extensive kit for healing even on short patrols."

"Unlikely!" The last came as a statement from Lorigan, not an allegation. "The item in question is unique, not known to many and only obtainable from the Fey."

The mere mention of the Fey seemed to register in Senteth's stature. He sat upright as if guarding something again, becoming wary and suspicious, yet still his face remained impassive.

"Then we cannot help you. I am afraid you must have been misinformed or misled. The Fey are a myth, a mere legend of a long-gone age. It is true, the people of these woods still believe they exist, but I am a man of proof and they offer none, but go," he swept his hand outwards towards the trees as if showing the way, "and speak to them if you must, they may be able to help you, but I doubt it."

Grabbit was struggling to keep his face straight. He longed to jump up and pull Lorigan's hood down, just to see the look on Senteth's face; he would have done it if he thought for a second that he would have been capable of doing it, and it would almost have been worth dying for. The revered Captain of the Royal Guard denying the existence of the Fey race whilst sitting opposite a Fey; today was getting better and better, he could not wait until he returned to Ishfern tavern, he would be able to dine and drink for free for weeks on today's events alone. Of course his version of it all would have him taking a more active part in the proceedings. He could even now almost picture himself jumping onto the horse, knife in hand, whilst Lorigan stood and watched. The sudden recollection that Lorigan could read his thoughts came screaming back into his mind from some dark recess, he suddenly felt cold and clammy and at the same time perversely sweaty; he looked over to where Lorigan had been sitting. His fear rose. He almost ducked, expecting to be hit as he heard footsteps behind him, but Lorigan just sat back down beside him, thankfully seeming unaware of his fantasy.

"What can you tell me of these?"

Grabbit almost choked as he watched Lorigan throw five identical silver rings onto the grass besides Senteth, each had the same silver fox emblem engraved on them. They fell loosely together onto the grass, the metal clinking together, the flames from the fire now reflected off their polished surfaces. He shot a glance of contempt over at Lorigan that also went unnoticed. His heart raced and he coughed out loud as

Senteth reached over and scooped up the five rings. Senteth glanced quickly over in his direction as he did so before returning his gaze to the rings. He rolled them over in his fingers, feeling them, assessing them, lifting each of them in turn close to his eye, studying in great detail the engraving on each as if they held an individual secret.

"They are all the same, one for each of the five, cut from their fingers."

Senteth continued to look at the rings, unhurried by Lorigan's words. Finally he looked up and then handed the rings over to Creaner who fastidiously and with equal intent studied each again. Grabbit watched each ring, calculating their individual worth with eager greedy eyes, following the path of each as if able to guard them from theft with his very vision. One of them by right was his and if he was able to convince Lorigan of his ability to source information with that one, he was sure the rest would also come his way. It would be better and quicker to use all five with different sources at the same time, rather than one at a time, he thought; he was sure this argument would convince Lorigan and secure him the rings.

He jumped up in anger before he could stop himself as Creaner deposited the rings in his tunic belt pouch. He had already taken a step towards the sergeant of the guard when the words hit him loud and clear, forcing their way into his head and compelling his brain to obey what his heart could not.

"SIT." The words were not shouted, yet they seemed to resonate inside his head. He sat, glaring at Creaner, who seemed to have taken little notice of him, yet when he glanced to his left he saw that two guardsmen were now watching him with their bows raised ready.

"You have him well trained, I am impressed." It was Senteth's turn to see if he could bait them and test Lorigan's control over Grabbit. He knew Grabbit well, an oaf of a man with the intelligence of an ox but a dangerous man who, when he set his mind on something, usually achieved his goal with little or no regard for the consequences, this was the dangerous part. He knew he would usually rise to the bait very easily, yet now this stranger seemed to be able to control him equally as easily. Interesting, he thought as he watched as Grabbit just sit there glaring at the two of them, his deep breathing easily heard from where they sat; it was obvious the man was dying to leap up and attack both of them. His intrigue satisfied for the moment, he returned to the matter of the rings.

"Interesting. I cannot tell you anything at the moment though about them. You say they came from the five who followed us? That again is interesting!" The lie came easily to Senteth, "When I return to the Keep I will make enquiries on your behalf regarding them, if that is what you desire?"

"You may keep three for that purpose!"

"As you wish. Sergeant," Senteth kept his eyes on Grabbit, watching for his reaction. He had seen the greed in the taxman's eyes earlier and wanted to see how he would react to them keeping three of the rings. Grabbit though had now achieved control over the emotions that had threatened to swamp him; any anger that he had was now tempered with relief as Creaner under his watchful and resentful eye removed two of the rings and returned them to Lorigan. He was no longer enjoying today but two rings closer to his grasp were better than none so he forced himself to be still.

"We have your permission to enter Crescent Wood?" Lorigan enquired as she replaced the rings in her pack, "To ensure the full recovery of my hawk."

Senteth looked over at his sergeant and nodded, the unspoken meaning in the nod, having spent years of service together, instantly understood. Sergeant Creaner took his leave with well-rehearsed courtesy and disappeared back towards his men.

"My Lord Luxor and Crown Prince Morkin are training in the woods," Senteth explained. "Sergeant Creaner and five of my men will accompany you for your safety, of course."

Lorigan was about to decline but Senteth pressed on, "They are hunting more of my men, a sort of training exercise, if you like, and they may mistake two strange horsemen riding in the woods as them. I would hate for either of them to give you further cause for offence."

The veiled threat, although subtle, was evident even to Grabbit.

Knowing that Senteth would send men to watch him anyway, Lorigan decided that she would like at least some of the men where she could see them. "Very well, will that be for the duration of our visit to the woods or just for today?"

"My Lord as of yet has not given me instruction as to the length of his stay here, but I can assure you that once he and the Prince are ready to leave, then we will leave as well and if you are still in the woods, well then, I am afraid you will have to fend for yourselves."

Lorigan ignored the further attempt to rile her, "How soon may we leave?"

"Eat and drink some coffee first; my men will be ready to escort you in an hour. Does that give you sufficient time to tend to the hawk, your horses and yourselves?"

Ah, a man who puts the care of his animals first, there is much to admire about this human. I wonder how many other men will follow us? Lorigan's mind stayed sharp and focussed on the task at hand; she would need to plan this well. "Yes, plenty of time."

The rabbit stew was good and very welcome for Grabbit, who at the same time longed for some ale to wash it down. It just does not taste the same without ale, he thought as he shook his head and burped. Lorigan ate little, and then picked small morsels of meat off the bone, which when she retired to her horse she fed to the hawk. Grabbit sat alone by the fire, taking little interest in anything bar the stew and the lack of ale. Lorigan returned just before the hour was up; it was close to dusk now, the sun low over the west, the shadows stretching out in its wake as the clouds turned from grey to pink, lending a false sense of colour and warmth to the world that would soon recede to darkness and cold.

"Listen well, human," she spoke in hushed tones, keeping her gaze away from Grabbit. "Carry on cleaning your plate."

Grabbit looked down with puzzlement at the tin plate he had eaten off, which now lay on the grass beside him. He had not intended to clean it, but now dutifully picked it back up whilst ripping some grass up with his other hand. He now proceeded to wipe the plate, smearing its contents with the grass over the surface and across his hand. He was concentrating now, trying to hear Lorigan, his tongue stuck out of his mouth subconsciously, a sure sign that his attention was now entirely on her.

"When we enter the woods I have a task for you. My hawk needs a special herb for her wing to heal properly. This herb only grows in the land of the Fey; a land which I cannot enter at the moment. You will need to gain entry and retrieve the herb for me. I will tell you how after we enter the wood."

Grabbit was still mindlessly wiping the plate with the grass long after Lorigan had finished.

Lorigan shook her head; she hoped this brainless human was up to the task, yet still his lack of imagination could work in their favour. It was essential that he believed in the herb though. "You can stop cleaning the plate now."

Grabbit shook his head as if to clear it, pulling his tongue back in now he realised it was hanging out of his mouth, a thin spittle of drool danced down to tickle his chin as he looked down disbelievingly at the plate and grass in his hands. He threw both down to the side as if they were now contagious and wiped his hands on his leggings.

"It is time."

Senteth meanwhile was busy, he had much to plan.

"Sergeant Creaner."

"Yes Sir." They were always more formal around the men.

"Keep your eyes on the stranger, he is dangerous and is not telling us all he knows. There is more to this than just a cure for his hawk, I feel that they are really after something else. I want two of your best men to follow them even after we leave. If Mr Grabbit is involved, it can only be for no good and I trust neither of them. As for the rings, make sure they reach the right people tonight. I want answers by the end of the week or else. Now go!"

Senteth had easily made the same mistake as many before him

in assuming that the stranger due to her ability and demeanour was male.

As Sergeant Creaner turned to leave, Senteth's hand grabbed his shoulder, turning him back towards him, their eyes met. "Be careful, do what you need to do and keep Lord Luxor and the Prince safe at all costs."

Sergeant Creaner nodded, a thin smile escaped from his lips, replaced immediately by his stony expression as he turned and shouted orders to his men.

Grabbit, Lorigan, Creaner and four royal guardsmen rode into Crescent Wood just as the sun, casting a last red streak of light across the darkening sky, dipped below the horizon. The shadows from the trees soon swallowed them up, smothering them into the greyish gloom, whilst off to their right, two men, dressed in black as if themselves mere shadows, drifted into the trees.

Chapter Fourteen

Vangor had spent the next hour trying to ascertain from his sergeant what had happened. The initial cold shock on hearing how Fent had howled and how he had thus been thrown to the ground had now worn off. It explained why he had been carried down the mountain over his horse and why the men had lost their horses, but something was missing. He was sure his sergeant was hiding something from him but he could not work out what it was; he had definitely appeared uneasy in the retelling of the story as if he somehow was embarrassed by something that had happened.

He had spoken to a few of the men after Graint; the stories in essence had all been the same but the men had been even vaguer about some of the events. Some stated that they had seen nothing after the wolf had howled and others appeared unsure who had rescued Vangor and put him onto his horse's back. It all sounded strange to Vangor, but what was of more immediate concern was Fent and the Ancients' Howl. Had he somehow lost it? Had he unwittingly given its power back to the wolf, and if so how? What had he done? He racked his brains but no answer came to him. Would he now still be able to control the wolf and get it to do his bidding or did he now have another problem on his hands? He needed Morkin and the wolves were supposed to fetch him, but he also now had no answer regarding the mages. He knew Fent knew of them; but where he could find them and how? He was now no closer to knowing the answer. He was not certain whether the current campaign would hinge on finding out more about them but he never left anything to chance and he did not want to make a mistake this time. The fact that he knew of their existence now meant that he needed to know if they were a threat.

"Sergeant Graint."

"Sir," the almost instant appearance of his sergeant was typical of the man's ability to predict his lord's needs.

"Send four men into Fennigan Mountain. I want to know what the wolves are doing, where they move to and what their intentions seem to be. I particularly want to know if they see any strange visions in the sky."

If the last part of the order sounded strange to Graint he showed no sign of it. He was good at following orders and keeping his men in line; he left the thinking and strategy to Vangor and if his lord wanted to know if strange things appeared in the sky, then he would ensure that his men would thus report it.

"Sir," he barked in confirmation.

"We move from here in four hours, with or without the horses, though I trust it will be with. Have you sent men to retrieve them? No, sorry, forget that, Sergeant! I know you will have done so. That will be all for now."

The dismissal was final yet Graint lingered on, "Where are we heading, my Lord?"

The look Vangor shot him cut him short and he backed out of the tent, leaving Vangor to his thoughts. A series of barked commands preceded a few discontented groans, an angry shout followed, then a flurry of activity before silence returned.

The four hours flew by for Vangor who spent it going over plan and counter-plan in his head as he used the ground at his feet as a makeshift map, leaves, twigs, sticks and a few piles of earth now marked out what he considered to be the relevant features of the Moon lands over which he now moved stones in what to the casual observer seemed like an entirely pointless random exercise.

His men, as he destroyed the map, busied themselves packing up his tent around him; it was an easy task, the tent a simple construction of poles and animal skins that collapsed quickly and was thus light enough to carry on journeys like this where speed was essential. Graint had recently acquired the tent for Vangor and had insisted on testing its suitability for patrols such as this. Vangor had only once slept in a tent before, it had been early in his military career, an eight-man tent and he had hated the claustrophobia. He had since that time, and even despite his rank, always slept out under the stars or if raining under a makeshift covering. Graint though had been insistent, Vangor thus had reluctantly humoured his sergeant this once and now, having spent an evening in it, in truth he had rather enjoyed the privacy it had afforded him, but he still would not like to spend all of his nights under its shelter.

The men Graint had sent out for the horses had not returned as of yet, and Vangor wore his displeasure openly on his face and his men did their best to avoid him. He was anxious though to get moving and to move quickly, his plan was set in his head and speed was essential with or without the horses. He ordered two men to remain at the site with his horse to wait for the others to return, hopefully, with the horses. He then led the way down the slope at a brisk jog, jumping from rock to rock with the sure-footedness of a mountain goat. Down they travelled over slippery scree and snow, across damp heather and gorse, its purple flowers a welcome sight amongst the endless white, grey and green; never once losing their footing or breaking their stride. The pace was relentless and easily as quick as riding would have been, considering the slippery surface and the steepness of the slope they now descended.

Down and down they went, snaking a path down the mountain, splashing through an icy stream, scooping up and drinking as they did so handfuls of the freezing meltwater that ran down from the snowy peaks that now towered up far behind them.

His men were sweating and breathing hard, yet Vangor appeared as fresh as when they had set off almost two hours ago and still he continued ever down and ever east towards the now imposing gloom of Sarken Wood; its ancient and gnarled trees jutting out into the landscape with an unsightly menace that invoked fear. Trees that were becoming more and more foreboding with each approaching step. The only sound they could now hear was the rushing water of the river Ces that now ran due north of them on a parallel course. Its course now lay hidden from their sight, deep within an ancient ravine, a ravine that Vangor knew would eventually peter out at the easterly edge of Sarken Wood. This along with the river that snaked down around the easterly margin of the woods and the high peaks of Fennigan Mountain to the west meant that the trees they were now heading for were protected on all but the southerly side. Despite the fact the trees lay in the shadow of the great Fennigan Mountain, it seemed as if it were the trees themselves that were producing the darkness, a darkness so complete within that ancient, thick canopy that not even the full glare of the noon's sun could lighten.

Vangor often came to these woods and they were his intended destination now. His men now knew where they were heading and shuddered, knowing full well what awaited them deep within the trees. As they approached the first of the trees, their great branches seemed to reach out to envelop them like grizzled, gnarled arms intent on drawing them within, on welcoming them and their shadows. Shadows which now cast out behind them in the last of the visible light seemed to falter in fear as if afraid to join their owners in the impending darkness of the woods. Vangor stopped unexpectedly; he signalled Graint to join him and after a brief one-sided discussion they continued into the trees, leaving two relieved men at the place where they had entered.

The first strides into the trees were the hardest; the almost complete blackness was only tinged with the dark greys of the trees around them. The silence seemed to suck at their senses, heightening the sense of foreboding; no insects, no birds and now no sound of the river, which only a few paces before had been a distant roar of water rushing over the bottom of its ravine. Yet the worst part of entering the woods was the thick undergrowth that grew around the margins where just enough light seemed to penetrate and facilitate the growth of brambles and thick nettles which were as tall as them. These now tugged, scratched, stung, pulled and tore at them, tearing their clothes and their skin. Vangor though seemed oblivious to them as he hacked and slashed, pulled and pushed his way through with a single-mindedness that made the effort look easy. His men followed in his wake, anxious not to lose sight of him, something easily done in their black uniforms which blended into the darkness within strides.

Eventually the going became easier, another natural boundary breached and they came out onto clearer ground. Vangor stopped for a moment, seemingly peering into the darkness all around him. Dark indistinguishable shapes seemed to move with each blinking of an eye, only to be still when looked at directly as if frozen on sight. A distinct smell of rotting vegetation hung nauseatingly in the air, accompanied by a dampness that had already within seconds soaked them to the skin. Seemingly somehow happy with their direction of travel, Vangor set off again, never once looking behind him or counting his men. His philosophy in such matters had always been that if they could not keep up with him or look after themselves then they were of no use to him and he was best rid of them.

The ground very quickly became wet under foot. One step onto damp, springy moss and the next was into ankle-deep water. No word was spoken between them but each man now followed in each others' exact footsteps, all coming behind careful not to stray from the path Vangor now trod.

A large splash, followed by a series of small frantic splashes and then a deep gurgling noise broke the silence momentarily. Graint, his job always to bring up the rear, jumped forward, filling the space that the new man only moments earlier had occupied in front of him. Nobody broke stride, nobody looked back, they followed each other, all aware that death was only a wrong footing away on either side. A dim, green light shone briefly through the trees, marking their destination, its appearance met with relief amongst his men. They were getting closer and the light was now slowly chasing back the darkness, forcing it to change from black to dark green and gradually, ever so gradually, it would lighten further, turning the trees around them rather perversely, thought Vangor, from grey to black in the now green-tinged air. The water of the swamp was now visible, appearing dark and oily all around them. Their silhouettes distorted grotesquely into dark shadows on its surface as they leapt between the grassy tussocks that lay concealed beneath the black liquid surface; their existence only betrayed by a few long blades breaking through the water's surface.

As they grew nearer still, the green light seemed to spread in wisp-like tendrils that stretched up from a hidden source beneath the ground, weaving their way up into the surrounding trees. At first the tendrils were sporadic and few in number, seemingly inviting them, luring them into their midst, and as they followed, walking in-between the green light, the tendrils slowly became more numerous, and before they noticed, they were walking between web-like walls of green that stretched up into the trees on both sides of them. The walls now also closed in on them, leaving only enough space between them to walk in single file. They were thus shepherded in a line first one way and then the next, the walls randomly, it seemed, barring passage between some trees and allowing it between the next.

The result of which kept them twisting and turning through a maze of light that was becoming brighter and more intense the further they ventured. The tendrils up close looked thin and weak, yet none of the men tested their strength, keeping well clear of them almost as if desperate to avoid contact. There were five of them now, Vangor still striding out in front, confident of his route, not that he had much choice, and Graint still bringing up the rear; he too felt comfortable at the moment, pleased with himself and the effortless ease with which he had taken care of one of his potential problems. Of the five of them left, only one was a new man, the tall figure of Pailnt, he now walked directly behind Vangor. His fate would have to wait as his sword might yet be needed but Graint, if the occasion arose and it was safe enough to do so, already had plans for him.

As they continued deeper and deeper into the maze of light, the light itself seemed to be developing a pulse; at first it went unnoticed, a mere trick of the light but now it was definitely growing brighter and dimmer with an unerring regularity that was disconcerting to watch, as if the web of tendrils were itself alive. The tendrils stretched upwards and now that the light was brighter, where before they had disappeared into the all consuming darkness, they could now see the lower branches and leaves of the trees that towered at least fifty feet above them, the green tendrils snaking around them before again disappearing into the dark grey canopy. The overall effect of looking up into the sea of pulsating light and shadows that stretched out to oblivion made them nauseatingly dizzy and did nothing to reassure them.

They had no real idea of how long they had been in the woods or the maze of light. With no sun or moon visible as an indicator they could only guess but it seemed as if they had been battling their way through the swamp for hours, and Graint knew that, at the earliest, they would not exit the woods until well after night had returned. He was getting hungry though, and his legs were aching from the constant strength-sapping leaps they had to do between each concealed grassy tussock. Although he had been here twice before he still did not know how much further they needed to go; each time the route seemed familiar yet different, the maze never appearing to have the same route twice. Everything around him looked exactly the same now, the constant green walls with their pulsating light and the constant dark pool they waded through. The only reference point for their progress being the growing height of the walls either side of him which marked their journey deeper into the depths of the Wraights' territory. He shuddered with the thought, remembering their first encounter with them four full seasons before, yet Vangor seemingly trusted them now, despite what had happened. He though would never feel comfortable or at ease in their domain.

They turned round another bend to the right, the walls as they did so opened out, finally and much to their relief it seemed as if they were going to be given room to safely move. They stepped over the fallen tree trunk that lay across their path, and then suddenly, their relief fading, they stopped. The way ahead was blocked by a third wall of light. They could not have taken a wrong turning, there had been no junctions for them to choose from, their only option the path the Wraights had chosen for them and now this path was barred.

Vangor looked around for a second or two and then, seemingly satisfied, returned to the fallen tree trunk and sat down. With unspoken commands and practised drills, the three other men apart from Graint spread out around the trunk, each finding somewhere dry to perch, each facing outwards, each guarding their lord, all watchful and alert, but still taking the moment to slake their thirsts from their water skins.

Graint sat beside Vangor and offered his skin to him. Vangor took it and drank deeply before returning it to Graint.

"Did you manage to acquire something suitable?"

"I did."

"You know what must be done." Vangor with the words swung his hand towards the wall of light directly in front of them.

"I don't know if it will be enough, remember the first time and the nex …"

"Sergeant Graint!"

Vangor needed to say no more, he very rarely emphasised Graint's rank, but when he did it was a sure sign that any further debate or discussion would not be tolerated. Vangor never needed to shout or raise his voice; he had Graint for that, so as always the words were spoken and they still carried an unmistakable clarity of meaning.

Graint hauled his pack off his back and proceeded to rummage about in it as if looking for something in particular. Eventually he pulled out an object about the size of his fist, which was wrapped in a muslin sheet. He looked up, calling over to Pailnt as he did so.

"No, Sergeant, you do it."

The words were unexpected but Graint hid his shock well, his only reaction to pause for a second as Pailnt looked over at him questioningly.

"Never mind, as you were."

Pailnt shrugged his shoulders and settled back onto the grassy mound he had found three paces away. Graint returned his attention to the wrapped package in his hand; he looked down at it and then over at the wall of light in front of him. As he approached it, the wall seemed to sense his presence, the pulsing light within it growing faster as his hand stretched towards it, its pace now quickening seemingly in time with that of his own heartbeat which now raced in his chest. Sweat stung at his eyes as he unwrapped the sheet of muslin to reveal a heart. It was the heart of a newborn lamb and had been cut from its chest within an hour of its birth, three days before. He had, ever since their first visit here, learned to always carry something of this sort with him just in case they returned. His hand was shaking as he reached out, he had to take a deep gulp of air to steady his nerves and then concentrate hard on his hand just to steady it. A low buzzing noise was now coming from the tendrils of light. Its pulse was now beating so fast that its light flickered past his eyes and seemed to occupy many areas along the tendril all at the same time. Its light now blending into one continuous presence that was both there and also not, at the same time becoming a mere ghost of an image that was merging and re-emerging, like the wings of a humming bird in flight quicker than the eye could take in.

He steadied his hand finally, his heart though as it galloped along with a thunderous beat felt like it would explode. His mouth was dry, yet sweat ran freely along his brow. He eased his hand gently into the space between two thin tendrils, carefully making sure his hand avoided all contact with them, subconsciously he held his breath as he did so. Now slowly, ever so slowly, his palm facing upwards, he raised his hand and, as gently as a butterfly's kiss, he touched the lamb's heart against the closest tendril of light. A mixture of emotions washed over him then. Fear, anxiety and relief. Relief that he had avoided contact with the tendrils so far, anxiety and fear because nothing had happened. The buzzing, a low drone like a hive of bees, continued at the same pitch. The lights continued to flicker at the same speed, constantly chasing each other up the thin tendrils to the distant canopy above. His hand, though still at the moment, was only so through great willpower; he longed to pull it away, scared of what he knew could happen.

The change was subtle at first. The heart started to change colour slowly as if the new colour were seeping into its surface, like dye onto a wet fabric. The veins in the heart changed first, from the black-red colour of dried blood, they gradually became lighter, then brown and slowly dark green and then finally light green, now matching the colour of the tendrils. Now that the veins had changed, the colour seeped outwards and inwards, into the flesh and the muscle, the change now quicker, more urgent, until the whole heart was now the same light green colour. And then it began to beat, a slow rhythmical beat, and the beat of the light now slowed to join it. It looked and felt to Graint that the dead heart on his hand was now controlling the pulses of light. It moved and thumped on his hand as if it were alive again. The bile rose in his throat, he gritted his teeth and swallowed, he was dying to look away, but knew he had to watch. He knew he had to pull his hand free at just the right moment.

That moment came suddenly, one moment the heart was there, beating on his hand and the next it was gone, seemingly absorbed into the light; he pulled his hand out quickly and carefully, glad now to be free, looking at his hand all over, frantically checking for any sign of green colouring. He half ran, half staggered away from the wall of light, back to where Vangor sat, watching him. He sat down in a daze, wiping sweat from his eyes before gulping down some water from his skin, wishing it were something stronger.

They sat and watched the wall, Vangor and Graint. The seconds dragged into minutes which then seemed to drag on yet further. The light eventually slowed, becoming a single slow pulse, a pulse that wound its way steadily upwards along each tendril at the same speed but at different intervals, one tendril's light would be at the ground whilst another's would be halfway up and yet another's near the top and others at various points in-between, the area around them becoming darker again as a result of the now dimmed light.

Graint looked at Vangor expectantly but Vangor still seemed content to wait, and Graint did not at the moment feel able to voice his concerns or opinions. Finally Vangor stood. Each light was now taking a little over a minute to travel from the ground in front to the top of its tendril. He approached the mesh-like structure which formed the wall in front of him, each tendril twisting around and intertwining with its neighbour as they ascended up to the heights. He waited, watching closely, choosing a particular point in the mesh where two pulses of light seemed to float upwards in neighbouring tendrils at roughly the same time. After they passed he grabbed the tendrils, one in each hand and pulled them apart, their surface felt moist and slightly sticky to his touch but each contained a hidden strength and rigidity that made the task more difficult and strength sapping than it looked. Once satisfied though that the gap was large enough, he very carefully stepped through, allowing the tendrils once through to spring back and close the gap behind him.

He left the others to come through at their own judgement and he walked forward a few paces and looked around. The area he was now standing in was covered in a light green springy moss which, after wading through the black swamp water for what seemed an age, was soft and welcome under his feet. There was sufficient light around now to see colours about him, a welcome tapestry of greens and browns as if he had just emerged from a world of sepia into technicolour. The light took the form of a soft yellow, almost whitish ambience that seemed to radiate out of various stones placed around the area he was standing in. Two clear lines of these stones lit up a path between them that led off in front of him to a structure that was built between two large tree trunks. From this distance it resembled a small hill of grass, only distinguishable as a building by the doorway in the surface that faced him. The door stood open and there was a figure standing there just visible in its doorway; the figure though seemed to float in and out of vision, depending on how you looked at it, appearing and disappearing at whim as if a mirage. If he stared directly at the figure, the doorway appeared empty, it was as if the figure just vanished, but when he looked at either of the tree trunks to the side of the building, the figure would then float back into his peripheral vision, only to once again vanish if he tried to return his attention to it.

Other paths branched off from the main one in front of him and led off in various directions towards the trees; these were narrower though and lit on only one side by the stones. As Vangor looked around, he counted another twenty figures in his peripheral vision;

they always seemed to appear after he had just looked directly at the area in which they stood, never before, as if the very act of staring at them and then looking away was the only way by which you could detect their presence. All the figures appeared to be stationary, as if they in turn were watching him. He was equally as sure that there would be others around that he had not been able to detect or had missed.

As he stood surveying the scene he was joined by two of his men, both of whom looked around with a mixture of initial awe and uncertainty. They both slowly relaxed though on seeing that their leader was seemingly unperturbed by the shadowy figures that they could see, and yet at the same time could not.

Graint followed moments later which was slightly strange, but Vangor thought little of it as he was followed almost immediately by the tall figure of Pailnt, who seemed to stumble and half trip his way through, such was his eagerness and evident fear of the pulsing light. He landed face first on the soft moss with a dull thud, pushing Graint forward as he did so. Vangor ever alert turned around fully on hearing the noise behind him and saw one of his new recruits lying on the ground with his left foot still stuck in the wall; his foot appeared to have been caught by a tendril that had snapped back and twisted around it at about knee height above the ground. A quick glance upwards and he just caught sight of the tendril's dim light above as it faded from view, a new brighter light appeared immediately at the base and started its ascent.

"Free him." The urgency in his voice sparked an immediate response from his men as they rushed forward. One pulled his sword free and swung it at the tendril in an indiscriminating, scything arc designed to sever not only it but many others. The sword clanged against hard steel though as it met, a fraction before the tendril, Graint's sword. Graint backhanded the off-balance man with his left hand, sending him flying backwards with the blow onto his bottom. The other man grabbed Pailnt's leg and pulled and lifted and twisted, trying desperately to free it as the light crept ever closer. Pailnt had now seen the light and started to panic, fighting against his comrade who was trying to help, kicking out, screaming, tearing at the moss which, such was his eagerness to get away, came up in big wet clumps in his hands.

Graint surveyed the scene and then strolled over. With one punch onto the side of his chin he knocked Pailnt senseless and his outstretched limb immediately became limp and malleable. His comrade lifted the leg again and eased it at what seemed an impossible angle through the entwined tendril, the pulse of light brushed gently against Pailnt's boot as his leg was pulled free.

Graint looked over at Vangor, who nodded.

"Remove his boot quickly and be careful not to touch the skin."

The Dark Knight that Graint had knocked to the floor picked himself up and came over to pull Pailnt's boot off. This was no easy task as they came up to his mid calf and had laces across the top to secure them tight. They were not standard issue boots, but Vangor's guard had very little equipment that was of standard issue. Each and every soldier under his command was allowed to wear what they preferred as long as the colour remained black and it had his emblem of a red raven emblazoned somewhere on the breast of either the plate, tunic or cape.

The boot eventually came free accompanied by a low sucking noise, the result of spending half the day wading through a swamp. Graint quickly examined the boot and then tossed it over towards Vangor, who was now once more facing the path with his back towards them; he glanced down at the boot.

"His small toe!!! And bind it well."

Graint grunted his agreement; having come to the same conclusion and anticipating the order, he already had his pack off his back and was now laying out the tools he needed.

"Hold his leg well," he commanded as he stood up. "Here, hold this until I ask for it." His men were well trained and very experienced but neither of them knew what was going on here; this did not stop them obeying his commands without question though, even if they were nervous.

He carried over a thin flexible piece of wire that was anchored at each end, to serve as handles, with a piece of thick wood about the length of his palm. Graint twisted the wire into a loop and very carefully so as not to touch the foot himself, he eased the wire over the small toe, pulling down on it until it hit the webbed space of the foot. He glanced over quickly at Vangor, who was still facing the other way, seemingly concentrating on something else; he looked at the two men helping him, who each returned his glance with the blank looks of trusting unconcern.

Will we need him later? He thought again as he looked at the toe, pondering his moment. He pulled on both ends of the wire together in a swift, rapid but controlled manner. The toe fell to the ground, small spasms in the muscles and tendons making it twitch faintly for a disbelieving second before its reality dawned on it and it was still. The blood oozed out, running down the foot, bright and red, almost frothy, dripping onto the wet moss, tainting it with a dark stain. Graint was handed the powder, before asking, which he then sprinkled onto the raw wound, he pulled out the muslin sheet from his pocket, sprinkled more powder onto it and then placed it directly onto the wound.

"Bind it tight, then you stay with him. When he wakes, give him this and wait here for our return."

He turned to the other soldier, the one who had held the powder, "You, come with me."

Chapter Fifteen

Earlier that morning, high up in Fennigan Mountain, amongst the trees of Fennigan Forest, a mist had settled during the night and was still clinging to the land, its pale grey fingers winding through the trees. Visibility was down to less than three paces, but Pareen and Neas had the scent now. They had noticed it almost three hours earlier, a faint tantalising and alarming scent that had been carried to them on a circling breeze, a breeze that had changed direction constantly. It had been difficult to trace the scent, many hours spent halfway up the mountain, slowly padding over the rocky landscape. They had had to change direction on numerous occasions, retracing their steps, it seemed, as often as the gentle breeze had changed its own course. It had seemed at the time to be teasing them with the faint elusive promise of their prey, their enemy, men on their land and then just as they had finally thought they had the scent it would change direction again to come at them anew, carrying again seemingly impossibly the exact same scent but now from a different direction. But now at last they had it. It was strong now and close, the surrounding mist which hid them from the sight of their prey played into their paws, they could smell man and he could not see them coming.

Neas pulled away to his left as they closed the distance, the men were now less than twenty paces away and at last they could hear their hushed movements. Four of them, heading back up the slope, heading south. The direction of the breeze changed again, becoming blustery, briefly gaining strength, able now to pull at clumps of the thick mist, revealing for brief seconds little pockets of terrain around them, before once again dying down, allowing the mist to slip from its grasp, to descend back once again into a complete blanket. The scent of man had again disappeared, replaced as the breeze carried Neas's scent down to Pareen in its stead, the difference remarkable and welcome, a sweet familiar warming scent of damp fur that was mixed with Neas's own individual aroma, an aroma he knew well and took great comfort in. The men in front of them by contrast had a smell as opposed to a scent, a bitter smell, a concoction of smells; sweat, tobacco, a mixture of animal smells, mainly horse, and the smell of dirt, not the clean sort, all thrown together and then in turn mixed with the human's own scent, a smell which to Pareen's sensitive nose was overpoweringly nauseous. These men were not locals, their smell differed, and if they were here tracking them, they had much to learn about the Wolves of Fennigan. Sure, they were light of foot and had been difficult to find and he had no doubt they would be good at tracking other humans, but the Wolves of Fennigan they would now find to their cost were different. He hoped though that they would not learn too quickly. He could scent Neas moving slowly up on his left, he matched his pace, closing on the men slowly, fifteen paces, ten paces. The mist was tugged away briefly from the slope, and for a tantalising second the terrain that lay ahead revealed itself.

Their eagerness was also their mistake. They were two against four and although they were big and powerful, these were soldiers, knights, some of the best in Vangor's own guard. The two wolves in their eagerness and inexperience both burst out of the trees at the same time, both now going for the same man at the rear of the group. He spun round with a frightening speed as he heard the noise of breaking branches accompanied by the low snarling of the wolves behind him. He saw two huge grey shapes hurtling towards him from either side.

Pareen and Neas realised their mistake immediately, but it was now too late, they were both mid leap and both closing on the same prey. The man was good, he was quick, he had his sword half drawn from its scabbard when Neas hit him on his right. Neas's teeth sank deep into the muscle and flesh, striking down to the bone, with a sickening crunching noise. With one powerful wrenching motion of his head, Neas ripped the man's arm free of its socket, sending a crimson fountain of blood that arced upwards and outwards, spurting out from the severed artery and painting the leaves, branches and grass around with a deep, dark red. His cries of pain, if they were coming, had no time to form as Pareen caught the man's throat in his powerful jaw, ripping away as he did so the windpipe and with it half of the neck less than a second later. A startled look in the man's eyes preceded his head flopping backwards, now only held on by the loose tissue at the back of his neck.

Both wolves crashed into each other as the man slumped lifelessly to the ground beside them. Pareen's vision was momentarily clouded in a red sheen as he tried to blink the man's blood from his eyes. A sword cut through the air over his head, its shine as it came just enough warning, giving him time to avoid its blow by ducking his head beneath it. Sensing rather than seeing an opportunity, Pareen lunged forward, heading for the midriff of the man in front of him as his sword, whistling harmlessly through the air, continued on its unchecked arc. The thump of a hard metal shield on his nose stunned him, making his eyes water, the tears, though helping to clear the blood, still made it difficult to see through; he yelped out in pain. He backed away. Three figures in front, distorted through his tears, now all facing them, two slightly to the front of the one. The one seemed to be holding something out in front of him in one hand and pulling at it with his other.

Neas barked a warning, "Pareen, move …" It came too late.

Realisation dawned on him as the arrow struck, driven hard from only three to four paces away, it hit his left shoulder, driving deep into his chest. He felt as if his chest was on fire, it sucked at his breath, it stopped him moving his head to the left, the last few inches of the shaft protruded out of him, only the feathers of the flight were still visible. He slumped forward onto his left side as his leg gave way, he could not believe it, he tried to stand again but his leg held no power, he became aware of a ferocious feral growl from his left and saw the huge grey shape of Neas charge at the men. He tried to command his friend to retreat, but no sound came. It now took all his effort just to breath, a great sucking noise from his chest accompanying every attempt, as bright red bubbles frothed up around the shaft of the arrow.

The men were momentarily stunned by the ferocity and power of Neas's attack; they were driven back as the great wolf in front of them moved from left to right with a speed and power that negated their efforts to attack it. They were forced to defend, to protect themselves, knowing that if they stayed together they would be safe and that the wolf would eventually tire. Yet at the same time they had to fight against their own fear that was rising in the face of such savagery; the great, white, blood-tinged fangs, the burning hate in its eyes, the huge powerful legs that were tipped with strong sharp claws. The beast was in a blood rage and they had seen the ease with which it had killed their comrade.

Their instincts told them to run; only their training now keeping them alive. They stabbed forward with their swords more to keep the wolf at bay than any attempt to attack. One of the men got lucky as his sword bit into flesh, his pleasure short-lived though, as the jaw of the wolf whipped round the pommel of his sword and bit into the hand. The sword dropped free from his grip as the tendons were severed by the wolf's teeth along the lateral side of his wrist. He pulled his hand back, as the wolf itself shook its head, tearing more of the flesh free with its jaw. His hand was still attached, a great rip of flesh missing though, exposing the bone, and his thumb was now useless as it hung limply at the side, unable to move. He swore. Neas had a small cut to his shoulder, it was not deep though and had already started to clot.

Only two swords now faced him, the man with the bow now having to use his sword instead in the face of Neas's aggression. Neas knew he could not keep up his attack for much longer; as powerful and strong as he was, his muscles were now crying out for oxygen and he could feel them tightening up. He knew this area of the forest well and he had wanted to drive them further back, perhaps another ten paces or so, on to and over the hidden cliff behind them. But he knew he no longer had the strength to do so and was now anxious to return to Pareen. He still wanted the man with the bow though, he wanted to rip his hands off and then close his jaw over his throat. At the moment the bow was hanging over the man's shoulder, down his back, still strung. He hated it more than the man himself, yet he was slowing, he could feel it and soon they would see it, soon they would have the advantage again, and then, forced to leave Pareen to them, he would have to run from them and the bow.

The men, unknown to him, had also had enough; they wanted away from the wolf. They were anxious to report to Vangor; only one would now make that journey and it would have to be their injured comrade. The other two did not relish following the pack, not now having seen at first hand the ferocity of these animals. The man with the bow knew he could no longer use it, the string was too wet having soaked in the damp misty air, it was now useless and would snap if drawn; he had others but he might have more need of them later.

They could see wisdom in the wolf, it knew it was tiring and they knew it would soon leave. When it did so they would make their retreat swift, helping their comrade as far as they could, knowing his survival in the mountains would rely on their speed. Vangor would need the information they carried, he would need to know where the wolves were heading.

Neas knew it was now or never. He put one last huge effort into an attack that was never meant to drive home. He lunged forward, pulled back and lunged again. The three men took a step backwards; it was the moment he had waited for. He hoped the opening would lead him to safety and back to Pareen. His change in movement was quick, one moment he was moving forward and the next he leapt over the low bush to his left that he had seen coming and hoped would give him enough cover for his retreat. He kept low, travelling fast, expecting the arrows to follow him as he darted between the trees, his soft belly fur was torn out in small clumps as he caught it on the fallen branches and undergrowth that littered the floor. The men though were also going. They had turned in relief barely seconds after he had jumped over the bush and were now running up the slope away from him. Both parties disappeared from each other's view within twenty paces, all absorbed back into the now clearing remnants of the mist.

Pareen was still alive, but barely, his chest rising and falling gently, desperately, despite the great gulps of air he was sucking in. The left side of his coat was soaked in red sticky blood which dripped down, pooling onto the rock beneath him, staining it a dark reddish-black. Neas had no problem finding his friend, the smell of blood was thick in the air and would very soon attract the scavengers and predators of the forest. He licked at the wound, staring lovingly and sadly into Pareen's eyes, hoping desperately in his heart that he would be able to repair the damage, yet knowing it was already too late.

"H-h-help …" The words came as a sigh barely louder than the breeze.

Pareen mistook the words for a cry of assistance, a plea for life and was about to reply.

"H-h-help F-F-F-Fent k-k-kill …," Pareen again struggled for the breath to form the words he was desperate to speak, "Vangor," he panted at last.

"I will help kill Vangor and I will do it for Fent, but the bowman, him I kill for you. His scent can now never hide from my vengeance."

Pareen tried to lift his head to look at his friend, but lacked the strength so looked at him with eyes that now only contained a husk of the life that had once burnt within them.

"T-t-thank you … my f-f-f-friend …"

Neas met his gaze, holding it, wanting his friend to remember his strength.

"Wait for me in the stars, my friend."

A last sigh of air escaped from Pareen's mouth and his eyes became dark and lifeless. Neas lifted his head to the heavens and howled, not the majestic powerful howl of the ancients, that could only be sung by Fent, but the death cry of his race, an unmistakable eerie howl that sung as one of pain, love and loss. It rang out over the trees, coursing over the mountain slopes, a short sharp bark as opposed to the howl of the ancients, a cry of despair as opposed to a howl of passion and pride.

It was answered in seconds, the howl echoing back across to him, down into the valley and out into every hidden gulley. It became a chorus as first one wolf and then another continued the cry, until the whole pack, it seemed, could be heard across Fennigan Mountain, singing Pareen's lament. The men heard it too. It seemed to chase them up the slope, hastening their flight as they now scrambled over rocks and loose stones, creating a mini avalanche that sped down the slope in their wake. It sounded to the men like the whole pack of wolves were now chasing them. Their howls now coming at them from every direction apart from the slope that lay ahead, thankfully this was the direction in which they were travelling. The men, so normally controlled and disciplined, were now in full unashamed flight, their swords were sheathed and banged and clattered heavily against their legs and the rocks around, limiting their movement, slowing their progress and it crossed their minds briefly at one point to discard them, such was their state of anxiety and fear.

Slowly the cries died down, melting into the mist and trees they had left far behind and below them. Their pace though still continued swiftly upwards until at last they reached the ridge they had occupied the night before. All three slumped to the ground, breathing heavily, no longer able to keep going at the moment, feeling that at last they were reasonably safe but at the same time too exhausted from exertion to care.

<hr />

Neas padded around Pareen's now still body. Blood continued to ooze out of the wound, but any movement had long since died away. The ground where he lay was rich with his scent, his bladder had emptied in death, the contents soaking into the soil to mark the spot of his demise. A fox had poked its head out of the scrub earlier, enticed by the smell, but on seeing Neas it had vanished again, at least for the moment. Neas was in two minds about what to do; Pareen was Fent's younger half-brother and as such he should be told by him how he had died. But Neas did not want to leave his friend on his own even for a second. He knew that if he did so the fox and the other scavengers would come and pick at his dead body. It was not that Neas minded his friend's body being a meal for others, that was the way of life in a forest, it was that Pareen deserved to be mourned and seen by his family in an unsullied state before that happened.

He decided to wait and risk Fent's wrath if the decision was wrong. His friend's honour was more important to him at the moment; he was sure that Fent would understand, so he lay down beside his life-long friend, feeling against his own fur, for the final time, the last of his warmth as he waited.

It was Fent himself who found them first; earlier that day he had heard of the humans' presence in the forest and as a result he had posted extra sentries and sent his patrols out further into the forest. He had been circling through the trees around the main pack on one such patrol, taking his turn, despite the pain in his left shoulder, as a roving sentry as they all moved south. The cry had sent a further chill down his back when he heard it. He had at the time of its call been drinking from a fresh mountain stream, lapping the icy cold water with relish, enjoying its refreshing taste and the chill that had cooled his hot body from deep within. His ears had immediately pricked on hearing the cry, a sense of foreboding creeping over him; he did not repeat it. That was the task of others. He had just set off at a run, seeking its origins. He headed north, sure that that was the direction it had originated from.

The smell of blood had hit him from over a mile away, fresh blood carried on the blustering breeze. Human and wolf blood, the aroma of each distinct yet similar, the component parts much the same, only the subtle differences in the quantities of each affecting the scent and allowing him now to identify each.

He ran fast, leaping over rocks, bushes and fallen trees in easy powerful bounds, his leg stiff and sore but equal to the task, his nose now guiding him to the destination, following a distinct path that was very clear to him yet invisible to the eye. He burst into the clearing, seeing the man first and gave him little more than a cursory glance, before he saw Pareen and Neas lying so tightly together it appeared at first as if they were one. At first sight he was unable to discern which of them was injured; such was their combined stillness on the ground, that his heart missed a beat, as the unimaginable thought of both of them being dead entered his head.

A lump rose in his throat as Neas saw him and stood. He swallowed. His relief at one of them being alive was tempered slightly by the fact it was Neas and not Pareen that now stood. He crossed over to the bedraggled form of the young wolf who, as he approached, looked away seemingly unable to meet his questioning eyes.

Neas felt sick, he felt like he was shaking from the inside. He had hoped it would be anyone but Fent who came first. In fact he never imagined it would be Fent; the thought had never occurred to him and now he was here he had no words for him, he knew if he tried they would only stick in his throat, and he felt ashamed enough as it was. They had failed, they had attacked the men without waiting, they had fought well, but ultimately they had failed; Pareen was dead and three men still lived. It mattered not how fiercely he had then fought and driven the men away. Nobody had seen that. The facts were there in front of him, lying at his feet, his friend and Fent's brother lay dead and now Fent was here to judge him.

He was sick; the thoughts had added to his despair and turned his stomach against him, it now spilt its brown bile out of his mouth, he coughed and spluttered, ashamed of himself yet again.

Fent seemed not to notice; his eyes took in the scene around him, the arrow shaft protruding from deep within his brother's chest and a wolf little older than a cub that had fought in battle and lost a friend, yet still stood beside him, waiting to honour him. He padded back over to the fallen man, looking briefly at the arm lying apart from him and his throat that had been ripped out. He went back into the trees, examining the trunks and the low undergrowth. He saw the broken branches on each side of the man, he understood, he blamed himself, he raised his head and howled, a short, sharp barking cry to honour his brother. Neas, hearing it, steeled himself and took up the cry, echoing it, relief seeming to wash over him as he did so.

Fent crossed over to him, looking deep into his eyes which this time he felt able to meet, and then unexpectedly Fent lowered his head and licked Neas; a long, tender, caring lick. The sort of lick a mother gives a newborn cub, a lick that said more to Neas than words ever could. Neas nuzzled into Fent's fur, for the moment a cub again, thankful for the gesture, a great feeling of warmth and love flowing over him and being shared between them in a private mourning for their friend and brother.

The questions could wait, Fent thought, he already knew there were four men and now three. He knew, even without the red raven emblem that was emblazoned on the man's tunic, that they were Vangor's men. One more reason now to kill the man, he thought. He bent his head down to Pareen's still body, gripped the arrow shaft between his teeth, tasting the salty, almost metallic blood that was soaked into it, and slowly using his strong neck muscles, he twisted and pulled. He used his front paws to anchor down Pareen's body and give him leverage; the shaft slowly eased its way out, bright jelly-like clumps of blood sliding out with it and slithering onto the ground. It took over five minutes of exhausting effort and patience to get the whole arrow out. Neas had offered to help but Fent had declined; he had to do it himself and by the time he was done, his muzzle and front paws were as red and matted with blood as they would have been had he dined on a fresh carcass.

Other wolves arrived, at first in ones or twos which soon became a steady trickle; the news had spread quickly and the packs, in particular Fent's own pack, were all anxious to pay their respects to a wolf who had been popular and well liked by all.

Up on the mountain ridge the three men now parted, their injured comrade the happier of the three as he headed east away from the

Wolves of Fennigan, back towards his lord, Vangor. The other two remained on the ridge, watching him with more than a little envy as he disappeared down the far side. They waited on the ridge for another hour as the sun climbed the sky, warming their cold bodies with its strong rays. They saw no sign of any wolves following and decided that their comrade was as safe now as they could make him. Their descent back down to the trees was slower than their ascent had been, their reluctance to get too close again to the pack slowing their steps despite the easier downhill going. Duty drove them on though. They knew well that they might not return, both ultimately willing to die for Vangor and the Dark Knights.

Graint stood beside Vangor, blinking at the figure in the doorway, trying in vain yet again to see it properly. It was always like this with the Wraights, even two years earlier when Vangor and he had stumbled across their hidden domain, their coming to the woods then of course no accident. Vangor had heard that none of the locals would enter these woods. The stories of ghosts and foul spirits kept them all away. Vangor was not superstitious and did not believe in such creatures, yet even he had nearly changed his mind when they first saw the Wraights' ghostly appearance. They had lost twelve of their men on that first occasion, twelve men who had simply disappeared, some lost into the black pools of the swamp to a watery, muddy grave as they had battled through, trying to find a safe path. But most though had died in the maze of light, devoured by it as the lamb's heart had been earlier. They had suffered a gruesome death that still made Graint shudder in fear and disgust. He and Vangor had made it to the end of the maze that time with only three of their men still alive. It was then that they had been attacked by the ghost-like apparitions of the Wraights. They had seemed to appear out of nowhere all around them, grabbing their men and dragging them away through the wall of light and beyond. They had fought of course, well, tried to fight back, swinging their swords, slashing into the air around them, cutting through the distorted forms of the apparitions, but their blades were useless, they had had no effect on their assailants, and their men were gone, taken in seconds, their shouts and screams disappearing as soon as they passed through the walls, as if they then had ceased to exist.

Vangor and Graint had prepared themselves then for a similar fate, expecting another attack, praying silently that their deaths would be quick, but at the same time determined to at least try and inflict some pain or injury on their assailants. The anticipated attack though never came; instead the end of the maze had opened, the tendrils forming the wall of light receding back into the ground that time, slowly revealing the land that lay beyond and welcoming their passage unharmed into the area they were now standing in.

Some of the secrets and the hidden power of the tendrils of light and the maze they formed were slowly revealed to them over the next two days. The emptiness of the surrounding trees becoming clear to them, as they discovered the source of the Wraights' power and the part their men's death had played in preserving that power. Vangor though had quickly set his anger aside, seeing immediately the opportunities such power had as a possible weapon to use to his advantage in the coming war, or, at the very least as a trap for the enemy or indeed, if need be, a sanctuary for his men. It soon became apparent that the Wraights had sensed something in Vangor too. They felt that he may be able to help them. They needed life energy, they needed flesh to feed the tendrils that in turn fed them, and after generations of feeding on the life that had lived in the trees, the wood had become barren, they had consumed nearly all of its life and now very little wandered through the trees and into their traps. They were starving, literally fading away, stuck in the woods, dependant on the tendrils for life, unable to leave and find the food which now no longer came to them. No humans dared to come, scared away by the legends and stories of ghosts, and those that were not scared of the stories had no need to come as there was nothing left to hunt or trap within the trees, nearly all the animals, birds and insects having been long since caught and consumed by the Wraights to maintain their now frugal existence.

The bounty of men that Vangor had unwittingly brought to them would sustain their existence for years; they were an intelligent race though and knew that whilst killing and consuming Vangor and Graint would have extended their existence for a further few years longer, they would then once again be stuck in the struggle to survive and left to the mercies of what nature delivered. They had sensed a need in Vangor, a need that they might be able to help fulfil, and they hoped he would in turn be able to help fulfil theirs and that was why Vangor and Graint still lived.

The effect of their men's demise on the Wraights had been instantly evident that day, the ghostly wisps of creatures that they had fought against so ineffectively had become more discernible in shape and substance. The thin transparency of their form had become a milky-green colour, more visible and now contained features which when seen close up were discernible as those of male and female, but as of yet they had not seen any children.

Their appearance still looked fragile though, a smoke-like presence that you would have thought would take a mere deep breath to easily blow away. But they both knew that there was a powerful strength there, a strength which seemed to defy any logic known to Vangor or Graint. This was something Vangor was anxious to learn more about, yet despite this being their third visit, he was still no closer to finding anything out.

They had traded though; the Wraights, it seemed, despite being confined to their woodland home, knew the Moon lands like no other race that had ever lived there. They knew it from the memories and thoughts of the life forces that had been consumed by the tendrils, memories and stories of men and women from all of the races that they had encountered, not to mention the animals, birds and insects and even the plants. Everything that had ever lived and then been consumed by them had a place in their knowledge. Unfortunately, the knowledge and information they possessed was all mixed together; memories, stories, experiences, tastes, smells, textures, sounds and emotions, all blended together with no reference to whom or what they came from or were related to. Like a huge encyclopaedia of knowledge with no index, no categorisation, no pages, no reference, no binding, just words, millions upon millions of words all mixed up and spread out across an unending floor.

The result was that Vangor always received a mixture of information from them that made no sense. Yet despite this he always listened, knowing that somewhere buried within this sea of knowledge lay the answers he needed. It was as if he were with no picture to guide him putting together a large jigsaw puzzle and whilst doing so finding out that someone had also mixed amongst the pieces he required the pieces of another thousand jigsaw puzzles. Graint thought he was wasting his time; he had never been a patient man and he would rather have seen Vangor try to utilise the Wraights' power somehow as a weapon. He imagined arrow tips coated in the power of the green light. Arrows which would then on striking their enemies consume them, which would in turn instil a fear into those that remained that would be impossible to counter; fear as far as he was concerned was what won battles, not useless facts.

The three of them walked forward towards the mound facing them; the figure fading in and out of vision in the doorway as they approached was Skaw, who was, as far as they could tell, the leader of the Wraights. His leadership though was a mere conclusion on their parts, based solely on the fact that ever since they had met he was the only one who ever spoke with them. Drawing closer to him did nothing for his appearance; he became more visible as they approached yet at the same time less so. His form was easier to see, now a deep milky-greenish cloud that hung in the air, shaped into the form of a man, yet everything about him was hard to define. It was as if he had been drawn with chalk on a blackboard and then somebody had taken a cloth to the drawing, everything about him was smudged and blended together, as if something had known the basic shape of a man when they put him together but were uncertain of the finer detail. The arms and torso were difficult to differentiate from each other; they appeared as an inverted triangular shape which blended together with a blob at the top and two oblong shapes that hung below seemingly serving as legs. The milky-greenish cloud seemed to blow around within the loose confines of the shape, changing and distorting the effect as it circled, eddied and flowed like something trapped, seeking an escape. The face though was worse, the eyes and ears seemed to blend into each other, if that was indeed what they were supposed to resemble, giving the effect of a rectangular hole in the centre of the face, the very margins of which extended outside the basic oval blob shape that resembled the face itself. The nose seemed to droop down like a shortened elephant's trunk, obliterating the mouth completely behind it, yet when he spoke the nose shrunk as if being sucked up like a drivel of hanging snot, disappearing almost completely to be replaced by a hole in the face, through which you could see right through to whatever was behind him at the time. It seemed as if the Wraights had assumed this form for them and were not very good at it, almost like a child that was making men out of dough for the first time.

Vangor and Graint had both found it unsettling at first, speaking with such a creature. It had no facial expressions to help them judge the mood of the Wraight and as such they had both been very mistrustful in dealing with it. Both parties though had kept to their ends of the bargain that were struck on that first visit. Every twelve months Vangor had returned with an offering of flesh for them. The size of the offering being in direct relation to its age as, according to the Wraight's, the younger the flesh, the more life power it possessed and it was this that they required to keep them alive. Vangor though wanted to keep the Wraights hungry and weak. He did not want them to have too much power yet, so he deliberately kept the offerings of flesh small and not too young.

He was afraid of their power and of the fact that he did not understand it. He was certain though that if he kept them weak then they would not be able to leave the woods. It was not clear, however, what would happen if they were given a feast of flesh to consume. Would they then be free to leave the trees, to seek out prey for themselves? That was the last thing he wanted; he had enough enemies in these lands as it was and did not want to empower another one. So for now they were in his power and he would keep it that way as long as he could. In return they had promised to tell Vangor all that they knew about anything he desired. They of course could not vouch for the information's accuracy, its source or its age; it would be left to him to decide on any of the information's relevance.

Vangor and Graint carried on through the doorway into the mound, signalling as they did so that the guard should wait outside. They greeted Skaw with a formal nod of their heads and crossed immediately over to the only furniture in the bare room; the same two plain wooden chairs that were always present for them in its centre. They sat down now, facing towards the open door. The room was lit from the centre by a small stone the size of a man's fist that sat on the bare earthen floor, its dull glow throwing out pale light that barely scraped the walls around them and revealed nothing of the ceiling that presumably must have lain somewhere up above them. As they sat the Wraight moved to the space in the doorway and they could now see their men clearly through his mouth as he spoke.

"Inn comee, backk youu welcomee aree. Goodd wass thee offeringg, youngg itt wass," the words, as on previous visits, coming out as a rolling voice that extended the ending of each, dragging it out as if each word needed an immense will of thought and mind to form and speak.

"A newborn lamb, less than two hours old at the time of its death," Vangor lied, the loudness of his own voice as it echoed around in the emptiness of the room took him slightly by surprise. He hushed his voice slightly as he continued, "I have need of information."

"Ourr deall iss ass, Ii telll willl askk andd."

"I have heard tell of a mage who walks these lands. What information do you have of their kind?"

Chapter Sixteen

Lorigan rode over close to Grabbit as they entered a small man-made clearing in the thick trees, the trees there having been chopped down, presumably by the local huntsmen to provide a clear area in which to rest and graze their pack animals. It now served as a welcome respite for Grabbit from the close claustrophobia of the tall trees and narrow paths that they had spent the last few hours negotiating. Thick grass grew wild and unchecked here and was littered throughout with the towering yellow heads of dandelions as they gazed over the sea of green. It was evident the clearing had not been used in many months. Sergeant Creaner and his men had ridden behind them the whole way, always staying within ten paces, and though it looked to the untrained eye that they were disinterested in them, it had been evident to Lorigan that they were listening to every word they spoke and watching their every movement and action. The clearing though now offered her her chance.

She swung her arm out suddenly, hitting Grabbit full on the chest with enough power to send him unsuspectingly flying from his horse and down onto the thick carpet of grass.

"What the …" The words had barely left his lips, when Lorigan jumped astride him, landing full on his chest, driving the air out of his lungs, followed quickly by a ringing, slapping noise as her palm stung Grabbit's cheek, marking it with a red hand print that flushed across his skin.

Before Grabbit could react, slap, the other hand stung across his other cheek. Now his anger rose uncontrollably, spurred on by the ripple of laughter that started with Creaner and quickly spread through his men, until they were all laughing openly at Grabbit's feeble and futile attempts to stop Lorigan slapping him. Slap, slap, slap, a trio of blows in quick succession; Grabbit's face, already reddened by the previous blows, was now turning crimson with anger. His fists swung upwards, trying to connect with the blurred image of Lorigan above him, but she avoided his lumbering blows with ease, moving her body and head left and then right, before once more slapping him again. The pressure on his chest suddenly lifted as Lorigan sprang to her feet; at first Grabbit thought he may have connected with a punch, but all too soon Lorigan was dancing around him, taunting him.

Grabbit reacted as Lorigan had expected. He scrambled to his feet, fixed his eyes firmly on Lorigan and then rushed at her, a wild lunge full of anger and power but lacking in agility and grace; a lunge meant to crush and pummel an opponent, a lunge that Lorigan easily sidestepped, waiting until the last moment and leaving her left leg trailing, she spun around and pushed the off-balance Grabbit over it, sending him sprawling face first into a smelly, putrid puddle of mud and manure. A spluttering, spitting face, covered in thick brown sludge emerged seconds later as he pushed himself onto his hands and knees.

Creaner and his men were now howling with laughter, such was their amusement at Grabbit's fate; a man they all despised now so easily humiliated in front of them. It never entered their minds for a second that it might all have been for a reason.

Grabbit was still spitting the brown mixture from his mouth when Lorigan jumped up onto his back, nearly knocking him back down again such was her force and weight. His arms buckled but he had just enough strength in them to push back, his nose just inches above the surface of the thick smelly mire.

"You leave tonight."

At first he never heard the words, his anger drowning out all sound. A savage pinch on his ear though focussed his mind.

"You leave tonight! Just keep struggling and I will tell you how."

This time the words did register and he nearly slumped forward again as he focussed on them and forgot his predicament.

"The herb I require is Willow Bark. It only grows in the Fey lands."

Grabbit roared out with effort and was rewarded by Lorigan springing off his back. He shot up onto his knees, looking around quickly, a blur of movement to his left, thud, a foot pushed him hard onto his side, accompanied by yet more laughter. He looked up, Lorigan's face was now inches from his own.

"Go with an open heart, my hawk needs it. The boy will show you the way back." The sole of Lorigan's boot pushed his face back down into the grass and then as quickly was gone.

Grabbit lay on the grass, a mixture of emotions coursing through his body: anger, frustration and confusion. Anger at the way he had just been treated, frustration at not being able to do anything about it and, finally, confusion; what boy? Lorigan had never mentioned a boy. I thought I was looking for a herb, where did the boy come from? His anger died slowly, only to be replaced by resentment though and thoughts of revenge. Lorigan had ritually humiliated him and, to make matters worse, she had done it in front of the Royal Guard. Grabbit knew that if the story became common knowledge he would never be able to live it down. All his bravado and dreaming of earlier had now gone, replaced by a morbid dread that tore into his stomach.

He glared over at Creaner and his men, looking each in the eye and seeing their mocking laughter still there. He took his time though, fighting the urge he had to look away, studying each face, committing all to his memory for a later date. Creaner saw the look in Grabbit's eyes. Initially he chose to ignore it, putting it down to injured pride and meeting it with an amused, scornful look of his own. Now though his concern was rising; Grabbit, he knew, was at his most dangerous when cornered. Creaner had seen it before and was now recognising the signs as Grabbit's eyes in turn seemed to bore into each of his men with an unblinking passion and cruelty.

He called his men over and sent them away to opposite ends of the clearing, not to do anything in particular but just to remove them from Grabbit's immediate vicinity in the hope of defusing the situation before it became out of hand. Grabbit watched them. He still sat on the grass and made no effort to move or say anything. Lorigan seemed, to the others, as if she were oblivious to the whole drama that was occurring around her as she tended yet again to her hawk. She was, however, fully aware of what was transpiring behind her and found it all highly amusing. Indeed, the fact that Creaner now seemed determined to keep his men clear of Grabbit worked perfectly for her plan. Humans, she thought, easy to rile and even easier to manipulate. The hawk let out a low screech seemingly as if in agreement with the sentiment, Lorigan immediately rewarding its perception with a morsel of vole she had caught near the stream at the campsite earlier that day.

It would soon be time, she thought, as she looked up to the night sky above as if judging the very quality of its darkness. The sky was dark as pitch, a complete, uninterrupted canvas of black that now blended into the leaves above and around her, creating shapes and forms that seemed to shift and blend into one another, dark sinister nocturnal shapes that were only able to come into being with the setting of the sun. Shapes that could excite your imagination or heighten your fears, shapes that could easily lead you to believe that the trees themselves had come to life and were reaching down for you, shapes that had been old familiar friends of the Fey for generations and would now come to her aid. The trees at night now making Lorigan feel as at home as she ever was going to after her exile, and now, they were going to play the part of the perfect host on the superstitious minds of their human guests.

She found a suitable spot in the clearing; there was nothing special about it but she judged it to be almost perfect for her purposes and now she sat down, crossing her legs and drawing them in close, her back held rigidly straight, her head held still, her arms resting lightly on her lap, palms facing upwards. She closed her eyes and sank into her meditation, slowly emptying her mind of all thought, slow, deep breathing; sucking in great lungfuls of air, deeply and slowly, as if the very act of breathing had become an art form. She sank deeper into herself, her head becoming light as all thoughts were banished. She started to feel the trees around her, their presence now registering in her mind; she stretched her mind out further, reaching out to them, into them and slowly becoming part of them. She could feel the grainy texture, see the layers of wood, feel the wind rustling through her leaves. The first time she had been able to achieve this the overpowering sensations had frightened her and she had had to pull free, but now she welcomed them like an old friend, she embraced them and felt comfortable in their caress.

Slowly the humans around her came into being as her mind became more focussed, more able to detect their presence, all of them appearing in the world within her mind as a faint, red glow of light. Light that represented their souls and that now moved around in her mind's picture of the surrounding woods, matching the movement of their bodies in the real world. Lorigan had never really understood why she could never see the true form of mobile creatures in this world as she could the trees, her education in such matters cut short by her disgrace and exile, but now was not the time to worry about such things.

Her mind's world was now becoming bluey-green in colour, as if seen through an eerie mist. She let her mind wander around the clearing, examining it, looking for the potential. It was nearly time, she was almost deep enough, small red glows were springing to life all around her, an army of insects, the smallest of all the creatures around, now finally visible to her as their glows scurried and crawled across the ground and over the trees around. The effect was stunning, an almost god-like power, she could now see every living creature around her without having to look for it, their presence in this world revealed to her as if by magic; over a million small specks of red, accompanied by six larger red glows representing the men, and now off within the trees, two further large red glows slowly revealed themselves, she had now found the last of the men. And finally the wisps of grey cloud floated into existence, each different and yet each the same, the ghosts and phantoms of all the creatures and races that had died within the trees, each cloud representing a replica of its owner, only now that they were dead could Lorigan see their true form in this world. Fey, human, troll and faerie to name but a few of the many races that now surrounded her. They came accompanied with the many animals and creatures of all description that had at one time resided in the Moon lands, too many to name and a few that she could not. All came floating through the trees, floating through each other, blending into one another only to then reappear again as one. None appeared to have a destination in mind; they seemed to all move randomly and aimlessly as if lost. A great sea of living, dead grey, a mist of souls that clung to the earth in desperate hope, each seeking an unknown sanctuary, an escape from their life in the dreams of the Fey.

Their presence now marked her arrival, she was ready, they were ready, it was now time. She sought out each of the human glows in turn, delving into the light with her mind, tapping into it, savouring it and tasting it. Looking deep within each for its strengths and assessing each for its weaknesses. There was no heat from the glow, yet it stung at her mind, a feeling similar to that of the slow burn of sunburn, the pain she knew would come later, but for now she could control it. None offered much of a challenge and only one managed to momentarily resist her, her power though soon reducing the resistance he had proudly and stubbornly offered to meaningless rubble.

Now satisfied, she picked her target and turned her gaze upwards, pouring her mind forward into the dark canopy above. The leaves started to rustle as the dark shapes took an even more sinister form, the branches creaked in pitiful protest, seemingly crying out in pain, as they were bent to suit her purpose. Lorigan ignored their protests, delving deeper and deeper into their midst, seeking out the shapes she required.

"DRAGON," the word was screamed in fear by one of the men as he looked up into the ever changing sea of dark shapes above and around him. In his mind the dark shape of a dragon leapt out through the trees, its wings bending and breaking the branches in a scream of splintering wood, its body black and sinister as its pure white eyes fixed firmly onto him. Lorigan had been slightly surprised to find this fear amongst the men, as most of them seemed to revere and almost worship the beasts, many aching and longing for their return. The result though now overcame her initial doubts, as the man leapt for cover behind a tree.

"WOLVES," another man shouted almost at once. Now this was a common fear amongst many of the men. Black shapes seemed to prowl around the margin of the clearing, hundreds of red eyes glowing back at the man as he drew his sword.

"DARK KNIGHTS," the shout seemed to carry from further out.

All of a sudden there was panic, fear and action within the clearing. One man was diving from tree to tree, desperately seeking cover from the unseen dragon that relentlessly swooped down on him. Creaner and another of his men had drawn their swords and were now circling around the clearing, dodging, parrying and striking into and at the dark shapes of the unseen wolf pack. Whilst further out, within the trees, two men were now cowering in a small ditch, both desperately trying to hide under the same rotten, fallen tree trunk. They were seemingly surrounded by a hundred or more dark shapes that took the form of an unseen army of Dark Knights which were now hunting for them.

The last man in the clearing was standing, watching with mild confusion and not a little amusement as his sergeant and two comrades seemed to have gone mad. They were either cowering behind trees, or slashing frantically into the trees and undergrowth around them.

"RUN. My arrow is coming for you."

Grabbit, who had also been watching what was happening with smug amusement as the Royal Guard seemingly had lost the plot, all of a sudden felt a cold wave of fear and panic wash over him. An arrow was coming for him. He had seen Lorigan sitting in the middle of the clearing only moments earlier, yet now he could no longer see her. Where is she? Where do I run to? he thought in panic, goosebumps pricked at his skin; he stood up, looking anxiously around him, peering into the dark shapes around, nothing.

"RUN, Grabbit."

The words seemed to light up in his psyche like a burning flame and he ran. Taking off like a startled hare, he crashed through the low branches with the ferocity of a charging bull. He heard the unseen twang of a bowstring in his mind, he ran faster, convinced he could outrun its flight, fear of the pain now driving him.

The last of the guardsmen saw him run. He looked to his sergeant for guidance, but Creaner did not seem to care. He looked at the other two briefly and then made his mind up; he turned and ran after Grabbit.

Creaner had seen Grabbit run. Good, he thought, the wolves will get him. He then also saw his man run; he jabbed hard at the unseen wolf in front of him, splitting its skull in two, yet another leapt immediately into its place, its red eyes the only truly distinguishable feature burning brightly in the darkness. He dragged his companion over into his place, having in his mind bought a mere second of time; he leapt at the fleeing guardsmen. It was one thing for a fat taxman to run but none of his guard would be allowed to flee the danger.

"Coward," he roared, "You will stay and fight, or die by my sword."

The two men collided, bouncing off one another with the force, each thrown to the ground. The young guardsman was stung and hurt more from the accusation of cowardice than the collision. His immediate thoughts now turning to his sergeant, his pursuit of Grabbit for now put to one side.

The collision though had broken the spell on Creaner. Where only seconds earlier the dark shapes had moved around him threateningly in the form of wolves, they now receded back harmlessly into the shadows and depths of the trees. Creaner looked momentarily confused, his brain trying to work out what was happening around him as the two of them picked themselves up off the floor. He looked at the young guardsmen he had just collided into and remembered Grabbit's flight.

"What did you see?" he ordered. "Quickly, man, tell me, what did you see?"

The guard seemed almost too embarrassed to talk now that Creaner was challenging him. How could he tell the sergeant he was behaving like a madman only moments ago?

Creaner sensed the guard's reluctance to tell him what had been going on.

"Listen, whatever happened, however strange it might have seemed, I need to know, I will not be angry with you." He hoped the words would convince the young guard, he did not want to force the matter too far, especially as he had, much to his own embarrassment, branded the man a coward only moments before.

The guard looked at Creaner. He knew that with every passing second Grabbit was getting further away, he had to tell the truth; duty and honour expected it of him.

"You all seemed to be … well, mmm, seeing things, Sergeant, or at least that is what it seemed like to me." Seeing no anger now in his sergeant's face, he continued, "You shouted out wolf, and he," he raised his hand to indicate towards his comrade who was now ducking behind another tree at the far end of the clearing, "he seemed to be concerned about dragons and …"

"Alright, but what about Grabbit?" Creaner interrupted, "did he seem to be seeing anything that would make him run?"

"I … I …," the guard considered his answer, he had a gut feeling that Grabbit had just run, but he could not be certain, perhaps he too had seen something in the shadows, "I'm not sure, he just seemed to get up really quickly and then he ran. I was going to follow him when," the young man was now anxious to explain his actions, "when you knocked me over and called me a …"

"Yes," Creaner interrupted again, rather more curtly than he had intended but he did not want to be reminded of his hasty judgement. "Never mind that now. Can you still follow him and where is …?" the question remained unasked as he looked around and saw Lorigan sitting on the grass. "Never mind, I see him, just follow Grabbit. We will follow shortly."

The young guardsman sprang into action and ran off in the direction Grabbit had gone, as anxious now to follow him as he was to be away from his sergeant. It was not hard to follow Grabbit's path, a trail of debris comprising of broken branches, snapped twigs and trampled grass littered the route he had taken through the thickly clumped trees. He could also hear the source of the destruction in the distance, the cracking and tearing of wood seemingly magnified by its ferocity, the sound easily reaching him despite the distance of Grabbit's lead. He felt confident though that he would be able to easily catch him up and then follow him until Sergeant Creaner and the rest caught up.

Meanwhile, Creaner now turned his attention to more pressing matters. He still had two of his men in the clearing, chasing or hiding from shadows. He looked over at Lorigan again, suspicion mounting in his mind. He made his decision, weighing up the consequences of each quickly in his head. Only one way to find out, he thought.

He strode over purposefully towards Lorigan.

"YOU," he bellowed, all courtesy put aside for the moment.

"Sergeant," came the unexpected and immediate replies from behind him and to his right. This stopped him in his tracks. He fixed his eyes on Lorigan, eyeing him suspiciously but the man had not moved, he still sat in the same pose as before, seemingly oblivious to the world around him; he had not even flinched when Creaner had roared at him. Right, he thought as he then turned to look at his men. They were both standing, looking over at him, feet firmly together, their arms pressed firmly down at their sides. His eyes moved between the two of them, they both just stared back at him blankly, as if waiting, expecting something more, a further command.

"Come here," he ordered.

Both men ran over to him, both halting and standing rigidly to attention about two paces in front of him.

"Look around you and tell me what you see."

They both exchanged quick glances with one another and seeing no support or understanding in each other, proceeded to quickly glance around as if looking for something obvious that they might have missed; something obvious like the horses having run away but they were where they had been left, heads lowered and happily grazing, quite content, it seemed, with life.

"Well."

"Trees, Sergeant," one offered hopefully.

"And grass, Sergeant," the other joined in enthusiastically.

Creaner resisted the urge to strike them both, his hands though seemed to be receiving the message more slowly as they clenched themselves in readiness.

"So no dragons or wolves then?"

Both men, equally half embarrassed and half confused, rather eagerly replied in unison.

"No, Sergeant, just trees and grass, Sergeant."

"As I thought. Now fetch the horses." He knew they were both half lying but now they had denied the existence of each to the other it would make his job a lot easier.

Lorigan listened intently to the conversation, her keen hearing easily picking up the strangely hushed tones of the sergeant's exchange with his men. I wonder how he will explain losing one as large as Mr Grabbit, she thought to herself mischievously. I imagine Captain Senteth will not be too pleased with his incompetence. She opened her eyes, judging that the moment had waited long enough; time to play again, she thought as she looked around, pretending to be puzzled by Mr Grabbit's absence.

"Where has my colleague gone, Sergeant Creaner? I hope he has not been taken by your Lord Luxor and the Prince. I thought you were here to protect us from that fate. What will your Captain have to say about it?" Lorigan now stood up as she spoke, she also had the attention of all three of them despite only addressing the sergeant. "I presume you will be sending your men to retrieve him for me. I need his services for my hawk, it will surely die if he is not found."

The words spoken without a trace of emotion still managed to cut deeply into Sergeant Creaner, whose suspicions were still centred on Lorigan. He lies, his instincts were screaming out to him, but he knew the words would become the truth if he could not find the loathed taxman.

"He ran off, seemingly frightened of something. I have sent a man to ease him of his fear and return him to us. But why do I need to tell you this, you were sitting there, surely you will have seen what happened?" Creaner's voice was full of threat and accusation as he spoke the words, his eyes openly challenging Lorigan.

"Ah, alas no, I was, as you saw, deep in meditation, Sergeant. My mind was shut off from the happenings of this world. I believed we were safe in your care and thus able to meditate secure in that knowledge. It saddens me now to find that this was unfortunately not the case."

Creaner bristled with pent-up anger. They should have just let these two enter the woods on their own. He could not understand why Senteth had made up the story of Lord Luxor training, and now he was stuck in the woods with a stranger, who he did not trust, and the fat, loathsome taxman, who he would rather leave for dead. It was times like this that he questioned his career choice; what he would give now for the life of a farmer as his brother had done. Yet duty was duty, he sighed, and he *was* good at following orders, despite any personal thoughts he had on the matter.

"He left on foot, we will ride after him now. You, Sir, are free to wait here if it pleases you. I believe you will be safe enough!"

To his relief, Lorigan agreed with his sentiments.

"You know what, Sergeant, I think I will."

⟫⟫◦◦◦⟪⟪

Grabbit heard the footsteps behind him. His mind was muddled, at first he thought he was running away from Lorigan and her dreaded arrows, but that no longer made sense. Yet there was someone behind him, someone that was chasing after him and if not Lorigan, then who? If that were not enough to confuse him the fact that the words 'Willow Bark' seemed to be stuck in his psyche certainly did. Every time he tried to push them away and forget, the words would rush back at him bigger, louder and brighter, determined to be heard and seen, screaming back into his head. And it now seemed to him as if the thing chasing him wanted to rob him of the words, to stop him accomplishing an important mission, a matter of life and death. He must deliver the words, he thought, he must, and he redoubled his efforts. He had no idea though of where he was going or even if he was heading in the right direction, but everything seemed to feel right and his body was screaming at him with every cell to run. So he did so, faster and faster, until it seemed as if it were his very weight now, having built up enough momentum, that was carrying him ever faster forward, driving him on through the crowded trees.

The guard chasing Grabbit was getting no closer to him now, this surprised him as at first he had closed the distance between them quite easily, but now Grabbit was keeping ahead of him. He had initially thought he would easily catch the lumbering giant of a man, who, let's face it, was not designed for speed, especially as he expected him to tire quickly. He had thus set off after him at a leisurely pace, unconcerned by the lead that Grabbit had over him, but now he was running just to keep up with Grabbit and he knew he would not be able to keep up the pace much longer himself as he now struggled to suck enough air in to feed his starving muscles. It seemed to him now that Mr Grabbit must have believed the devil himself was chasing him and he was obviously as equally deter-mined not to be caught.

Back in the clearing the three guardsmen had finally mounted their horses. Creaner though was now having misgivings about leav-ing Lorigan but he knew that he could not now back down from his decision without making it obvious to Lorigan that they were there in fact to watch him. Damn my impetuousness, he thought, never mind though, he still had the two men in the trees to watch him. Had he known that those two men were still hiding in a ditch under a rotting tree trunk and totally oblivious to what was happening around them, he would have swallowed his pride and insisted on either Lorigan coming with them or on leaving one of his men. As it was he did not know and the three of them rode off none the wiser, leaving Lorigan on her own.

Lorigan wasted little time; as soon as she was happy they were out of sight and earshot, she took Grabbit's horse and her own by the reins and led them out of the clearing, following the path that led to the north. Soon the boy Prince would be with them, she had much to do still and it would require a little preparation and not a small amount of patience on her behalf to be ready in time.

In the trees over a mile away to the east, the air around Grabbit changed as he ran. One moment the air was thick and clingy around him and the next it was light. Similar to the feeling you have after being stuck indoors all day with the doors and windows shut up tight and then you step out suddenly into the cool light breeze, the air all of a sudden feels and smells so much fresher and blows away the stuffiness inside you within seconds. This was what Grabbit was experiencing; it felt as if for the first time in his life, he was actually breathing and feeling fresh air, as if he had been stuck indoors all of his life and had finally stepped through a door, sadly though he was too preoccupied with running to notice.

The differences were not just in the air quality though, the colours, although it was still night, were brighter and richer as well; it was still dark and the colours were not as vibrant as those seen in the full light of day but these colours were less dark, less grey and less gloomy. Whereas before the trees had been shades of black and grey, they were now dark browns, dark greens and dark blues, lending a splash of deep colour to the surroundings. Colours so vivid that even in the poor light they held the faint promise of riches for the coming day. Slowly the depth of the change registered within Grabbit's mind and he noticed that the shadows and dark shapes that had only moments before seemed so hostile and threatening were, as they lightened and receded, no longer so and though not appearing exactly friendly to him yet, he could imagine that they would if given time.

Slowly as his fear died so did his need to run; he almost felt if not safe then at least less threatened here. He could no longer hear the footsteps that had been chasing him, their disappearance so sudden and absolute it was as if they had never existed. He slowed as if only now his body was able to register its fatigue and he ground to a halt, bending forward as he did so, his huge hands resting wearily on his bent knees, sweat dripped down over his face and onto the ground as he panted for breath.

Several minutes passed before he felt he was able to raise his head and take in his surroundings properly. When he did, he nearly jumped with surprise; six silent figures in dark grey cloaks were standing, blending half in and half out of the shadows of the trees, about ten paces away, all seemingly looking directly at him, though it was hard to say as the shadows hid their features from view. His immediate thought though was of Lorigan, so similar was their stance and their attire that they could all have been her. Frighteningly for him at first they all, bar one, had bows hung over their shoulders, yet something was different; these Fey seemed less threatening to him and he slowly relaxed. It felt almost like they were expecting him yet at the same time had not made up their minds whether he was welcome or not.

He smiled at them awkwardly, lacking the words and courtesy that he might have offered had he been schooled in such matters. His toothy grin though seemed to register, as one of the figures stepped towards him, emerging from the shadows. As the tall figure drew closer, Grabbit could see the similarities between him and Lorigan more clearly; these were definitely Fey! He had somehow managed to arrive in their fabled lands. His excitement mounted within; the last time he had been this excited was when as a teenager he had spied through the washroom window of Mrs Fult's Finishing School for Young Ladies. He never saw anything though, much to his regret, as he was caught in the act by a royal guardsman before the girls had undressed, but he could still remember his excitement.

"Step this way quickly, Mr Grabbit!"

They know my name! His puzzlement though did not stop him stepping forward such was the authority in the voice and, just as he did so, he felt and heard the air behind him fizz, hiss and crack. The sound made him leap forward another couple of paces as the hairs on the back of his neck rippled with static, sending a judder down his spine. He shook lightly with the effect and then rubbed his hand down his neck to settle the hair; only then did he turn around to see what was happening.

The very air where he had been standing seemed to be condensing in on itself, becoming thicker and thicker, distorting and blending the view behind it into a mixture of streaks of green, brown and blue, as if somebody having just painted the scene had spilt water over the canvas and the shapes of trees, grass and sky were rapidly becoming one. The condensed, distorted air centred itself into a ball, a thick mass about the size of a man's head, that hung about waist height over the ground and, even as they watched, it visibly grew thicker and thicker, sucking in the air around it, feeding on it, the surrounding grass now bending in towards it, sucked swaying inwards in a giant green circle by its power and thirst.

Grabbit took a step backwards in fear as he felt the force of its pull grab and tug at his tunic but on seeing that the Fey around him were unconcerned, he decided to swallow his fear down. It was harder than he thought as the wind pulled at him, leaves shot past his head, sucked into a vortex that seemed to grow stronger and more powerful by the second, yet he persevered, chewing on his fear, tearing it into small bits until it was again manageable, he now stood his ground, watching with the Fey.

Sparks of pure white flew outwards from the ball; the air around it had now become so thick that it obliterated entirely the view behind it. The centre remained a mixture of greens, blues and browns though, streaks of colour that were just visible deep within as if the very colour had been sucked from all around. The air around the centre of the circle changed outwards in ever decreasing levels of denseness as it was sucked inwards, creating a tapestry of distorted images within them that hung in the air. Trees appeared in places that they had no right to be, some thicker than they were, others shorter, some had thin bases and thick branches and yet others had long thin middles with thick tops and bottoms and, even more bizarrely, others seemed to now hang upside down in the air as if the world itself had been turned around and had left them the wrong way up. Grabbit was having real difficulty taking in the spectacle in front of him; just looking at the strange, distorted view of the world beyond made him feel giddy but he could not pull his eyes away from it as the image which was constantly changing in front of him made compelling viewing.

In the centre, the ball was still growing denser and denser, a wave of colours now flashing over its surface, blues, whites, greens, browns, purples, reds and yellows, the colours tumbling around within the ball like a kaleidoscope of light that was now being matched by the sparks and crackles that resounded in the air around them. When the ball had grown to the size of a giant pumpkin, the colours changed again into a rotating circle of light green, blue, white and pink, the colours spinning around becoming slower and slower, each seemingly having a position in the circle and each keeping its place. As the colours slowed, the ball began to shrink in on itself, slowly at first, then it seemed to gain pace. Soon it was the size of a fist and then bang, it exploded, its force nearly flattening Grabbit who seemed to be the only one of the spectators not expecting the great rush of air that had whistled past him in its fury to be free.

When he looked again in the space where the ball had been, there was now an arch, an arch as tall as that of two men standing on each other's shoulders, reaching upwards towards the leaves above. It was not a structure as such but an existence; where once there had been the ball and before that the floor of the wood, there now stood a black darkness in the air itself that was shaped like an arch, its dark outer margin the only defining border to its existence, standing out in contrast against the background of trees, grass and sky behind it. It was as if someone had just painted a black arch onto their world in front of them. Grabbit peered into the blackness but he could see nothing, the air was still now and no sound filtered through to them. It was as if the whole world now stood still holding its breath, waiting and watching to find out what would happen next. The silence and waiting stretched on and on until Grabbit's impatience and curiosity got the better of him; he took a step around the arch, looking over at the Fey as he did so and, seeing no indication to stop, he continued. He walked all around the arch and from every angle it was the same, an impenetrable hole of black that seemed to just hang inexplicably in the air.

The Fey seemed content to wait, as if expecting something further to happen. Grabbit's curiosity, though sorely tempted, did not extend to sticking his hand into the blackness, and after several minutes of seeing little else to rouse his curiosity, he decided to return to the Fey and wait as well.

Several more minutes seemed to pass and just as his patience was again beginning to fray, he saw something in the corner of his eye. He was sure of it, he peered into the blackness in front of him. Had he just seen something in there? He rubbed his eyes as if disbelieving them but when he opened them again, it was still there. It was, he almost smiled at the absurdity of it, it was a small man, spinning around. Yes, definitely, and as he watched, he was growing bigger as if getting closer and closer, larger and larger, but how, where from and what was this? He had no time to ask the questions though, as now the man was, well, man size, not Grabbit size granted, no, just a normal man sort of size, and then he was there, lying on the grass in front of them. Even as he emerged, the arch was shrinking, pulling itself off the ground into the air, wrapping itself up back into a ball, the air again sucking in, quickly now as if in a rush and then a low, popping sound like a bubble being burst and then it was gone. The view of the surrounding trees returned to normal, there was no sign of the arch and no distortion in the air.

The man stood up in front of them, took a couple of awkward clumsy steps and then fell down again, only to then stand again and this time the steps were to the side instead of forward; he fell again, his dizziness conquering his efforts and this time he just sat there and laughed, the sort of laugh that is infectious, the sort of laugh that before you know it, without knowing why, you have joined in with. Grabbit joined in, the Fey did not, they stood and watched, seemingly impervious to the infection that had now affected their guests.

The laughter continued, tears ran freely down Grabbit's cheeks, his ribs ached yet still they laughed, each feeding off one another, until eventually neither of them knew why they were laughing and with the realisation of this it slowly died, replaced by small snickers and smiles which in turn also died away. They looked at each other smiling, sensing in each other a common bond that only they had shared, each instantly liking the other.

"We were beginning to think that you might not be able to make it, Master Ranabin." The elder Fey bowed his head slightly. "I am Fengar of the Fey, welcome once again to our realm."

Ranabin tore his eyes away from Grabbit and focussed on the figure who had spoken to him, the words of Sin jumping back at him, pricking his conscience, reminding him of the urgency of his task. Thankfully his head had now eventually caught up with his body and had stopped spinning. He stood up tentatively this time, conscious all of a sudden of the spectacle he had already created.

"Thank you. I am not too late! Am I?"

"Not at all, Master Ranabin, your timing is impeccable as is always the case with your kind. Come, you must be anxious to meet the boy Prince."

The boy Prince, the words seemed to tug at Grabbit's mind; he knew something about this, but at the moment it again seemed as if the only thing he could consciously think about was Willow Bark. Even when he tried to shut it from his mind and think of something else, it would not be denied, it would twist and turn and force its way back into his thoughts like a really catchy song that despite hating it seems to stick in your mind and then, despite its annoyance, you find yourself humming along to it for the rest of the day. Almost as if the song itself has taken over your mind and now controls your thoughts instead of the other way round; well, that was how Grabbit now felt, and he wouldn't have minded so much but he had no idea of what or who Willow Bark was; he had never heard the word before today and now it was there constantly in his head.

"Mr Grabbit."

The words shook him gently out of his thoughts.

"You may join us as well."

He looked up and saw that Ranabin and the Fey entourage were now standing twenty paces ahead and were all looking back at him as if he were an errant puppy. He dutifully followed them though, as they made their way through the trees.

It was hard for Grabbit to really appreciate the differences between the trees of Crescent Wood and those in the Realm of the Fey; he knew they were different somehow but he was blind to the subtlety of the differences. To him a tree was, well, a tree; it grew in the ground, it had a trunk, branches and leaves. Its sole purpose as far as he was concerned was to provide timber for his house or his fire, further than that was of no interest to him. Yet if he had known what to look for, he would have seen the richness in the colours, the browns of the trunk, not one brown but a collection of brown hues that appeared more vibrant than normal, that seemed to possess a magical quality of its own that was able to repel all attempts of the fungi normally found on tree trunks to grow and colonise on its bark. The rich, dark hues of brown were thus unblighted, unblemished, a virgin brown colour of purity and strength, yet these were no virgin trees. These were trees as old as the land itself, trees whose age spanned many lifetimes of not only man but the Fey as well; trees that stretched up, straight and true, like proud sentinels of an age long since departed, their trunks thick and sturdy, trunks which would require six men linking hands just to circle their girth, their leaves and branches growing in accordance with their neighbour, each fitting seamlessly into a giant jigsaw puzzle of greens and browns that maximised their own space and that of the shelter they provided for their guardians and carers, the Fey.

Ranabin was not blind to these subtle changes; he walked around with his head almost constantly looking upwards, taking in every inch of his new surroundings, drinking in its beauty. Not only because of its beauty, but also in relief; after the claustrophobic sulphuric caverns of the trolls, it felt fabulous to be back out in fresh air, even a swamp, he thought, would have been welcome. He even welcomed the sounds of birds singing in the trees but only after that brief, heart-stopping, dreading moment when he had first heard them and had to listen to their song just to make sure. It was joyful and non-mocking, thankfully, just normal birds doing whatever it was they did, so he relaxed and swam joyfully in the magic of his new surroundings.

Chapter Seventeen

Morkin had just woken up. It was still dark but only just, the last remnants of the night, dawn was not far off. The small signs of the new light that dawn offered were already around if you knew what to look for. The shadows were longer and darker as if making a last futile attempt to keep their grasp on the land, the darkness was lighter, greyer. Colour was slowly seeping back into the sepia of the world around him. He stretched, cat-like, easing his muscles to life and then proceeded to look around. Luxor was lying on the grass snoring peacefully, content, it seemed, in his dreams. Carebin too seemed to be asleep; he sat leaning back against a tree trunk, his grey hood pulled down over his face, hiding it from view, his chest though betraying the long, slow rhythmical breathing of those at rest.

Something had woken him, some sound which now evaded his senses. He waited in anticipation of its return, each passing second of silence raising doubt in his mind but then it slowly came back to him, singing. A light voice singing and, from the sound of it, it was coming from not too far away. He rose and followed the sound, silently slipping away, leaving Luxor and Carebin in their peaceful slumber.

He followed the gentle notes, their sound no more than a whisper floating gently on the breeze. A whisper that was sometimes lost, blown away from his hearing, so fragile were some of its notes and at other times the notes came strong and true as if the words originated from behind the very next tree. They led him on a path down a gentle slope, through a thick forest of grass which in turn was thick with wild spring flowers. A wash of colour and scents assaulted his senses, each competing for dominance over the other. His particular favourite, the light blue of the bluebells, stole his attention, reminding him of a mother that he could not remember. They had been her favourite flower, he had heard the stories of her, of how she had always come to these very woods each spring to pick the bluebells. It was the main reason that they had in turn become his favourite, but if truth be told, he also in himself liked their colouring and shape, their name so accurately describing their form, and even if his mother had hated them, he still would have liked them. Sweet and simple, he thought, he only wished it was truer of all things in life.

The music came at him more loudly, as if by momentarily ignoring it, it had gained force. It was calling to him now, pulling him away from the flowers and onwards down the slope. The ground slowly evened out, the trees fell away, leaving an area in front of him that was bathed in the first rays of the morning sun. Tamora sat there on the grass in the centre of the clearing, her white robe radiant and glowing in the light, her copper coloured hair now plaited into ringlets hanging over her shoulders. In her hand she held a small, golden-coloured, stringed instrument, shaped like a harp but smaller, its four strings drawn taught across its surface. She seemed oblivious to his presence as she plucked gently on the strings, a lush, beautiful, single note sang out which was then accompanied by her voice. A voice so sweet and gentle, that Morkin imagined in that moment that this was surely how the angels sang.

The words meant nothing to him, an ancient song of the Fey. Yet as he listened silently, transfixed by the beauty of the whole scene, he found he could almost hear his name. Not his name as in Morkin but of something else. A sense somehow that the song was for him, about him and telling him something he was for now unable to understand. The tune called to him, stirring his spirit, the words tugged at his soul and made his heart sing with them.

"Plador ley Ce ne cay
Se as a ney fel ar pe."

He would have stood there forever, happily listening, indeed he might have such was his happiness. Yet the song ended minutes later, and he felt an immediate emptiness and longing for its return. The tune whilst sung had been with him, in him and part of him but now even that evaded him as if it had never been, never existed, a mere figment of his imagination. But surely even if that were true, he could have at least guessed at it but no, it was now as if the very song had never been thought of and would be impossible to compose.

Tamora turned, seeing him for the first time standing there, and smiled; it was the sweetest smile he had ever seen, a smile full of beauty, grace, peace and love, the smile of a child given to another when sharing a secret. A smile a parent gives to a child when giving them a gift they have longed for. It was a smile full of happiness; she had just given Morkin a very precious gift, a gift that would in turn help him on his quest, a gift whose power he knew nothing of, as yet. He instinctively returned the smile, his face lighting up; he raised his hand as he did so in a nervous wave.

Tamora giggled, the sweetness of the sound etching itself into his heart. She leapt to her feet and before Morkin could move she was gone, leaving a huge emptiness as if her very departure had now robbed the entire place of its beauty. Morkin thought he would feel sad but he didn't, he felt strangely at peace; he wanted to feel sad but it would not come. He wished she had stayed, he longed to talk to her but her absence seemed to make the memory of her all the more sweeter and he had that fixed firmly into his thoughts.

He smiled to himself, shrugged his shoulders and turned to slowly pick his way back to Luxor and Carebin.

They still slept when he stepped back into what had become their campsite. He was about to settle down on the grass again, intending fully to concentrate on the day that lay ahead instead of returning to sleep. It was then that he saw him. He stood in the shadow of the trees, watching; though now sure that Morkin had seen him, he stepped out into the light. Fengar, such was his light-footedness, seemed to float over the grass towards him.

"Young Prince."

"Is it time? Are the council ready to speak with me again?" He had tried to keep the excitement out of his voice but the words seemed to gush out none the less.

"No, not yet, but soon!" Fengar noticed the slight slump in the Prince's shoulders on hearing the first words. "The other two have arrived and thus revealed their identities. It is as we saw. The third though chooses not to enter our realm and is still hidden from us. I thought you might like to meet them before our council reconvenes."

Morkin looked up, took a deep breath in which he then let out as a sigh.

"Perhaps that might be prudent."

He was now thinking of the one that would betray him. Would it be one of these two or the third? I wonder what he has to hide? Perhaps nothing, maybe. No, best to think logically. Meet them first and assess each on their own virtues. Should I wake Luxor though? No, best not, he would only serve to cloud my opinions and if we are to be apart after this, then it is time I learnt to take more responsibility for myself.

"Yes," he said with more conviction now, having made his mind up. "I would love to meet them."

Fengar studied him for a second as if trying to work out what had been going on in Morkin's mind.

"Come then, they await us."

So for the second time that morning, none the wiser to his absences, Morkin left the sleeping forms of Luxor and Carebin behind, and made his way through the Realm of the Fey.

"I will take you through the heart of our home this time. It is a place only a handful of non-Fey have ever seen," Fengar offered.

Morkin's excitement mounted; he had no idea what he would see, but the thought that he might in that place catch a glimpse of Tamora being all the encouragement he needed. If he was expecting the grandeur and glamour that he would find in his own home, then he was sorely disappointed. What he did find though was in itself grander than his mind could ever have imagined. His eyes struggled to take in all they saw. They walked into what appeared at first to be a low hanging mist, which looked totally out of place amongst these trees. It seemed to appear as if summoned, conjured up, one moment not there and the next existing in front of them, the whole area in front now a rolling cloud of impenetrable grey.

He expected to walk into a wall of wetness, after all that was what the mist at home felt like. This was not wet though; the air was dry and fresh, and now he had entered into it he could almost see clearly through it. And as he turned his head, he was astonished to find the very same impenetrable grey sheet was now behind him, obliterating the view of where he had just come from. His concern was only momentary, overcome immediately by his curiosity and Fengar's reassuring presence beside him. His eyes marvelled at the world around him; it seemed to be coated in a silvery sheen that sparkled and shone but this was not on the objects themselves but actually in the air, an almost silvery glow that hung all around them.

Fengar's hair, the bushes around, the cobweb hanging from a nearby branch, the trees and the Fey who walked around; all now bathed in it. He held his hand out in front of his face, turning it slowly, studying it, marvelling at it, it was as if it had just obtained a metallic silvery coating to the skin. He looked up at Fengar, who offered a small knowing smile in return, the corners of his mouth just curling upwards and no more.

"Shall we?"

Morkin needed no further invitation. So this was the real world of the Fey, he thought. It was almost as if where they had been before was a poor substitute for the real thing, a mere mirage for visitors who, it seemed, were not deemed worthy enough to enter the real realm. No sooner had he thought this though, did he then feel guilty. Did he not do the same with his own people, never mind some of his guests? They entered his hall, yes, but very few came into his own home and his rooms. This was their home, out there was their hall, he was honoured and now felt very humbled.

Fengar sensed the emotion but chose to say nothing. Wisdom, he thought, comes from experience and reflection. The boy had no need of his advice on this matter. He learns quickly and is so much more than a child of the Fey could ever hope to be at his age; so do not judge him as one, he happily chastised himself.

They made their way through the inner Realm of the Fey. Wooden ornate steps carved into the shapes of leaves curled and spiralled upwards around the tree trunks all around them, leading high up into the silver-green canopy above to where bridges and walkways hung suspended by thick vines which then snaked back upwards themselves to higher hidden anchorages. The place was full of Fey, too many to count, old and young; the children playing, the older Fey working, carving wood, stringing bows, twisting vines together to make strong rope, each going about their lives and unperturbed by his presence. Here and there a few of the trees had openings carved into their very trunks. Great big halls carved into the largest of the trees, some of them serving as communal eating areas for the Fey, with wooden tables and chairs adorning the wooden floor. Others were evidently meeting halls, their size shrinking back into the depths of the tree itself, full of mystery and life. The very wood of the trees around them was soaked full of the history and lifeblood of the Fey race; these trees belonged to them as much as the Fey belonged to the trees, each would no doubt be only a shadow of themselves without the other. As Morkin looked more closely on passing one such hall, he noticed that all the furniture possessed such a dark rich texture and brown earthy grain that brought its very life to the fore, that it seemed as if they were still living, furniture that seemed to be actually carved out of and into the very wood.

All around him now he could see the objects that the Fey had lovingly carved out of wood. A sort of living testament that spoke of their love of the trees and highlighted their skills in woodcraft; a plethora of intricately carved symbols and shapes littered the trees around, some having an obvious purpose like the ornate steps, plates and cups, some, however, not as obvious to Morkin, like the small round discs of wood that were sitting on the floor close by.

"Have you eaten?"

"Huh?"

Morkin suddenly realised that Fengar had spoken, the words slowly filtering into his thoughts through his wonder.

"No, not yet." He shook his head as if to confirm the statement.

His mind though was not really interested in food as it feasted on the unfurling scenes around him as they continued walking through the trees; his stomach though growled in protest.

"Here!"

Morkin looked around this time and saw that Fengar was indicating that he should enter one of the carved wooden halls within a great oak tree.

His eyes followed Fengar's hand and rested on the table; two silvery-green plates rested on its surface each having on them, piled up high, a delicious-looking selection of breads, nuts and fruits. He could almost taste the bread already, his taste buds salivating at its memory.

They entered the hall within the oak. Never had he seen the beauty of wood so intricately displayed. This was raw wood in its natural form, unlike the blackened preserved wood his craftsmen produced; he marvelled at the simplicity of its beauty, his eyes tracing around the visible rings in the ceiling, and the grain running up the walls. He would never have believed anyone if they had told him that such a place existed or could be; the trees he knew of could barely accommodate squirrels, mere dwarves in comparison to this. No, he would have dismissed their story with scorn, as fantasy, yet here he was now, sitting on a chair, its very wood part of and at the centre of the heart of a living, standing oak tree.

He ran his fingers over the surface of the table in front; it was rough in texture, not smoothed to a fine finish as those at home were and somehow it felt better for it, and he thought as he did so that he could almost feel its very life deep within. He ate in silence, his eyes taking in the walls around him. Above him on each of the walls he now noticed the small emblems of woodland creatures that were engraved gently, lovingly and intricately into the wood. The faces of foxes, badgers, mice, squirrels and deer seemed to gaze down at him with mild fascination.

Fengar noticed where Morkin's gaze now fell.

"The symbols of our race. Each hall holds a different meaning, tells a different story. This hall is to honour our woodland neighbours for the essential part they play in our lives. Other halls tell their own story, each depicting a small part of the Fey culture, each small part becoming the essence of the whole. One tells our own story, another depicts that of other races we have met," Fengar offered in explanation.

Morkin let his gaze fall onto the Fey, the coming question obvious in his eyes.

"We have no time now. Perhaps though at some future date it may be possible!"

Morkin's heart sank just a little bit, he almost knew already that that time would as likely now never come, yet despite the feeling he still hoped that it would.

"Come now if you are replete. Our guests await you!"

They continued through the inner realm, their journey far too quick for Morkin; the time seemed to fly by and, before he knew it, his preoccupation had brought him effortlessly back to the grey mist. He took one last look behind him, trying in that final second to etch every detail into his memory and hoping against hope for a glimpse, however briefly, of a girl. It never came though, and once more he stepped back out into the Realm of the Fey, its colour and beauty once so vibrant and enchanting now seemingly uglier and bland in comparison.

A short walk took them down to a stream, and there to his great surprise, he saw Mr Grabbit, the royal taxman, sitting on the grass and stuffing huge great lumps of bread into his mouth, making no attempt, it seemed, to savour its rich flavour. He managed to cover his surprise well though.

"Mr Grabbit, how nice to see you here," surprisingly he had almost managed to sound pleased to see the man.

Grabbit, his mouth full of bread, almost spat crumbs as he tried to reply. Morkin stopped his attempts though by raising his hand.

"Please, finish your meal," and he then turned his attention to the old man who now was looking at him.

"Master Ranabin," Fengar cut in, "may I introduce you to Crown Prince Morkin."

Ranabin let his eyes take in the boy who stood before him; he was thin and lanky, with a mop of thick unruly brown hair. It looked to him as if the boy had only recently been stretched and his body had had no time to fill out with muscle. Despite his appearance though, the boy had obvious power and strength in his stance and his eyes burned with passion, pride and wisdom. He had no idea what he had expected but it certainly was not the boy that stood in front of him; none the less, this was apparently the Prince. He cleared his throat, swallowing down the piece of bread that with its rich dreamy flavours diffusing over his taste buds had been slowly melting on his tongue. He stood and bowed his head.

"My Lord, it is an honour and pleasure to meet you."

———⟫•◆•⟪———

At that very moment deep within Mark Wood, high up inside Icebar Tower, four mages breathed a collective sigh of relief and, thankfully for Ranabin, managed to resist the strong urge they had to shout out his name as they peered into the flames of their fire, watching him, their youngest, meet the boy Prince. They had been afraid he would not make it in time. For a while in the troll caverns it had seemed that the fates were conspiring against them. But there he was and so far, much to their relief, he had not embarrassed them or let them down. Sin now could not resist shooting a knowing, accusing smile over to Acab. He did so though mainly to hide some of his own trepidation.

———⟫•◆•⟪———

Meanwhile back in the Realm of the Fey, Morkin now studied the old man as he stood up. The most striking thing about him was his eyes, each a different colour that seemed to be both friendly and distant at the same time. He was sure the man's light green robe should signify something of importance; he tried desperately to think if he had ever seen one before in his court but his memory for the moment was not compliant.

"No, Master Ranabin, it is I who am honoured. I trust your journey here was not too arduous."

Ranabin nearly laughed, suppressing a small chuckle, "You have no idea, my Lord."

Morkin noticed the mirth and made a note to pursue this strand of conversation at some other time, sensing perhaps a story that was well worth hearing.

"Please, Morkin will suffice. I am lord of no one here for the moment."

Grabbit looked around on hearing these words; he had until that time taken little interest in the conversation. Just call him Morkin, he thought. Ah, what simple joys there are in life.

"I am afraid time is short, we must return to Carebin and Luxor and from there we will go to the council," Fengar cut in.

Ranabin and Morkin had been expecting this but Grabbit was nearly knocked sideways. *Luxor*, no, not Lord Luxor surely, but there could be only one. His heart pounded in frustration, it seemed at the moment whenever something good happened to him it was immediately ruined by something else, why me? But wait, Willow Bark, he thought again, this time the words were greeted like a long-lost friend, a saviour perhaps? He needed it for something. Perhaps this Fey would know where I can find it and then I can leave without having to meet Luxor.

"Willow Bark," he tested the words out loud softly, they sounded good, he shouted, "WILLOW BARK!"

They all stopped and turned to look at him; it was Fengar though that spoke.

"All in good time, Mr Grabbit. It takes some time to harvest and prepare, but rest assured it will be ready in time for your departure. Now please, come along, you have nothing to *fear* here."

Grabbit heard the emphasis on the word fear. He is doing it as well, he thought, he remembered how Lorigan had read his thoughts. A sharp pain though shot through his head as soon as he thought of

Lorigan, driving the word immediately away as if he were ashamed by its sudden presence. Willow Bark, Willow Bark, the two words returned with a vengeance that rattled his mind.

Fengar stopped again, this time deep in thought, as if an idea had just come to him; he turned his head once more to look at Grabbit. The man though was now walking towards him, seemingly undisturbed. Had he just felt that right? Surely not, but for some reason a name had just sprung into his thoughts, a name from long ago, a name he had hoped he would never hear again. Had it come from Mr Grabbit or had he just thought it? Surely too much of a coincidence. Had Lorigan of the Fey returned to these lands? It would certainly explain why the identity of the third remained hidden from him and the ancestors; but the question is why would she be involved in this? And should I now mention my fears to the boy Prince or leave things as they are?

He looked up; the others were now standing at a crossroads waiting for him, unsure which of the paths ahead they should take. He walked on deep in thought, leading them back in silence to Morkin's campsite.

As expected, Lord Luxor's dislike of Mr Grabbit was immediately evident. His eyes flared in anger when he saw the taxman follow Morkin into the clearing. He pulled Morkin aside immediately, completely ignoring the other man that followed, such was his desire to find out why the taxman was there.

"What is *he* doing here?" He made no attempt to disguise who his contempt was aimed at as he pointed directly at Grabbit and almost spat out the words.

Morkin was unsure of what to tell Luxor, he had considered telling him what he thought but decided to err on the side of caution for the moment, anxious not to antagonise either man.

"I do not know rightly but he mentioned something about getting Willow Bark, something I believe the Fey have. I am sure he will be gone soon." He tried to dismiss Luxor's anger lightly, but seeing Luxor's face now he doubted he had made any inroads.

Luxor continued to stare for a moment at Morkin as if trying to assess the truthfulness of his answer. Morkin returned the stare, daring him to question him further, until Luxor, seemingly satisfied for the moment at least, turned and strode off back towards Carebin.

Morkin was fully aware of how Luxor felt towards Grabbit and knew he had justifiable cause. He too had reason to distrust the taxman, he knew that Grabbit routinely and methodically cheated and stole from him and at the same time persecuted his people, the only problem being that they had never been able to catch him doing it. The discovery that the royal taxman was going to be one of his three companions on the next part of his journey had initially horrified and frightened him. But the more he had thought about it on the walk back, the more unsure he had become.

He already knew that one of those companions was going to betray him and the obvious candidate as soon as he had seen him was Mr Grabbit. But at the same time he knew nothing of his other companions. One seemed to be an old man, dressed in a light green robe, some sort of master of something or the other, but, he knew not of what. So despite his faults, at least he knew who Mr Grabbit was and what his character was like. No, he had decided, he could not now afford to let his past experiences cloud his judgement, despite his own hatred of Mr Grabbit. This was too important a matter and his life and that of his people may yet depend on it.

Ranabin had watched the exchange between Morkin and the strange man. He had never seen so much evident hatred and anger caused by the presence of another before; he had thought his own exchanges with Acab were bad but they had been nothing compared to this. He liked Grabbit and the fact that this man could so obviously detest him puzzled him.

Grabbit for his part hung back, wisely keeping clear of Lord Luxor who was now sitting on the grass opposite, deep in conversation with yet another Fey, one he did not as of yet know.

Fengar had not expected the open show of hostility he was now confronted with. He knew very little about any of the humans or the mage in his midst but he thought they could at least be civil to each other whilst in his realm.

"It is obvious that Mr Grabbit and the Lord Luxor are acquainted," his voice rising and now holding all their attention as a welcome distraction. "However, I am sure, Lord Luxor, that you are not acquainted with Master Ranabin here and that my friend," the last aimed at Ranabin and Grabbit as he pointed to Carebin, "is Carebin of the Fey. I will leave you now for a moment, please refrain from killing each other." The last few words were aimed directly at Lord Luxor, who on hearing them had enough grace at least to look mildly embarrassed.

Ranabin and Grabbit sought solace in each other's company, Luxor's distrust of Ranabin now growing from that moment but he chose to remain beside Carebin. Morkin stood in-between the two groups, isolated and perplexed. Where do I go now? he thought. Lord Luxor was his lifetime friend and guardian and to cross over to join him was in its warm familiarity sorely tempting. But he knew he would now be spending his immediate life with Mr Grabbit and Master Ranabin, who he was eager to get to know. But there was also the possibility that he would not see Lord Luxor now for who knew how long or if indeed they would ever see each other again.

But if he joined Lord Luxor, how would that appear to Mr Grabbit? There were too many ifs and buts so in the end he chose neither and unhappily sat down where he was on the grass in-between them, hoping that in doing so, he would not offend or distance himself from either.

The laughter from both sets which started as genuine now heightened his misery, but soon it became evident that Grabbit and Luxor were now only trying to outdo each others' joviality. To their credit both Carebin and Ranabin looked suitably embarrassed by the whole charade and finally decided, much to Morkin's relief and happiness, to join his company in the centre. They each shared knowing glances as Grabbit and Luxor both too proud and stubborn to join the other three now fell into a silent sulk.

Their pleasure, discomfort and embarrassment did not last long though, and before Morkin and Ranabin could get past the initial pleasantries of opening conversation, Fengar returned.

"It is time," he announced. "The council awaits you."

Morkin stood and walked eagerly over to join the Fey Elder. The rest looked over hopefully, either to join him or, in Grabbit's case, to be left in peace.

"All of you are to attend!"

Grabbit heard the words and wished he had not. Luxor heard the words and wished Grabbit had not. Why must I attend? thought Grabbit. Why must he attend? thought Luxor. Ranabin rose eagerly, his excitement evident. Carebin rose as if it were inevitable that he was going.

Morkin, Luxor and Carebin of course knew what to expect and were greeted by the cold familiarity of the circle of elders in front of them. Grabbit had reluctantly followed behind, dragging his heels like a petulant teenager who knew his attendance was inevitable but was equally determined to show his reluctance and that he was not going to enjoy the experience whatever happened. Ranabin by contrast was practically buzzing with enthusiasm and was as equally as determined to enjoy and relish the whole experience as Grabbit was not.

Ranabin was stopped though just as he approached the circle, a grey cloak stepped out from behind a tree, barring his way, a stick held out across his path. It took him a few seconds to recognise it.

"Yours, I believe!"

Ranabin practically snatched it from the Fey's hands in his enthusiasm.

"Yes, thank you, but where?" His happiness now complete with its return.

"Strange thing really, four what seemed like identical birds dropped it here an hour ago, then flew off. We are also certain, bizarre as it might sound, that they were singing your name as they left."

Ranabin laughed, thankful for his stick's return and equally thankful he had missed the birds but grateful to them none the less. He twirled it in his hand, relishing the familiarity of its touch, feeling once again complete.

"Please enter the circle," the Fey now stepped back, clearing the path onwards.

Grabbit hung back still, trying once more desperately to evade the invitation, hoping against hope that somehow he would now be forgotten.

"Please, Mr Grabbit, your presence is required and is essential."

The other four were now already sitting inside the circle. Grabbit looked around a circle of hooded grey cloaks covering hidden Fey faces, none seemed to be looking at him, but none the less, he could feel their eyes. He really had no choice, he had nowhere to go and so finally he stepped reluctantly through into the circle, crossing over to the last chair that seemed, as all of the others did, to have sprouted out of the very ground.

He was the only one that fought the experience, trying with a huge effort of force and will to tear away from the chair which now held him in place. Futilely he tried to swim against the tide of pure white light that now blinded him. The pain he felt was non-existent, but he felt it just the same, an excruciating pain that ripped through him, making his muscles spasm and jerk as he held his breath, afraid to breathe, his muscles tore as he fought in a futile attempt to free himself and battled against the voices urging him to calm. All the pain he felt was of his own doing yet he denied it, blaming everyone around but most of all Luxor.

The others saw their paths or an image of it, small clips of what may yet come to pass. To Morkin it seemed initially to be the same as before but slowly he began to see the difference. It was as if the others' very presence was now feeding his dream with more images from their own dreams, adding their flesh to the skeleton of his. He caught glimpses of Grabbit and Ranabin, yet there was another, something or someone lurking in the shadows, presumably the third still hidden from sight but at least now having a detectable form. He tried to peer into the shadows, seeking it out, anxious for more detail, the blackness absorbing him into it, a figure emerging from within. Tamora, standing by a sheet of ice that towered up reaching high into the heavens and beyond, an impenetrable wall, its surface smooth, reflecting and shining almost as one. It dazzled his senses that were still trying to adjust; he pulled away, driven by the brightness, his fear inexplicably rising, an inner instinct awoken by something. The growl was almost welcome when it came, as if justifying the fear; a blurred shape, shaggy, matted fur like a dishevelled dog, leapt out from behind the ice, smashing through it, shards of silvery frozen water spun sparkling and twinkling through the air like a million stars.

The beast headed straight for him, blood dripping from its fangs, its breath stale and putrid, its sheer size obliterating the view as it grew larger and larger, drawing closer and closer. He tried to jump out of the way, he was rooted to the floor though, unable to move and the image shot right through him, he could have sworn the blow knocked the air from him as he clenched his eyes shut, raising his hands up to protect his face, holding his breath. He lowered his hands, the beast was gone; a man or at least that is what he presumed stood now before him. The image tall and dark, his armour though black seemed to absorb all the light from around it, casting the surroundings into darkness and bathing the figure in a dark foreboding glow. The sword rasped free of its scabbard, the sound taunting him as the scabbard curled up like a coiling snake. The figure's eyes burned into Morkin, the sword rising, now pointing its tip at him and marking him as its destination. The chill felt real as it crawled and slid down his spine. His world went black, a complete void empty of all light and sound. He waited, hardly daring to breathe such was the loudness of its sound in that place.

Luxor was greeted by the familiarity of his hall. The twelve, it seemed, had gathered, their pendants with his hung on poles, fluttering against the breeze. He swooped into the hall, gliding in noiselessly, he could feel and breathe the air, smell the roast boar, stale ale and sweat. He expected to see joviality and merriment; he was met by hostility and anger. Lord baited lord. Five stormed out, passing straight through him, the rest waited. The fire in the hearth blazed more and more angrily as if feeding on the emotions around it, its force drowning out the noise, its flames reaching upwards, outwards, consuming the scene. He blinked, raising his hand up as if to ward off the heat. The coolness washed over him, he rode astride his battle mount, men of his keep either side, the horses' armour resplendent and perfect. The horn of battle rang out, a long single note that rose and fell in pitch;

they charged and an unseen mass seemed to emerge in front. He swung his arm, red sprayed across his world. He saw Morkin briefly, a giant wolf in close proximity, he called out, his voice noiseless as they disappeared again, replaced by Carebin, a thousand arrows, a dark sky. Then a knife, small and black, it spun endlessly in front of his eyes, tip to hilt, blood washed across its surface, he tried to reach out to it, it was close. The void was absolute, it consumed him, and he waited expectantly, hoping for more.

Carebin flew across the plain, it was real, the wind pulling at him, rushing over him, his mare ran free, his heart almost sang. Hidden eyes watched his path, peering out at him. Eyes of men and others, small faceless creatures, too afraid as of yet to show face but knowing soon. They could feel it, he could feel it, their power was rising, all was not well. The boulder seemed to come from nowhere. At first a shadow, growing on the ground, the thunder of its landing nearly knocking him sideways. Mud and grass danced briefly for him in mid-air and then pelted him unashamedly as if his lack of applause had offended them. The shadows came faster now, raining down on him, each bigger, louder and closer than the one before; he raised his hand, the last loomed over him, about to consume him. He died in that moment, reopening his eyes to trees, home yet not so. Fey around him but not his, he fell, or that is how it seemed, backwards, spinning slowly in the air. Arrows, thousands of arrows, each brushing past him, the feathers on the flights gently caressing his skin. He looked down, each flight had coated him in blood, he opened his mouth to scream, the howl drowned him out, the void consumed him, he waited, at peace.

Ranabin skipped through the lush, rich meadow, revelling in the joy of the warm rays of the sun and the smells that greeted his nose. Grabbit laughed at him, sharing his joy momentarily. Morkin in contrast glared at him, accusingly. He pirouetted in mid-air, the world flashing past his eyes as he spun, he landed on air, where there should have been ground, plummeting down through the hole, deeper, faster, the walls of earth a blur of brown. The icy water stole at his breath, trying to snatch it free from him. He breathed it in, the cold darkness flooding through him as if he were an empty vessel.

A light blinked above, dancing in small circles, weaving out an endless pattern that hung loosely in the air before being finally snatched away by the darkness, only to be replaced again by another moments later. He coughed out loud, or at least it sounded like it, the water released him, spitting him out. Small creatures fluttered by singing, he reached out his hand, one landed, its touch on his palm as gentle as a butterfly's wing. It turned to face him, Sin's face reared up on his hand, growing, filling the space; he almost jumped back with anger and surprise. Acab now appeared, his face shouting soundless taunts that his mind filled with words, Fazam and Anabar watched silently from behind. The faces converged, blending into one, a grotesque mask that quickly changed to resemble that of his own staring back at him, his or its mouth opened as if to speak, four identical birds came flying out of it straight at him, he raised his hands to scare them away. Red burning eyes blazed at him in their stead; he stepped backwards, he fell, the heat flashed across his skin, it blistered and sizzled, then he burst into flame. A small silver fox leapt through the flames, stopping briefly to look at him before the world faded to black, the void welcomed him in. He tried to echo, his voice carried on, fleeing him, deserting him, leaving him to his fate.

Grabbit still fought but now it was against images as real and as terrifying to him as the real thing. A giant wolf clawed and tore at him; a troll, its eyes flaming sockets of hate, smashed its fists into him; arrows pierced his flesh, turning him into a human porcupine; men on horses trampled him; flames licked painfully at his flesh; water fell in torrents over him, pulling him under its life-sapping watery cloak; all manner of things and creatures tormented him, kicking him, scratching him and biting him; it was as if he were in hell itself. Finally he remembered the knife, it bit into flesh, red washed across him, spraying him, consuming him, the colour tainting his vision which turned from red to black as the void sucked him in.

They woke, or so it seemed, as one, each agitated and confused. They shared quick glances, all were exhausted but Grabbit, it appeared, had fought an entire war on his own. He was soaked in sweat, his hair, ragged and matted, stuck to his scalp; he was slumped back in his chair, his breathing as loud as a hurricane.

In Sarken Wood Vangor sat on the damp grass; it seeped into his cloak and leeched against his skin, its cold bite stabbing him, demanding attention. He ignored it, he was deep in thought and had no time for such discomforts. Graint cast his eyes momentarily towards him, deciding in that moment whether to disturb him or not. It appeared that they had not been quick enough; thin smoke-like wisps of light green snaked over Pailnt's foot, the man was still unconscious, it was perhaps for the best.

Vangor's concern though was not for this man. The words of Skaw still hung in his head like a cloud. A cloud he was now trying to wade his way through, searching for a few raindrops, perhaps only a handful amongst the millions present that were of any use to him.

Ow, that hurt. You're a fool. Beer. I was sober. Mage. Scratch, sniff. Food, hidden food. Tweet, tweet, cheep. Twittering birds, damn. Five. Tower. Cold mist. Invisible. Wall. Drunkard. Pain, intense pain. Wolves. Land. Scratching. Ripped claw. Too hard. Dead. Magic. Five. Old, very old. Dragons. Men. Wall. Tower. Moves. Woods. Explosion. Sin. Towers. Travelling. Home. Air. River. Water. Oldest. Reborn. Ages. Power. Black. Moon. Knights.

The words were flowing past in his mind like a river of thoughts and feelings. A few repeated, thousands still to come.

Graint watched as Pailnt's leg turned green, a light luminous colour that almost glowed, he grinned smugly to himself, one more dealt with. His two remaining men kept a silent vigil, horrified and afraid to watch but at the same time too fascinated not to. Glad it was not them and determined never to come into contact with the green wall of light themselves.

In the Realm of the Fey the elders sat in cold silence, each in their own thoughts, each in each other's thoughts; the entire council one continuous mind that tried now to piece together the deluge of information they had just encountered, their vision of the dreams not as bright and vivid as the individual's, a greyer shade as if seen through a deep mist and making them harder to see. All their images also came blended together, which served to confuse the issue more, as they now struggled to trace each image back to its owner. It was always the case when they had multiple beings in the circle and they had never discovered, despite centuries of trying, how to make it any easier. They would have liked more time but it was no longer a luxury that they could afford; they had to offer their decision and advice now. The five were now leaving the circle, guided by Fengar, leaving them to decide on the fate of their people and ultimately the Moon lands.

It was time; the ancestors had spoken and now the Fey had decided. It was rightly so as this was their land and their burden to carry. Fengar as always would speak for them as was his right; he would tell the five of their decision and help guide them onto the path revealed by their dreams and as such chosen for them. Fengar turned to face the five; he was troubled, not only by the decision of the elders but by the constant nagging sensation of Lorigan that tugged at his conscience like a persistent itch that would not be satisfied.

The five now looked at him, each since the circle had also been trapped by their own thoughts. He looked at each in turn, mapping their faces and images into his mind, seeing a mixture of emotions on each; fear, excitement, anxiety and worry. This is what their fate and the rest of these lands rested on, it did not inspire confidence within him. Would anything he had to say ease their emotions, he pondered, either way it mattered not, it was time and they must know.

"My friends," he began, choosing his words and his tone carefully, trying to sound familiar, yet distant, friendly but not intimate. "Your dreams revealed much yet told us little. Your path is clear yet shrouded in mystery. It is the way with dreams. All that you saw will come about, its effect on you though is not yet set, much will depend on your own reaction to it. Remember though, all is not as it first may seem."

A look of shared puzzlement stared back at him, increasing as he spoke with the riddle of his words. Fengar chose to ignore it and pressed on, "It is clear that Morkin, Grabbit and the one who waits outside this realm are to look for the Ice Crown. Its discovery is essential, if only to bring back unity to the army of men. Beware though," he looked directly at Morkin as he spoke, "the dangers you face will be many. The Dark Knights seek you out and one known to you will betray you. You should seek out our cousins, the Faeries of the Snow. Their realm lies to the north, hidden within the Snowy Peaks, across the Plains of Iyce. They are not known for their hospitality though. Do not fret as there are others that may assist you; unfortunately, there are more that would happily see you fail, including some of your own kind."

Morkin listened to the words intently, trying hard to marry each to the images that still squatted in his head, searching for any further clues hidden between the two. Grabbit seemed nonplussed by the words; either he did not care or he was not fully aware of their meaning to him. He just longed to be away from Luxor and was relieved to hear he soon would be.

Fengar pressed on, turning now to Luxor.

"You, my Lord, have the unenviable task it seems in trying to unite the Lords of the Moon. The army you raise must meet the Dark Knights, a task that will lead to bloodshed, a task that has to be done, a task that only you can fulfil. Beware though, not all the lords will welcome you. Do not lose hope though, the discovery of the Ice Crown should be enough to persuade them in time."

Luxor nodded his head, he knew it would come to this and had accepted his fate.

"Luxor, you must not dally though, if a lord will not join you freely, you will have no time to persuade them, you must move on to the next. You have little time, one cycle of the moon perhaps, little more definitely, before you must meet their army in the north. You must stop them from crossing the river Ces for as long as possible; that alone is essential to our success, Lord Luxor."

Luxor's frown creased across his brow, the task he had now been set seemed almost impossible; time was too short, his mind was now reeling as he tried to seek out possible alternatives to the puzzle.

"Carebin," Fengar at last turned to the young Fey, "you may yet be the key. The Fey of Crescent Wood will fight for these lands but only if the other Fey decide to do likewise. Your task it seems is to persuade them as you have us. I can offer little else that you do not already know other than our desire for your success."

Carebin nodded once, a small confirmation, content with his task and relieved that his Fey at least were willing to fight.

Luxor had to bite down on his tongue, a feeling of abandonment and betrayal rising in his stomach to match the words he had just heard. He had thought he would have at least been able to rely on the archers of the Fey. Why else was the sky in his dream dark with arrows? A rising dread gripped his heart at its core, if not Fey arrows, then whose? He left the question unanswered in his head, afraid now even to think of it.

"Master Ranabin, your path is more than can clearly be seen or discussed, your purpose here and now is to accompany Prince Morkin and Mr Grabbit. The reasons, I believe, are already known to you, yet remain hidden from us. Beware though, your path may lead you over steps you have already trodden. The darkness may serve as a blessing; your power is the ultimate hope, only you can discover how to release its potential."

Ranabin smiled at the Fey, his stick resting comfortably across his lap. He had already worked out the meaning behind much he had seen but still wondered where Morkin, Grabbit and the hidden other would fit into it.

"My people wish you all a safe passage. We will aid you as we can and in many ways you will not be aware of. Food and horses for the two without will be brought to you shortly, please take all that you want with our blessing and thanks, and for Mr Grabbit," he paused for effect, "the Willow Bark you requested!"

They made to rise.

"Prince Morkin, if I may?" Fengar signalled to the young Prince to join him.

"I debated long and hard about telling you this."

Morkin looked up at the older Fey, waiting for him to continue, intrigued by what he had to say.

They walked out of earshot from the others, who readied themselves for their imminent departure, a group of Fey children entering amongst them as they did, carrying packages of bread, fruit and nuts all wrapped within giant green leaves that had a waxy texture to the touch. The packages themselves were tied loosely together with a thin strand of some sort of vine. Mr Grabbit received a smaller package from one of the children, wrapped in a similar way.

"I fear the third to join your party may be one of our kind," he raised his hand to stop Morkin from speaking. "Please, I will answer your questions but let me finish first. Her name is Lorigan, she was sentenced to the long death by our people, she somehow survived and has since been in exile. I fear that it is she who will join your party. It would explain why the third remains hidden from us but not why she has returned. I am forbidden to tell you why she was sentenced to death; that is a matter for Fey ears only. I tell you this though not because I believe she will betray you, I have no idea who that will be, but to make you aware of my fears. If this serves to cloud your judgement then I apologise; however, I felt you needed to know. It may be that I am wrong but her name now haunts me and I believe it can only be for that reason."

Morkin considered what he had just heard; another Fey and this time an exile. Could she be worse than Grabbit? Perhaps, only time would tell.

"If you cannot tell me the nature of her crime, can you then tell me if her death sentence still stands, and if so, can she earn a pardon?"

Fengar looked momentarily stunned by the question; he composed himself and smiled down at the boy. This time the smile lit up his face as if for the first time in his life he was truly amused.

"Now that is some question, young Prince, and in truth something we have never had to consider. No one of our kind has ever survived the long death before, she is the first, so the situation you can see has never come about. I imagine though that if she can prove that she is once more worthy of a Fey name, then anything might be possible."

"Then for that at least I thank you and look forward with intrigue and curiosity to perhaps meeting this Lorigan, exile of the Fey. I will though bear in mind your advice and concerns and now thank you for them."

"Young Prince," Fengar bowed humbly towards Morkin, "for too long we have not known you. I look forward eagerly to our next encounter and hope in time to get to know you better. I am also aware that this sentiment is shared by at least one other of our kind. Please go in peace and return safely."

Morkin returned the bow and the smile, liking this Fey more with each encounter and warmed by the reference to Tamora.

He returned to the others, happy and sad, eager and reluctant. He embraced Luxor openly, like a son to a father. Would it be for the last time? Doubt slowly rising its ugly head. He stamped on it immediately, sending it scurrying back down the hole it had crawled out of. No, it would not be the last time; the words with force and aggression were almost shouted inside his head as if to emphasise the point and thus make its sentiment an assured reality. They broke off, Luxor's hand ruffling his hair as they did so.

"Be careful and watch Grabbit; if ever there was one to betray you it would be him, and if he does, rest assured I will even rise from the dead to pursue him."

"Thank you, my friend, but I am sure it will not be necessary. Besides he is far too slow to catch me!"

He tried to make light of Luxor's fears but the joke failed to register on his mentor's face. His oath to protect the young Prince was now hanging tightly around his neck like a noose he no longer had any control over and was now slowly strangling him.

"Go, boy, I have trained you well, you are ready and if not

I will kill you myself." Luxor's voice nearly cracked with emotion; he had no children of his own but Morkin was as a son.

They shared one last look and then Morkin turned to join his new companions. His adventure was just about to begin.

They left soon after, Morkin and Luxor the only two to gaze back as each went their separate ways. And as Morkin stepped out of the Realm of the Fey the sound of a girlish giggle lifted his heart another few beats. He saw her, she waved; it was a brief, flitting appearance that promised much, and delivered hope and determination to steel his will.

As they left, the Wolves of Fennigan hunted their next prey, a farmer disappearing from the world of the living, his soul joining the eternal wanderings of his new brethren. The wolves hunted again, their prize far off, but near, his scent not yet present, but promised on the cold wind that blew onto their blood-soaked faces. War was coming, arriving sooner than expected for some, the howl sounding out their intent.

Graint watched in silence as Pailnt faded from existence, he was now just another memory in the unfathomable sea of souls the Wraights had caught. Vangor gazed over, his concern non-existent, the man's own foolishness had cost him his life and he was well rid of fools. He never for one minute suspected his sergeant's involvement. He had a new prey himself, the Mages of the Moon. He was sure now that there were at least four of them, and somewhere in this land there was a tower that contained the hidden power of these lands and in it his key to victory.

End of Book One